Riding the Snake

Also by Stephen J. Cannell

THE PLAN

FINAL VICTIM

KING CON

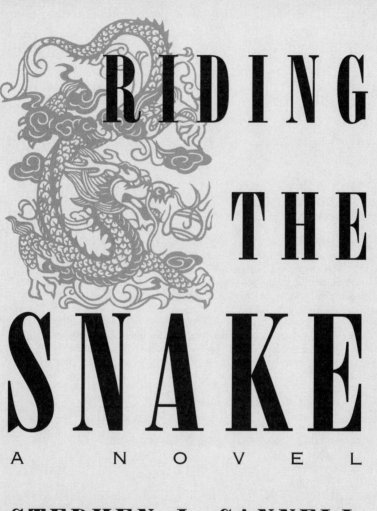

RIDING THE SNAKE

A NOVEL

STEPHEN J. CANNELL

WILLIAM MORROW AND COMPANY, INC.   NEW YORK

Library of Congress Cataloging-in-Publication Data

Cannell, Stephen J.
  Riding the snake : a novel / by Stephen J. Cannell.—1st ed.
     p.   cm.
  ISBN 0-688-15805-6
  I. Title.
  PS3553.A4995R5   1998
  813'.54—dc21   97-49674
                                                                   CIP

Printed in the United States of America

First Edition

1 2 3 4 5 6 7 8 9 10

BOOK DESIGN BY ELLEN CIPRIANO

www.williammorrow.com

To my wife, Marcia; my children, Tawnia, Chelsea, and Cody; and my mother, Carolyn, who all support me

And to Ralph Salisbury, who turned the lights on

ACKNOWLEDGMENTS

Many heartfelt thanks, first, to my army of loyal colleagues who were there for me again: Grace Curcio, Kristina Oster, and Christine Trepczyk, who cleaned up behind me, straightening out my hopeless spelling, inputting the manuscript, and managing my countless rewrites; and Wayne S. Williams, who tirelessly and scrupulously helped me edit. Jo Swerling did numerous reads and made helpful suggestions. Thanks to Paul Bresnick, Paul Fedorko, and Bill Wright at William Morrow for continuing to believe, and to Eric Simonoff and Mort Janklow, who provided counsel, advice, and friendship.

Michael Browning was the novel's heavy lifter. He was crucial in helping me research China, contributing both ideas and details. Anita Addison is a true friend who read and helped me reshape. Reuben Cannon, a lifelong buddy, shared his insights and feelings. Thanks to Jack Green, who contributed many observations about Hong Kong, and to William T. Park and Ross Ari of the L.A. Asian Crime Investigation Section, who gave me wonderful background material on that important LAPD unit.

It is man that makes truth great . . .
Not truth that makes man great.

—Confucius

Riding the Snake

1994
The Year of the Dog

H e sat in the back of his beautiful new three-engine Falcon jet as a setting sun turned the silver wings bright orange. He watched in fascinated silence as his "dirty" blood was transferred, snaking out of his arm in the transparent plastic tubes, then shooting into the large dialyzer where it was washed of urine and body toxins. Then his blood would return from this grotesque laundry and be inserted back into him. The process was debilitating and caused "Willy" Wo Lap Ling tremendous fatigue. He looked up at his full-time physician, a young Chinese doctor from Hong Kong named Li Dayu. He was narrow shouldered and skinny with thick prescription wireless glasses. Dr. Li checked the dialysis machine, which was built into the private jet's lavatory. He pushed his glasses up on his nose and noted the blood flow rate that measured the fluid processed by the hissing, gurgling monstrosity. Next, the doctor checked the permanent plastic tips that had been surgically implanted in Willy's arm and abdomen, and to which the dialysis machine was now attached. Then he looked at the withered sixty-nine-year-old Triad leader critically.

"I think it is time. We must go to Beijing," he said in Mandarin Chinese. "I sent your blood panels to them. They have notified me they have a donor."

"I have enemies there," Willy sighed. "I have ignored the wishes of Chairman Deng. I cannot lose face. I cannot now crawl there like a wounded animal, drag myself up onto his porch, and ask forgiveness."

"Zou Hou Men," the doctor said, looking into Wo Lap's jaundiced eyes, using the Chinese expression meaning "Go in the back door." "Use your Guan-Xi with the Chinese Academy of Social Sciences." Guan-Xi was the time-honored Chinese tradition of influence that still controlled most social and business relations in China. The head of that new Academy was Chen Boda, who also headed the Chinese Communist Party's Military Commission and was, arguably, the most powerful man in China. Even more powerful than the ailing Chairman Deng Xiaoping.

The Chinese Academy of Social Sciences had been formed only one month before and had been heralded by President Clinton as an important step by Chinese Communists to find bridges of understanding with the West. Willy Wo Lap Ling had been invited by Chen Boda to be part of the Academy. The invitation had surprised him, because he lived in Hong Kong under British rule and had engaged in a life of crime there, but Willy had been told it was extended because he was an expert on U.S. commerce. After all, didn't he steal billions in cash annually from an unaware and stupid America?

Chen Boda had identified the United States as China's sole global enemy in his address before the Communist Party's Central Committee during a closed meeting at Beijing's Jiangxi Hotel in January of 1994, the Year of the Dog. In the view of the Chinese Academy of Social Sciences, Willy Wo Lap Ling was actively engaged in poisoning the American fabric from within with his drugs, guns, and illegal immigration. He was known to have great influence with corrupt American officials. He had invested heavily in American politics and had influence with many U.S. Senators and

Congressmen. Willy Wo Lap had even been to the White House and had his picture taken with President Bill Clinton. The picture was hanging in his Hong Kong office and displayed for all his incredible Guan-Xi with the American leader. It was this criminal activity and political influence that caused Chen Boda to invite Willy to be an adviser to the powerful new Academy, which was hardly a bridge to better understanding with the West. It was a Chinese think tank solely dedicated to the total and absolute destruction of American interests around the world.

Wo Lap Ling had been born in the New Territories inside the Walled City of Kowloon in 1925. At the time there were nineteen members of his family living in a one-room concrete flat. The Walled City was the perfect place for Willy. History had prepared that ghetto for him years before he was born.

The New Territories had been ceded to the British from China for ninety-nine years in 1898. The Walled City of Kowloon, as a result of a poorly worded agreement, became disputed property, with both the British and the Chinese claiming sovereignty over it. It was a pocket of lawlessness, governed by neither country, where crime and violence flourished. Soon criminal Triads became the ruling power in the Walled City, where there was no wall. The Japanese had it torn down by POWs when they occupied that area during World War II. The ghetto kept its name because the place had been designed without streets. Narrow alleys randomly transected the crowded mass of buildings. As the population and need for new housing grew, the ghetto swelled. "New" top floors were built precariously over old. With no Planning Commission or City Council to oversee design, stress, and load requirements, the new floors were balanced unevenly, like randomly stacked boxes, giving the ghetto the look of a wall of concrete. The narrow alleys became tunnels which were closed in by top stories. Even at noon, no sunlight penetrated these walkways. Water and electricity were stolen from nearby conduits. Makeshift water mains leaked; jerry-rigged wiring sparked and zapped in the fetid darkness. Sewage and the entrails of animals were thrown down into the dark pathways from one-room factories that churned out pork balls and fish cakes. In most places, the narrow walkways were filled almost two stories high with human excrement and rotting garbage. At some places, the alleys were only a few inches wide.

The small industries that operated in the Walled City hummed twenty-four hours a day, turning out everything from hair oil and bicycle parts to sex toys for Western consumers. Theft, murder, and intrigue always hovered in the dark.

It was in this criminal environment that Wo Lap Ling grew up. His family lived on the fifth floor of a ramshackle old building. Since there were no streets, no apartment had an address, and children from an early age learned to navigate in the teeming black tunnels, finding their homes by instinct almost like blind ants returning to the nest.

Wo Lap Ling had to share a bed with five other members of his extended family. They used a "hot-cot" method. He had the bed from nine in the morning until four in the afternoon, then he would turn it over to his cousin, Sun Yee. By five P.M., he was out in the swarming alleys of a city that housed factories, opium shops, and humanity with equal disregard.

No Occidentals dared go into the Walled City of Kowloon, except, that is, for Jackie Pullinger. She had lived there since she arrived from England in 1929. She was an evangelist missionary who taught the children the vague customs of the West that were now the rule in Hong Kong. She also ran a drug rehabilitation program. Her success rate was staggering. Since she provided a service for these Chinese children, she had at first been tolerated, and eventually became a fixture that everyone accepted. She had taught Wo Lap Ling English and had given him his Western name, Willy.

Jackie Pullinger was the only Occidental he had ever loved.

Willy had been so adept at feats of criminal balance that he had risen from a street urchin who ran errands for the area Triad leader to become, at the age of twenty-three, the powerful Incense Master or Vanguard of the Chin Lo Triad. As Vanguard, it was his duty to wreak punishment on delinquent Triad members, a job he performed with great relish. He became an expert on all forms of punishment, including the painful Death by a Myriad of Swords. He resurrected several ancient tortures involving rats and insects. He rose quickly to become the White Fan (Consigliere), and now Willy Wo Lap was the "most powerful Shan Chu" and ran the entire Chin Lo Triad in Hong Kong. The Triad's current annual take from its worldwide illegal activities was eighty billion dollars and growing.

The largest market for his criminal empire was America, which had focused almost all of its law enforcement energies on the Italian Mafia and Colombian drug cartels. Willy was astounded. Together they netted only twenty billion. Yet the stupid Americans concentrated on them while Willy's Triad poisoned American society with guns, drugs, and illegal immigration, extorting three times that amount, while having his picture taken with the American President. It had been an exciting, exhilarating ride.

Now at age sixty-nine, the trail seemed to be coming to an end. He had applied to Sloan-Kettering hospital in New York for new kidneys and been told by the Americans that there was a donor. He had flown there in his new three-engine Falcon jet, only to find out at the last minute that a mistake had been discovered in the tissue match. He had been turned away without explanation or regard for his desperate condition.

"You will die if you do not get new kidneys immediately," his doctor said, interrupting Willy's thoughts.

Willy's life had been a mixture of violence and power. Women, enemies, and wealth had all been conquered, like helpless children. Wo Lap Ling had been riding a vicious tiger. In his youth, he sat the beast easily. The tiger carried him fast and far and, at his direction, had savaged his enemies. But now he was desperately holding on, barely able to stay aboard. If he fell, he knew the tiger would turn and savage him.

"Tell the pilot to refile the flight plan for Beijing," he whispered.

The doctor turned and moved away as the blood-cleansing, lifesaving machine, squatting on the toilet behind him, hissed and throbbed at the end of two plastic tubes that coiled out of him like hooded cobras—one snake sucking his blood, the other spitting it back inside him.

The problem with riding a tiger was that when the ride was over, it was impossible to get off the vicious animal's back.

The Friendship Hospital in Beijing was clean but not very friendly. Gray walls and yellow tile floors made the sterile environment foreboding. The Communist doctor had given him a complete physical as well as a new blood work-up. He checked Willy's vital signs, then told the dying Triad leader that he was in immediate need of a kidney transplant. Any wait would make his chance of survival more difficult. This was hardly news. When Willy asked in Mandarin Chinese if this could be accomplished, the doctor only looked down at him and clucked his tongue in a very peculiar way before leaving Willy's private room.

Willy Wo Lap's dreams had been getting very bizarre. He assumed, in his waking moments, that it was probably all the toxins in his blood that were poisoning his mind. But there was a part of him that wondered if he was getting a sneak preview into the dark hallway of his spiritual future. If so, the dim light under that door was grim and held evil promise.

The dream he was having in the Beijing hospital was strange indeed: He was sitting up in bed but needed to urinate. The floor was alive with writhing poisonous snakes. They hissed and bared their fangs at him. He needed to walk to the bathroom but had no shoes. The snakes would surely strike his bare feet and kill him. Two large, snow-white Akita dogs were also in the dream, sleeping at the foot of his bed. Willy called to them. They looked up, then came over and sat obediently next to him, one on each side. Suddenly a knife magically appeared in Willy's hand. He turned and drove the knife deep into each dog's back. They sat patiently as he opened them up, making long cuts, exposing their innards. He stuffed his bare feet down inside them, pulling the carcasses up like huge furry white bedroom slippers. Then he stepped down off the bed, into the sea of snakes, walking carefully in his new dog shoes . . . but then, slowly and powerfully, the dogs began to move in their own directions—one right, one left. In panic, he knew he had been fooled by their trusting beauty. He could not control them. Soon he was caught in awkward peril, unable to stand, his legs spread, his genitals dangling inches above the snapping reptiles. Willy was hopelessly off-balance and began falling face down into the sea of hissing snakes.

He woke up with a start and was looking up at the smooth liver-spotted face of Chen Boda. The Chinese politician had been sitting in the room, staring down quietly at him, saying nothing. It was strange, even frightening, to wake up in the middle of the night and find one of the most powerful men in China—perhaps the whole world—sitting silently at his bedside, observing him, making plans while he slept, but saying nothing. Chen Boda was seventy-one, his hair slicked back on his small, bony head. His skin was the color of an old calligraphy scroll, an aged wheaten yellow. He was only five feet tall. Western diplomats refused to take him seriously because of his size, thinking him diminutive in spirit as well as stature. It was a mistake they were just now beginning to regret. He had soft brown eyes, an angelic complexion, and a ruthless core.

"This has been an eventful year," the Chinese politician said to the dying Hong Kong mobster, a moment after Willy's eyes opened. Only two years in age but fifty years of contrasting and tumultuous political activity separated them. Chen Boda had risen in the Chinese Communist Party in the same spectacular fashion Wo Lap Ling had risen in the Triad hierarchy. What made them brothers under the skin was that both reveled in the luxury of power in a way few can understand.

"I'm dying," Wo Lap said softly in Mandarin, the chosen language of the Chinese Communist Party. "That will certainly make this year eventful for me."

"How you arrive and how you exit are the only two things in life that count," the old politician said, a smile playing at the corner of his thin lips. Both men knew this particular Confucian philosophy was inaccurate, if not ridiculous, at least for them. They had both been defined by the ruthless acts they'd committed in between those two sacred events.

"You have come here to give me the Master's wisdom?" Willy Wo Lap said, his voice weakening to a whisper in the already quiet hospital room.

"It has been a year of *jing-shen-wu-ran*," the Chinese politician said, talking of the spiritual pollution of China that the Communist government claimed was the sole fault of American intervention in Beijing's internal policies.

"I am not a politician," Willy Wo Lap said softly.

"This is not so. You are just a politician with different goals. You steal from America, you attack them from the inside. You can become a different kind of warrior in this battle. This is what I want to talk to you about."

The two men looked at one another in the dimly lit room. Each waited for the other to speak. Finally, it was Chen Boda who continued:

"The Americans challenge us at every turn. They attempt to be the sole force in the Pacific theater. This year, they sent their aircraft carrier *Kitty Hawk* into the Yellow Sea to threaten us over our attempt to repatriate our renegade province, Taiwan. This is a direct threat against our national sovereignty. . . . They attempt to chastise us over our necessary reorganization of Tibet, tying that important internal matter to their Most Favored Nation trade status; complaining about our supposed Human Rights atrocities, while they burn their own citizens at Waco and castrate Black children in Alabama."

Willy Wo Lap closed his eyes, both from fatigue and lack of interest. He had never cared about these things.

"I am boring you, comrade?" Chen Boda asked.

"The lowly swallow cannot possibly understand the lofty ambitions of the eagle," Willy Wo Lap said, using another Confucian wisdom, then watched as the smile reappeared momentarily on the politician's face.

"Let me propose to you a bargain," the five-foot-tall head of the powerful Chinese Communist Military Commission said. "I will give you the kidneys you desperately need, but you in turn will work for me. . . . I want your river of pollution to become a flood. We will attack their society from the inside with even more narcotics, Russian AK-47s and illegal Chinese aliens who will steal from their welfare state. I will direct your efforts. You will increase and control the flow. You will continue to buy favor with American politicians. Increase your already sizable Guan-Xi. If you are caught, it will be you—not the People's Republic of China—who will be guilty of this act of aggression. In return, I will give you life."

The two men looked at one another. There seemed to be nothing else to say. It was a great deal for both of them.

They took him by ambulance past the gates of the Forbidden City. The gold tiles on the roofs of this ancient part of Beijing shone up defiantly at a three-quarter moon. They left the city on the Qianmen Dajie highway and finally arrived at a huge *lao gai*, or "reform through labor" camp. It was located in the Chinese countryside south of the capital. The camp was a mammoth, windowless fortress of gray concrete. Dismal, even from the outside. The *lao gai* housed prisoners who had been arrested for political crimes. There was a hospital there for medical experiments. The *lao gai* was full of the very men and women that President Bill Clinton was claiming were victims of Chinese Human Rights violations.

Chen Boda walked to the operating room on the sixth floor, where three of China's best urological transplant surgeons had been rushed and were now awaiting him. It was four-fifteen in the morning.

"Is the donor here?" Chen Boda asked.

The doctor nodded and led the diminutive politician to an adjacent room where they looked through a window at a young student dissident strapped to a table. He looked back at them through the glass in wide-eyed fear.

The student was named Wan Jen Lam. He had been arrested for distributing brochures proclaiming the New Democratic Front in Tiananmen Square during the uprising five years before. He had been held under "strict supervision" for his crime without ever being formally charged, let alone facing trial.

"He's a five-out-of-six tissue type match to Mr. Wo Lap. A good donor," the lead surgeon said.

"Are you ready to begin?" Chen Boda asked the doctors, and they all nodded.

"Then wheel the patient in here so he can witness our generosity on his behalf."

A few minutes later, Wo Lap Ling was on a rolling hospital bed that was parked in front of the observation window where Wan Jen Lam was strapped down. They cranked Willy's bed up. Once the ailing Triad leader was in a position to see, Chen Boda went into the operating theater and nodded to one of the doctors. The surgeon, a narrow-faced man whose eyes were hidden behind the gleaming circles of his thick glasses, stepped forward and picked up a scalpel from a tray of instruments. He approached the frightened student, who wriggled helplessly under his restraints.

"You have a great love for American Democracy. It appears you think the Western moon is rounder than the Chinese moon," Chen Boda said without preamble. "But it is time for you to make a contribution to the Motherland."

"What are you going to do?" the terrified student asked.

"I am going to give you a chance to give valuable aid to your beloved country," Chen Boda said, smiling at the terrified youth. His smile was surprisingly warm and gentle, his voice soothing. Despite the horrifying situation, it seemed to calm Wan Jen Lam.

"How will I contribute?" the young man finally asked.

"You will give to the Motherland something she desperately needs. . . ."

The student was puzzled by this and furrowed his brow. Chen Boda motioned to the doctor, who advanced to the table, holding the scalpel as if it were a calligraphy brush: two fingers high on the outside of the handle, thumb in powerful opposition, lower two fingers resting on the inside of the handle near the blade. It was a grip that permitted extraordinary strength and precision.

The blade flashed as he swung it down and buried it in the student's heart. The student convulsed once, exhaling a gust of air. Chen Boda watched impassively as the dissident quivered and shook; the scalpel protruding from his chest twitched like a small dark arrow as his nerves and synapses rioted within his skinny, undernourished body. Quickly and painfully, the young man died. Blood from the wound ran off the table and pooled on the floor. Then Chen Boda walked back into the adjoining room and faced Willy.

"I have done this for you, Wo Lap Ling. Do not forget that when you were about to perish, a good friend shielded you from the storm." Then he turned and walked out of the room.

As the sun came up on Tiananmen Square, the three-man surgical team was already deep into it, removing Willy Wo Lap's disease-shriveled kidneys and replacing them with Wan Jen Lam's healthy ones.

Willy Wo Lap was wheeled into recovery at nine-thirty-five A.M. His vital signs were stable and he was about to begin a long journey of healing that would lead him back to power.

Wan Jen Lam was wheeled to an elimination chamber and disposed of quickly and efficiently. His body was shredded and washed with harsh acid. Once liquefied, it was drained away without a trace.

If Bill Clinton wanted examples of Human Rights violations, Chen Boda was only too happy to oblige.

Willy Wo Lap slept a peaceful sleep and dreamed of his father. The old fish-factory worker had once sat in their crowded

Kowloon apartment, with the sound of crying babies and electric saws ripping pig carcasses nearby, and told him, "No feast lasts forever." Willy had been ten and listened while his ailing father spouted Confucian wisdom dictated by Chairman Mao. These last painful years had proven Confucius and the old fish factory worker right. Willy had suffered renal failure . . . and with it had come a loss of all his appetites. The feast that was his life had ended. He no longer craved women, food, or luxury. All he wanted was a few moments free of pain. Now he had been given a new chance. Once more, the crafty Chinese mobster had managed to stay on the vicious tiger. Once more, he could savage his enemies from a seat of power behind the beast's shoulder blades. Willy was back.

A new feast was about to begin.

PART ONE

SIBLINGS

1998
The Year of the Tiger

ONE

Wheeler and Prescott

T he locker room at the exclusive Westridge Country Club was Wheeler Cassidy's "spot." He arrived every morning around ten and flopped down on the tan leather sofa, then browsed the *L.A. Times*. Of late, he had just been scanning the front page, then going directly to sports, reading the racing results and ball scores. The rest of the paper failed to interest him. He used to read it cover to cover, but now the pointless articles on the Metro page about police brutality or campaign finance abuses didn't concern him anymore. He had been vaguely aware of the fact that his world had been narrowing but had managed to flush those thoughts with Scotch shooters.

The beige couch was also good because it was in front of the picture window that overlooked the tennis courts, which afforded him a prized spear-fishing spot. He could either tag up on a new member's wife coming back from her tennis lesson or pick up a golf game with some middle-aged walk-over. By one P.M., he had usually moved from the comfortable On-Deck Circle to Home Plate, which was the last stool at the bar in the grill. From there, he would swing lazily at the slow curves that wandered past in sexy tennis skirts.

Wheeler was thirty-seven, tall and good-looking in a careless, bad boy sort of way that women of all ages seemed irresistibly drawn to. His curly black hair hung loosely on his forehead. His square jaw and white teeth were babe-magnets, although his once rock-hard abs were beginning to take on some extra padding and his hands were starting to shake at eleven each morning. Once he got his first Scotch shooter—Blended Vat 69—they calmed down.

Wheeler had not turned out the way he was supposed to. He had not lived up to his father's expectations. His first spectacular failure had been sixteen years ago when they'd thrown him out of the University of Southern California for being drunk and disorderly, and according to one University Regent, "an irredeemable scholastic project." The final incident that propelled his expulsion was a fist fight he'd gotten into at Julie's Bar after the S.C.–Stanford game. He had endured three Bay Area assholes for almost two hours before slipping his thousand-dollar Cartier watch off his left wrist and putting the misplaced Stanford alumni in the U.S.C. Trauma Ward. Wheeler had a solid punch and, even drunk, he could still bang one off you. His left hook was lethal. He preferred talking to hitting, but occasionally had to "step outside" with somebody. Fighting was a necessary skill when you were periscoping other people's women.

Wheeler Cassidy had been famous at U.S.C. He was that guy that everybody talked about . . . the tuna fisherman's tuna fisherman. The stunts he'd pulled were legendary: like jumping off the roof of the Tri-Delt House on a dare or driving his VW into the L.A. Coliseum at half-time during the U.C.L.A. game. On the side of his paintbrushed-cardinal-and-gold VW Rabbit, he had written, "Have one on me, Bruins." Then he sprayed the U.C.L.A. rooting section with warm beer from a supercharged keg. He'd been arrested six times for various violations and pranks before finally being expelled. His exploits were written up in the *Cardinal and Gold,* the student paper, at least once a month during his colorful three-year academic career, but that was a long time ago. Now he was what some people would call a country club bum. The West-ridge Country Club in Bel Air, California, was his haunt.

The W.C.C. had all kinds of strict membership requirements: Your family and ethnic background had to be acceptable; you needed to be well placed in society; and no members of the entertainment community were ever accepted. Wheeler got in on a junior membership when he turned twenty-one because his father, Wheeler Cassidy, Sr., had been a longtime member.

However, Wheeler Jr. was currently up before the W.C.C. disciplinary committee. They were trying to decide whether to kick him out for a one-nighter he'd had with the beautiful but restless wife of a senior member who was also, unfortunately, head of the club's rules committee. The affair had resulted in the couple's messy divorce. It was the memory of Wheeler's late father that so far had stayed the axe, but this time it looked like his expulsion from the club was inevitable.

Wheeler Sr. had been an investment broker and portfolio analyst who had made it big, eventually opening his own brokerage firm. He had died last year, taking with him Wheeler Jr.'s sole reason for being. There was something exhilarating about being the bad seed son of a domineering, humorless father that lost its thrill when Dear Ol' Dad hit Boot Hill. Now all of Wheeler's pranks seemed more desperate than funny. His father's anger had always been the rimshot that saved the joke.

Wheeler started drinking more after his father died, and now, in the morning when he got up, his head was dull as racial humor. His eyes were filled with grain, his stomach always on the edge of revolt. He was approaching middle age and, apart from three years at U.S.C. and another two in the Marines, he'd never accomplished anything.

He'd joined the Marine Corps only to fend off his father's threat that he would lose his inheritance for being chucked out of college. Then, just when it looked like he'd straightened out, being accepted for elite Special Forces training, he'd been dishonorably discharged from his unit for fornicating with his Commanding Officer's wife. Since then, he had never finished anything, except for hundreds upon hundreds of bottles of blended Scotch. He'd once read about an old eccentric in the desert who had built a house out of empty beer bottles. If Wheeler had had any architectural ambition, his empties could have built a small city.

It was twelve-thirty and Wheeler's hands were beginning to tremble. It was still a little early, but he moved down the narrow hallway toward the grill, and his first shooter of the day. On the way he passed framed pictures of club pros and golfing celebrities who had achieved recognition or glory on the W.C.C. links. As he walked, he glanced through the glass doors of the private dining room that catered lunches for members, and saw his younger brother, Prescott, gathered with five or six businessmen. All of them had yellow pads in front of them, their finished meals pushed off to the side, making notes while Pres lectured. Pres's secretary, Angie Wong, spotted Wheeler, tapped Prescott's shoulder, and whispered. Pres glanced up. His narrow face and intense expression darkened at the sight of his brother. He shook his head slightly as if to say "Don't come in."

Jeez, Pres, I'm not a typhoid carrier, Wheeler thought. But he was ashamed of his younger brother's reaction to him. Wheeler knew he'd been an embarrassment to his dead father. He knew his mother had long ago tired of making excuses for him, and now Pres seemed afraid his older brother might stumble in, vomit on the table, and ruin his business meeting. Before moving on, Wheeler waved at his brother and smiled an apology through the glass door. Then, unexpectedly, Prescott's face softened and, for a moment, Wheeler saw on his brother's narrow features the same look of awe Pres had always given him during their childhood . . . a look of envy and respect that Wheeler hadn't seen in almost sixteen years.

Back then, Pres had thought his big brother could do anything. Wheeler had been Pres's god, his idol. It was a time when if Wheeler had told his little brother to run through fire and jump off the Santa Monica cliffs, Pres would have ended up on the beach with his hair burning. Now things were different. Wheeler was a gravy stain on Pres's huge success. Prescott Cassidy was the family superstar now. At thirty-four, he was arguably among the most important lawyers in Los Angeles. One of the biggest names in the local political spectrum, a huge Democratic Party fund-raiser and power broker, Prescott handled complex legal problems and political deals while Wheeler honked down shooters in the W.C.C. grill. *Oh well, shit happens.*

That look of admiration that Wheeler thought he saw on his brother's face must have been a weird reflection in the glass or bad lighting. Even still, it made him stop . . . made him wonder why things had turned out this way.

He was sitting in the beautiful dining room that overlooked the third fairway, eating alone, when Pres and his secretary, Angie Wong, walked out of the club. Angie was a small, thin Chinese woman in her late forties who never seemed to smile, but had laser intensity and a personality as tough as federal taxes.

Angie looked at him, or through him, and didn't react. Pres never slowed as he moved on with the rest of his party. Pres was always in a hurry, always late to a very important appointment.

Wheeler was looking out the window, his mind far away, when he suddenly heard Pres's voice.

"Wheel?"

He looked up and saw his younger brother. Prescott's narrow face and intense manner hovered restlessly at the edge of the table like a dragonfly over a pond, afraid to land.

"How ya doin', Pres? Big deals, huh?"

Pres shot a look out to the front door where his party was just pulling away in valet-delivered cars. "Yeah, right. Got a minute?"

Wheeler was surprised. Everybody knew time was the big loss leader in the department store of disappointment he was managing. Wheeler had minutes, he had hours, he had years.

His time had become so cheap, it had almost no value except as chronology.

Wheeler motioned to a chair and Pres lowered himself into it. Pres glanced at his big brother and then the look was there again.

Just for a second; just for a flash. It was little Prescott's look from their childhood, an expression that said, *Wheel, can you show me how to catch a football? Can you help me learn to skateboard? Can you get her to go out with me?* Blue eyes looking at Wheeler Cassidy in worship and wonder; a look he'd once dearly treasured.

And then it was gone. Now Pres was looking down and frowning. A moment of business came next, so Pres could regain control. "I have your check," he said. "If I'd known I was going to see you today, I would've brought it. There are capital gains taxes on the big sale the estate just made on the O.T.C. Preferreds, so it's a little less this month than usual. But we had to sell that shit off. The portfolio was overloaded on media stocks." He looked up. "I know you're always running short around the twentieth but the Fed upped the estimated quarterly so I had to hold some back on the account."

"Right. That's okay."

"But if you get pushed, call me. I'll shoot you an advance against your quarterly dividends."

Wheeler lived on the estate money his father had left. It paid out over $180,000 a year, after taxes. But Wheeler lived high and had expensive tastes in women, gambling, and cars. He often ran short and, even with his golf winnings, was sometimes mooching hundreds from friends by the end of the month.

As Wheeler looked at his brother, he saw something else he wasn't used to seeing. He saw tension. It was in and around the eyes, with maybe a tinge of panic. Usually Pres was all business. The white rabbit of the legal profession hurrying out the door, clutching his oversized watch. *I'm late, I'm late, for a very important date.* Business, of course, not pleasure. Prescott was "happily married" to Elizabeth, the Ice Goddess of charity and consciousness-raising. He had a twelve-year-old son, Hollis. Prescott was the eight-by-ten family man in a gold frame.

"Are you okay?" Wheeler asked, because his brother still looked uncharacteristically troubled.

"Uh, yeah, sure. Of course," Prescott smiled, but the smile was the one you give the dentist so he can check your incisors. "Listen, Wheel, I . . . I wanted to tell you something . . . something I haven't said in a long time. . . . It's something I've been thinking about a lot lately."

"Get a job?" Wheeler said, trying to preempt what he suspected was his younger brother's latest attempt to knock him back onto the road of responsibility.

"I wanted to say I . . . that I love you. . . . Sometimes, with all the bullshit, that gets lost. I know things have been difficult since Dad died, but the memories I have of you, the important ones are . . ." He stopped, took a breath, then went on, "You're the reason I made it. I just wanted you to know I haven't forgotten."

Wheeler was instantly choked. Tears rushed into his eyes. He looked at his brother and wondered what to say. He loved him too, but he also hated him. Why did Pres have to be such a damn world-beater? Why couldn't he just be a good guy to go drinking with? Why did he always have to be first?

"Remember when you taught me to drive and we took Dad's car and I went too fast on Angeles Crest and lost it?" Pres said unexpectedly.

"Jesus, you were nuts that night," Wheeler contributed to the memory. He'd been sixteen. Pres had been only thirteen. Pres was driving and had slid their dad's new yellow Corvette into the guardrail on the mountain highway, busting the fiberglass front fender, exploding it like fine crystal. The next morning Wheeler had told his father that he had taken the car out alone and had done the damage, which was more or less true. It had been Wheeler's idea. Prescott had always been scared of their father, so Wheeler had taken the hit. Wheeler was grounded for two months, which didn't mean much because he snuck out the upstairs window every night after his father went to bed anyway.

"I just wanted you to know I remember all the great stuff you did for me when we were growing up, and I want you to know that I've always loved you and always respected you. Even now when, when . . ." He didn't finish it but sat there, looking at Wheeler, his hands clasped formally on the table in front of him. "Well, I just wanted to tell you that." He looked at his ten-thousand-dollar watch. "Guess I better go. Got a full calendar this afternoon," the white rabbit said, but he didn't move. He didn't leave the table or rush off. They looked at one another across the W.C.C. silverware and crystal. Time slowed, became more valuable. Seconds ticked. Precious seconds, precious even in Wheeler's discount store of failed expectations. They reached out to each other with their eyes and tried to find their childhood.

In the half-minute or so of silence, it was magically recovered. It was okay. They were brothers again. Sort of. And then Prescott said a very strange thing.

"Whatever happens, promise me you'll do the right thing."

Then Pres got up and walked out of the dining room without looking back.

Wheeler was unsettled by the incident.

It was almost as if his brother had been saying good-bye.

TWO

Fu Hai and Xiao Jie

hang Fu Hai awoke as the train lurched violently on a switch-back turn, then rattled and groaned down the east face of the Tianshan range, the huge Mountains of Heaven in northwest China. Shortly after he was awake, a middle-aged woman moved unsteadily down the crowded aisle of the car. She was carrying a steaming thermos of *kai shui* and knocked on the board he was lying on with her knuckles, asking in Mandarin if he wanted tea. He nodded and she poured him a steaming cup, which he paid a few *fen* for, then she moved on. Fu Hai was traveling "hard sleeper," which, on Chinese trains, meant second class. Only high-ranking political figures, foreign tourists, and wealthy company chiefs could afford "soft sleeper," or first class. He had spent extra money to avoid the uncomfortable "hard seat," or third class, where he would be cramped and have to sleep sitting up. It was worth it. This escape from the Taklamakan Desert had been his goal for almost fourteen years, since he'd been exiled to the boiler room of the No. 3 Silkworm Factory in Khotan for political crimes his father had committed.

His father, Zhang Wei Dong, had been a calligrapher in Beijing and had been turned in by Fu Hai's older brother, Lu Ping, for practicing the "Four Olds," which were forbidden by Chairman Mao. The Four Olds—Old Thoughts, Old Habits, Old Customs, and Old Ideas—were difficult to defend against because they were so general. His father had been taken from their house in Beijing twenty years ago when Zhang Fu Hai had been only seven. He had watched in sorrow as his father had been made to daub his face with black ink and wear the dunce cap of social degradation. He cried as Zhang Wei Dong was led from the house while an angry mob of Communists shouted, "Leniency for those who confess, severity for those who do not!" He had never seen his father again. His older brother, Lu Ping, was rewarded for his act of patriotism with a commission in the Chinese Army and was stationed at a secret nuclear base somewhere in northern China. In one letter to his little sister, Xiao Jie, his brother had bragged that he was helping to develop a nuclear arsenal that would bring great glory to Mother China.

Fu Hai was taken from his mother's house shortly after the letter arrived. It was determined that he was a product of bad parenting by his politically corrupt father—that his mother had fallen into the trap of the "Four Over-dones": Over-indulgence, Over-protection, Over-caring, and Over-interference. It was decided that he was a candidate for "reeducation," so Fu Hai was shipped to Khotan, which was a place as close to hell as he could imagine.

Khotan was in the northwestern section of China, near the Pakistan border. The Turkic-speaking natives called Uighurs hated the Chinese. The dusty desert town sat on the east face of Khafa Gumbaz, the Domes of Wrath Mountains, on the edge of the vast Taklamakan Desert. *Taklamakan* meant "You go in, you don't come out." Fu Hai was never tempted to try.

He had been assigned to work in the black, windowless boiler rooms of the silk factory there. The intense heat was almost unbearable. Fu Hai's job was to make sure the boiling water continued to flow across the huge metal trays on which the silk cocoons were soaked before being spun. The working conditions were slimy and dank, and Fu Hai spent almost fourteen miserable years sweating in that hell-hole. He soon realized that he could not stay in that place much longer. He had seen older laborers who had been in the boiler rooms for fifteen or more years slowly go blind; a blindness, he learned, caused by being made to stare at the white cocoons in the inky blackness, hour after mind-numbing hour, surrounded by steaming silk, screaming spindles, and unbearable heat. In a sense, the boiler room had become a cocoon of political hatred for Fu Hai . . . hatred for Mother China, which, as an innocent child in Beijing, he had once adored. He decided he would find a way, not only to leave Khotan, but to leave China. He would find a way to "Ride the Snake" to America. "Riding the Snake" was the dangerous practice of illegal immigration out of China. The criminal Tongs in Guangzhou and the newly repatriated Colony of Hong Kong provided this service for anyone willing to pay the price. Fu Hai had heard it was exorbitant, over thirty thousand American dollars. A figure so vast he could barely conceive of it. The only way a penniless worker like Zhang Fu Hai could afford it would be to sell himself into slavery to the Tongs.

He knew this would be frightening and dangerous and that he would have to put his life at risk, but he had already decided that if he stayed in the silk factory, he would soon die from the abysmal conditions.

The food was like nothing that he had ever before encountered: horrible concoctions that he could barely force down. Flatbread and stinking gray mutton with raisins that, it was rumored, the Uighurs blew their noses in to show their contempt for the Chinese workers.

By the age of sixteen, Fu Hai had already begun to save the majority of his meager wages. He lived in a one-room hovel with five other men, and at night he would sneak out of the one-street town of Khotan to the edge of the desert. There he would hide his savings in an old pot that he buried in a Muslim cemetery, under a cracked clay dome whose interior was strewn with dry bones. Twice a month, he would make deposits in his "bank of freedom."

The captured years moved as slowly as the silkworms crawling from their annual cocoons. The boredom and wretchedness of his life stretched out behind him like a ribbon of snail slime that he could barely believe was his own personal history. When he was twenty-seven, he finally got his chance to escape in the person of a greedy, contemptuously corrupt Assistant Communist Party Secretary named Wang Ming Yang. Strangely enough, in Chinese, that name meant Bright Force. Wang had charged him three thousand *yuan* to sign a Party Relocation Permission slip, allowing Fu Hai to return to Beijing. The money was almost everything that Fu Hai had saved during the entire fourteen years he had been in Khotan. He gladly gave it over and watched in the Party Secretary's one-room apartment as the slip was signed and stamped with the official Chinese red government seal.

He traveled by rattletrap bus from Khotan to Kashgar, then through the dusty oasis town of Aksu, finally arriving after three long days at Urumqi, the provincial capital.

He waited at the train station, with his heart pounding, as the "Iron Rooster" pulled into Urumqi. The train was covered with black dust. The windows were impossible to see through, having been pelted relentlessly by the *Kara Buran*, the "Black Hurricanes," that blow apocalyptically out of the western deserts, starring and cracking the glass with flying rocks and gravel.

Carrying his one knapsack of meager belongings, Fu Hai boarded the "Iron Rooster" and found his bed in hard sleeper on the first tier. After one day on the train, they were winding down the east face of the huge Tianshan range. Then they would head east on the five-day journey toward Beijing.

After waking, his fellow passengers started their morning ritual, coughing and spitting globs of phlegm down on the floor of the car. Then they would jump out of bed, making sure to step on their own glob, much as one would step on a cigarette. It was considered impolite to omit this "step on it" courtesy, despite the fact that all of the train cars had signs that demanded: NO SPITTING. HELP BUILD SPIRITUAL CIVILIZATION.

There was a festive atmosphere aboard the train. People spoke freely, laughing, even making fun of things political. It was talk that would have gotten you locked up or even shot during the Cultural Revolution. Fu Hai discovered that trains were the only place in China where people could speak freely, because the passengers knew they would never see each other again. The moving, rattling conveyance provided a sense of safety that temporarily allowed them unheard-of freedom of speech. This free-flowing speech was also helped by liquor called *kaoliang*, which was made from sorghum and was as powerful as moonshine and plentiful as beer.

It was almost New Year's, 1998, the Year of the Tiger. Fu Hai was excited to be on his way to America.

The soldier who was sitting across from Fu Hai on the hard sleeper was from the Lop Nor nuclear proving ground in far northwest China. Fu Hai asked him if he'd ever heard of his brother, Zhang Lu Ping, but the soldier had not. The soldier had a medal on his uniform that he showed to everyone he talked to. It had been awarded to him for "Excellence of Political Thought," and Fu Hai decided not to say anything more to him. By noon, the soldier got very, very drunk and vomited in the aisle. Fu Hai and the other passengers screamed and yelled at him until he cleaned it up. The incident made Fu Hai feel stronger. They had made the soldier bend to their collective will. Fu Hai had become one of the group.

Two days later, Zhang Fu Hai was a practiced traveler. He had learned to get off at the stations they encountered and buy sunflower seeds and hot dumplings from the traveling station vendors, whose prices were much cheaper than at the shops in the station kiosk. He would quickly reboard and climb back on the first-level board bed. The train would lurch out of the station and he would ride in silence, spitting sunflower seeds on the floor and smiling as they headed to Beijing.

———

Three days later, Fu Hai looked out the cracked train windows as they passed the huge chemical smokestacks of Lanzhou.

In Gansu Province, the landscape gradually turned greener and he saw the terraced hillsides and green rice paddies he vaguely remembered from his youth. He had a surge of homesickness for his father and mother and his beloved little sister, to whom he had written once a month for fourteen years, without ever receiving a reply. He wondered if she was alive or if his letters had been stopped by the party officials in Khotan. Or perhaps, if they ever got through, maybe her return letters had been opened, read, and just thrown away. He had been told by Government Communication ten years before that his mother had died of tuberculosis. Fu Hai would never forgive Chairman Mao for what he had done to his family. He remembered his father, forced to leave home wearing a dunce cap in shame and humiliation. He remembered the days after, the anger building in him as he sat in his classroom singing the Mao anthem. The lyrics were repugnant to him: "Mother is dear and Father is dear, but Chairman Mao is dearest of all." It had been the beginning of a political dissatisfaction that had ended with his exile to Khotan.

The train rattled on, a lurching, winding metal snake, taking him back to the city of his birth.

After five days, the train finally pulled into Beijing's bustling "Fire Cart Station." Zhang Fu Hai got off and looked around in awe at the same railroad station he had left fourteen years before. Only the building remained the same. Its twin clocks chimed in watch-towers above the station roof. Red flags were flapping in the late winter breeze from silver poles at the end of the huge new concrete concourse. Outside lay a wonderland of capitalism. There were shiny American and German-made taxis lined up, waiting for rich travelers. Fu Hai couldn't afford one of these, so he hired a three-wheeled trishaw with a pedal-boy to take him back to his old neighborhood.

Beijing was totally transformed. No more dark colors and drab clothing. The city was alive with activity. It was February 8, 1998, the day before Chinese New Year, which would mark the beginning of the Year of the Ox. The national bird of China had become the construction crane. The steel-armed monstrosities seemed to be perched on top of every other building. There were department stores with plate-glass windows filled with modern appliances, which more and more people could afford: "Snowflake" refrigerators and "Great Wall" color TVs. Record stores advertised Aiwa stereos. A huge McDonald's restaurant was right on the edge of Tiananmen Square. Fu Hai passed the old Forbidden City and Bei Hai Park with its placid, beautifully landscaped lake. They peddled past Coal Hill with its five gold-roofed pavilions.

Beijing seemed money-mad. He could barely believe Wang Fu Jing, the big shopping street with its T-shirt shops and music stores. He gawked at the Chinese shoppers in bright clothing and western blue jeans. He marveled at the fancy bars, restaurants, and karaoke clubs.

All of this had been happening while he'd been in a dank, dark room sweating over steaming silk cocoons. Instead of being thrilled by the changes, he became even more bitter. Because of the "Four Olds," he had lost his chance to be a part of it all. And even worse, he knew he never would be. He was no longer from Beijing. He was now a hated refugee from the Western Provinces. A peasant scorned for his very presence here, forced to constantly show his relocation permission slip.

Fu Hai finally arrived at his father's old house. It was as he remembered: a large gray brick building with an ornate carved wooden door, which had been freshly painted red. After asking for his sister at the second-floor apartment where he was born, he was told by an old woman that Wang Xiao Jie was now living in the abandoned porter's room near the street entrance of the house with her husband, a night soil collector named Wang Ping An. His sister, the old woman said, had one child, a girl. It was said with contempt, girls being of little value in New China. Fu Hai walked slowly across the tiny courtyard, passing coal bricks drying in the sun. The bricks were made by scraping coal dust out of the stoves, mixing it with water, and pouring it in wood molds to dry. Later, it would be cut into bricks and reused. Everything in China was reused—even old wood matches were saved. A wood splinter could still carry a flame from one fire to another. Eggshells could be sprinkled on potted plants as fertilizer. Old Ping-Pong balls got faces painted on them and with a little cloth became finger puppets to entertain children.

Fu Hai walked across the yard feeling the harsh stares of the families now clustered in the building. He walked down the stairs into the dark porter's room. A cloth hung over the threshold of a ten-foot-square windowless space that was now his beloved little sister's home. When he saw her, he could barely believe it was her. She looked ancient. A twenty-six-year-old crone. Her teeth were rotted, her body stooped, her spirit broken. After they hugged, their eyes filled with tears.

"Why are you living down here?" he finally said. "This is a place for an animal. Our rooms were in the second courtyard."

"After mother died, I had no choice," she told him. "I became pregnant with my second daughter, which was against Party regulations. I was forced to have an abortion and I was badly injured by the operation. I have never been the same."

That evening, he met his ten-year-old niece, who was extremely slender and said nothing, looking at Fu Hai with large black eyes. He also met Xiao Jie's husband, Ping An, the night soil collector. He was uneducated and couldn't read. Even worse, he stank from his work. He had the horrible job of scraping up human excrement from the public latrine catch basins and loading it in containers to be taken to the fields, a position so low that nobody challenged his sister's politics anymore. She had sunk below the radar.

Later, the Block Warden came into their room unannounced.

She was sixty years old, wearing a civilian uniform, and said she had heard from the neighbors that the Wongs had a visitor.

"I need to see your permit to be in Beijing," she demanded.

Fu Hai got the stamped permit out of his bag. He had already showed it many times as he crossed four provinces of China. He had never had a problem with the permit, so he was shocked when the woman first seemed puzzled by the document, then angered.

"Where did you get this?" she asked, harshly.

"It was issued by the Assistant Party Secretary in Khotan," Fu Hai said, his breath now in spurts, fear creeping up and grabbing his throat.

"This is a forgery," the Block Warden said, glowering at Fu Hai. "Did you buy this with money? Did you use Guan-Xi?" The remark was ludicrous. One look at Fu Hai said he had no influence. He had paid for it with fourteen years of drudgery. He was almost penniless.

"It is not a forgery!" he said. "It is a valid relocation document."

"It is not," the Block Warden said, and she turned to leave, carrying the permit with her.

"I need that permit!" Zhang Fu Hai cried out.

The old woman spun back on him. "We have peasants coming from inland China or the Western Provinces trying to take our jobs, jobs that belong to the citizens of Beijing. You flood our markets. You work for peasant wages that we can't live on. You steal. We don't want you here."

"I'm from Beijing. I was born here. This is my sister."

"A night soil collector's wife is not going to save you from this crime of deception," the Block Warden said angrily, then left.

"You must go," Xiao Jie said softly to her brother. They both knew the woman would be back quickly with the police to arrest Fu Hai. Without his permission slip, he would be sent to jail. Wang Xiao Jie hugged her big brother.

He could feel the bones in her back. "I'm going to Ride the Snake," he told her. "If I get to America, I will work very hard

31

and I will pay to bring you there. In America, everybody has money, and everybody lives like a Party Secretary."

"But the travel fee is very expensive. We have no money to help you."

"I will sell myself. If I have to I will commit crimes for the Triads. I will do anything to get to America," he said hotly, channeling his anger toward this goal. "I will bring you there to be with me," he promised her again.

She cried and held his face between her hands. The fourteen years had completely reshaped both of them. They could barely recognize one another.

Despite the changes, with all of the new department stores and colored T-shirts, Beijing was still not a friendly town for a silk worker from the Western Provinces. It opened its arms only to the politically elite, or to people who could make money by their Guan-Xi with the politically elite.

He left his sister and walked quickly out of the courtyard of the old building. He moved up the narrow, teeming streets, soon losing himself in the crowd. Without his permit, he knew he wouldn't last long. He had to find a "Snakehead," who could organize illegal immigration to America. The Snakehead would tell him how to pay for a ticket.

With the loss of his relocation permit, he had become part of China's huge floating population, a population of disenfranchised people that numbered in the millions.

He remembered studying a philosopher in school, long ago. "Turning toward the light," the philosopher had written, "is initially confusing, painful, and even blinding. But if not now . . . when?"

Zhang Fu Hai had turned toward the light, and, as promised, he was blinded by it. His heart pounded with fear and uncertainty, but he had to keep going. He was going to Ride the Snake. He would save his little sister. He would somehow make it to America.

If not now . . . when?

THREE

The White Rabbit Takes a Dive

Several days after the strange encounter with his brother, Wheeler sat in the W.C.C. grill bar and watched for Lois Atwater. She had been playing tennis on court three when he'd finished the front nine. Her long, tan legs had flashed invitingly under her short tennis dress. Lois was high up on his spear-fishing list. She had a tight, gym-trained body and an over-weight, out-of-shape older husband. Her black hair was cut short and she seemed to constantly display her beautiful white teeth when Wheeler was standing around. She had that model's trick of being able to smile so that her bottom row got into the act. He knew he was close to pay dirt when she mentioned that her older sister had been at U.S.C. when he'd stolen the University fire truck and driven it up the steps of Annenberg Hall, crashing into the pillars of that august monument to higher eduction. This reckless stunt, pulled during the Middle European History exam, resulted in its postponement until after Christmas. *Rimshot. Another Wheeler Cassidy masterpiece.*

"Freshen that up for you, Mr. Cassidy?" Ramon Delgado

asked. Ramon was a handsome Mexican, short and muscular, about ten years older than Wheeler. He had witnessed many of Wheeler's spear-fishing tournaments from his penalty box behind the bar.

"Might as well keep the barley farmers in business," Wheeler said as a new shot was poured into his glass.

"John Haverston was in here this morning," Ramon said, his voice sort of ending in a question. John Haverston was on the membership disciplinary committee, which had been deliberating for almost a week on whether or not to give Wheeler the boot. "He was looking for you," Ramon continued. "I said you was out playing golf."

"I think we're about to have a W.C.C. execution," Wheeler mused. "I'll be beaten to death by old lawyers with putters."

"I don't know, sir. I think they just gonna tell you you gotta be more discreet. . . ."

Ramon polished the bar, trying to find a way to put difficult thoughts into words. Wheeler always thought it must be strange for Ramon to deal drinks to bums like him all day. Ramon, who had come across the border in the back of an empty, stinking gasoline truck, who had worked in the lettuce fields in central California to support his family until he got a job through his cousin on the maintenance crew at Westridge Country Club. Ramon, who learned near-perfect English and worked like a peon, and who now found himself behind the bar listening to millionaires' sons bitch about their lives.

"See, I think if a woman member is married but she don't respect the sanctity of her marriage vows and decides to take liberties in the bedroom, this is not totally the gentleman's fault . . . because, sir, this was not a good marriage, I think, to begin with."

"That's got nice Latin spin on it, Ramon, but I don't think this bunch of pooh-bahs is gonna see it your way."

He knocked back the drink in one swallow as the phone on the bar rang and Ramon moved down to answer it. Wheeler could hear him say, "He's right here, sir."

Ramon brought the phone over to him. It sort of bothered Wheeler that most people now knew they could find him at the W.C.C. bar any afternoon, but it didn't bother him enough to do anything about it. Still, it was discouraging, as if he'd dropped another notch on the social ratchet wheel. He put the phone to his ear.

It was Jimmy, a willowy, overtly homosexual blond man who was his mother's secretary.

"You must get here immediately," he lisped.

"Why? What is it . . . is Mother okay?"

"As if that matters one whit to you. . . ."

"Come on, Jimmy, cut the shit. What's up?"

"I'm not going to say. It's not my job to say. Better she tells, but you just better get your little white ass over here, Wheeler," and Jimmy hung up.

He thought it was also noteworthy that his mother's secretary felt he could sass Wheeler out. On the other hand, Jimmy was an expert on men's asses, so maybe it was just a nice compliment. With that amusing thought still rattling in his liquor-soaked head, he got up off the bar stool, dropped a twenty for Ramon, and left.

The Cassidy mansion was in Beverly Hills, on Wingate at the end of the cul-de-sac. It was a choice seven-acre spread, the house sitting in Colonial splendor on the top of a rolling hill of bright green, freshly mowed summer rye. He parked his new red XK8 Jag convertible out front and walked into the house, his hands in his pockets, linen pant cuffs flapping over polished Spanish leather loafers, feeling like a road-company Gatsby.

He had never lived in the house. His father had bought it just after Wheeler got thrown out of Special Forces. Wheeler had decided to live in sexual splendor with two topless dancers who worked the summer shows at the Trop in Vegas and were now wintering in Los Angeles, trying to open a health food restaurant. *Why* does *everybody in L.A. want to open a restaurant?*

Jimmy was standing by the banister with his hands on his hips, feet in fifth position, glowering savagely. "You're going to have to help her. You're the only one she has left," he said. "She's going to need a lot more than a half-drunken bum."

"I really wish you'd just tell me what the hell is happening, Jimmy."

The young man chose to say nothing, but moved to the side and pointed to his mother's room upstairs. Wheeler climbed the long circular staircase to the upstairs hall. He could hear his mother crying. When he entered the bedroom, his mother looked up from the chaise longue by the front window.

It happened again, as it had for all the years he had known her. He was momentarily startled by her incredible beauty. She was sixty-five but looked forty, and it wasn't Beverly Hills plastic surgeons who had performed the miracle. He knew he had received his looks from her gene pool, but there was something about Katherine Cassidy, something so beautiful and restrained and elegant, that she always required a moment of reappraisal. As if his memory wasn't strong enough to carry her perfection. She turned to him.

"Prescott, Prescott . . . is dead," she said, and her hand wandered up to her mouth and covered her lips, almost as if she was afraid the evil sentence would return.

"What?" Wheeler said, his mind in full gallop. "Dead? How?" Three one-word sentences. *Mr. Bullshit comes up dry.*

"How could this happen?" his mother wailed.

"Mom, who told you? Are you sure?"

"The police. They came by two hours ago. We didn't know where to find you."

"I was at the club," he said, instantly regretting the remark. "Did he . . . ? Was it . . . ?"

"Heart attack," his mother whispered. "They found him in his office, at his desk, when they came to work this morning." And then she started to cry again.

It was such a mournful wail that Wheeler rushed to her and put an arm around her, trying desperately to comfort her. He felt the racking sobs. Her muscles quivered with the sickening effort.

"Mother, mother, I'm here," he said, as if that made any fucking difference. "I'm here," he whispered, and she reached down and squeezed his hand. The squeeze sort of said it all. It was the way you'd squeeze a child's hand when you want him to be quiet.

"What can I do? How can I help?" he asked, his mind still racing. Somehow, just like that—in a heartbeat—Pres wasn't part of the race anymore. He'd been scratched on a coronary technicality. Wheeler's world had shifted again. Prescott Cassidy had checked off the planet.

"Why? Why Prescott . . . ?" Kay said.

And immediately, Wheeler knew that the full sentence went: *Why Prescott and not Wheeler?* After all, Wheeler was the foul-up. The country club lush who was only trying to screw other people's wives. Wheeler was just taking up bar space while Prescott was taking up political causes. Wheeler was a much better candidate for a medical crack-up—he'd been processing ninety-proof Scotch through his kidneys and liver faster than a mid-sized distillery. Why Prescott and not Wheeler? *Goddamn good question.*

"The office has been calling," Kay finally said. "They're frantic. I don't know what to tell them."

"What office?" Wheeler said, dumbly.

"*His* office. Nobody knows what to do. Can you go see if you can help?" she asked, not looking at him, her eyes out the window as if maybe Pres was out there winning another race, about to come in and surprise them with a new gold trophy.

"Mom, what do I know about Pres's law office? What do I . . ." He stopped, speechless, because she looked at him with such a pained expression of anger and regret he felt dismembered by it.

"Okay, I'll go. I'll go over there."

So, with very little else to say, that's exactly what he did.

What he found made absolutely no sense at all.

Madhouse

Wheeler's thoughts about Pres were complicated. So complicated that he suspected they would never become totally clear to him. First there was love; Wheeler had really loved his younger brother, loved him unconditionally, loved him for who he was and what he had become. While Wheeler was getting drunk, Pres was getting rich and famous, and you had to admire that, because it was what Dad had wanted for both of them and Pres had taken the chance, stepped up and hit the ball. Wheeler had chosen his own path, which, lately, was winding in tighter and tighter circles around the nineteenth hole at the Westridge Country Club. Still . . . still, there was that early training, those fatherly lectures delivered to Wheeler earnestly and without deviation; lectures that had somehow managed to find a spot and fester malignantly in the back of his head. Now he could hear his father's warnings. *"Wheeler, you're wasting valuable time. Your life is about nothing."*

Pres had become the things they had both been told to be, and Wheeler truly admired Pres for taking the more difficult road.

Okay. So that said, there was also the other side of it. There was Pres, the fucking prince; Pres, the family kiss-ass; Pres, who, with his immense success, had made Wheeler's failure even deeper and more important. And for this, Wheeler had started hating his younger brother. Now his little brother was dead. Pres's heart had blown up like an old Studebaker engine. Wheeler was finally back out in front. He was alive and Pres wasn't. *So who's better off now, buddy?*

Wheeler's thoughts were a jumbled mixture of sadness and guilt. Then his mind flashed back to a drunken conversation he'd had one afternoon, a year ago, at the W.C.C. bar. He'd been looking into the rum-dimmed eyes of Stockton C. Tanquary IV, known around the club as "Tank." Alcohol had ravaged Tank, and tuned his Harvard-educated engine down to a dieseling, coughing idle. His complexion looked like a blueberry pie that had exploded in the oven.

"Fucking Suzanne Peiser . . . 'member Suzy?" Tank was referring to a younger member's athletic wife. "Fuckin' brain cancer. Deader'n dog shit in less than a year," he slurred, wheezing musty breath over the rim of his tub glass at Wheeler, who nodded, not sure what to make of the abrupt statement. "Yep, she's right there with the Colonel," Tank continued. "The Spudster is one dead military son of a bitch. Fucker's doing close-order drill with Jesus now."

"Right," Wheeler had said, wishing he didn't have to smell Tank's alcohol-rotted breath. Colonel Warren "Spud" Westwater had had a fatal traffic accident coming home from his horse farm in Santa Barbara. His wife, Sissy, had also been killed in the crash.

"An' how 'bout Kip Lunsford? How 'bout that? Huh? The fuckin' guy died in the shower. Can you believe it? Thirty-nine years old, head of his own trucking company, and that bozo slips goin' for the soap, hits his fuckin' head on the tile ledge, and . . . kaboom! Adios, motherfucker."

Even in his dumbed-down stupor, as Wheeler looked at the ghost of his own future, he had known what Tank was saying: "I might be a drunk, I might look like two hundred and thirty pounds of yellow shit in a bag, but dammit, I'm better off than all these other world-beating assholes who are now gazing up at their own coffin lids."

The traffic was light on Beverly Glen, but Wheeler was so lost in thought he almost hit a pedestrian who was crossing the street at Wilshire. He was on his way to Century City, where Prescott's law firm was housed in two floors of antique-furnished splendor. Those ornate offices had always managed to give Wheeler the finger every time he dropped by to get his estate check, which his mother thought should be delivered each month by his reliable younger brother. *So, fuck you, Pres! Who the hell is winning the race now?!* Wheeler wanted to cry for his dead brother, but the tears wouldn't come. So he drove stone-faced, all the way down Santa Monica Boulevard to the Avenue of the Stars, and down the underground garage ramp of Prescott's building to visiting parking. Although he couldn't cry, he was broken-hearted because he would never be able to see his brother again or root for him or be proud of what he'd accomplished.

Like he'd said, his thoughts about Pres were complicated.

The office was a madhouse. Phones were ringing; there was an air of funereal reverence amidst confused, frenzied activity.

"Angie didn't come in this morning," the pretty redhead said, looking at Wheeler, trying not to flirt. She correctly reasoned this would be a bad morning for it, even though she found Wheeler terribly attractive. "We met last time you were here. I'm Georgette, I was in Legal Research then," she said. "I'm so sorry. We're all . . . we're so . . . I just don't know how to say it. Prescott was a wonderful . . . just a wonderful person."

"Yeah, he was," Wheeler said softly and looked around at the chorus of faces watching him, all of them wondering how he would surf the crest of this wave. He showed nothing.

"It's been crazy," she said. "Clients have been calling. I'm just temping up here, but somebody apparently broke into your brother's house last night and set off the alarm. And now Angie didn't come to work and she's the only one who knows where everything in his office is. . . ."

"Somebody broke into Pres's house?" Wheeler said, concerned. He knew that Pres's wife, Liz, and his son, Hollis, were in Connecticut at Liz's parents' house for Hollis's winter vacation. Pres had been planning to go there on Tuesday. Now they were flying back, or at least that was what Jimmy had said as Wheeler left for Century City.

"The police called. We gave them a key. They shut the alarm off. I tried to find Angie. She's got her machine on and she's not picking up."

Wheeler remembered the last time he had seen his brother's secretary. Angie Wong had breezed by him on her way out of the country club a week before.

"Is his Rolodex in the office?" Wheeler asked. His mind was still whirling and skipping beats, nibbling at stray thoughts but locking on nothing. She shrugged, then nodded, and he moved into his brother's huge corner suite filled with certificated Chippendale furniture.

Chip and Dale—aren't they cartoon mice?

Wheeler started to look through the Rolodex for the number of the alarm company so he could contact them to see if a window or door had been broken. It was then that he noticed the first strange thing . . . all of the little cards were out of order, as if somebody had removed them and stuck them back in without looking. None were under their correct alphabetical listing. Pres would never do that. Pres was over-organized; even his closets were color-keyed.

"These are out of order," he said, looking at the hundreds of cards, thinking it would take forever to find the alarm company in this jumbled mess.

"Well . . . uh, he . . . that's strange." She couldn't explain it, *but then, she was just a temp, transferred up from—what was it?—*

Legal Research. He sat down and went through the cards, finally finding the alarm company in with the Q's, where there was almost everything but a name starting with Q.

He handed it to Georgette and asked her to call the company and make sure the house was secure. While she went out to call, Wheeler sat in his brother's high-back swivel chair and looked out the window toward the ocean.

The offices were on the twenty-fifth and -sixth floors and the view was spectacular. This particular L.A. afternoon was better than most. A light Santa Ana wind had cleared the basin of smog, blowing it out to sea, giving Catalina Island a good dose of twentieth-century reality. He felt strange sitting in his brother's chair, where Pres had died. He'd never sat there before. He didn't belong in this chair . . . *or did he?*

The next thing that happened was downright spooky. Pres had died at his desk, working late . . . and his car was still in the garage. It had been, for some reason, parked across two spaces. Orderly, compulsive Prescott would never do that.

W*ho's pulling this shit?*

The building's parking garage had been asking that it be moved. Nobody had the key. Georgette came back in and told him that the police had not reset the alarm, but the house was secure. He nodded and went down to move Pres's car.

It took no time for Wheeler to get Pres's classic brown Mercedes sedan open. He popped the chrome strip off the door with his penknife, reached in through the hole under the strip, and pushed the lock up. He hot-wired the car by reaching under the dash, disconnecting, then touching the ignition wires together. The engine coughed and purred to life. Prank car theft was another of Wheeler's deft social accomplishments.

"Stop," Prescott said, his voice clear and commanding in the car interior. Wheeler's heart jumped up into his throat. He spun around, looked in the back seat . . . empty! *What the fuck?*

"New paragraph, Angie," his brother's voice continued. It was coming from the speaker system. The radio in the dash had a digital readout on the LED screen that now said "Tape." Wheeler's heart slowed. It was just a dictation recording:

"All our contacts at I.N.S. will remain intact, and John will continue to process the account on your end. However, I must caution our friend in Hong Kong against continuing to increase the flow in all three divisions. At this level of activity, he will surely have political trouble at the highest level of the U.S. government. Stop. New paragraph, Angie. Lastly, I regret to inform you that, as of this date, I will no longer be able to continue to participate. Stop. I have been making all of the above arguments to the White Fan here, but have basically been ignored. I have no other choice but to withdraw from the equation. New paragraph, Angie. I wish you well and hope all is successful, and that everything we worked for will eventually happen in mid-'98. Please make no further contact as my decision is final. Sign that with the usual closing, Angie, and get it off immediately. Then erase this tape and shred the file."

The tape was over.

Silence.

His brother's voice had shaken him deeply. He wanted to get the fuck out of there.

He reparked the car between the lines, replaced the chrome strip on the door, then left the tape in the tape deck, locked safely inside the newly orphaned Mercedes.

When he went back up to the office, he was approached by the office manager, a narrow, hawk-faced man with a perennial scowl. "It would really help us if you could find out what happened to your brother's secretary. Pres confided only in her, and frankly, she's got to get in here and untangle some of this mess. There are arrangements, details only Angie knows about. Pay-out schedules, court calendar dates . . . I know it's a horrible time, but some of these situations won't wait."

"I'm . . . I don't really know how I can help," Wheeler said, wanting to get the hell away. Being in this place where his brother had mounted his successful rise to power on the very day of his death was unsettling. It was as if Pres's spirit hadn't quite left yet.

Hearing Pres's voice on the tape had only made this feeling worse.

"If you could just go out there, we'd really appreciate it," the office manager pressed. "I'd go myself, but I'm trying to deal with half-a-dozen things right now. This has really knocked us sideways."

Wheeler wanted to get out of the office and still be able to tell his mother he had helped out, so he reluctantly accepted the assignment. Angie Wong's address was in Torrance, California.

Where the fuck is *Torrance, anyway?*

It was off the 110, south of the airport. The houses were small, wood-frame jobs, most with neatly trimmed gardens. Angie Wong lived at 2467 Clarkson Street.

When he pulled up, he could see a red Toyota in the driveway. He got out, walked across the neatly trimmed grass, then rang the front-door chimes. They were just like the ones at his grandmother's house in Baldwin Park. He vaguely remembered standing on his grandparents' porch as a child, maybe only three years old, ringing the doorbell of their huge old white Spanish mansion, then running to hide every time they came to answer, until his grandparents finally stood on the porch and begged him to stop. What a jokester. Wheeler was driving his family nuts even before he could shit sitting down.

Nobody opened Angie's front door, so he walked around to the back. There he found another strange thing. The back door had been jimmied. The wood door had been pried, leaving a deep hash mark by the lock. The door was ajar.

Wheeler pushed it open with the flat of his hand and walked into a very small kitchen. He could tell the place had been searched, even before he got all the way inside. He moved slowly through the disheveled house and found that, from one room to the next, things had been strewn everywhere. He called out for Angie, but there was no answer. The last door he saw led to the basement. He turned on the light and moved cautiously down the wooden stairs.

The basement room was a small gym with mirrors on the walls.

Angie Wong was reflected in most of them.

Her dead body was tied down on the workout bench. It was naked and bleeding. The corpse was covered with cuts. With hundreds and hundreds of incisions, the dead woman had been mutilated and bloodily desecrated. Her flesh was riddled and had retracted. The cuts had puckered and now oozed. Angie glistened red. Her eyes were open, her cut-up mouth fixed in a silent scream. It didn't look like her tongue was still in there. On her stomach was placed a framed picture of a young Chinese man, maybe about thirty years old.

Vat 69 was a damn good Scotch, but it was a lot smoother going down than coming up. It spewed on the carpet and all over his Spanish shoes. It stained his shirt and floppy linen trousers.

Rimshot. Another Wheeler Cassidy masterpiece.

FIVE

Tanisha and Kenetta

I t was the second new moon after the winter solstice, which was February 9—Chinese New Year.

Ray Fong and Al Katsukura didn't want to drive all the way out to fucking Torrance, because they had plans to celebrate. Al, of course, was Japanese, but never passed on any drinking holiday, regardless of its ethnic origin, so they reluctantly gave the squeal to Tanisha Williams.

The homicide dick at the scene thought the killing looked ritual and wanted somebody in LAPD Asian Crimes to take a look. The vic was Chinese, or so they thought. She was so cut up it was hard to tell.

Ray moved across the linoleum floor in the run-down fifth-floor rented office that housed Asian Crimes and dropped the green slip on Tanisha's desk. She was on the phone, trying to talk Mandarin Chinese to someone. It was pathetic, but at least she was making the effort. Ray Fong was good in that dialect, almost fluent, but he didn't help her because he'd been told by Internal Affairs to leave her alone. Everyone had.

Tanisha Williams, known to her friends as Tisha, was departmental poison. She had been parked up here by I.A.D., and everybody knew a Black female had no chance of conducting a successful "field shake" on an Asian male. Asians didn't trust other racial groups, especially Blacks. Being female just made it worse, no matter how trim her body or how beautiful and smooth her coffee-colored complexion. Nonetheless, Ray had to respect her, because as soon as she had been assigned there, she immediately went to work to learn the terrain. The first day she had checked out an armload of library books on the many Asian cultures, and she had been reading constantly, even during lunch. It was almost as if she didn't know she was supposed to be up on blocks while the I.A. Shooflies crawled around under her career, looking for wet spots. I.A. had taken her off the LAPD Crash Unit because, as a teenager, before joining the Department, she had been associating with Crip gang members in the neighborhood. They now suspected she was giving up her investigations to old gang-banger boyfriends. The Crash Unit worked the Black gangs in South Central and Tanisha had grown up in that hood. Her grandmother, niece, and nephew still lived there, south of Manchester, and she visited them on her old turf during her days off.

Tanisha hung up the phone and cocked her eyebrow as she picked up the greenie.

"One eighty-seven in Torrance, Asian woman hit the slab. The lab techs are already rolling. It's all yours," Ray said and moved back to his desk. The address was 2467 Clarkson Street.

She grabbed her sweater and her purse and left before they changed their minds.

Tanisha got in her Department-authorized P.O.V. (Personally Owned Vehicle), which was parked across the street from the rented fifties building on Hill Street in downtown L.A. where the Asian Crimes Task Force was officed. ACTF was located miles from the steel-and-glass efficiency of Parker Center. The unit had been an orphan division from inception. It had been formed by Chief Redden in the mid-sixties as a political unit to deal with the problem of rising Asian crime in Los Angeles. Back then, the actual criminal investigations had been done by regular detectives out of Parker Center, the Asian detectives on ACTF spent most of their time explaining American police tactics to wary Asian groups at specially arranged Department lunches. Gradually, with the rising tide of politically correct thinking, their charter was expanded and now they handled all Asian CAPs—Crimes Against People, which included the whole gory smorgasbord of human atrocities: rape, theft, assault, child abuse, and murder.

The reason Tanisha left so quickly was that for the six weeks she'd been on the Asian Crimes Task Force, this was the first greenie anybody had handed her. She knew it was because Ray, Al, and the other on-duty Asian cops were trying to slip out early for Chinese New Year, and the murder in Torrance threatened to be an all-nighter. She coaxed her rusted-out yellow Mazda up 6th Street on her way to the Harbor Freeway. When it was cold, the little Japanese bumblebee chugged and spit like a cat coughing up a furball.

The Harbor Freeway took her through her old neighborhood in South Central, where she had once been a student at Martin Luther King High School. She knew that the I.A. dicks were now down there, crawling through her personal history, talking to all the people she had grown up with.

She'd been told by her friends in the hood that I.A. had even tailed Li'l Evil. He was her last homeboy lover from almost fifteen years ago and was an O.G. (Original Gangster) in the neighborhood Crip set. He took over when C. went upstate. Monster C., another old friend, was back in the brickhouse at Lompoc, doing a long bit.

Kenetta had died in Li'l Evil's arms, not two blocks from where she was now driving.

She thought about her little sister. Blood gurgling up through the huge 9mm hole in her five-year-old chest. Tanisha, just sixteen then, standing over her, screaming hysterically, unable to process what she was seeing, unable to do anything as her baby sister died in her boyfriend's arms. There were three paybacks after that, including six people who died because of her little sister: three from her neighborhood Crip crew, two from the Rolling Sixties, who her homies thought (though they weren't sure) had busted the cap at Li'l Evil that mistakenly killed Kenetta. The last victim of that useless violent exchange was another innocent bystander, a sixty-year-old grandmother who obligingly stepped in front of a thirty-ought-six hollow-point Devastator and inadvertently saved the life of a Rolling Sixties banger named Russell "Hardcore" Hayes.

Tanisha had never joined the gang, because her mother, Lilly, made her promise she would never start Crippin'. Her mother's dream for her was that Tanisha would go to beauty school and open her own hair salon. Tanisha bought the dream, and despite their poverty-level existence, she grew up with solid middle-class values, believing, despite the evidence, that anybody could succeed in America. A belief that distanced her from schoolmates who grew up with desolate views of the future. This difference between Tanisha and her classmates caused her to become a social outcast. As she thought back on it in later years, she realized it was probably the reason she had started dating Li'l Evil, who was a Crip ghetto star. . . . Their romance gave her position in her neighborhood, but it had culminated with the drive-by shooting. A bullet intended for Li'l Evil had ended Kenetta's life. The guilt she felt because of that was overpowering, and still influenced her life.

Back then, Tanisha's nickname was "Rings." In her first twenty years, nineteen people she knew well had died from street actions. The last and most devastating being her own little sister. After Kenetta died, Tanisha had forgotten her dream of beauty school and had shocked everybody she knew when she joined the LAPD. Her goal was to somehow make up for Kenetta's death—but no matter what she did or how hard she tried, she had been subtly dissed by the Department. It was almost as if because she'd been born in South Central, she could never be anything more than "Rings" Williams, a sly sixteen-year-old homegirl. It didn't matter that after Kenetta died, she'd gotten straight A's in high school . . .

didn't matter that she'd enrolled in junior college and transferred to U.C.L.A. to finish her degree in criminology. She was marked by her beginnings. No matter how much they said they respected her journey, they really didn't. It was all hoo-rah.

When things went bad, her grandmother used to say: "Can't kill nothin' an' won't nothin' die." And that was what her new life on the LAPD felt like. Because she refused to stop going down to South Central to visit her family they distrusted her. And then, because she wouldn't let Lieutenant Hawley at the Crash Unit jump her bones, she was facing a full-scale I.A.D. investigation. Lieutenant Darnel Hawley, who wore his black skin like a preacher's coat but couldn't take the fact that she didn't want to sleep with him. Now, rather than face her on a daily basis after she rejected him, he'd decided to get rid of her, charging her with leaking confidential case-related information to old homies. He didn't have any evidence, so he couldn't suspend her. As a result, she had been banished to Asian Crimes, where she was now trying, without luck, to talk suspicious Asians into communicating with her.

Now, because of Chinese New Year, she had finally caught a squeal. She looked down at the clipboard where the green slip fluttered in the breeze from the open window. She wondered what she would find at 2467 Clarkson.

"Whose vomit is this?" Tanisha asked a lab tech. "Is this the vic's puke? This smells like booze."

Cindy Masatomi was a Japanese forensic scientist who worked for the LAPD Crime Lab. She was in a blue hospital jumpsuit with paper slippers and headgear. Tanisha had worked a few cases with her when she'd still been on Crash.

"Belongs to the guy outside . . . the good-looking one who found the body."

Tanisha nodded. She'd seen him when she came in. He was dressed like a golf pro, leaning against a new red Jag like he owned the neighborhood. She had already made a cursory check of the body and instantly knew that she was looking at a punishment kill. Punishment and a warning. The person being warned here was the thirty-year-old Chinese man in the picture on top of the victim's body. It was a Triad message. A picture placed on a body meant: "You're going to get this next." She'd been reading about this stuff now for almost six months. Some of these Asian gangs, like the Bamboo Dragons and the Ghost Shadows, made her old neighborhood set seem quaint by comparison. The corpse was probably the homeowner, Angie Wong. The body was too mutilated for anybody to make a visual ID, but dental records and prints should nail it. One strange thing: On her forehead, in Magic Marker, was written "1414." She didn't know what that meant. She'd never seen it before. The body looked fresh, no lividity, no rigor, no insect infestation. She had already asked Cindy for a T.O.D. estimate, which the lab tech would do with a liver thermometer. After she rolled the corpse, Cindy would drive the pointed thermometer down into the liver, which was a chemical factory and the hottest organ in the body, usually 102 degrees. It cooled about a degree an hour. They could estimate time of death by rate of temperature loss.

Tanisha wondered if there was a Death Doll anywhere. The Chinese Bamboo gangs were big on death symbols. It wasn't enough to just kill you, they had to scare the piss out of you first. The Death Doll was often used as one way to do this, the picture on the corpse was another.

She knew there wasn't much she could do with the crime scene until the lab techs finished with the body, did a hair and fiber scan, and bagged the vic's hands. She went outside and started digging around in a residential Dumpster out back. She had her head down in the metal container, trying to move an old box of cereal out of the way, when she heard:

"What're you doing?"

She jerked her head out of the trash and was looking at the man who had found the body. The residue of vomit on his shirt and linen pants confirmed him as the upchucker who had hurled all over her crime scene.

She got a better look at him now. Her immediate impression was that she'd seen him before, that she knew him from somewhere and he'd pissed her off, but beyond that, she couldn't place him. Up close, he looked like he thought that even with vomit all over him, he was still somehow totally irresistible. Maybe her reaction to him was chemical or maybe she was just horribly upset at the sight of the dead woman cut to ribbons, but she instantly took a dislike to the handsome man standing in front of her. She put on her police poker-face and addressed him with cold departmental politeness.

"You want to step back? This is a crime scene," she said and watched as he looked for a place to stand. "Over there," she commanded and pointed to a spot on the driveway. She followed him over and took out a notebook and pen.

"I'm Detective Williams, LAPD Asian Crimes Task Force. You're the one who found the body, is that correct?"

He nodded.

"What's your name?"

"Wheeler Cassidy," he said, his voice soft in the cold February night.

"Wheeler? Is that a nickname?"

"It's a family name. My great-grandfather, on my mother's side, was Jefferson Prescott Wheeler the Third. He was a Confederate General, 27th Richmond Regiment."

"Write down your address, please, and a number where you can be reached," she said and handed him her notepad and pen. He wrote down his address in Bel Air and his phone number.

"Why did you come over here, Mr. Cassidy?" she asked.

"Miss Wong was my brother's secretary. She didn't report to work and the office asked if I would come over here and check on her. My brother was a lawyer in Century City."

"Was a lawyer? Past tense?"

"He died last night, at his desk. And Miss Wong didn't come in this morning. The people in Prescott's law firm got concerned."

"Prescott . . . that's your brother?"

He nodded.

"How did your brother die?"

"I don't think it has anything to do with this," Wheeler said.

"Let me do the thinking, Mr. Cassidy. Tell me how he died."

"Heart attack. At least that's what the L.A. cops said."

"Prescott Cassidy was his whole name?" She wrote it down.

"Yes. Well, no. Prescott Westlake Sheridan Cassidy was his complete name." Off her look of disbelief, he added, "Southern names—they're calculated to piss people off."

She wrote it down. Then her gaze dropped and from this new angle out on the driveway, she saw a box behind the Dumpster she'd been digging in. A wood crate. The top was off and lying beside it. She moved over and looked down. Inside the crate was a small white paper doll about ten inches tall. "There it is," she said.

He had followed her to the box despite her instruction to stay back, and now he started to reach down and get it for her. She stopped him. "Don't touch it. The lab techs go nuts when you do that."

"Oh," he said and they both stood looking at it.

"What is it?"

"Death Doll. It was probably delivered a day or two ago. That's what I was looking for. It confirms this as a Chinese gang murder. You get a doll like this, it says you're going to die. Usually in a terribly violent way. Some Chinese who've received these just go out and commit suicide rather than wait for the inevitable."

"If what they do to you is like what happened to Angie Wong, I don't blame them."

"That's a ritual slaying called the Death of a Thousand Cuts. It's a Triad kill, also called Death by a Myriad of Swords." She was showing off for him now. She wondered why she was even making the effort. "The victim was kept alive while all of her main muscles and tendons were severed, in particular the calves, thighs, forearms, and biceps."

"Jeezus," Wheeler said, his expression darkening.

"You knew the victim?" she asked, and after a moment he

nodded. "Can you make a positive identification? The body is pretty mutilated."

"It's about her size . . . I just assumed . . ." He didn't finish.

"She didn't come to work for how many days?"

"Uh, I don't know. I don't work there. One day, I guess."

"Where do you work?"

"Where do I work?"

"Yeah."

He smiled a boyish smile. "I don't . . . I'm retired."

"Retired? What are you . . . thirty-five?"

"Seven."

"What kind of work did you do before you retired?"

"I was a Prankmeister," he said, the smile disappearing. "I pulled practical jokes on friends. Since my retirement, I mostly work on my golf game. It's pretty grueling. I'm simply killing myself trying to break par." There was a bitter self-loathing in the way he said it.

"I see," she said and flipped her book closed.

He didn't say anything more. He just stood before her; his face now seemed cut from stone.

"That's about it," she said, "unless you can tell me anything else about Miss Wong I should know, like whose picture was placed on her abdomen?"

He shook his head.

"You can go. I'll be in touch, probably tomorrow. If you think of anything, let me know. Here's my card." She handed it to him.

And then Cindy Masatomi stuck her head out the back door and called to Tanisha. "Detective Williams, we've called for a Coroner's wagon. The M.E.'s standing by at County."

"What's up? There's usually at least a two-day wait for an autopsy."

"I think something's alive inside her."

Another Opening, Another Show

T he autopsy room was on the third floor of the County Medical Building across from Parker Center.

Dr. Paul Dickson, known in the "canoe factory" as Dr. Death, was doing the organ recital. He always referred to the cadaver he was working on as the "guest of honor." They now definitely knew from prints and identification it was Angela Wong. He had made a thorough examination of the corpse, then photographed it before and after washing it. The knife cuts were gruesome and everywhere. He was bent over, studying the wounds through the pull-down magnifying glass mounted above the metal-drained autopsy table. He began reading observations into the microphone over his head in a friendly, almost conversational voice. He'd seen too much to be shocked by anything.

That was about to change.

The room was white tile and uncomfortably cold. Air conditioning hissed valiantly but still failed to completely remove the collection of distasteful smells in the morgue: chemicals, preserving fluids, and the sweet, sickening odor of rotting flesh, naturally dissolving in a self-liquefying bath of butyric acid.

Tanisha was standing near the corpse's feet, watching the autopsy with a small recorder in her hand so that she could make her own observations as well as gather stray thoughts that hit her during the gruesome procedure.

"Looks like a very narrow, very sharp blade . . . extremely honed, like a razor at its edge. Most of these cuts are only two- to three-eighths of an inch deep. All major muscle groups and tendons have been attacked. The tendons have all been severed and have snapped back, recoiling against the bone. Must've hurt like a bitch." Dr. Death pushed the mike back and put his hand on the abdomen. Then, for a second, he also thought he could feel something moving inside. He turned to Cindy Masatomi, who was just entering the room with the Stryker-500 oscillating autopsy saw.

"Found it," she announced. "It was in Calvin's room. His burned up an hour ago." She set down the saw. It was an extremely ugly little tool that cut bone by rapid forward and backward strokes . . . almost like an electric kitchen knife. Dr. Dickson took his hand off the abdomen. "What's your estimated T.O.D., Cindy?" he asked.

"When I got to her house, her liver temp was ninety-nine point three. At one degree an hour, starting at a normal liver temp of one-oh-two, I'd guess she'd been dead maybe three hours when we got there." She looked at her watch. "Over four now."

Dr. Death put his hand back on Angela's abdomen. "So, what the hell is this? It's not a uterine pregnancy. With no blood flow, the fetus would've been dead hours ago." He picked up a scalpel from the tray. "Guess we aren't going to find out by just talking about it."

He began to work on her vaginal area, carefully making an incision, widening the canal. After making the preliminary cut, he washed the area with a small, flexible tube to clean off the small amount of blood that leaked out of Angela Wong's already pale, blood-drained body. Then he pulled the ceiling-mounted magnifying glass back down and looked carefully at his incision.

"Whatever this is, it's way up there. Hand me the Rigby six-and-three-quarter-inch vaginal retractor," he demanded, and Cindy grabbed a pair of long scissor forceps and handed them to the Coroner, who used them to probe deep inside the body.

"Son of a bitch, what is this?" he said again. He couldn't grip it, so he picked up the scalpel and made a slightly deeper and longer cut. Rewashed, then reexamined.

Tanisha found herself holding her breath. She was looking right at the dead woman's reproductive system, and, as had happened before when she attended autopsies, she couldn't help but put herself on that table. Autopsies were sterile postmortem procedures that reduced human beings to meat. The cadavers were turned into body canoes opened with Y-cuts from clavicle to abdomen. All the organs were removed, examined, weighed, measured, and returned, but not to the place they were in originally. They were just dumped back in and the incisions were sewn up with the same crude stitches you would find on a supermarket turkey. If anything had police value, it was preserved and sent to the holding vault for later legal use. The scalp was peeled back and the head opened, and the brain that had once contained all of life's intimate thoughts was poked and examined like a shellfish on the beach. When Tanisha let herself think about it, about this woman, who had laughed and cried and made love, it devalued Angie in ways that were indescribable.

"Can't get the damn . . . What is this?" Doc Dickson said, as he reinserted the vaginal retractors and finally got a solid grip on something and started to pull it out.

"Son of a bitch is fighting to stay in there. . . ." He pulled harder and finally, after almost two minutes, dragged a half-dead rodent of some kind out of her.

"Jesus H. Christ," he said in awe. "It's a fucking rat."

The animal lay on its side, starved of oxygen but alive, with its red eyes open. Then it squeaked once and a few moments later died.

Tanisha Williams had never met Angela Wong, but she was appalled at the poor woman's torturous ending. She promised herself that she'd get the sadistic motherfucker who did this.

Easier said than done.

Ray Fong wanted the case back. He was standing in front of Tanisha's desk at the Task Force headquarters on Spring Street, looking down at her through holiday eyes rimmed in red.

He was half-tilted.

It had been midnight when he'd stumbled over to the pay phone at the Red Dragon Bar in Chinatown and called the Duty Desk to check in. He'd heard about the Wong killing from the Officer On Duty. The O.O.D. told him about the Death of a Thousand Cuts and the rat Dr. Death had found in the vic's vagina. Ray had instantly known it was a "Hot Grounder," police terminology for any high-profile case. Ray had pulled himself away from the bar and driven his P.O.V. the twelve blocks from Chinatown back to Spring Street, hoping he wouldn't get stopped by some Dudley Do-Right with a stick up his ass. Ray knew he would never beat the needle with the load he was packing. He used his magnetized I.D. card on the security elevator and eventually found the Soul Sister at her desk, talking quietly on the phone.

"Can't have the case, Tanisha. Sorry," he said drunkenly as she hung up the phone.

"Can't hear you, Ray."

"This is a fucking Triad hit. You can't have the case. Gonna be a Hot Grounder. Needs Asian policing. You'll get blitzed. Nobody's gonna tell you shit."

"Am I the wrong color, Ray, or the wrong sex?" she said, six weeks of isolation, inactivity, and anger heating the exchange. They locked gazes. Each knew she was both, but the new P.C.

Department guidelines made this the pink elephant standing in the room that nobody ever mentioned. Even on Chinese New Year.

"I'm the primary on this homicide," she continued. "I've just about had it with this shit. I'm a licensed experienced investigator, and if you try and take it from me, I'll file a discrimination suit against you and the Department."

Ray looked at her, wishing he hadn't had the last two Tsing Taos. He was definitely swacked and not up to this. "We'll talk about it in the morning," he said, retreating, buying time to get sober.

"We're not gonna talk about shit, Ray. This is my D.B. I went to the autopsy. I policed the crime scene. I'm on it. Go eat a fortune cookie."

He left without replying.

Of course, she knew it wasn't going to be that easy. She also knew this was going to be a high-profile media case. There were always leaks in the Department, especially in the Coroner's office. The rat-in-the-vagina story was worth a couple of hundred at any TV station in town. It would probably make the A.M. news.

After the rat had been cleaned up and photographed by Doc Dickson, she had taken it to the evidence vault and booked it as part of case HF-235-98, which made Angie the 235th homicide in L.A. in the first two months of 1998. The city was off to a brisk start. She didn't leave the rat downtown. She signed it out and took it home in the shoebox her new Pearla low-heeled sandals had come in. She stopped by her apartment and put the rat in her freezer. The things a girl will do for her job. Then she had gone back to ACTF to finish the paperwork.

The rat in her freezer was different from any rat she'd ever seen. It had loose, hairless skin and was cylindrical in shape, with short but powerful forearms and legs. Dr. Dickson had said it was a male rat and had measured him. Head to tail, he was thirty centimeters long, about a foot. He weighed 1.7 kilograms, three and three-quarter pounds. She was going to take him to her vet tomorrow and find out everything she could about the rodent. As a girl in South Central L.A., she'd had more than a passing acquaintance with rats, growing up with a houseful of the uninvited bastards. She didn't think it was a native American rat, at least she'd never seen one like it before.

She would find out where this rat came from and what, if any, pet store had sold the animal. It would probably turn out to be a long, exhausting quest, but she knew that was what homicide investigations were about. Her training officer at the Academy had told her probationary class that police work was like piloting airplanes—endless hours of boring, uninteresting drudgery, punctuated by a few seconds of ass-puckering fright. She was used to the drudgery, but she didn't count on the ass-puckering fright that was coming her way.

While Angie Wong was getting the hairless rat taken out of her vagina, Wheeler Cassidy was getting his sister-in-law's luggage out of the United baggage claim. He hauled the suitcase out to his Jag and put it in the trunk. Liz and Hollis seemed determined not to speak to him. He tried to comfort Liz first, then his twelve-year-old nephew, but Liz snapped at him.

"He'd really rather not talk right now," she said, hotly turning her anger and distress over Pres's death directly on Wheeler, as if Pres hadn't been his little brother. As if he didn't love Prescott, too, way down deep under the anger and resentment.

He and Liz had never quite found a level place to stand. Everything about Wheeler seemed to annoy her. She preferred ladder climbers, upwardly mobile world-beaters who saw their futures in terms of milestones of accomplishments: that new house in Bel Air or that Young Presidents Organization membership. You had to be under forty and be president of a firm that employed at least one hundred people to be in Y.P.O. Pres had been president of Y.P.O., so let's hear it for Pres . . . give Pres the long cheer. Give Wheeler the Bronx cheer, which his sister-in-law, Liz, had done quite adequately last Christmas.

All of them were gathered around the Christmas Eve dinner table at the mansion on Windgate, the warm glow of Christmas schnapps smoldering in their bellies.

"Life isn't about golf, other people's wives, and goofy pranks," she'd said, bringing his mood of holiday cheer to a bone-chilling halt. "Honestly, Wheeler, it's one thing to shoot beer into the Bruin rooting section when you're nineteen. It's another thing to do it at thirty-seven."

Of course, he hadn't done it at thirty-seven, but the point was made. He sat there at his mother's long, elegant dinner table in a two-hundred-year-old high-backed Queen Anne chair, feeling lower than lizard shit. He looked up at his aunts and uncles, nieces and nephews. Cassidys all. Nobody said anything. Neither Pres nor his mother had come to his defense. His mother had just picked at her oysters Florentine with a fork. He had been forced to endure Liz's criticism without comment. "Honestly, Wheeler, it's sad the way you just do nothing, just hang out at that country club bar, swilling vodka all day."

It wasn't vodka, it was blended Scotch, Vat 69, his trademark hops, but he didn't correct her. He endured the criticism, his cheeks burning in humiliation.

What made it so devastating was that the very things that had defined him as a young man and brought him glory at U.S.C. were now the same things that were labeling him and bringing disgrace. He knew that he had been on a threshold of some kind for almost six months. Like a kid on a high cliff, overlooking a swimming hole with his toes hooked over the rocky edge, he'd been looking for the inner strength to jump to a new kind of life. But he was stuck, afraid to go forward, afraid to stay where he was. He'd been teetering there, waiting for courage, hating himself for his indecision.

They pulled up the driveway at Prescott's three-million-dollar Bel Air French Provincial. Wheeler got the suitcase out of the trunk and led them, without comment, up to the front entrance. Once on the front steps, he froze. The front door had the same brutal hash marks next to the lock that he'd seen on the back door of Angie's house. Then he heard movement in the house upstairs in the master bedroom. He backed up and set the suitcase down. Liz was coming up the cement steps. He grabbed her arm and led her and Hollis back to the car.

"Wheeler, what on earth . . . ?"

He shushed her, putting his finger up to his mouth, then handed her his cellphone and pointed to the foot of the drive.

"What is it?" she said, whispering now.

"Somebody's in the house. I want you to call the police."

"But . . ."

"The alarm went off earlier yesterday. The cops were here. They shut it off. Now your front-door lock is broken. I heard someone inside. Gimme the keys to the pool house."

She reached into her purse and gave him her key ring, then he moved quickly up the driveway, his heart pounding.

Who the hell is pulling this shit, anyway?

He got to the pool house and silently unlocked the glass door and slid it open. He slipped inside, then slid it shut. His brother kept his hunting rifles and some target pistols locked up in there. Wheeler went to the cabinet where the guns were stored, but none of the keys on Liz's ring worked in the lock. Finally, he found the gun cabinet key on the ledge over the door.

He opened the cabinet and took down two 9mm Beretta target pistols, both nine-shot semiautomatics. He grabbed a box of ammo, checked the clips on both guns. They were empty. He started thumbing cartridges into the first clip, dropping four or five in the process. They rolled loudly on the white terrazzo floor. His hands were trembling. He slammed the first clip home and tromboned the slide. He had the second clip loaded with five rounds when he heard a noise out by the pool . . . a lounge chair scraped. He stopped loading the second gun and moved silently to the door and peered out.

Sitting by the pool, having a cigarette like he owned the place, was a Chinese boy. It was hard to tell at this distance, but he looked to be only seventeen or eighteen. He was very skinny and dressed in black: baggy black gangster jeans, a shiny black windbreaker, and a red headband.

Holding his breath, Wheeler watched the boy, his heart slamming harder in his chest.

"Breathe, you dirt-eating asshole," a Southern voice in his memory instructed. It was his old Special Forces training officer, Kale McCoy.

McCoy had told the platoon in his South Carolina drawl that under combat circumstances, your body gets fed large jolts of adrenaline, which causes you to burn oxygen faster. If you don't breathe, you'll get light-headed. *"Light-headed gyrenes end up as junk on a bunk,"* he had warned them.

Wheeler took a deep breath, tried to steady his nerves.

He watched, not sure what to do, as another youth came out of the den in the main house. He could faintly hear their voices floating across the garden in the night air. They were speaking in Chinese; a singsongy, high-pitched melody of language and laughter. Then both of them put out their cigarettes and went back inside.

"The fuck am I supposed t'do now?" Wheeler said to himself. He chambered the second gun, then tucked it in the back of his belt. He held the other in his right hand. "This is nuts," he whispered, and heard his own voice echo in the empty pool house.

He'd been poised on that cliff wondering what he should do for too long. Suddenly it seemed clear. He was going to find out what was going on; why his brother's secretary had been murdered and why these Chinese boys were in Pres's house. He was going to find out who was pulling all this shit and, more important, why.

After many months of soul-searching, gut-wrenching indecision, Wheeler Cassidy, Jr., slipped his watch off his wrist to protect the expensive timepiece and put it into his pocket. Then he slid open the glass door to his brother's pool house and finally got into the game.

Night Maneuvers

"*T*his is a night maneuver. Work on purple vision,*"* the six-foot-four South Carolina Platoon Commander screamed in Wheeler's distant memory.

Wheeler stopped and gave his eyes a minute to adjust to the night, then, as he'd been taught fifteen years before, he softened his focus slightly and let his peripheral vision come into sharper play. Suddenly, his bowels went soft. He needed to shit. Combat runnies. *Damn. Fuck it!*

He forced himself to ignore the feeling. He moved slowly, keeping his back to the wall the way his Special Forces training had instructed, keeping the light in front of him so his shadow wouldn't announce him. Then another voice inside his head spoke. The Prankmeister wanted to go home and have a tall one.

"What're you doing, you asshole? What're you trying to prove? Cut the crap. You're no hero."

He moved up to the glass door that led into his brother's den and stopped, remembering something important.

"When you're goin' through a kill zone, you become a snake.

Slide on your belly, scope the fire zone before you clear your position."

Wheeler dropped to his stomach by the den door and slowly slid forward to look around the threshold into the room. He could see the legs of tables and chairs, but nobody seemed to be in there, at least as far as he could tell.

He slid the door open from the floor, inching it slowly so it wouldn't make noise. Then he held his breath and listened.

He lay there as he'd been taught, his ears probing for any sound that would give him an edge. After what seemed like an eternity, he wriggled into the den, careful not to scrape his belt buckle on the metal track of the sliding door.

The den had been thoroughly searched. His brother's antique-book collection was emptied onto the floor. Old leather volumes of Dickens and Poe were spilled, face open, on the carpet. The drawers in the big TV credenza across from the bar had been pulled out and dumped. Then he heard distant voices upstairs speaking in Chinese. . . . He froze while the Prankmeister shrieked at him: *"Hey asshole, listen to me! How's it gonna help anybody if you get killed? You're a fuck-up! They threw you outta Special Forces, or maybe you forgot that?"*

Wheeler moved slowly in the den, staying on his belly, re-membering how they taught him to clear a building. *"A well-trained force will deploy. Watch your back,"* his Platoon Com-mander cautioned.

Still on his belly, Wheeler snaked out into the hall. Then sud-denly, a racket in the kitchen. Someone was opening and closing drawers, spilling the contents loudly out onto the tile floor. Simul-taneously he heard two, maybe three more voices upstairs, speak-ing Chinese. He felt a tinge of panic.

"You're in between two fire zones. Preserve your exit line. Regroup."

He back-slid out of the hall, into the den again, and sat up with his back against the curtain wall.

And then the intruder in the kitchen moved down the hall,

past the den door that Wheeler was hiding behind. Wheeler could see the man's Nike tennis shoes and black pant legs as he climbed up the stairs.

"Go vertical," his training officer whispered.

Wheeler slowly stood up and edged toward the stairs. He put his weight carefully on the first step, thankful that the house was new and the staircase didn't creak. He kept his back pressed against the wall and began slowly climbing the stairs, remembering to keep his knees bent for quick lateral movement.

"This is nuts, Wheeler. You're gonna get killed here. Use your fucking head."

Wheeler crept slowly up onto the landing. So far, so good. He could hear drawers opening and closing in the master suite. He had turned to move in that direction when, unexpectedly, somebody came out of Hollis's room behind him. Wheeler spun with the Beretta in front of him and found himself face to face with a young Chinese man. He was about five-six, rail-thin and around nineteen, dressed in black with a red bandanna.

There was a moment frozen in time while the two just stared at each other. Then the Chinese intruder started to reach under his jacket . . . and Wheeler aimed the Beretta directly at the boy's chest. The drama was playing without sound until the Chinese boy yanked his gun out and screamed something in Chinese. Suddenly, still frames went to fast-forward. In milliseconds, the youth was blasting at Wheeler with an ugly square-barreled foreign automatic. For some godforsaken reason, Wheeler hesitated and then watched dumbly as the automatic in the gangster's hand spit fire at him. He felt a searing pain in his thigh that blew his leg out from under him. His gun flew from his hand unfired, landing at his feet. Blood oozed ominously out of his wounded thigh.

"You happy? Is this what you wanted, asshole?" the Prank-meister screamed in terror.

The boy ran up and grabbed Wheeler's Beretta. Two other Asian gangsters came out of the master bedroom. They all held guns on him, chattering at each other in Chinese.

"Who are you?" Wheeler asked, his voice shaking from the adrenaline pump.

They ignored him and kept jabbering, their high-pitched conversation singsongy and piercing. It seemed they were deciding what to do. Whether to kill him. No . . . how to kill him.

"Does anybody speak English?" he asked, his voice almost a whisper now.

"No English. You dead," the oldest and tallest said.

Wheeler then propped himself up on his elbows, while his right hand snaked unobserved behind his back where the second Beretta was tucked and chambered.

"Make this good, soldier."

The oldest, who Wheeler assumed was the leader, aimed a revolver at him, about to fire. Then Wheeler did something the gangster didn't expect, and it bought him a few seconds. Wheeler smiled. It was his old Prankmeister smile. His U.S.C. frat-house grin.

"Lemme show you guys something," he said pleasantly.

They looked at each other, puzzled by his attitude, as he pulled his right hand away from the small of his back and, without warning, started firing the second Beretta.

The sound was deafening on the enclosed landing.

He got the oldest one on the first shot. The bullet went right through his neck, blowing him backwards. The one who had come out of Hollis's room pulled down on him with Wheeler's own Beretta. Wheeler's second and third shots blasted him in the chest and knocked him over the banister rail. He fell, cartwheeling, hitting the big chandelier in the entry, taking it down with him in a loud shower of breaking crystal. The remaining gangster ran back into the master bedroom. Wheeler fired twice, missing him, and then he heard sirens out front as the balcony door slammed.

Wheeler had emptied all five shots from the second Beretta and was still lying on the hall floor, clicking the trigger maniacally on the empty automatic. Finally he became aware that he was reflex-firing and stopped.

The silence was overpowering. Then he heard running and shouting outside, two more gunshots, then quiet. The front door opened and a man's voice called to him.

"Mr. Cassidy? Police! . . . are you okay?"

"I've been hit! Think I'm okay," Wheeler tried to call out, but now his voice was barely a whisper. Feeling dizzy and weak, he lay back on the hallway carpet. He heard footsteps coming up the stairs to the landing.

"Good fucking ground op," Lieutenant Kale McCoy drawled proudly.

"Whatta you talking about, you cornbread asshole?" the Prankmeister whined. *"We almost got fuckin' killed here."*

Before the cop reached him, Wheeler had gone into shock.

EIGHT

Willy's Garden

L i Xitong didn't get out of the black Hong Xi (Red Flag) limousine. He was extremely fat and the effort it would require to exit the car and climb the steps to the lobby of the Kun Lun Hotel was not worth the gratitude it might engender. Instead, he sat in the car with the red window curtains pulled shut and struggled to breathe. His belly, when he was seated, pressed up on his diaphragm and his exhales came in gasps. It was the day before Chinese New Year and a fitting time for the meeting that was about to take place, a meeting that he knew might well determine the political future of Hong Kong.

The Kun Lun Hotel was large and ornate, with beautiful sculpted gold pavilions on all four corners. It was located on the east side of Beijing. Everybody knew that the silent partner of the Kun Lun Hotel was the Chinese Public Security Bureau, which was just the fancy name for the State Police, who made a small fortune running the place.

The visiting Triad leader from Hong Kong had made a wise decision when he elected to stay at that hotel. Li Xitong was forced to revise his earlier estimate of the man, because the choice showed a delicate understanding of Guan-Xi. The visitor from Hong Kong could have also chosen the beautiful Palace Hotel in central Beijing, because that establishment's silent partner was the People's Liberation Army. In either hotel, he would appear politically respectable.

The meeting about to take place was with Chen Boda, the head of the Chinese Communist Military Commission and, therefore, also the head of the Public Security Bureau.

Li Xitong was the ex-Mayor of Beijing. He had retired because of health problems, but was often called upon by Chen Boda for special assignments that included escorting and hosting important visitors. Li Xitong was fun to be with, or at least he had been until his prodigious girth made him perennially uncomfortable and consequently grouchy. His nickname was "Five Oceans" because of the awesome amounts of fiery white Mao Tai liquor he could consume.

The door of the Red Flag limousine was suddenly opened and Willy Wo Lap Ling entered the car.

Ling appeared surprisingly fit. In 1994, he had been a shriveled old man with dying kidneys and a yellow-gray complexion. Now the seventy-three-year-old Triad leader seemed reborn, trim, with carefully barbered white hair and robust red cheeks.

Aside from exchanging brief introductions, the two men didn't speak. They rolled along Beijing's busy streets listening to a mixture of sounds: the faint purr of the car's engine; the red flags flapping on the front fenders; Li Xitong's labored breathing.

The meeting was to take place in the beautiful restaurant on the twenty-fifth floor of the CITIC building located on Chang An (Boundless Peace) Avenue. Willy Wo Lap knew that CITIC stood for China International Trade and Industry Corp. CITIC had many connections with Poly Industries, which was the commercial arm of the People's Liberation Army, a lucrative business that sold arms to everybody. Poly Industries had almost single-handedly made the market on Russian ordnance after the break-up of the

Soviet Union. Willy had felt that sales of Russian nuclear weapons would be a lucrative market and had been trying for several months to purchase, through Poly Industries, some Russian suitcase bombs. It was rumored that one hundred of these highly portable nuclear weapons had gone missing from the Russian war lockers, and Willy was very close to arranging the purchase of ten of them. Poly Industries was already responsible for supplying the very Russian automatic weapons that Willy's Triad sold to Black teenagers in the streets of America for top dollar.

The elevator doors opened onto the top-floor restaurant, where Chen Boda was waiting. The diminutive head of the Chinese Communist Military Commission seemed ageless. It had been four years since Willy had lain on the rolling gurney in the Friendship Hospital and watched through the glass as the slight politician ordered the surgeon to plunge the scalpel into the young radical's chest, beginning the lifesaving kidney harvest that "protected" Willy from the storm.

The two men shook hands. Willy had been summoned here, and he knew, just like the last time he had been invited to Beijing, that something important was about to happen.

Several military attendants set up folding screens around a corner window table. The Chinese screens were thin, delicate silken artworks, decorated with dragons breathing gold-threaded fire. It would be easy to hear through them, but Willy knew that nobody else would be allowed into the restaurant this morning. Willy was given the view position that looked out onto the city of Beijing, which sparkled under a bright February sun. The preparations for New Year's were well under way. Flags and decorative banners flapped from spires below them. The American Embassy compound could be seen a few blocks away to the east.

They said very little as the first course of steaming mushrooms was served. The dish had been prepared in ginger sauce in the traditional Cantonese way.

The deal they had made in the Year of the Dog was perfect. Chen Boda had given Willy the gift of new kidneys and in return

71

got the gift of Willy's smuggling routes. It was a very Chinese solution. One gift extracted poison from Willy's bloodstream. The other had inserted it into the American enemy. Better still, Willy had established even stronger Guan-Xi with American politicians. China had again received Most Favored Nation trade status, despite the protest of the U.S. Congress over Human Rights violations. Both men knew it was the money that Willy had poured into U.S. political campaigns which had helped to accomplish this. Investigations into campaign funding violations were still taking place in the American Congress, and China had been accused of trying to subvert the U.S. political process, but nobody had mentioned Wo Lap Ling. In fact, quite the opposite had happened. He was now on many U.S. corporate boards and had achieved great recognition as the Vice President of the American Red Cross in Asia. Now it was time to discuss a new arrangement.

The diminutive politician began a careful conversation that played on two levels because of the hovering waiters. "I hear the lichees in Guangdong are the sweetest in the world," Chen Boda began, referring to the sweet fruit that abounds in the province that contains Hong Kong. This fruit symbolized Hong Kong, which was now in China's hands.

"That is true," Willy said in Mandarin. "The summer crop was especially rich," referring to the hand-over of Hong Kong to mainland China that had happened last July.

"I understand that your own garden is flourishing, that many Americans now buy your fruit," Chen Boda said, referring to the Triad leader's Guan-Xi in America.

"Yes. When one has the right gardeners, things grow."

Chen Boda added, "But I have heard that to protect the garden, you had to pull out several weeds quickly and without mercy. I hope you got them all and that none will grow back."

"Yes. When weeding, it is very important to destroy the roots."

Both men smiled at this casual exchange, which referred to several influential Americans who had worked for Willy, but had been murdered recently because they had been contacted by the American FBI. Willy had judged them to be dangerous liabilities.

The mushrooms were soon devoured. Waiters cleared used plates and placed the ivory chopsticks on small ceramic props beside each diner's elbow.

Now other waiters in Red Army captain's uniforms brought the main course, enormous "dragon" shrimp, called Long Xia. Again, the two men ate in silence. The only sound was the clicking of ivory until the course was completely finished. Then came the Beijing Kao Ya, which was a delicious Peking roast duck. It arrived completely chopped up in a large dish. Chen Boda and Wo Lap Ling wrapped it in thin pancakes and added a sumptuous plum sauce. The skin of the duck, the "crackle," was the choicest part of the dish. They also had a side dish of chicken cooked inside a clay coating, which was known as "Buddha Jumping the Wall," because legend had it that the Lord Buddha interrupted his prayers when he smelled it and jumped over the garden wall for a taste.

Chen Boda nodded to one of the officers, indicating it was time for all of them to withdraw. The waiters closed the screens, leaving Willy and Chen Boda alone in the enclosure.

"It is time for you to play a larger role," the head of the Chinese Communist Military Commission said softly. "The Americans and the British do not trust us to rule Hong Kong with benevolence, and they are probably shrewd in this assessment. It is difficult to control some of the powerful tides of reform, and while we open our Motherland to the outside world, sometimes it is almost impossible to manage our destiny. Politics, like love, makes fools of everyone."

"But if you change the 'One Nation, Two Systems' agreement promised in the Sino-British accord, Western business will flee from Hong Kong. You will have inherited an empty house. It achieves nothing," Willy said, watching Chen Boda carefully.

"I see that you have finally become a student of the Master's wisdom," the politician said softly.

"Sometimes observers can see a chess game more clearly than

the players," Willy replied. He knew they were close to the reason he'd been brought here.

"Crows are black the world round," Chen said, sighing slightly. "And only rats know the way of rats." Chen was referring to the nature of men, and Willy was surprised to hear such blatant skepticism from the politician whose career had flourished because he refused such narrowness of thought.

"You have great Guan-Xi with the Americans," Chen Boda continued. "The West trusts you. They seek your wisdom even while you smuggle guns, drugs, and immigrants into their country. You have done your part skillfully."

Willy lowered his head to accept this compliment.

"And you are right. . . . It is imperative that we live up to the joint accord and have the free elections in Hong Kong in mid-1998, just as we promised Mrs. Thatcher when we signed the agreement. As you say, to fail to do this would be disastrous to Hong Kong's economy." Chen Boda hesitated, then smiled, "However, as you know, water can both sustain and sink a ship. The trick here is to give the impression of compliance. In this regard, I have finally persuaded the Central Committee that the free elections must take place, that this course is mandatory."

"But the Hong Kong Democratic Party is bound to prevail in an election. They will throw your Chief Executive and the Beijing-appointed legislature into the sea," Willy said.

"Not if it is you who runs for Chief Executive. You are the candidate to lead the Colony. You will be the first elected Chief Executive of the Hong Kong Special Autonomous Region. It will be a master stroke of world diplomacy. We will get all of your new friends in the U.S. government, the ones we helped to elect, to endorse you. Bill Clinton will support you as you have supported him. You must no longer run the Chin Lo Triad. We can't accept the risk that your criminal past will become known. You must turn the Triad over to your White Fan. After the election, you will run only the government of Hong Kong. It is the perfect deception, because you are from the New Territories with a dual passport.

Born in Kowloon, you have strong ties to the West, but you owe your life, hence your allegiance, to Mother China . . . and to me."

"I can still run the Triad. Nobody has discovered my association yet. Nobody will. I have taken great care to shield myself."

"There are rumors. . . . Already, several Hong Kong police have had to be weeded from your garden. There will be too much scrutiny. You must choose. One man cannot stand on two boats."

"This was your plan all along," Willy said, realizing he had been skillfully maneuvered to this place by the canny politician.

"You proved to be exactly the man I was looking for."

"I don't aspire to politics," Willy said.

"You will learn to love it. We are much alike. You will see the way. . . . I will not speak of this with you any longer. It has already been decided. You are already very wealthy. How much money can a man spend?" Chen Boda asked. "I offer the real elixir of life. I offer unrestrained power."

"Money is power," Willy said, still doubting the prospect of a life in politics.

"I will give you more power than you ever dreamed of."

"How do I know?"

"You have my word."

"We both know the satisfaction of longevity, but even the longest river eventually reaches the sea. What will happen when I no longer have your personal support? My White Fan, Henry Liu, is violent and strong. Once he has tasted the sweet nectar of control, he will spit out only seeds of vengeance if I cross him. I will have a dangerous time trying to reclaim my seat. I could lose a lifetime of work for a four-year term in the Chief Executive's office. I could end up with nothing more valuable than a title."

"Then there will be a paper between us. The terms will satisfy you—I promise. Sometimes a man must rise to important occasions or face the pain of a friend's disappointment." The threat against him was clear. Chen Boda had already made the decision. The two men locked gazes.

After a long moment, Willy Wo Lap nodded.

The next morning, Willy was picked up again by the limousine. This time "Five Oceans" was not in the car. Wo Lap Ling rode alone across Beijing to the impressive vermilion gate of the Zhong Nan Hai garden. The car passed between four Red Army soldiers perpetually on guard with fixed bayonets.

Willy was greeted on the grounds by Chen Boda. They walked across the beautiful flowered compound with its perfectly manicured lake. In the middle of the lake was an island that was dominated by a modest but elegant pavilion where Emperor Kuangxu had lived under guard after the failed "Hundred Days" coup of 1898 until his death in 1908. Kuangxu had attempted to bring democracy to China and had paid a heavy penalty. His advisers were beheaded or had fled the country. He had been kept like a caged bird in this pavilion for the rest of his life.

They walked across the wood bridge to the pavilion where the new President of China was sitting on a small bench, waiting. The President was dressed in a black suit with a starched white shirt and black tie. Wo Lap Ling knew that as China's economy grew, this man would one day become the most powerful man in the world, but to Wo Lap Ling, he looked strangely nondescript on the rosewood bench. He was tall, with a flat face, domed forehead, and heavy black-rimmed glasses. Chen Boda stood back and motioned for Willy to take a step forward. Above their heads were two beautiful scrolls hanging from the pavilion's rafter. These two scrolls were crafted by Emperor Kuangxu, as he lived out his life in captivity here. One said: "Obedient to Heaven, I gaze at the Blue Lake." A metaphor for hope and freedom to come with Buddha's blessing. The other banner said: "Ten thousand years are not enough to honor a good parent." This was a futile attempt to win the favor of the terrible old Dowager Empress, Ci Xi, who had quashed the coup and made the Emperor her prisoner.

The President of China stood, and as he stood, a strange thing happened. He seemed to grow larger in power and stature, as if he represented a new beginning. Wo Lap Ling instantly knew he had been foolish not to see it before. The realization of Willy's new status swept over him as he found himself standing before the President of what would soon become the most powerful country on earth. Despite his wealth and stature, until now Wo Lap Ling had just been an outlaw, nipping at the heels of the world, tearing off pieces of flesh, eating well but hiding from his true destiny. As China accepted her role as world leader, who knew how far Willy could eventually go? Politicians had always been his enemy. . . . In Hong Kong, the British leaders had launched attacks against his Triad. But the British were gone and now there were new rules. Now he could be the attacker. He felt his tiger suddenly lurch under him, restless to stalk new prey. Willy looked at the powerful man before him, knowing this man could transform him instantly from a pirate to a prince. Not since he was a boy in the streets of Kowloon, being asked by the powerful White Fan to join the Triad, had Willy felt such awe in the presence of another human being. He stood, head bowed, and waited.

"No progress is possible without stability and unity," the President said to him, implying that the current political systems of China and Hong Kong must remain unchanged.

"The Yellow River flows for thousands of miles, but eventually it reaches the sea," Willy said, his voice lost in the vastness of the moment. The Yellow River had always been the symbol of a powerful China.

The politician nodded his agreement. "But remember," he said, "a river that is too clear will never grow fish."

This was the very sentiment that had always defined Willy. Corruption was the soil of his garden.

The President of China extended his hand to Wo Lap Ling, then took one step backward, indicating that the meeting was complete.

Willy Wo Lap Ling had been born in the stinking ghetto of Kowloon. Now he turned and walked off an island that had once been the home of an Emperor. He and Chen Boda stood for a moment on the other side of the bridge. Willy did not want the moment to end. He had new ambitions, new goals. Chen Boda finally took his elbow and walked Wo Lap Ling out of the magnificent garden.

It took until evening to hammer out the terms of their agreement. Chinese New Year had just started as Willy boarded his private jet to head back to Hong Kong. He had altered his goal but not his quest. . . . Power, as the politician had implied, was the earth's fertilizer. Power made things grow.

There were no weeds left in Willy's garden. His river would grow many fish.

NINE

Aftermath

sian Crimes was a hung-over division the day after Chinese New Year. The detectives moved at their same pace for the benefit of their Occidental Captain, but the din of conversation was several decibels lower than usual. Tanisha had gone to the Homicide Board to make sure that the Wong murder was still up in her column. Ray Fong could have swiped the case if he got the Lieutenant to okay it. She'd been right about it hitting the news. There was a story on the Metro page of the *Times* and all the local TV newscasts had led with it this morning.

As she stood in front of the case chalkboard, she noticed a homeowner shooting that had taken place last night in Bel Air—a botched residential burglary where three Chinese John Does got killed. Ray Fong had rolled after the responding patrol unit called. It was the practice in ACTF to assign cases to detectives of the same ethnic origin, if possible. It facilitated the investigation, especially if the detective was fluent in that dialect. Tanisha went back to her desk and fished in her purse for the spiral notepad with Wheeler Cassidy's address on it. 1243 Belaggio Road, P-3. Penthouse? Probably a condo, she thought. Then she turned on the computer that she shared with four other desks and entered the triple case number. The computer told her the shooting had taken place on Canon Drive, not Belaggio. She was about to shut it off when she saw that the name of the owner of the residence was Prescott Cassidy.

"What the fuck?" she said to herself softly. That was the dead lawyer's house. Then she pulled up the full case report, and her amazement grew. The computer screen gave her Ray Fong's detailed and colorless account of the shooting. She was dumbfounded when she got to the name of the shooter. It was her smug, vomit-speckled asshole, Wheeler Cassidy.

"What's going on here?" she said to herself softly. She instructed the computer to hard-copy the case to her printer, then shut off the console. She sat in her chair, looking at the blank screen, trying to piece it together. She ran the beats, chronologically.

Prescott Cassidy had had a heart attack. *Maybe.* She made a note on her pad to get a look at Prescott's autopsy report. After Prescott Cassidy died, Chinese bodies started dropping like bunny shit. First Angie Wong gets a Death Doll from a Tong street gang, then she gets a punishment kill, complete with a rat gnawing her insides. A young Chinese man's picture is left on the body. Identity still unknown. No prints or trace evidence at the scene, so the perps had been thoroughly schooled in peri- and post-mortem crime scene behavior. She had asked patrol to interview the neighbors to see if anybody had seen anything unusual, a car, people who didn't belong. Nobody had. So far, the Wong killing was a complete "Who done it?" The Wong house appeared to have been thoroughly searched. Then, three Chinese gangsters were caught apparently burglarizing Prescott Cassidy's home. Wheeler, who is bringing his sister-in-law home from the airport, walks in on it. He gets his brother's target pistols out of the pool house. Next comes the O.K. Corral. Wheeler acquits himself surprisingly well and puts two of the three gangsters in the county freezer. The patrol unit skags the third one as he's running off the property. According to

Ray Fong's detailed report, Wheeler took one in the leg and spent the night at Cedars-Sinai in Beverly Hills.

Way too much activity in one place.

Something much bigger was going on. She looked over at Ray Fong, who was leaning back at his desk, his feet up, reading a Chinese paper. She wondered how this would go down. Only one way to find out. She got up and walked over to his desk.

"You have a good New Year last night?" she asked conversationally, playing dumb and smiling at the Chinese detective.

"I caught a squeal right after I left here. Triple kill in Bel Air. Brother of the homeowner dropped two. The responding unit got the other. I was up all night with it," he complained. "My D.B.s had no I.D. Prints can't pull up anything. They're probably illegal immigrants. Maybe Tong members. So it's gonna be a stonewall out there."

"How do you know they were Tong?" she asked.

"They had more drawings on 'em than a South Central overpass. From the tattoos, I'd say they're Bamboo Dragons."

"I think those three shootings may be connected to the Wong hit."

"Yeah?" he said, putting the paper down. "How come?"

"The guy who found Angela Wong's body is Wheeler Cassidy, the brother of the guy whose house was being burgled. The same guy who lit up two of your Bamboo Dragons."

Ray sat up and took his feet off the desk. "Nobody told me Wheeler found Angie Wong's body. He didn't say anything last night. 'Course he was going into shock."

"And it wasn't in the computer," she said, stating the obvious.

"All the more reason you've gotta give me the Wong case," he said.

"Look, Ray, I don't want to fight with you over this. Department guidelines say that everything that stems from one killing is under the direct control of the primary on the lead case. That's me."

Ray stood up to look Tanisha directly in the eyes. "That's

what it says, but if they *are* connected, we got two burglaries, three shootings, and a punishment kill in less than twenty-four hours. You're not gonna get anywhere on this because nobody is going to talk to you. I tried to tell you that last night, and you laid all that discrimination shit on me. You don't belong in this unit. You and I both know why they put you here. It wasn't my fault. But if you learned anything from all that Asian culture you read, you should know by now how things work."

"I'm sorry about last night, Ray. That rat thing spooked me. I know I need help, but you've gotta let me at least run with you. These two deals are connected. You can't freeze me out." She knew if the three dead Chinese in Prescott's house were Snake Riders and Bamboo Dragons, then information was going to get scarce. She'd need somebody like Ray, who was fluent in Mandarin and Cantonese, maybe Fukienese and Chin Chow, or any of the other dozen Chinese dialects. She could see he was teetering on the brink of saying yes, so she decided to give him something to help push him over. "I dropped the rat off at my neighborhood pet store. Don, who runs the place, is good with rare species. He told me it was a naked mole rat. Originally native to Ethiopia and Somalia." She looked at her notepad. "Its scientific name is *Heterocephalus glaber.*"

"Sounds like a venereal disease," he said.

"It sure was for Angie Wong. They mostly come to the U.S. from Hong Kong . . . illegal exports to the pet store market here. In the wild, they live mostly underground in narrow tunnels and can survive for a long time with almost no air, making them ideal for that kind of torture."

Ray started to write this down on a pad.

"The thing about putting it up the vagina . . . last night, I looked it up and read about it," she continued. "It's an old Chinese torture developed by the ancients. It all but died out, but recently it was reintroduced. The Royal Hong Kong Police saw it a few times in the old Walled City of Kowloon, the last few years before Hong Kong got handed back. Apparently there was no governing body that controlled the Walled City while the British ruled there. Some pretty weird shit happened."

He looked up at her but didn't say anything. He had developed the Chinese poker face used by inveterate Chinese gamblers. His flat features showed overpowering boredom, his eyes registered disinterest.

She went on, "Obviously the Cassidy house wasn't being robbed, it was being tossed, just like the Wong house. These guys were looking for something. It's too much of a coincidence to be just a straight burg."

"Okay, Tisha, we'll work this together. But right now, for the purpose of noninterference, let's keep the two cases technically separate. Once the Lieutenant finds out they're linked, he'll have to notify Major Crimes and we're gonna have a platoon of Parker Center cowboys in here, scooping everything up. We'll both be standing out in the rain."

"Fair enough," she said, and then, unexpectedly, he put out his hand, and without hesitation she shook it.

And that was how Tanisha Williams and Ray Fong both turned up in Wheeler Cassidy's hospital room at ten A.M. that morning and caught him arguing with his mother.

His leg was bandaged and hanging in a pulley hoist. She was in her mid-sixties and incredibly beautiful, wearing a Givenchy cocktail dress with a single strand of pearls. The woman had just taken a silver flask from Wheeler and was holding it, accusingly, as Ray and Tanisha entered.

"This is a private room. Unless you're doctors, we were having a personal discussion," the older woman said.

"Detective Fong and Detective Williams. We have some follow-up questions about last night," Ray said, pulling his badge case and showing his shield and plastic-covered I.D. to her.

"When will it end?" the woman sighed in disgust and set down the flask on the bedside table as she moved to the window and looked out. Tanisha could tell from her body language that she was under a great deal of strain. From the resemblance to Wheeler, Tanisha also assumed she was his mother.

Then Wheeler flashed a glassy smile and confirmed it. "May I present my mother, Katherine Cassidy," he said with alcoholic largesse.

"My God, Wheeler, your brother is gone, his secretary has been murdered. You have shot two men dead. How can you be drunk? I just can't . . ." She didn't finish, nor did she turn away from the window to look at them.

"Maybe I'm drunk because of all that, Mother, not despite it," he said, slurring a few words.

She turned and fixed an angry look on him but said nothing.

"You had a very busy day yesterday," Tanisha said to him, trying to change the energy in the room.

"Yep," Wheeler grinned, looking through her. There was a desperate gleam in his eyes when you looked close. She'd seen it the night before when he'd mocked himself, only now it was more pronounced.

"That was quite a shootout," she said.

"I got real lucky, you want my opinion," he said. "Damn fool bullshit thing ta do. . . . 'Scuse the language, Mother."

"Mr. Cassidy," Ray said, "we think the people you shot were illegal aliens, mainland Chinese who are in a local Bamboo street gang. The fact that they were searching your brother's house and had also, most likely, searched Angelica Wong's house and murdered her is more than slightly significant. All of this happened shortly after your brother died. Do you have any idea what they might have been looking for?"

"No," he said.

"It could have to do with your brother's business," Ray added.

"What on earth are you trying to say?" Katherine blurted. "Are you trying to say that Pres was involved in something illegal?"

"We don't know anything yet, Mrs. Cassidy," Ray said. "The timing of his secretary's murder right after his death and the fact that both houses were searched indicates—"

"You can't possibly be serious," she interrupted. "Do you have any idea the clients he had, the political contacts? He was a central part of the Clinton re-election campaign. Bill and Hillary Clinton had him to the White House twice. He was on the Presidential Commission on International Trade Alliances."

"That's very commendable," Ray said, wilting badly.

"Mrs. Cassidy, I'd like the name of the doctor who's doing the autopsy on Prescott," Tanisha said, deciding to break in and give Ray a rest.

"There is no autopsy," Katherine said. "It was judged a heart attack by the attending physician at the hospital that received the body. It was confirmed by Pres's own doctor. He had high blood pressure and was being treated for it. We didn't see why there was any reason to mutilate his body before the funeral, so we got the autopsy waived."

"Under the circumstances, don't you think it would be a good idea to make sure his death was from natural causes?" Tanisha asked.

"I certainly do not. He had a heart attack. You people will clear out of this room immediately or I will make some big trouble," she said.

"I'm going to have to order an autopsy," Tanisha said. "Mrs. Cassidy, I know you're upset—"

"Do you? Do you have any idea what it's like to lose a son? A son who had the most wonderful future in front of him? A son who had demonstrated the most wonderful skills in business and in life . . ." She was near tears now. "Do you have any idea what it's like to have him snatched away, just taken like that? And then to have the police insinuate that something sinister was going on?"

Tanisha's mind flew back to the neighborhood street corner. Her own screams echoed in her memory as she watched the life disappear in her beloved little sister's eyes. Katherine Cassidy's voice brought her back. "You two people get out of here right now," she growled.

The interview was blown. Wheeler was half in the bag. His mother was hysterical. Tanisha decided to talk to Wheeler later. She nodded at Ray, and as they excused themselves, Wheeler gave her a lazy wave. That was when Tanisha remembered where she'd seen Wheeler Cassidy before. It was back when she was finishing her criminology degree at U.C.L.A. Some classmates had talked her into going to the U.S.C.–U.C.L.A. football game. They had an extra ticket and she needed a break from her twelve-hour marathon study schedule, so she'd gone along. It was half-time and a crazy bastard in a hand-painted cardinal-and-gold VW had driven out of the south turnstile of the Coliseum and squirted warm beer into the Bruin rooting section. He'd stained her blue sleeveless silk blouse. He'd given the U.C.L.A. rooting section that same careless wave before being chased by security police, pulled out of the car, and arrested. "Son of a bitch," she finally said, as they walked to the elevator.

"Huh?" Ray asked.

"Nothing."

"Whatta you think?" Ray said as they waited for the elevator door to open.

Tanisha was thinking about that football game fifteen years ago, remembering the drunk Trojan frat boy laughing as he drove in circles at mid-field, two dozen security men running after him. He had ruined her best silk blouse. She didn't have the money to replace it. Her world was too grim back then to understand somebody like Wheeler Cassidy, and she still thought the prank was pointless and unfunny. Then her heart softened as she remembered the look of pain in his eyes a few minutes before, as his mother lavished praise on her dead son, while heaping contempt on her living one.

"No wonder the man drinks," she finally said.

TEN

A New China

Z hang Fu Hai found his way back to Beijing's Huo Che Chang, the central railway station. He waited until after ten o'clock in the evening and then moved furtively across the tracks, looking for a boxcar that was heading south. He found a string of cars parked in the switching yard that had paper transit slips noting their destinations. The cars in this line were not hooked to an engine but were marked for transit to Shanghai. He had heard from other workers at the silk factory that the Triad which ran the immigration business in China was the Chin Lo and that its China branch was located in Guangzhou, the capital of Guangdong Province. The cars on this track were headed south to Shanghai, not the exact location he needed, but he had to take what he could get. The Master's wisdom taught him that: "It is better to make a net than yearn for fish at the edge of a pond."

The cars were padlocked and he was wondering what he would do to get inside when somebody yelled in broken Mandarin mixed with Cantonese, "Hey you, get away from there!"

Fu Hai spun and saw a burly man with an angry expression

moving toward him. He had on greasy work overalls and no shirt, even though the February night was very cold.

"What do you think you're doing?" the man growled as he moved up on Zhang Fu Hai. He was almost a foot taller and much heavier.

"I am . . . I need . . ."

"You were trying to break into this car," the man said. "I will have to call the police."

"No. No, please. I have no travel papers. My permission slip was taken from me for no reason by a Block Warden," Fu Hai said, knowing that he would have to run to get away. This man was too big to fight.

The man reached out and unexpectedly grabbed Fu Hai's shirt, pulling him close. Fu Hai could smell coal and oil on his clothing.

"Do you have any money?" the burly man demanded.

"Why?"

"Perhaps we could make a bargain. Perhaps I could sell you a ride in one of my cars. My job is to watch to make sure nobody steals or tries to board the boxcars, but I have the keys," he said, grinning and showing teeth made brown from chewing sugarcane and brown seeds.

"I . . . I . . . how much would this cost me?" Fu Hai asked, wondering how he could ever trust this man who looked like a street thug.

"What do you have?" the man asked. "How much?"

"I can pay you fifteen *yuan*," Fu Hai said.

"You pay me a hundred or I will take you to the police right now."

A hundred *yuan* was a fortune. Two months' work at the silk factory. All the money Fu Hai had was in his pocket and added up to a little less than sixty *yuan*. It had to get him all the way to Guangzhou. But Fu Hai was frightened, so he pulled out the money and handed it to the rail guard, who counted it quickly.

"Is this all?" he demanded.

"It is all," Fu Hai said.

Then, without argument, the man folded the money and stuffed it into his pocket. He moved to the boxcar, took out a key and unlocked the padlock, then pulled the chain free and opened the door wide enough for Fu Hai to get inside. "I will lock it now, because the cars are inspected before the train leaves. All the doors have to be padlocked, but I will come back and unlock it before the train pulls out of the station," he said.

Fu Hai got inside the freight car, sure he could not trust the man, but before he could say anything else, the door was pulled closed and he could hear the chain rattling in the metal hasp and the big padlock was snapped shut.

Fu Hai cursed himself. He had let the man take all of his money and lock him in a rail car. He was helpless. The rail guard could just go and get a policeman. Fu Hai had been stupid, outfoxed by an uneducated brute. Fu Hai could tell by his accent that the man had no schooling. Like so many in China, the burly man had been forced into a labor market to help feed his family before he had learned pure Mandarin, as dictated by the Cultural Revolution. The man would certainly turn Fu Hai over to the police. Fu Hai would be sent to a *lao gai*, a work camp. He would die in prison and all of this would be for nothing. He would never get to America, never be able to get his beloved sister out of the horrible porter's room where she lived.

He looked around the car and saw that it was filled with wooden crates of "White Elephant" batteries on their way to Shanghai. Finally, he sat on the floor and put his head in his hands. His thoughts turned to his family, the way it had been when he was a child, before his father had been targeted as an enemy of the Revolution.

He remembered the first time the Red Guards had come to his father's calligraphy studio. He had been six. They accused Zhang Wei Dong of neglecting one of the "Four Bigs" which were mandated by the Cultural Revolution. They included speaking out freely, airing views fully, holding great debates, and writing "Big

Character" posters. The Red Guards said that on one of the posters he had not written Chairman Mao's name in big red letters as mandated by the government. They demanded he undergo a "struggle session." His father said the poster was not his work. He tried to explain to the soldiers that he, Zhang Wei Dong, would never violate this rule of the Revolution. After much violent shoving and shouts commanding him to confess, the Captain of the Red Guards said he had decided to show pity. He said he would not arrest Wei Dong. Instead, he had his men hold Fu Hai's father's hands on the wood table. While Fu Hai watched, the Red Guards slammed their wood batons down on his father's hands, breaking all of the finger bones. His father screamed and cried for mercy. He tried to say, through his pain, that he was a calligrapher and needed his hands to feed his family. They paid no attention and beat him until he was unconscious from the pain.

Mother is dear, Father is dear, but Chairman Mao is dearest of all.

His father's hands had healed without medical attention, but they became useless claws. He could no longer hold a brush. It had been the beginning of the end of the Zhang family's good life in Beijing. Their "rice bowl" was broken. They had no livelihood. From then on, nothing went right and the bad luck had continued for Fu Hai, right up to this moment.

Fu Hai was sound asleep on the wooden floor of the boxcar when he felt the train lurch. He woke up with a start and instantly knew that the switch engine had backed into the line of waiting cars to hook them up. He waited, listening for the door to be unlocked by the burly man, but he never came back. In five minutes, the train lurched forward and then slowly pulled out of the vast gray station.

Fu Hai was still on his feet an hour later as the train pulled out of Beijing, leaving the new construction and concrete streets behind. He wondered how he would get out of the train as it rattled and creaked along the tracks toward Shanghai. He finally sat with his back against a crate of batteries and wept.

By sun-up, he could see through a crack in the boxcars' worn slats that he was passing through the cotton, corn, and melon fields of northern China. He could smell the damp soil and see vectoring insects whirl above the colorful new crops, planted in dewy green rows, shining against the yellow earth.

He had begun to view the time he spent in the padlocked rail car as pleasant. In a way, the confinement was comforting to him. He couldn't get out, but nobody could get in. He hid behind a fort of wooden crates every time the train came to a stop. He knew that getting out of the car once they were in Shanghai would be a difficult problem, so he set his mind on it. He finally decided to empty one of the White Elephant battery crates and hide inside, but the large wooden crates were nailed shut. Furthermore, it was going to be hard to get the batteries out of the boxcar. He gave it some more thought, then lay on his back and kicked an opening in the side of the car at the worn spot in the slats. He worked feverishly, kicking splinters loose. His feet ached from the blows. His thin cloth shoes offered almost no protection, but slowly he widened the gap between the slats. Then he spent almost half a day getting the nails out of one of the crates. He started by kicking the underside of the top of the crate up with his swollen feet, loosening it slightly, until he could push it back down enough to get his teeth around the nail head. By pulling up hard, he finally got the first nail out. It took almost two more hours to remove six more nails. A few of his teeth were badly chipped by the time he was finished. Cold air stung the nearly exposed nerves in the broken teeth. The inside of his mouth was cut and bleeding when he got the top loose enough to pull it off. Slowly, he began to push the batteries out of the widened hole he had made in the rail car. He emptied the crate and made his hiding place.

At four P.M., the train reached the Yangtze River, which was known as the Chang Jiang, the River Without End. He looked through the slats at its huge girth and turbulent brown waters. For hours, they traveled downriver. The train rumbled along, following the rushing current to the sea.

He looked in awe at the outskirts of Shanghai as they moved into that historic city. He could see that whole sections of the town were being torn down. Turn-of-the-century colonial houses were ripped out to make way for new construction. Rubble and old broken colonial masonry were stacked all along the tracks. Farther down the river, he could see new concrete high-rise buildings being put up. It was as if China was eating her own past, chewing down the old and excreting new monuments of concrete, terrazzo, and glass.

The train rattled through the green rice fields of Jiangsu Province, where he had read in the provincial papers that people were being forcibly removed to make way for new commercial construction.

Fu Hai had known a wretched man from Jiangsu Province who had been sent to Khotan for questioning the redistribution of land in 1952. The man's house had been taken by the government. He had been made homeless, paid nothing for his family's property. When he objected that he only owned five *mu* of land, a little over an acre, he was told that he was a "landlord" and a "class enemy." In that part of Jiangsu, four *mu* was the maximum land one could own. He had been sent to Khotan for this offense. There was no redress of grievances in China. It was best to understand that and not stand before a force that could crush you without fear of reprisal.

The train finally slowed and pulled into Shanghai Station. The celebration of Chinese New Year had already begun. In the distance, the sky was lit by fireworks. He hoped the celebration would help him. He knew he had to change cars here. It was a dangerous proposition. He had heard that the train stations on the coast were patrolled by the People's Armed Police, who would look for escaping members of the floating population. They were not wanted anywhere in eastern China and were arrested on sight, then, without benefit of a hearing, were put on buses which took them to detention centers.

Fu Hai waited fearfully inside his crate as the boxcar door was opened. He listened as a man counted the crates of batteries, out loud, tapping on them to make sure they sounded full. Another man came into the car, and Fu Hai heard him say that they should hurry, the celebration for the New Year had already started. Both men left, and Fu Hai guessed that because the car only contained batteries, they didn't relock it. He got out of the crate, slid the boxcar door open, and jumped down onto the gravel between the tracks. He needed to find a car that would take him to Guangzhou. He knew he couldn't walk around out in the open. His shabby dress and cloth shoes would give him away. He had no money; no way to bribe anybody if he was caught. Then he saw a car he could climb into. On the door was a slip of paper, a waybill, saying the car was destined for Guangdong Province. Close enough. The load inside was angle-iron rods, too heavy for anybody to steal, so the door was loosely chained. He pulled it as wide as it would go and slithered up into the boxcar.

At ten o'clock that night, the boxcar he was in was connected to a tug engine, pulled out of the yard, then slammed into the back of another car and hooked up. At a little past midnight, Fu Hai was again headed south, away from the fireworks that lit the Shanghai sky.

The angle-iron rods had stickers on them that said they had been forged at Shanghai's Baoshan (Treasure Mountain) Steel Mill. The metal beams would undoubtedly be used for construction and were twenty feet long. It was impossible to find a comfortable place to lie down. Fu Hai was accustomed to misery and he made the best of it, often being forced to balance on his feet for hours, rocking unsteadily on the long grooved steel angles. The train shook and creaked and lumbered on.

They moved through dimly lit stations. Fu Hai could barely read the signs through the slats. The next morning, they passed the beautiful willow-clad city of Hangzhou in Zhejiang Province, where, it was said, Mao Zedong spent his summers in splendor. Zhejiang Province was the Chinese land of fish and rice (milk and honey). While Fu Hai's father's hands had been broken for the glory of the Revolution, Mao and his concubines were quartered not half a mile from where the train was now passing, on a willow-fringed lake in a green-roofed villa cooled by powerful Russian-made air conditioners.

Mother is dear, Father is dear, but Chairman Mao is dearest of all.

The next morning, the train pulled into Guangdong. Fu Hai cowered in fear as People's Armed Police (P.A.P.) guards moved through the yard banging on the wood doors of the cars with their trenchant sticks. "Open up, we know you're in there," they shouted at each car.

Fu Hai had no place to hide in the car full of angle irons. He huddled in the corner, trying to stay out of the sunlight that was streaming through the slits. He heard the door being opened; then someone was climbing in. Suddenly he was face to face with a man who was wearing a uniform of the People's Armed Police. As Fu Hai looked closer, he saw that the soldier wasn't much older than eighteen. The guard reached for his electric baton, and Fu Hai launched himself across the opening, diving at the young man and knocking him out of the car. The two of them rolled on the ground as the soldier began yelling in terror for his comrades. Fu Hai grabbed the electric baton away from him and jabbed the young guard in the head, neck, and privates. The baton arced blue agony from its power source. The boy whimpered and curled up into a ball, stunned but not unconscious.

"You be quiet," Fu Hai hissed at him, not wanting to sting him again, but also not wanting his own soft heart to cost him a life in prison. Then Fu Hai threw down the baton and started running. He didn't know where he was headed. He didn't have any plan of escape or even know what direction he was going. He ran blindly on the loose gravel, his chest heaving with the effort, his cheap, rubber-soled cloth shoes barely supporting his swollen, aching feet.

He finally found two wood buildings split by a narrow road. He ran between them and miraculously was out of the train yard, running along a small, dusty street lined with brick walls. Barbed wire was strung on top.

He saw a small smelting house made of concrete and old bricks. It was one of the "backyard steel furnaces" left over from the disastrous "Great Leap Forward" of 1958–1960. Another lunatic fantasy of Mao Zedong, who wanted to industrialize China overnight. Instead, thirty million people starved to death.

Out of breath and unable to go on, he crawled inside the smelting house. His heart was pounding. He could taste the blood in his mouth from pulling out nails with his teeth—teeth that stung as he inhaled cold air over exposed nerves. He could still feel the shape of the electric baton in his hand. He could remember Xiao Jie's whisper with the pounding heartbeat in his ears. "You must go. They will come for you," she had said as he looked at his beloved little sister who had aged to twice her years.

"Don't worry, little sister, I will get to America and I will send for you. I will get us a new life there," he had promised her.

ELEVEN

China Boy

T hey were face up on steel trays, laid out like patrons at a Beverly Hills tanning salon, stripped naked but cold as marble. Next door, the decomp room in the morgue leaked unsavory odors. The three young Chinese corpses stared up vacantly as Ray Fong and Tanisha Williams examined the graphic, colorful tattoos of snakes, dragons, and Chinese symbols which adorned their young, bloodless bodies. Then Tanisha noticed a homemade tattoo on the right arm of the oldest boy. A faded "1414." It was exactly like the one that was on Angie Wong's forehead in Magic Marker.

"What the hell is this?" she said, looking at it closer. "What's it mean?"

"Fourteen K is a Tong," Ray said as he examined it.

"I know," she said. "It was formed in Taiwan under Chiang Kai-shek, as an anti-Japanese political organization. Later, they became a secret brotherhood called Hung Fat Shan. Ten years after that, they moved to Hong Kong and switched to heroin, gun smuggling, and extortion. It was nicknamed 14K because 14 was the street address of the Tong's headquarters in Canton. K stood for Karat, the common measure of fineness for gold." She was showing off again, trying to prove to Ray Fong that she knew her stuff and deserved to be with him, even though she suspected she was a far superior detective. She silently cursed herself for this need to impress. Why did she always have to over-perform to just be allowed in the game? She had never been taken seriously, until she had killed the two O.G.B.s.

They'd been Original Ghetto Bloods, off-brand G-sters from Hawaiian Gardens, which was known among gang-bangers as the Jungle because the developers had over-planted the crummy box-like ghetto apartments with ferns to disguise the tasteless architecture. She'd only been sixteen when she'd done the two Bloods. It was just two months after Kenetta was killed. She'd been buying groceries for her mother at the 7-Eleven. Without warning, the two smoked-out, chained, and federated ghetto stars rolled on the market. Both decked out in gold jewelry and the Bloods' "federated color" red. They were waving banana-clipped AKs and Trey-five-sevens, and immediately started splashing on everything, first killing the cashier, then two other shoppers. One hapless victim was Miss Bradley, her third-grade gym teacher. When they were through hosing down the market, they saw Tanisha. They pulled her into the back room and started ripping at her clothes.

"C'mon, sweet meat," one hissed at her, "we gonna do some bone dancin'." They were both tugging at their zippers and not paying close enough attention to her.

Anger over Kenetta's death fueled her attack.

She got the nearer one with a shiv she'd been packing since fourth grade. She shoved it into his stomach, right through his leather jacket, and he fell to his knees. His road dog stopped fumbling with his pants and grabbed for her as the first G-ster yelled for help. She slashed the road dog, opening his throat up ear to ear, cutting his jugular. Then, as the first Blood grabbed for her again, she slashed him the same way. Both G-sters fell right there in the back room of the market and were bled out and ash-gray when the police arrived ten minutes later. Tanisha was long gone. She had run through the carnage, out of the 7-Eleven into the night. She had been seen in the market and was later picked up and questioned, but no arrest was ever made.

To this day, she had nightmares about it. She could feel the narrow blade in her hand, feel the soft rending of flesh as she ended the count for the two dope-sprung dust-bunnies who had actually tried to rape her in the middle of a robbery where they had already killed three people. She hated the memory, but in her neighborhood, she had finally been made by that horrible act of violence. Monster C. said she had "come from the shoulder on the Blood stripers." The ultimate compliment. Li'l Evil said that she'd "ring around the collared" the "off-brand" motherfuckers.

From that day, she'd been "Rings." It was seventeen years ago and she was still uneasy every time she thought of it.

As Tanisha looked down at the three dead Bamboo Dragons, she wondered how Wheeler Cassidy felt about the two he'd dropped. She wondered if he felt devalued; wondered if it would stay with him the rest of his life as it had with her.

"I don't think 1414 stands for the 14K Triad. I never heard of that before," Ray Fong said, changing his mind and interrupting her thoughts.

"Well, we've gotta find out what it means," she said. "It meant enough to him so he carved it into his arm with a knife, and if these are the guys who killed Angie Wong, they put it on her forehead. I'll get it up to Symbols and Hieroglyphics."

There was one other tattoo that looked promising in terms of getting an identification. On the right biceps of one of the Bamboo Dragons was the name "China Boy."

When they got back to the Asian Crimes Task Force, Captain Rick Verba was waiting for them.

"What the fuck's going on with you?" he said, looking at Ray but not Tanisha.

"Whatta you mean?" Ray asked.

Then Verba motioned for them to follow him. They moved through the squad room, past the questioning looks of the on-duty Asian detectives. The Captain's office was at the end of the room. They entered and Rick Verba closed the door. There was a glass window that looked out at the squad room. Verba pulled a curtain, shutting his office from view.

"What's going on, Skipper?" Ray asked.

"You fucking amaze me. I get a complaint from some Beverly Hills grande dame named Katherine Cassidy who says you two are out at Cedars together, kicking dirt on the memory of her dead son, Prescott. Making it worse, the complaint is personally delivered by Deputy Chief Matson. Then I find out it's her other son, Wheeler Cassidy, who shot the three home invaders, and he's the same guy who found Angie Wong's body yesterday. These two cases are somehow connected. You two didn't put up a flag. You outta your minds?"

"We didn't want Major Crimes to jump it. We've got a much better chance of clearing it. It's an Asian situation," Ray said, but he was back on his heels again. "Deputy Chief Matson?" he added in awe. "I never heard of a Deputy Chief delivering a field complaint."

"Wait outside, will you?" Verba asked Fong. "Don't drift. I'll need you back in here in a minute."

Ray left the office while Captain Verba glared at Tanisha. He was a middle-aged, heavyset man with gray eyes and a bad case of pattern baldness. The Ab-Roller he got for Christmas wasn't helping. His stomach was mushrooming over his belt. Still, he was not a guy Tanisha wanted to screw around with, especially since Internal Affairs was all over her anyway. It was noteworthy that the two of them were the only non-Asians in Asian Crimes.

"I'm putting you on a desk, Tisha. I gotta take you outta the field."

"Why? Because we hooked up on these two cases? We thought if we put 'em together, we'd—"

"I know what you thought," he interrupted, "and you're right. I probably won't give it to the Major Crimes Cap Unit at Parker Center either . . . but you've got Internal Affairs scoping you, Detective. They don't want you in the field. If you were smart, you'd cool off. Instead, you're scrambling after corpses. I got a call this morning. I.A.'s getting set to file on you. I think you need to go talk to your Police Association rep, get some legal advice."

"Captain, this is all bullshit."

"The I.A. dicks say you hang out in the hood on weekends. That you go to your grandmother's, which is a known drug house, and you also go to some other house south of Crenshaw every damn Saturday."

It was true. Her nephew had started dealing, but Tanisha had run him off. She also had a standing appointment at Zadell's every Saturday. Zadell's was a two-chair unlicensed beauty parlor in the back of Zadell Falk's garage south of Manchester. It would do her no good to try and explain to Captain Verba that African-American women can't get their hair done by White hairdressers. Working on Black hair was an artform. Most of the African-American women she knew, from prosecutors to judges, had Black hairdressers. Some still went to hot-comb parlors in the ghetto to get their trims. Before she was a cop, she would wait with the hoo-chie mamas, who sat on metal chairs in open-toed shoes and talked about babies they'd had with three or four different neighborhood rock stars. Rock stars, south of Manchester, weren't singers—they were boned-out, jive-ass turf-ballers who dealt smack or rock and looked at you with dusty eyes. Tanisha had slowly become a cultural alien in her own neighborhood. It had started when she wouldn't join the Crips, and talked about her middle-class dreams. She made no sense to her friends. They said she was uppity and full of herself. Then after Kenetta died and she started getting A's in school she became more of an outcast. Joining the LAPD was the final defection. She had emigrated to Baldwin Park, but she had a standing weekly appointment at Zadell's. She didn't know why she kept going there. Pride, she guessed. She wasn't about to be run off. Conversation between the hoochies kicking there always stopped abruptly while Tanisha was in the chair, her head drenched with hair relaxer to loosen her Afro curls. The hoochies put out a kill-vibe as they painted their nails or looked at their feet until she was gone. Tisha was "the Man," the "PO-lice." She'd been coming to Zadell's since she was sixteen, but now she felt uncomfortable and couldn't get out fast enough.

Captain Verba looked down at a pad where he had written some notes. "This gang killer, Parnell Davis, called Li'l Evil. I.A. thinks you gave up a Crash case to him. When they rolled on Parnell's crack house, the place was clean as Crisco."

"Captain, that was a very sloppy bust. Crash was working half-a-dozen zooted-up informants for info. Any one of them could've given up the operation. I admit, I've known Parnell since I was ten. We went to junior high together. My baby sister died in his arms, but I didn't give up any case to him. This isn't about that anyway."

"What's it about then?" he said softly.

"Lieutenant Hawley in the Crash Unit couldn't get in my pants, so he sold me off to the Shooflies."

"If that's true, I'm sorry. It's also not my problem. I.A. wanted you out of commission 'till they could get enough on you to bring a hearing. They finally think they have enough. You need to get the police union into this. Either way, you're off the Wong killing."

"Who's going to work it?"

"Turn everything you have over to Ray Fong."

The LAPD had targeted her for extinction.

Tisha and Ray went to lunch. It was an awkward meal where not much was said. Ray told her he thought she'd been handed a raw deal. Then he followed her over to her house and she gave him the rat, which was still in her freezer.

"Really sucks. I'm sure you'll win the I.A. review," Ray said without much conviction.

"I have a girlfriend who's a homicide lieutenant. She's married to a patrol officer who beats her up. One night, a month ago, he's feeling particularly frisky, she's finally had enough so she calls the cops. They live in Santa Monica, so naturally the Santa Monica P.D. gets the squeal. When the responding unit found out her husband was in L.A. Patrol, they didn't arrest him, even though she's an LAPD loot, and she's standing right in front of them bleeding like a club fighter. The next morning, *she* got pulled in front of an Internal Affairs review board and chastised for calling the Santa Monica cops and bringing disgrace on the L.A. Department. This bullshit that's going on with me is just more dog pound protocol," she said.

"Y'know, from time to time, I'd like to swing by," Ray said unexpectedly. "Maybe we could go over the case. I could sorta keep you involved, so once you get through this I.A. thing, you'll still be up to speed."

"Who's gonna buy the wine?" she said sarcastically.

"Look, Tisha . . . it wouldn't be so bad."

"You're a good guy, Ray. Let's not spoil it."

Finally he just smiled and shook her hand. "Good luck," he said and left her there. He moved down the walk, got in his car, and drove away.

That night, at a little past two A.M., Tanisha's phone rang. She rolled over and fumbled it out of the cradle.

"You okay?" It was Rick Verba calling.

"Yeah, Captain, why?"

"Just checking . . . Go back to sleep."

"Captain . . ." But he was gone. She lay in bed trying to get her mind to work. A Division Commander didn't call you at two A.M. just to see if you were sleeping soundly. She rolled up and sat on the side of the bed. Then she called the office.

"Asian Crimes Task Force," the operator said.

"This is Tanisha, who's this?" she asked.

"Ellen," the operator said. Ellen was one of four Asian operators that worked the phones at ACTF. She was a civilian employee who spoke seven different Oriental languages, including the three most common Chinese dialects: Mandarin, Cantonese, and Fukienese.

"Is everything okay down there?" Tanisha asked.

"Not exactly . . ."

"What's up?"

"Somebody got Ray Fong. . . . He's dead. Shot in the head!"

"Goddamn," she said. A sickening feeling swept over her.

"I gotta go, Tisha. This place is going nuts."

Tanisha dressed without even looking at what she pulled out of the closet. Twenty minutes later, she was in the squad room getting the gory details.

Ray's car had been found on Hill Street, one block away from Chinatown, by a cruising patrol car. Ray had been slumped over, his face on the wheel. When the officer tipped him back, he had seen that the detective's forehead was missing.

Al Katsukura had the case. He didn't have much time to talk to Tanisha, saying only that the shot appeared to have come through the driver's side window. Ray had apparently rolled down the glass to talk to his killer and had been shot in the face. She told Al that Ray had been working a trace on one of the dead Bamboo Dragons. His possible street name was "China Boy." Al nodded, made a note, and hurried out the door. That was it. Ray Fong was E.O.W.—End of Watch.

She stood in the squad room while detectives streamed in with their hair badly combed. It was three-fifteen A.M., but they stood around in the corridor and leaned on the walls. She'd seen this kind of thing before when cops were shot. Everybody came to work and just hung there, hoping somebody would get lucky and bring the killer in. All of them stifling fantasies of being allowed to walk into a holding cell while the rest of the watch was magically off getting coffee, then slowly and efficiently kick the doer's nuts up between his eyes. It was powerful hatred.

Tanisha was one of them, but then again, she was not. She felt like she did at Zadell's every Saturday. So after about a half-hour of playing eye-tag with the complement of Asian cops, she went down and got in her car and drove over to Hill Street. She knew she'd have no trouble finding the crime scene. It would be taped off and guarded. There would probably be half-a-dozen lab techs and some TV news crews hovering.

She drove past the spot where Ray Fong had gone E.O.W. As she imagined, there was a lot of police and news activity, despite the hour. She cruised on by and rolled slowly into Chinatown. The neon was off, the streets eerie and quiet. She wondered what Ray had been doing down here.

Two blocks from where he was killed, she saw something that made her put on her brakes and pull to the curb.

It was a Chinese "social club," local headquarters of the Chin Lo Triad in Los Angeles. It was an unimpressive stucco building with a red door. The shabby, plain architecture revealed little about the activities inside, but Tanisha had done her research. She knew it housed the L.A. branch of a huge international criminal Triad, also known in Chinatown as the "Neighborhood Welfare Society." A misnomer if ever there was one. The Chin Lo certainly didn't have neighborhood welfare as a goal. Again, as she'd been taught to do at the Academy, she tried to arrange the facts to construct the story.

Known facts: The three men whom Wheeler Cassidy surprised in his brother's house were undoubtedly Snake Riders, illegal Chinese immigrants. The Chin Lo Triad was one of the largest smugglers of immigrants from China to Hong Kong to America. They also used their influence over frightened Chinese businesses in Chinatown, forcing them to employ the Snake Riders. Then the Triad would collect the immigrants' wages as payment for travel services rendered. The one clue Ray had was "China Boy" tattooed on the dead boy's arm.

Now some suppositions: She wondered if Ray had gone to the name file database. In the Crash Unit, cops would enter gang-bangers' street names into the system so they could pull up a real identity from the colorful gang handles. ACTF also had a street name database. Questions boiled in her mind. She wondered if Ray had found out who China Boy was. She wondered if the Chin Lo Triad had brought China Boy to America and if China Boy had figured out that he would never pay off his Triad Snake Rider loan working in a restaurant. All his earnings there would barely keep him even with the vigorish. She wondered if, like so many before him, China Boy had joined the Bamboo Dragons and had begun committing more dangerous crimes to pay off his debt. She questioned if that was why he might have been in Angie Wong's basement and Prescott Cassidy's bedroom and then finally had become a guest of honor in Dr. Death's canoe factory. Lastly, she wondered if Ray had come here to ask questions, parking a block and a half up the street, and if he'd come away with something—something big enough and scary enough that somebody inside had followed him back to his car and pulled the trigger, sending the Asian cop off to be with his sacred ancestors.

She wondered all of this and more as she sat there looking at the unimpressive front door of the Los Angeles branch of the most dangerous criminal organization in the world.

Tape

When he was released from the hospital the next morning, Wheeler went directly from Cedars-Sinai to the W.C.C. grill. Two reasons: First, he needed a drink and some company to calm his nerves, which were pretty damn jangled; and second, he had made all of the network news feeds, often being referred to as a neighborhood hero. He didn't think it would hurt his precarious situation at the club to make a show and "aw shucks" his way through a few hours of complimentary bullshit. Shallow reason, but there you have it.

He hobbled in there on crutches at around ten-thirty, his left leg bandaged like a mummy's, waving and smiling at people who hated him. He eased himself down on Home Plate, leaned his crutches in the corner, and told Ramon to "hit the gas."

An hour later, he was still accepting compliments.

Dr. Clay "Rusty" Collins and Luther Harrison were his current hero worshipers, sipping beer and commiserating enthusiastically.

"I tell you, Wheeler, the way things are going in L.A., you can't drive your car without some asshole trying to take it away from you at gunpoint, or make a freeway lane change without dodging gunfire. Our wives and daughters aren't safe. The cops are so compromised they don't even try and catch the criminals anymore. The courts are a joke, the prisons overflowing. The whole L.A. basin's a war zone." This paralyzing social complaint from Dr. Rusty Collins, a plastic surgeon whose own hold-up weapon was a number ten scalpel, which he wielded maniacally, doing nose, tit, and tummy-tucks on Beverly Hills housewives who didn't need them.

"Just happened to be in the wrong place at the right time," Wheeler aw-shucked.

"God, and right after your brother dying. Pres was such a first-rate guy . . . talented, unassuming, brilliant. First that, now this. Tough break, Wheeler," Luther commiserated.

"Yeah," Wheeler said, feeling both sadness and relief over his brother's death.

Why should there be any relief?

" 'Nother Scotch, Ramon," he said, trying to drown his self-contempt.

By noon, he was alone at the table in the dining room. He'd had plenty of offers to join members for lunch, but had already grown tired of his own humble hero bullshit and his leg was killing him. The morning's pain pills had worn off and, like a moron, he'd left the bottle of Percocets his surgeon had given him at the hospital.

That was where she eventually found him. Tanisha arrived at the club dressed in a rayon blouse and two-year-old mini-skirt. It was what she had grabbed at two-fifteen in the morning when she heard Ray had been killed. She was carrying an imitation leather bag and had on her old sling-strap faded red shoes. Older women in expensive dresses and single-strand pearls played bridge in the lounge to the left of the door. They turned to study the apparition in the club lobby.

"Can I help you?" the W.C.C. Assistant Manager said, rushing out from behind his desk near the entrance to cut off her vile intrusion. He was thin and geeky, with glasses.

Tanisha turned to face him. His narrow face showed consternation.

Homegirl alert! We have niggers in the entry!

"I'm Detective Williams. I need to talk to Wheeler Cassidy. I understand he's here." She badged him.

"Oh, I see . . . of course . . . about the shooting."

"Right," she said, wishing she'd gone home to change before coming up here. She had a few really great designer knock-offs that looked stunning on her.

"Mr. Cassidy's sitting in the dining room. Allow me to escort you," he said politely, but with a subtle ring of accusation, as if he suspected she was going to swipe an ashtray unless he herded her in personally.

As they walked into the dining room, Tanisha saw Wheeler sitting alone at a corner table. The Assistant Manager led her to him, then left, and Tanisha put her purse on the adjacent chair.

"I'd stand but my leg might buckle. Have a seat, Detective."

She looked around. More than half the faces in the room were turned toward her. "Did I do something?"

"Yeah," he said, going back to his salad. "You had the balls to come in here without your maid's uniform on."

It was a racial remark, but she could detect no racism in it. He sounded more hurt by that fact than she was. It was usually impossible for Whites to enter this emotion-filled terrain. Only those who were truly color-blind could avoid the subtle potholes. Again, there was such self-loathing in his delivery that it made her wonder about him. He was a boat full of tippy emotions. "I'm sorry to intrude on this enclave of upper-class American gamesmanship, but I have a few more questions," she said.

"You mock me," he said, and looked up from his salad and held her steady gaze. In his eyes was a complete lack of judgment.

She looked down at a notepad she'd been carrying in her

108

hand. "Mr. Cassidy, you and I both know that something very strange is going on," she said. "And until I figure it out, I'm going to be asking questions."

"Really?"

"Yeah, really."

"I don't think the three people in Prescott's house were connected to Angie Wong," he said, "if that's what you're talking about."

"That's also what you said about Angie's death and your brother's. I've ordered an autopsy. Your mother is trying to block it. I can take her on and I'll win. It won't even be a contest. Angie Wong is now a high-profile media-hyped homicide. Whichever muckety-muck in the Department got Prescott's autopsy waived as a favor to your mother must now know he made a boo-boo. With the press involved, he's gonna have to crawl under his desk. Still, it serves nobody to have a public debate about it. Maybe you could talk to her. . . ."

This was mostly horseshit. She'd been removed from the case by Captain Verba. The only reason she was here was she thought Wheeler Cassidy might be holding something back and she figured Al Katsukura wouldn't get around to back-checking him for a day or two. She was risking her job following up on it after being benched. She wasn't sure why she was gambling everything over this . . . probably a mixture of desperation over what was happening to her and Ray Fong's shocking murder. There was definitely a lot of anger. Was it because of the unkept promise she'd made to her dead sister, or the violated corpse of Angie Wong? She wasn't sure.

Now the Manager came over to the table. He was a tall, handsome man with a gorgeous smile who turned the full force of his personality on them. "I've finally been able to get that private dining room you requested, Mr. Cassidy. If you and your guest would like to move in there, I can have your order transferred."

"This is fine. Could you excuse us, please?" Tanisha said to him.

"Could I do what? I beg your pardon," he said softly.

She put her badge case on the table, open and face up, then shoved it across to him. "And I beg yours, toots. Now run along."

He hesitated, re-evaluated, then walked away. She put her badge back in her purse.

"You'll never be offered a chance to join our little club if you behave like that," he said, deadpan.

"Listen, Chuck, I'm in absolutely no mood for your bullshit," she said, letting her anger and remorse spew out on him. "Now, you either start dealing with me or we're gonna have this conversation downtown." Another bluff.

She watched him closely, then he smiled at her. It was a lovely smile, beautiful actually.

"Listen, Detective Williams, my leg is killing me. I don't think I can even drive. I'll make you a deal. . . . If you'll take me back to Cedars-Sinai and run in and see if you can find the Percocets I left there, I'll cooperate with you fully. Until then, with this leg throbbing, I can't think about anything else."

"Let's go," she said. She couldn't help herself . . . she was beginning to like him.

He lumbered up, grabbed his crutches, and they headed out front.

She gave the skeptical valet her ticket. In a few moments, her listing, coughing little Mazda rumbled up. They left in a cloud of black exhaust and baffled stares.

On the ride to the hospital, they said nothing. She parked in the big lot across the street, went inside, and got his meds, which they were holding for him at the admitting desk. When she returned to the car, she handed him the bottle through the passenger window and watched as he swallowed one dry, then looked up at her.

"Do you think Pres was doing something illegal?" he asked.

"I don't know, Mr. Cassidy," she replied. "Those three guys who got shot were all illegal aliens. I've got a trace going on one.

He had a street name tattooed on his arm, 'China Boy.' According to the gang name index, that makes him one of two people we have records on in L.A. He's either Bob 'China Boy' Chin or he's Lewis 'China Boy' Lee. From the preliminary description on the arrest report, my guess is he's Bobby Chin. I'm having his picture e-mailed from Records and Identification. I also have a print run started. Maybe it will turn an address and we can go through his house, find out what those three were up to. I should know more in an hour or so."

She assumed that Ray had already done all that and that's what might have got him killed. She also knew Al Katsukura would be all over that angle and had already decided to stay away from it to avoid suspension. Both China Boys, Lee and Chin, had arrest records for extorting money from Chinese businesses. She continued, "Neither Lee nor Chin had immigration or citizenship papers, and once arrested, they applied for diplomatic asylum, which was granted within twenty-four hours. Both were allowed to stay."

"Allowed to stay?"

"Yeah. It's a big scam in Chinatown. You got an hour sometime, I'll run it down for you. Basically, these illegal, non-English-speaking immigrants have lots of American political juice. It comes from the Chin Lo Triad, which basically owns them. There are I.N.S. guys on the pad who write up favorable 'Request for Asylum' reports or just supply counterfeit green cards. We've got Chinese illegals with rap sheets that look like shopping lists wandering around with diplomatic asylum provided by our federal government. The whole system on Chinese immigration has been bribed and compromised."

She was still standing at the passenger side window, looking down at Wheeler, who suddenly seemed troubled. "I.N.S.?" he asked, and she nodded. "My mother's gonna kill me," he said softly.

"What have you got, Mr. Cassidy?" she said, watching him closely.

———

Prescott's old Mercedes had not been moved. It was still squatting on the third level of the Century City parking garage where Wheeler had left it. They got out of Tanisha's car and she looked on in amazement while Wheeler, balancing awkwardly on his crutches, pulled out his penknife, popped the chrome strip off the door again, then reached through the hole underneath and clicked the lock mechanism up.

"You're also a car thief?" she said.

"I used to steal cars from my friends and park them in funny places, like fraternity living rooms or courtyard fountains," he said without humor. Then he got in the front seat, opening the passenger door for her. As she settled into the Mercedes beside him, he again hot-wired the car. The engine purred to life, powering up the radio, then he ejected the tape from the dash sound system. He started to reach for it, and she stopped him.

"Prints," she said. "Remember?"

He cocked a skeptical eye at her. "This is Pres's car. It'll just have his prints. He used this mike, here, to dictate letters while he drove." Wheeler picked up a headset mike which had a plug that attached to the car tape deck. "Had this rig custom-designed so he could drive and fire off a legal letter at the same time. Pres never wasted a minute."

"Mr. Cassidy, this is a murder investigation. Let's do it my way." Then she pushed the cassette back in with her fingernail and hit "rewind." It went back to the beginning and stopped, then she hit "play."

"Angie, I want this to go out immediately to Hong Kong," his brother's voice said, mixed with the sounds of traffic and engine noise. *"Once you've typed it, destroy the tape. This will be keyed to ten and sent hand-delivered by security courier in a locked mail container."*

"What's with this James Bond shit?" Wheeler muttered.

"Hold on, I'd better pull over while I read this so I don't transpose a number," Pres said after a horn blared. There was a click and the tape started again. This time, no background sounds.

"Dear 16-10/15-2/12-1. . . . My worst fears are now coming

true. I have been recontacted by the 12-2/15-6/11-9. This time they were much more insistent. I warned you about the level of volume we have engaged in the last two years. There is only so much damage control I can do before I am totally compromised. I do not intend to stand for federal indictment if it should come to that. I have made my position abundantly clear to 16-9/16-16/11-5 in Los Angeles, and all he does is continue to threaten me. I don't need to remind you, I am one of the few in this country who is exposed and I don't intend to sink by myself. Stop. New paragraph, Angie. I have made all of the direct contacts with 12-9/17-7/15-23. I'm becoming very frightened. I never expected a plot of this dimension. If this comes out, we're all finished. I am listing, under code, the last group of animals who have been fed. The following have received what is due them: d 34-13/66-9/12-5 (22), d 88-12/12-8/22-6 (12), d 66-15/3-55/8-22 (8), d 1-88/9-77/7-6 (71), r 77-8/99-20 (12), r 78-88/5-3/22-6 (16), r 22-4/5-33/2-9 (53). New paragraph, Angie. The payments from Hong Kong have increased but still have not kept up with the flow. Stop. Our friend should be notified that 9-2/6-15/12-1 has indicated he will continue to process the documents. Stop. All of our contacts at I.N.S. will remain intact and John will continue to process the account on your end. However, I must caution our friend in Hong Kong against continuing to increase the flow in all three divisions. At this level of activity, he will surely have political trouble at the highest level of the U.S. government. Stop. New paragraph, Angie. Lastly, I regret to inform you that, as of this date, I will no longer be able to continue to participate. Stop. I have been making all of the above arguments to the White Fan here, but have basically been ignored. I have no other choice but to withdraw from the equation. New paragraph, Angie. I wish you well and hope all is successful, and that everything we worked for will eventually happen as planned in mid-'98. Please make no further contact, as my decision is final. Sign that with the usual closing, Angie, and get it off immediately. Then erase this tape and shred the file."

They sat there in the car for a long moment, Prescott's voice echoing in their ears.

"The fuck was he doing?" Wheeler finally said, not looking over at her. "What's with all those numbers?"

"I don't know. I'll get somebody in Cryptology downtown to take a look at it."

"Wait a minute . . . take a look at what?"

"At the tape." She started to reach for it, and he blocked her hand with his.

"Don't you need a warrant?"

She stopped and looked at him. "You aren't going to turn into a problem for me, are you, Mr. Cassidy?"

Wheeler didn't say anything, just looked at her with concern for his brother's reputation.

"He's dead. And Ray Fong is dead. We can't hurt your brother now. I need to know what this is all about."

"Maybe it's not about anything," Wheeler said.

"That seems to be your standard response to everything. Let me give you a few more maybes. . . . Maybe that file, whatever it was, didn't get shredded. Maybe that's what those Bamboo Dragons were looking for in Angie Wong's house and your brother's bedroom. Maybe they found it or Ray got it and got killed for it. Maybe half-a-dozen other things happened. Don't make me write a buncha paper on this, 'cause if you do, I'll make no effort to conceal what I find when I find it. If you help me, and your brother *was* slipping, I'll try and downplay it." Again she was bluffing. If he or his mother made one phone call to Rick Verba, I.A.D. would scoop her up and take her away in a gunny sack.

Wheeler sat in his seat and listened to the tape deck hissing. Then he shut it off. "Was Prescott really doing something illegal?" he finally said, his voice so small it surprised her.

She looked at him and tried to judge the moment. "It sure looks that way," she said.

"What was he doing? What's your guess?"

"It sounds like something to do with illegal immigration—maybe bribing I.N.S. officials. We can't tell for sure until we break that number code."

He turned his head and looked at her. "So all of this . . . all his wealth—his legal success was just bullshit?"

"You tell me. He was your brother."

They sat and listened to the motor purr.

"Can I take the tape?" she said.

He reached out and hit a button. The little tape ejected from the dashboard, sticking its tongue out at them. Tanisha reached into her bag, got a tissue out of a package, pulled the tape out, and wrapped it up. Then she put it in the side pocket of her purse.

"He was my little brother. He looked up to me once. I was supposed to protect him. Instead of getting drunk, I should have been paying closer attention," he finally said.

They both sat in silence inside the luxury Mercedes and wondered what on earth Prescott Cassidy had been doing.

THIRTEEN

Snakehead

Fu Hai stayed in the small concrete smelting shack until night, then got out and moved cautiously into the city of Guangdong. The February night was exceedingly cold, and his clothes were thin and gave him almost no warmth. He had decided not to sleep but to keep moving all night. He had heard that the police in Guangdong searched the parks and doorways for peasants from the provinces. He would never allow himself to be captured and sent to another hell-hole like Khotan.

Guangdong was a madhouse of activity. Even in the late evening, cars from Europe and Japan roared down the streets, honking their horns. Police patrolled everywhere in their bright green uniforms. He marveled at the new architecture going up everywhere. He could see the wealth and power, feel the vibration of economic growth. He realized that he stood out terribly. One look at his shabby clothes and haircut and the police would know he didn't belong.

Fu Hai was soon spotted by a policeman, who yelled at him from the other side of the street. He ran and the policeman chased him, blowing the gold whistle around his neck. Fu Hai dashed downhill toward the vast Pearl River. Halfway to its bank, Fu Hai spotted a "honey cart" full of human excrement. The night soil collector had gone into a latrine to empty the trench, and Fu Hai realized instantly that dressed as he was in peasant clothes from the provinces, he could easily pass as the workman who managed the cart. He grabbed the old worn handle of the reeking conveyance, turned it around, and began pushing it back up the hill, toward the pursuing policeman, who ran right past Fu Hai without even looking at him.

Later that night, he abandoned the cart and found his way across the bridge over the bay to Shamian Island. He moved down the crowded street to the huge Ching Ping Market. Even though it was almost midnight, the market was still buzzing. Fu Hai gawked in wonder at what he saw there. Headless haunches of skinned dogs hung from hooks out in the open, still dripping blood onto the sand. Cats, not yet old enough for slaughter, meowed loudly from tiny cages. The vendors had all painted their booths the same deep shade of green, and Fu Hai marveled at the vast array of products on sale there. Everything from badgers, to monkeys, to rare pythons in circular wire-mesh cages. There were hard-shelled pangolins, which were armadillo-like beasts whose ground scales were thought to be good for rheumatism. The cages that contained the hapless animals were only a few inches wide. He saw aquariums full of colorful, grotesque, celestial telescope goldfish with their eyeballs at the ends of long swiveling stems that came out the front of their heads. Fu Hai continued to wander, not sure what he was looking for. He had been told that one might find a Snakehead in the Ching Ping Market, but he didn't know whom to ask. Which of these people could he trust to tell that he was a traitor to the Revolution, looking to escape China?

He saw a flight of stone steps that led down to the terribly polluted Pearl River. He moved halfway down and sat on the cold stone and watched several vegetable vendors wash cucumbers and ginger roots in the reeking water.

Fu Hai did not know what to do. He looked off across the river at a huge structure lit like a Chinese festival. As one of the vegetable vendors carried his basket of "clean" produce up the steps, Fu Hai spoke to him in Mandarin.

"What is that beautiful lit building across the river?" he said, trying to pick a subject that wouldn't be dangerous.

"Who are you that you don't know that building?" the man asked accusingly. Then he stared at Fu Hai's clothing, his cloth shoes, light linen pants, and frightened eyes.

"I . . . I am . . ."

"You are a peasant from the provinces. You are looking to steal a job from a Guandong citizen."

"No, I . . . I want to go east to America," he said, standing in case the man should call the police and Fu Hai had to run.

"I understand," the man finally said, his expression softening. "I have many times dreamed of leaving this place . . . but now I am married with a child. My lot is fixed."

Fu Hai was not sure what to say next, afraid to ask how to find a Snakehead.

"That building you asked about is the Pearl Hotel," the man continued. "It is the most luxurious and beautiful hotel in all of China."

Fu Hai nodded.

"If I were you, I would not stay here, dressed like that. You will be arrested."

"Where should I go?" Fu Hai asked.

"Go to the Catholic cathedral. Ask for John White Jade. He will help you." And then the man picked up his basket of vegetables and climbed the steps. Before he got to the top he turned and looked back at Fu Hai. "If you are looking for a Snakehead, be careful," he warned. "Tigers and deer do not walk easily together." Then, without waiting for Fu Hai to respond, he continued up the steps with his basket and was gone.

———

The Catholic cathedral was not hard to find. Fu Hai stood on the steps and looked at the place. Most of the first-floor windows were boarded up and several of the religious statues in the niches of the cathedral wall had been knocked down.

Fu Hai walked up the steps and entered the huge, cold place. He sat in a back pew and looked at the cross on the distant altar. The cathedral was magnificent, with high arched stone ceilings. The boarded-up windows made it very scary; the only light came from flickering candles. His head ached from lack of sleep. His body was sore from fighting and running. His broken teeth throbbed. He wanted nothing more than to get some sleep, but was determined to stay awake. In consciousness, there was control—in sleep, only danger.

He was awakened when a hand shook him gently. He sprang to his feet and was looking into the face of an old Chinese man who was not dressed in religious vestments.

"Who are you?" the man asked, his voice soft and nonthreatening.

"I am . . . I . . ." Fu Hai was afraid to reveal his name, afraid to say anything. Then, almost without thought, he added, "I came to see John White Jade."

Father John White Jade stubbornly used his Christian name despite years of persecution. He was maybe a few years older than Fu Hai. They were seated in the rectory office on hardwood furniture that had no padding. Father John, in a black robe and clerical collar, was exceedingly thin, with a nose that appeared as if it had been broken many times.

"You have come a long way," he said.

The old man who had found Fu Hai asleep in the cathedral returned with a platter of steaming rice and chicken from the church kitchen.

"I feel strange being here," Fu Hai said, not knowing how to begin. "I do not believe in God."

"That is never a prerequisite for kindness," Father John White Jade said. Then he reached over the desk and pushed the plate of food toward Fu Hai, who was starving, but had not looked at the food. It was at this moment that Fu Hai noticed that the priest's hand was misshapen, frozen into a withered claw. The bones had all been broken, just like his father's.

"Were you a class enemy during the Cultural Revolution?" Fu Hai asked as he began to eat with the bamboo chopsticks that had been brought with the meal.

Father John held up both hands and showed them to Fu Hai. "The Cultural Revolution was not an easy time. The Red Guards attacked this beautiful place, swinging their hammers, breaking our stained-glass windows and the statues outside. I was eighteen. I had just taken the Sacraments of Priesthood. I was foolish and tried to prevent it. My hands were held down on the stone steps of the cathedral and beaten until no bone was left unbroken. Now I cannot administer the Sacraments. I cannot even hold the body and blood of Christ in these broken hands."

"The same thing happened to my father for violating the Four Bigs," Fu Hai said, instantly feeling affinity for the priest, knowing they had shared some of the same terrible evil. He told the story of the persecution of his father, Zhang Wei Dong. When he finished, Father John White Jade nodded.

"Men do strange and ugly things in the name of politics and culture," he said. "But it cannot be helped. I have learned that rivers and mountains are more easily changed than some men's natures."

Fu Hai knew this was true. He had decided to spill out his needs to this kindly priest.

"I need to find a Snakehead," Fu Hai said, "but I have no money. I'm sure I will need money."

"You will need a down payment, but this can be arranged. I have some Guan-Xi with these people."

"Then you know a Snakehead?" Fu Hai said, his heart quickening.

"I know a man who does these things. He is a *tou she*." The Chinese words for Snakehead. "They call him 'Big-Eared' Tou. He works for Henry Liu, a powerful White Fan of the Chin Lo Triad in Hong Kong."

"I must get to America. I must find a way to get my beautiful little sister and her family there." When he spoke of Xiao Jie, he tried to remember her as a child, blotting out the memory of the prematurely aged crone with the brown teeth and skinny body who had looked into his eyes and cried.

"I will talk to some people. In the meantime, you must get some sleep. You look as if you have gone many days without rest."

Finally, Fu Hai felt safe, and after he finished his meal, he lay down on the hard bench where he was seated and immediately fell asleep. The polished oak felt as soft as a mattress of clouds.

He was awakened after dark by Father John and led out into the cathedral, where a young, ugly girl with big teeth and a flat nose waited. She spoke in Fukienese, a dialect that Fu Hai couldn't understand. Father John talked to her for a minute, then turned back to Fu Hai.

"She will take you to meet the Snakehead. Good luck." And then Father John White Jade said a prayer over Fu Hai in a strange language he couldn't understand, but assumed must be Latin.

Without looking back at him, the ugly girl led Fu Hai out of the cathedral and down the wide steps. She led him back to Shamian Island, and finally, after going down many narrow streets, she stopped, turned to him and put her hands on his shoulders, then pushed him down onto a stone bench. She didn't talk to him, but he knew he was supposed to wait. She left him there.

An hour passed and then she came back and led Fu Hai down several more narrow streets into a crowded restaurant at the edge of the Ching Ping Market. She pointed to a man sitting alone at a table in the back of the murky, dark place. He had huge meaty ears, an undershot jaw, and big teeth. Three black hairs, nearly a foot long, grew from a large wart on his chin, and he stroked them as he sat waiting. As Fu Hai approached, he guessed that the man was the ugly girl's father. Fu Hai stood at the edge of the Snakehead's table, with his eyes down, and waited respectfully.

"You want to Ride the Snake?" Big-Eared Tou asked in Mandarin, without introducing himself.

"I am determined to get to America."

"It is very expensive."

"I have heard this."

"Over thirty-five thousand American dollars. Do you have enough money?" he asked, smiling for the first time, showing big teeth.

"No, sir, but I will do anything to earn my way."

"You would kill? You would wreak havoc on my enemies? Commit violent crime?" Big-Eared Tou said, looking intently at Fu Hai.

"I have never killed or done any of those things."

"But you said '*anything*.' A man willing to do anything could have great value, if this is not just a boast to impress me."

"To get to America, I would do anything," Fu Hai said, again thinking of his little sister and her plight.

"There was a time when I would ask you to give me a hostage to secure the debt, somebody in your family who would be my slave and work if you should flee. But Father John White Jade is my countryman. We come from the same village in Fukien. He has spoken highly of your honor and trustworthiness and he has Guan-Xi with me, so I will take you at your word. You must work seven days a week until your debt is paid. However, if you fail your responsibilities to me, I will collect your life as payment. You agree with this?"

"It is a fair bargain," Fu Hai said.

"I am a man of great patience and understanding," the ugly Triad mobster said piously. "I perform this service not so much for money as for the love of my fellow man."

"That is very noble," Fu Hai said.

"Then it is a bargain. I will get you to America and you will do what I ask," the Snakehead concluded. He motioned to a waiter, who stepped forward holding a wriggling black indigo snake with a flickering tongue. The mobster nodded, and the waiter severed the snake's head with a single chop of his cleaver and cast the still wriggling head into an enameled basin. Blood oozed from the twisting coils. With a sound like a zipper, the waiter pulled back the serpent's skin, exposing the pink pearly flesh. He fished amid the glistening meat for a small black pill-shaped organ and placed it in a glass of rice wine at the gangster's elbow. Big-Eared Tou swallowed the wine and the snake's gallbladder at a gulp, eyeing Fu Hai as he did so.

"You must be very careful I don't swallow you too," the ugly Snakehead said with a horrible grin.

FOURTEEN

Would You? Could You? Should You?

I t was Wednesday afternoon and Wheeler was in his brother's den helping his sister-in-law straighten up the mess. Wheeler was by the bookcase, teetering on his crutches, rearranging volumes, while Liz and Hollis crawled on the floor gathering up and reshelving Prescott's priceless leather-bound editions. Full first-edition sets of Emily Dickinson, Poe, and Herman Melville, which Prescott had collected. Some volumes ran as high as ten thousand dollars. The perfect gift for L.A.'s most promising young lawyer. Each one unwrapped to a chorus of "aahhhs" on Christmas morning.

Wheeler was now restacking, in order, the twelve leather-bound volumes of John L. Stoddard's *History of California.* John Stoddard had been a Dominican monk who published this historical work in 1898, and he had an undoubtedly cloistered view of the debauchery and death surrounding the California gold rush. Also ready to be put back on the shelf was the *Complete History of the World,* by Henry Smith Williams, L.L.D., twenty-five dust-covered first editions, published in 1904. Prescott was a history buff.

Wheeler had actually given his brother three of them. A Christmas bargain at five hundred a copy. Money spent on historical thought was not deemed to be pretentious over-spending, and beat the shit out of rings and watches in Cassidyville.

Wheeler had just started sliding Henry Smith Williams back onto the shelf when his mother arrived.

"Arrived" was sort of an understatement. She flew through the door, tears streaming off her high cheekbones, and immediately started to rail at all of them and at none of them. "How can they say, how can they even hint that he . . . that he was . . ." Unable to finish, she started to cry. Both Wheeler and Liz rushed to her and helped her across the living room to the sofa, where she sat and continued sobbing.

"What is it, Mother? What happened?" Wheeler said, assuming this wasn't about Prescott's death. That had been three days ago, and this hysteria was over something recent, something that had just happened.

"What is it, Kay?" Liz echoed.

Both Liz and Kay looked drawn and sleep-deprived. Wheeler was holding up better. Except for the bullet hole in his leg, he had weathered the emotional storm of his brother's passing with the least visible strain.

"The police. The police say . . . they say . . . that Prescott was . . . that he was killed!"

"Murdered?" Wheeler asked.

"The autopsy. The police just called. They said somebody stuck an acupuncture needle into his heart. They want us all to make appointments to come down and talk about what Pres was up to. They want to take our statements," she said, finally looking at Liz and Wheeler, as if they would somehow magically know how to avoid this.

"That's ridiculous," Liz said hotly. "What he was up to? He wasn't *up to* anything!"

Wheeler held his silence.

"How could he even be dead?" Katherine wailed. "And now

they say killed . . . murdered. I'm not going to be questioned like a common criminal. That Negro detective . . . she'd love to find something horrible. You just know it."

"Mom," Wheeler heard himself saying, "I think we should cooperate." He'd long ago learned to overlook his mother's slightly racist Southern upbringing.

She turned on him, venom and anger mixed with extreme loss. "*You* think . . . *you* . . . ?"

'Nuff said. It was clear to all of them, even Hollis, that she meant: *You have no say. You're not good enough to even be part of this. All you do is drink and hold this family up to ridicule, blah-blah-blah.*

"Mother, the police think—"

"You've been *talking* to them!" she all but screamed. "You've been talking about our family? Good God, Wheeler, this is a time to band together, to put up a front. We need to put family before everything. Do you want to read about this in the *L.A. Times*? Do you want us treated like that Ramsey family, for God's sake?"

"Mother . . . I had no choice . . ."

"You always have a choice."

"I found Angie Wong's body. She was murdered. Cut to ribbons. It's some kind of Chinese punishment murder. I reported it. The police questioned me. Then I shot two Chinese gangsters right here, in this house, two nights ago. The police think it's all connected. How am I not going to talk to them?"

"Connected? Connected to what?" She had stopped crying and was now alert, feral, and fiercely protective. Wheeler was the problem now, not the police. They were back on familiar ground.

"Connected. Just . . . connected," he stammered.

"How . . . ?"

"Mother, c'mon . . ."

"No, you come on. I demand an answer. Tell me what they think. I don't like that colored detective. She can't wait to cause trouble. In the hospital . . . she indicated Prescott was involved in something. *Why are they saying this?*" This last sentence shot out with force and venom.

"Mom . . ."

"What are they thinking, Wheeler? At least tell us that, for God's sake."

"That Pres . . . maybe was . . . that he could've been involved in illegal Chinese immigration. That perhaps he was fixing I.N.S. visas, buying off politicians." He watched an expression of utter disbelief cross his mother's features, distorting her high-cheek-boned beauty. The room was unnaturally quiet. You could almost hear dust settle.

Then, unexpectedly, Liz took a few steps closer to her mother-in-law, and Hollis followed, leaving Wheeler in the center of the room to hold his vile, traitorous position alone.

"Did you hate your brother that much?" Katherine finally whispered.

"No, Mother, I did not hate him. I didn't always understand him, and sometimes I wished he would've understood me, or dealt with things differently. But I didn't hate him. How could I? I loved him. He was my little brother."

"Deal with things differently?" his mother said, seizing on just that one statement. "Deal the way you do? Take a permanent seat at the bar? Thank God that wasn't his solution."

"No, Mother, I didn't want him to do that. I wanted him to . . . understand. He was the only one who could see things from the same place as me. If he got talked into some bribery scheme to gain influence, so he could live up to Dad's impossible expectations, then maybe it wasn't completely his fault."

Katherine's mouth actually fell open. Then she stood and took the two steps across the room to him. "God damn you," she said softly. "If you try to balance the scales for your miserable performance on your dead brother's back, I'll never forgive you for it."

"Doesn't it matter to you that Prescott was murdered? That somebody drove a needle through his heart? They killed him, and now, because of some mistaken sense of family loyalty, we're going to let them walk away from it? Don't we need to stand up for him in death? Can we let him get murdered and then turn away just to save the family's reputation?"

"To save *his* reputation. To save your *brother's* reputation," she shrieked.

"He's dead! He's gone to the next level. Let's deal with what's here."

"What you want, Wheeler, is to bring Prescott down to your level. You want to find some made-up crime against him to soil his memory, to take the heat off so you won't stand out as such a monumental and colossal fuck-up!"

He'd known her for thirty-seven years, he'd watched her in times of extreme crisis, he knew every side of her layered, complex Southern personality . . . yet, this afternoon was the first time he'd ever heard her swear.

He left without saying another word. . . . Their stares burned holes in the back of his jacket. He stood on the front porch of his brother's beautiful house, looking out at the maple trees lining the expensive street. His emotions boiled. He felt like a traitor to his little brother. He felt like he had turned on him, and yet, somebody had killed Prescott. Wheeler was beginning to feel rage about it and a need for revenge. And he also felt something else. For a moment as he stood there, he couldn't pin the feeling down . . . then it hit him. In this tragedy, there was opportunity. It could be a second chance for him. Maybe it was his last opportunity to re-claim his wasted life. Maybe Prescott had died so Wheeler could be reborn.

"Will you teach me how to throw a football, Wheel?"
"Will you get her to go out with me?"
"Will you destroy everything I stood for?"
"Would you? Could you? Should you?"

FIFTEEN

Tea Money

U sing latex gloves, Tanisha made a copy of the tape from Prescott's Mercedes on her home recorder. She typed a transcript of it on a groaning Selectric typewriter that had a sticking ball element. Then she left her cluttered Baldwin Park apartment and headed to Parker Center, where she left the original tape off at Symbols and Hieroglyphics with instructions to have it dusted and then analyzed. The Cryptology unit was in the neon-lit, white-walled basement at Parker Center. It had a computer link with the FBI, which had a large database on numerology and cryptology patterns. Tanisha had read up on cryptanalysis deprogramming at the Academy and knew that certain letters in the English language appear more frequently. It is possible to assign a frequency index to each of the twenty-six letters in the alphabet. By keying on this, a number could get assigned a letter. The problem was that the sample in Prescott's dictation was pitifully small. It would be a slow, tedious process, without much chance of success. She also put in a request to find out what the significance of 1414 might be.

She filled out the paperwork and returned to Asian Crimes to check in. She ran her magnetized I.D. card through the slot. The door lock clicked and she entered; then she took the old elevator up to the eighth floor and walked out into an empty squad room. It was six P.M. She hadn't been at her desk long when Al Katsukura entered carrying a surprisingly thick case folder which she assumed was Ray's murder investigation. Thick folders didn't necessarily mean progress. They just meant the Department had thrown a lot of "blue" at the investigation and twenty cops were out interviewing everybody within a mile of the crime. Al moved to his desk, glancing up at her without giving her much expression. It was obvious he didn't want her to come over, so she got up and moved to his desk.

"Did you get an address on China Boy?" she asked.

His expression seemed to say, *Gimme a break here.* Then Al glanced at the Watch Commander's office. Captain Verba's blinds were still pulled. "I thought you had your Internal Affairs hearing tomorrow."

"Nobody told me," she said, and no one had, but that didn't surprise her. They would probably spring it on her. She had met with her police union legal adviser once, but since Tanisha was only guilty of visiting her grandmother's house and getting her hair done in South Central, they had decided to go to the hearing and find out what was being alleged before mounting a defense.

"Did you get an address?" she asked Al again.

"Look, Tanisha, you're supposed to pull off this."

"I'm just interested. Ray was a friend. We were working together. Don't freeze me out, Al. I just want scuttlebutt."

After a minute, the Japanese detective nodded. "Okay, but you didn't hear it from me. The address on Bobby Chin's arrest file was bogus, but it looks like Ray got lucky on a field shake before he died. A restaurant in Chinatown where Bobby Chin once worked had an address. They told Ray where Bobby really lived. It musta been yesterday afternoon, shortly after he left your house."

"He sure got there quick," she said.

"Ray had great contacts in Chinatown. Anyway, the address

they gave him was an old metal fishing barge tied at a dredging dock down at the marina. We rolled on the place. The barge was a rat hole—hot, no toilets, but empty. Everybody had left. It'd been used to house a lot of people. It stank like nothing you ever smelled. Old chicken bones, piss in mayonnaise jars, a real Third World jackpot. I've got half the off-duty guys canvassing the two blocks down there by the docks . . . it's all commercial boat yards. So far, nobody saw Ray or his car Thursday night, before his murder."

"My guess is, after the restaurant gave him the address, he probably went there," she said. "Something happened . . . he saw something or somebody, or got something. Then he got tailed back to the Chin Lo headquarters off Hill Street and one of the Chinese O.G.s did him." Al Katsukura nodded, without commenting. "You know anybody at I.N.S. who'll pass a scratch and sniff test?" she added.

"Tisha, leave it alone. Verba's gonna go tits-up if he catches you messing with this."

"Is that a 'no,' Al?"

"Stay off it. We're gonna cover all those angles. Don't free-lance the investigation—you'll just fuck things up."

Solid advice from a seasoned professional, but not what she intended to do. He looked up at her, his jaw set. His information window had just slammed shut. She moved back to her desk, picked up her stuff, and went back to the L.A. Public Library. She'd decided to find out more about the Chin Lo Triad.

That night at home, she went through half-a-dozen new books and printouts she had found. At almost midnight, she was deep into a report written by somebody named Willard G. Vickers, who was head of a private think tank called the Pacific Rim Criminal Research Center in Cleveland. She had found him in the Nexis computer at the library when she cross-referenced the Chin Lo Triad with U.S. crime. He had been to Washington half-a-dozen times to testify before both the U.S. House of Representatives and the Senate. She had printed out his Congressional testimony and was hardly able to believe what he had told Congress under oath.

According to Mr. Willard G. Vickers, the Chinese crime syndicates were mostly located in the Fukienese-speaking communities of Asia, which included parts of mainland China, all of Taiwan, and Hong Kong. The Triads were responsible for staggering amounts of crime in the United States. It was a criminal conspiracy, he said, being orchestrated at the highest level of the Chinese government in Beijing. According to Vickers's estimates, the combined Chinese Triad criminal take in the United States had escalated from eighty billion in 1994 to over three hundred billion dollars a year. He had told the startled Joint Committee on Organized Crime that the Chinese Triads had managed to infiltrate all areas of our business and political life, removing this huge sum from our economy by importing three illegal commodities—drugs, guns, and illegal immigrants—and by exporting counterfeit intellectual properties, securities, and stolen goods. The double whammy was that while stealing billions, they were simultaneously poisoning our country with Chinese criminal activity.

Chinese "cutouts" or front men, he told Congress, had infiltrated the political spectrum in America, bribing government officials and investing illegally in political campaigns, right up to the President of the United States. These intermediaries had become rich and powerful, and had curried political favor and influence. When she read that, Tanisha remembered what Kay Cassidy had said in the hospital about Prescott's political clout. She wondered if Prescott Cassidy was a "cutout."

Vickers testified that this huge theft from our country had gone virtually unreported and unprosecuted. He went on for pages, talking about how the Chinese crime problem completely overshadowed the American Mafia and Colombian drug cartels, taking easily five times the combined amount of those two criminal enterprises annually.

According to Vickers, the surprising, unprecedented rebound

of heroin use in the United States was due almost entirely to Chinese efforts. China was the largest producer of heroin, growing inland poppies like no other nation on earth. Since it was a cheap commodity in China and worth billions in the United States, the Chinese had imported it without much U.S. government interference and had priced it to undercut the Latin American cocaine cowboys. This had caused a flood of "China White" into U.S. schools and inner cities. The Chinese drug lords had set up pipelines that were now feeding America tons of pure heroin annually.

Vickers told Congress about illegal immigration, saying that in California alone, the Triads were responsible for smuggling over a hundred thousand people a year into that beleaguered state, without almost any prosecutions—an astounding feat. The Chin Lo Triad in Hong Kong shipped these non-English-speaking peasants halfway around the world, fed them, housed them, clothed them, and supplied them with false documentation . . . all right under the noses of U.S. government agencies chartered to protect us from this very penetration. Obviously, he concluded, this couldn't happen without people in those agencies looking the other way. Even more devastating was that many of these illegal immigrants sold themselves to the Triads in return for passage. In order to pay the Triads back, they turned to crime in the United States. "The problem of Chinese crime," he told a shocked Congress, "escalated dramatically since 1994, the Chinese Year of the Dog."

As Tanisha Williams read all of this, her level of skepticism rose. How could this be true? Willard G. Vickers broke the crimes down by category: Weapons smuggling netted over five billion a year; theft of luxury automobiles, yachts, and consumer goods netted around twelve billion; counterfeit currency, credit cards, access devices, trademarked goods, and securities over one hundred billion; intellectual properties in the growing computer field close to a hundred billion; illegal trading in stock market commodities another two billion; illegal immigration ten billion. The list was staggering. Yet, none of this was even hinted at in the press. Nothing had been said about it on Capitol Hill or in the White House. The reason for this, he had told a silent Congress, was self-evident. It was because of "Tea Money," which, he explained, was what Asians called government bribes.

She had never heard any of this discussed at the Asian Crimes Task Force. They all knew that Asian crime was on the rise, but how could it be this pervasive unless the majority of it was going unreported? She finally put down the printout.

Either Willard G. Vickers was crazy as a street-corner Jesus, or this was the biggest, best-run criminal conspiracy on the face of the globe. She was determined to find out which it was.

She woke him up at four A.M. She could hear him muttering and fumbling with the latches on the other side of the door of the beautiful tenth-floor Bel Air condo that overlooked the country club on Bellagio Road.

Finally, the door opened and Wheeler was standing there in surgical greens and no shirt, leaning on one crutch. His hair was mussed. He looked like a Calvin Klein ad for hospital wear.

"You have interesting technique, Detective," he said, glancing at his Rolex watch.

"May I come in, Mr. Cassidy?" she asked.

He nodded and hopped out of her way as she moved into his beautifully color-coordinated, antique-laden penthouse. He flipped on a few lights in the entry hall and followed her into the living room, where she was looking out the balcony window to the golf course below.

"This is nice," she said, thinking of her own cluttered railroad flat in Baldwin Park.

"Right," he said, leaning on the crutch, studying her.

"I need your help," she finally said.

"You've already got my mother climbing the drapes," he said slowly. "She's not used to being told to report to the police station to be interviewed on a homicide."

"That wasn't me," Tanisha said. "Not that I don't agree. Your brother was murdered. Maybe he let something slip. Maybe he told her or his wife something. Tell your mother to stop fighting and help us. We're not challenging her or accusing her. We're trying to solve her son's murder."

Wheeler decided not to tell her that his mother had no interest in cooperating.

"I've been taken off your brother's case," she said, "and off of Angela Wong's."

"Why's that?"

"I'm undergoing a probe into my background by my superiors."

"I like you better already."

"Mr. Cassidy, I think I may be on to something. I'm not sure exactly how much weight to give it, but I need to go to Cleveland and check it out."

"So you decided to come here at four in the morning to keep me informed?" he said, cocking an eye at her skeptically.

"I need to borrow the airfare. It's four hundred, round-trip. The Department won't cover it, and I don't have it, but if I'm right, it might help solve your brother's murder. I can pay you back at the end of the month."

"You wanna borrow four hundred dollars?"

"It's just a loan. I figure you want this solved. I'll sign over the pink slip on my Mazda as collateral."

"I can hardly wait to get behind the wheel of that little wheezing bumblebee." He moved to the bar, took down a beveled crystal glass, and, using silver tongs, dropped two ice cubes into it. They rang as they hit the fine Baccarat. Then he picked up the Vat 69 and splashed a liberal dose into the glass. "Anything I can fix you?" he asked.

"No," she said, moving away from the window.

"Why Cleveland?" he asked.

"Police business. I need to check out a source."

"If it's really police business, I wouldn't have to pay for it. Besides, didn't you just say you weren't on the case anymore?"

He took a big swallow from the glass as she looked down at the carpet.

"Something wrong?" he asked, picking up her look.

"No."

"He was my brother, and I do want to find out why he was murdered. But if I'm going to loan you the four hundred, you need to tell me why," he said, and watched as she struggled with it for a minute.

"I think your brother was a 'cutout' for the Chin Lo Triad, a powerful Chinese criminal organization. A 'cutout' is a money conduit, usually handling payoffs to politicians or agencies like the I.N.S. They're used so the Chinese government, or in this case the Triad behind the bribes, doesn't get identified. It's possible Prescott was handling political payoffs in America to facilitate Chinese criminal activity. It was probably no accident that his secretary was Chinese. I think, among other things, she was his interpreter. I've been checking her background. Angela Wong was born in Fukien Province, which happens to be the province where the Chin Lo Triad originated. She was fluent in Mandarin, Cantonese, and Fukienese, as well as several rare dialects like Hakka, Chin Chow, and Hoi Ping."

"You already said you thought he was doing payoffs this afternoon. What's so different now?"

"This evening I read about a man in Cleveland who runs the Pacific Rim Criminal Research Center, on Asian crime. He sounds like the best expert in the field. I think he may be able to fill in some pieces."

"Why don't you just call him?"

"This guy knows all about the Chin Lo Triad and other Chinese criminal organizations. He has research materials, a computer database, but . . . he may also be a problem. I need to get a look at him."

"A problem?"

"I got his personal profile out of the computer. He's a disbarred lawyer, a radical in the sixties. A long-haired, bomb-throwing, William Kunstler–type liberal. He's also been busted a buncha times for possession, mostly ganja."

"Terrific . . ."

"But he's an acknowledged expert on Chinese crime who's testified three times before Congress."

"And you can't call him?"

"I could, but if he's a flake, I need to be looking at him to make that judgment."

He took another huge gulp of Scotch, draining the glass. He turned back to the bar and refilled it. This time when he turned back, he caught her scowling. "My drinking bothers you?"

"You don't drink, Mr. Cassidy, you guzzle. Ever think about backing off a little?"

"I . . . no. I . . ." Then he set the refilled glass down. "I want to know why you're doing this," he said. "If you're off the case, why don't you leave it alone?"

She didn't say anything, but glared at him in frustration.

"You're asking me to help destroy my brother's reputation. What's your motive? Why are you doing this? Is Pres going to get a fair shake here?"

She studied him in the dim light, next to the bar. She couldn't see his eyes, which were cast in deep shadow. "I'm doing it because of Ray Fong. He was my partner. He was murdered. I have an obligation to him."

"Bullshit."

"Bullshit?"

"Yeah, bullshit. I watched you and Detective Fong at the hospital. I've seen more cooperation at bankruptcy hearings. You guys had nothing."

"You're a mind reader, too?"

"I'm a shrewd observer of people, especially women. It's how I get laid. You didn't really like Ray Fong. You were tolerating him. Sort of like you tolerate me. So what's in this for you?"

Of course he was right, but she couldn't tell him her real reason. She couldn't admit that to fail now would effectively end a ten-year journey. Even though her stay on the LAPD had not been what she had planned, she couldn't admit the mistake. At least not yet. This desperate attempt to solve a red-ball double homicide would be her way of saying they were wrong. They should have taken her more seriously.

"For now, let's leave it at friendship for Ray, even if you think it's bullshit," she said.

"Then I'm going to have to go with you."

"I won't be needing any help."

"You think my brother may have been involved in something criminal. . . . My mother is about to cut me off. If I help you and she finds out, I'll be hanging on the fence at the estate sale. I've got a lot at stake. But most important, I've promised myself I'd try to find out who killed Prescott. It's very important to me. But I'm not sure of your motives, Detective Williams, and since I don't know where you're aimed, I'm coming with you or you can get the money somewhere else."

"That's crazy."

"Maybe so, but I don't want my little brother framed for something he didn't do."

SIXTEEN

The Pacific Rim Criminal Research Center

They arrived in Cleveland at four-thirty in the afternoon. They had no luggage, so they moved directly out of the terminal. Tanisha put her cellphone on "Roam," and while Wheeler looked for a cab, she dialed the Cryptology unit of the LAPD. She got hold of Mark Watson, a bespectacled scientific technocrat who displayed an absolute absence of personality. At least she'd never detected one.

"Nothing we can break," he told her after she asked how they were proceeding. "Looks like a key book code, and without the key book, we can't decipher it."

She asked how a key book code worked.

"It's one of the easiest to use and hardest to crack," he sighed. "It was developed by the Germans and used by spies during World War II. The way it works, both parties in the communication have to know the book. Then you simply use any page number of the book and count to the letter you need on that page. For instance, if you're looking for a W, you turn to any page, let's say 22, and then count to the first W. Let's say it's the fifteenth letter on the page . . . so the first letter is 22-15. I'm pretty sure that's what Prescott Cassidy was using. We aren't going to be able to break it without knowing the book. Sorry," he said. He sounded like he was in a hurry to get off the phone.

"Shit," she mumbled. "Anything on the 1414?"

"It's not in any databank we have," he said, "but the Chinese love numerology, so I'm getting somebody on the outside to see if there's a number significance."

After saying good-bye, they both hung up.

On the plane ride to Cleveland, Wheeler had read Willard G. Vickers's testimony before Congress, while a ten-year-old boy kicked the back of his first-class seat. He handed the file back to Tanisha once they were in the taxicab heading to the address she had found for the Pacific Rim Criminal Research Center.

The address turned out to be a clapboard house on a run-down street in a racially mixed area of South Cleveland. They stared apprehensively at the unpainted house and graffiti-tagged neighborhood.

The cab driver glared back at them. He wasn't happy about the neighborhood either. "This is it!" he growled in some Middle Eastern accent.

"This can't be the Pacific Rim Criminal Research Center," she said, looking at the house, then back at the address in her hand.

"Expecting something with a lobby and a revolving door?" Wheeler mused as they got out. Before they could stop him, the cab driver sped off.

"Maybe we should've held the cab," he said after it was gone.

"You're a shade late with that, Chuck," she sighed, and they moved up the weed-strewn path to a rickety wooden front porch.

There was a wood plaque leaning against the side of the house. It had fallen off a metal bracket by the front door. Wheeler picked it up. In faded, hand-painted block letters it said:

P.R.C.R.C.

PACIFIC RIM CRIMINAL RESEARCH CENTER

"I don't know about you," Wheeler drawled, "but I just felt a shiver of pure excitement."

She frowned and knocked on the door. Then she rang the bell, which sounded the last five notes from a seventies rock-and-roll song.

"Isn't that from 'Truckin',' by the Grateful Dead?" Wheeler asked.

"Jesus," she muttered, disgusted. They'd come all the way to Cleveland to visit the Pacific Rim Criminal Research Center and it turned out to be a clapboard house in a slum, with a doorbell that played drug music from the seventies. She rang the bell again, and the door was opened by a very pretty Chinese girl, about twenty. She stood at the threshold in a tank top and torn jeans, and looked at them through unfocused eyes. "Yeah," she said. "Do we know you?"

"Is Willard around?" Tanisha asked.

"Willard's flying Mexican Air. Won't land for about an hour."

"Out of town?" Wheeler asked, and the girl shifted her bored look over to him.

"He's laced," Tanisha groaned. "Mexican marijuana. He won't be straight for an hour. Am I right?" she asked. The girl nodded, then Tanisha pulled out her LAPD badge and flashed it, not leaving it out long enough for the girl to see it was no good in Cleveland.

"Shit, you guys're blue dogs?"

"You have a name, precious?" Tanisha glowered.

"Kelly Ching."

"Okay, Kelly . . . we need to talk to Willard, so stand aside." She pushed the door open with the palm of her hand, and they moved into a cluttered, totally disheveled house.

Willard G. Vickers, like his doorbell, was a throwback to the seventies, big and barefoot with long, stringy gray hair, a full beard, and too much turquoise-and-silver Indian jewelry. He was dressed in coveralls, and crashed on a sofa, staring glassily at a video game which kept recycling its opening advertisement. A cyber-warrior galloped maniacally around, killing floating objects that looked to Tanisha like Portuguese man-of-wars. Willard Vickers shot them a wide smile.

"S'up, kids?" he said with lidded eyes.

Three hours later, they were sitting in the shabby dining room of the Pacific Rim Criminal Research Center. Willard G. Vickers had landed. He was off his ganja ride but having a bad sugar jones.

"Kelly, see if there's some Hershey bars in the kitchen. Second drawer, left of the sink," he said. Kelly jumped up obediently and went off in search of blood sugar for the boss.

Tanisha handed him a copy of the typed transcript she'd made of the recording from Prescott's Mercedes. She wasn't expecting much from this disheveled pothead and watched skeptically as he placed the page in front of him on the dining-room table, which was obviously not used for eating. It was stacked high with Asian crime research reports. Vickers read the transcript once, carefully.

"Well, obviously the writer of this missive didn't want us to know what he was talking about. But let us do some calculated guessing," he said, looking up at them with bloodshot eyes. "He mentions the White Fan, which is a subleader in a Chinese Triad, like a Consigliere in the Italian mob. Most likely, the man who wrote this is a cutout for the Chin Lo Triad, but you already know that, or you wouldn't be here," he said. Then he picked up the sheet of paper by its edges, rereading it carefully while they waited.

"I like this," he said, then he began reading part of the transcript out loud: " 'I am listing, under code, the last group of animals who have been fed,' and then we get this list of letters and numbers: d 34-13/66-9/12-5(22), r 78-88/5-3/22-6, and so on."

Tanisha took a moment and explained to him what she'd learned about the key book code.

"Who are the animals?" Wheeler asked. His hands were trembling slightly. He needed a drink. He put them in his lap to hide them as Vickers looked critically at the transcript.

"Just a guess, but back in 1994, when China first identified America as their global enemy, they decided to invest in young political comers in the U.S. by donating to their campaigns. China's leadership realized if they could buy influence with hot-shot pols on their way up, once these elected officials became important players in Congress, China's influence would grow, and their agenda would grow with it. It was a long-range plan, so 'd' could stand for Democrats, 'r' for Republicans. The animals could be donkeys and elephants. The Chinese love animal symbols . . . snakes and tigers, stuff like that. With respect to the key book code, the numbers could be initials. Hey, Kel, how you doin' with the candy?"

Kelly Ching came back carrying a half-eaten candy bar with the wrapper still on it. He peeled it back and took a bite, then went on.

"Later in the letter, he talks about increasing the flow in three divisions. The divisions could be Triad product lines. Like guns or drugs."

"Shit," Wheeler said softly.

Vickers finished the candy bar and wiped his hands on his pants.

Willard Vickers was hardly what Tanisha had been expecting. She could barely imagine this large, unkempt bear sitting at a polished desk in front of a joint Senate-House committee, sporting his long gray hair, beard, and four pounds of turquoise jewelry. He was bizarre and slightly comic. No wonder they hadn't acted on his alarming statistics. But somehow she sensed that what he'd been telling everybody, without success, was true.

"How did you get so interested in Asian crime?" she finally asked.

"Accident. I was handling radicals during the sixties, before I got disbarred for smoking bud on my lunch break, inside a federal courthouse. Back then, I did a lotta pro bono work, specialized in draft dodgers who got snatched for crimes in Canada and were facing extradition back to the U.S. Along the way, I picked up a few Snake Riders who were dissidents being sent back to China. They'da been killed by Mao if they were returned, so they were petitioning our government for diplomatic asylum. I was pretty good at winning those cases. Then the Chin Lo Triad contacted me, wanted to put me on retainer. Something about those Triad criminals really stuck to the roof of my mouth. The more I saw what was happening, what they were doing, the more I realized this country was under attack."

"I thought you were anti-government," she said.

"You cops never get it right!" he said hotly. "I'm a patriot. I love this country. I just hate bullshit. Vietnam was bullshit. Kent State was bullshit. Waco was bullshit. And stealing three hundred billion dollars a year from the tax base of this country—money that could go to feed starving kids in the inner city—is also bullshit.

"I got disbarred right about then, so I formed the Research Center . . . mostly volunteers, like Kelly. The deeper I dug, the smellier it got. We've got us a full-scale, secret war against the United States happening here, and our President is afraid we're gonna piss off the Chinese and close that huge market. He's afraid his buddies like Bill Gates and Steve Spielberg won't be able to get their products into China. So nobody is doing shit." There was a long moment, and then he stood up. "You want my opinion, this letter is about the '98 elections in Hong Kong."

"What elections?" Tanisha asked.

"The first democratic elections ever being held in a Communist province."

They sent out for pizza and were eating it in the living room off TV trays while Willard G. Vickers continued:

"That reference in your transcript to mid-1998 makes me wonder if a lot of what's going on in L.A. might be connected to the Hong Kong elections this year. In order to see the nature of all this, you've gotta understand the complex history of Hong Kong.

The way people are behaving today has to do with the way things happened historically."

They ate the greasy pizza and listened while Willard gave a remarkable political lecture:

"The whole thing started in 1839," he began, and they stopped chewing. "I know, I know . . . that's almost a century and a half ago, but to understand China, you've gotta understand two things. They revere history, and they never forget." Willard pushed up the sleeves on his long-sleeved shirt and exposed furry, snow-white arms.

"In 1839, China pulled a massive drug bust on the British, who had been trading opium for silver at Canton for years. This started the first Sino-British Opium War, which the Chinese promptly lost. When the treaty of Nanking was signed on August 29, 1842, part of the spoils of war given to Britain was a barren little island with a terrific harbor, just off the southeast coast of China. Only about three thousand people lived on it, mostly fishermen and incense-makers. The incense is why they called the island Xiang Gang, the Fragrant Harbor. The Chinese sign it over to Britain 'in perpetuity,' and it becomes Hong Kong."

"Right," Tanisha said. She had her notebook out and was writing it all down, although Wheeler didn't see how the Opium Wars could have anything to do with the murders of Prescott and Angie Wong.

"Okay, then comes the second Opium War, 1856 to 1858, which breaks out when the Chinese board a British trading ship named *The Arrow*. Sure enough, the Chinese lose again. This time they have to give up the Kowloon Peninsula, right across the harbor from Hong Kong Island. Then—and this is the important part—the British lease the New Territories, a big chunk of land behind Kowloon, for ninety-nine years. It's this lease, signed in 1898, that ran out at midnight, July first, last year."

"So why did they give everything back?" Wheeler asked. "You just said the Brits got Hong Kong and Kowloon in perpetuity."

"That's right," Vickers replied, "but Hong Kong can't function without the New Territories and the islands and waters around them. Take away the New Territories and you take away the economic base for Hong Kong. There'd be damned little left. So in 1983, when China said they wanted it all back, Britain saw the handwriting on the wall. They said they would turn over the whole deal and get out."

"Okay," she said, scribbling furiously. "Got it."

"The Japanese conquered Hong Kong during World War II, but they ended up surrendering the Colony back to the British on September 16, 1945. This is only important in our context because the Triads came into renewed political prominence during the Japanese occupation. During World War II, the Triads fought the Japanese invaders. They were national heroes because of it, celebrated for their acts of courage and their attempts to free the country from the hated Japanese. It's one of the reasons the Triads still have some measure of respectability today, despite the fact that they've since become total criminal organizations."

He got up and threw the rest of his pizza in a trash can. "Okay, next comes Mao Zedong." Willard was pacing, prowling the small, cluttered room like a predator. "On October 1, 1949, Chairman Mao founded the People's Republic of China, and in 1966 he started the Great Proletarian Cultural Revolution. Lotta people got messed with big-time by that. Everybody has to dress in Mao coats, walk around like zombies, quoting from the Red Book. Even when I was a Socialist in the sixties, I thought that sucked. Lots of Chinese escaped during the 1950s and '60s, and some became wealthy business owners in Hong Kong. They love China, but they fled Mao to escape political persecution. They know the Communist government today ain't much more tolerant than Chairman Mao's gang, so even though they're smiling in public, they're very leery of the Chinese being back in control of Hong Kong."

"Okay, keep going," Tanisha said, her pen flying across the paper to keep up.

"In 1966, the anti-colonial riots break out in Hong Kong over increased fares on the Cross Harbor Star Ferry. Obviously, that head-bashing tournament wasn't about the fares. It was about British rule. The Communist-backed labor unions wanted to run the Colony. That's why these elections coming up are so important. But I digress," he grinned.

"Okay, now let's jump to current events," Vickers said with a flourish of his hairy arms. "Margaret Thatcher—the Chinese call her Sa Cha Fu Ren, or 'Wife Thatcher'—goes to Beijing in 1984 and signs the Sino-British Joint Declaration in the Great Hall of the People. This Declaration is a real piece of bullshit, in my opinion, 'cause I don't think it's ever gonna work. It says that after the Chinese take over Hong Kong in July of '97, there will be 'One Country, Two Systems.' The one country, of course, is China. The two systems are a laissez-faire economy for Hong Kong, side by side with a repressive Communist dictatorship for the rest of Red China. No fucking way! These two diverse ideologies can't coexist, and deep down, everybody knows it, and that's why everybody is so jittery. The U.S. and other world powers are trying to buy into this bullshit idea because they don't want to piss off China and lose that huge market, and they don't want to lose Hong Kong as a banking and shipping center that links East and West.

"This Joint Declaration also states that China will not change the capitalist system in Hong Kong for fifty years from the date of repatriation. Again, I say, good fucking luck."

Now Wheeler was leaning forward, listening intently.

"In June 1989, the Chinese scare the piss out of all the Hong Kong citizens when they kick ass in Tiananmen Square," Vickers said, still pacing. "After that massacre, a brain-drain ensues. Wealthy Chinese business owners leave Hong Kong like a flock of pigeons taking off after a backfire. The Chinese don't want Hong Kong to be an empty shell now that they finally have it, so they're trying to make it look like they're going to live up to the Sino-British Joint Declaration and not change anything for fifty years like they promised.

"Plus, the Brits did one thing that really infuriated the Chinese. A little going-away present, if you will."

"What was that?" Tanisha asked.

Vickers grinned toothily. "Democracy. Can you believe it? For one hundred and fifty years, the Brits run the place like a kingdom. They treat the Chinese citizens of Hong Kong like serfs and peons. They have no political rights. There's no such thing as habeas corpus. Forget British citizenship! The only elected officials Hong Kongers can vote for are the Urban Council, which supervises sidewalk peddlers, garbage pickup, and street names—I'm serious! Then, six years before they are due to sky out, the Brits decide to hold free elections for the Legislative Council. You can imagine how pissed the Communist Chinese up in Beijing were! They never had any intention of keeping the Joint Declaration. Now they've got to go in, just eight years after the massacre in Tiananmen Square, and deal with another democratic movement in full view of the whole world. If they fuck over Hong Kong, they put their own Most Favored Nation trading status in jeopardy. So they have to act cautiously.

"In December of last year, they appoint Tung Chee Hwa, a shipping tycoon from Shanghai, to be their first Chief Executive of Hong Kong. Two hours after midnight on July 1, 1997, they boot out the elected legislature and replace it with hand-picked puppets of their own. They send in two mechanized divisions the next morning to garrison the place. Hong Kong is now a Special Autonomous Region of China. 'Autonomous' my ass. Although it's on a lease, it's still the golden goose, producing forty percent of China's foreign exchange. They can't treat it too roughly. As of today, twenty-nine percent of the Colony has fled. We are poised and waiting. The whole world is watching, wondering what will happen. . . . This year, the first Chinese-controlled democratic elections are supposed to take place. These are supposed to be free elections to pick a new Chief Executive and Legislature. The Chinese Commies in Beijing obviously don't want a bunch of Western-leaning Social Democrats to get installed, but if they stifle the election, everybody will know the Joint Declaration was bullshit, and the remaining banks and world businesses in Hong Kong will take off. So I think something very evil may have happened, and now I'm into pure speculation and rumor."

"What?" Tanisha asked.

"A man named Willy Wo Lap Ling recently made a trip to Beijing. It was reported on CNN. Nobody knows why he went, but I have a suspicion."

"Who is he?" Tanisha asked, pausing from her note-taking to look up at Vickers.

"Wo Lap Ling is one big-time gonif. I keep running into his name. So far, he's just smoke on the radar. . . . Can't quite identify his game, but I think he's involved in a lot of bad shit. There's even an unsubstantiated report he's trafficking in black market Russian nukes—he's been trying to purchase some suitcase bombs missing from the Russian armory. I got that from a spook in the CIA named Carter DeHaviland who's pretty reliable. He's officed out where you are in L.A. He thinks Willy's already got his hands on some of those nuclear weapons. If that's not enough to scare the shit out of you, he's also rumored to be involved in big-time smuggling of drugs and illegal immigration into the U.S. Some Hong Kong Royal Police I know think he's connected, somehow, to the Chin Lo Triad, which is one of the most powerful criminal organizations in the world. I've represented some Snake Riders who whisper about Willy Wo Lap. A few Hong Kong detectives who started to investigate him met with violent ends. Nobody can prove it, but in my opinion, anybody who walks like a duck and quacks like a duck is a fucking Chin Lo Peking duck. The Triad is responsible for a good deal of the burgeoning crime and political corruption here in America. So why is Willy Wo Lap, who is supposed to be a Hong Kong businessman, in Beijing talking to China big shots? I think Wo Lap Ling is being groomed to run for Chief Executive of Hong Kong. If I'm right and this deal has been cut, and if Wo Lap Ling is connected to the Chin Lo Triad, it will mean that Hong Kong, the third-largest banking center in the world, has been flat out sold to a worldwide criminal organization."

"And the U.S. government will let this happen," Wheeler said.

"These guys aren't stupid. Wo Lap Ling has big-time Guan-Xi with the U.S. government. He's on the board of directors of the American Red Cross. He gives millions to charity every year in Hong Kong and America. They throw dinners to honor this guy. He dines with Clinton in the White House, sleeps in the Lincoln bedroom, donates big to everybody's campaign. Both our political animals get fed by this guy. He builds soup kitchens and hospital wings. The Americans like him because he was born in Kowloon, not Communist China. He's a free market economy kind of guy, with strong ties to the West. You may have noticed, our government guys only see green."

"But you can't prove any of it," Tanisha said.

"No, I can't. But let's suppose . . ." He waved the typed sheet Tanisha had brought. "Let's suppose the payoffs on this transcript have something to do with this rigged election in Hong Kong in 1998. Then maybe a big piece of the cover is flapping up."

SEVENTEEN

The Man with Good Shoes

The ugly girl led Fu Hai out of the restaurant and through the Ching Ping Market. She reached back and took his hand and pulled him along so they would not get separated amidst the teeming crowds of people. He followed her obediently, watching the soft swell of her haunches moving under the fabric of her baggy trousers. He had not had a woman in months. He wondered what it would be like to make love to the ugly girl. Then he reminded himself that her father was a dangerous criminal and a Snakehead who would be getting him to America. Only a fool would attempt such a reckless act.

The ugly girl led him to a warehouse down by the Pearl River. Beyond the metal building, he could see old Chinese junks and a rusting metal freighter tied to a concrete dock being loaded by peasant laborers. The girl took a key out of her sock and unlocked the warehouse door.

The inside of the building was dank and smelled of rotting fruit and engine oil. He was led to a place in the back, and again the girl put her hands on his shoulders and pushed him into a sitting position on a row of wooden pallets. Then she turned and left.

Fu Hai sat quietly, wondering what would come next. He thought of all that had happened on the journey to Beijing. What had surprised him the most was how China had changed. No longer a sleeping giant, she had awakened. New buildings and roads were everywhere he looked. All over the Eastern Provinces the cities were changing. From Jiangsu Province, south to Zhejiang, from Fukien to Guandong, China was bustling with new architecture, life, and ideas. Had he picked the wrong time to leave? Would he miss the opportunity the awakened giant would bring to her people? What was he going to find in America?

He had heard wonderful stories of America, about immigrants who had gone there with nothing and, in a few years, owned huge houses and had many American cars. But how on earth did one make this happen? What if it were not true? Perhaps he *had* made a mistake, but even as he had these thoughts, he knew China did not want him. China might change, but its new face would not welcome him. He would never be happy here. With new resolve, he was determined to go to America. He would become his dreams. But he was frightened. Confucius said: *Good medicine is often bitter to the taste.* Fu Hai gritted his teeth. He would take the bitter medicine of change and leave the land of his birth forever.

Three hours later, the ugly girl returned with a man who spoke Mandarin. He was tall and had good shoes.

"*Chi fan le ma?*" the man asked, without introducing himself. This meant "Have you eaten yet?"

"I have. Have you eaten?" Fu Hai replied. In China, because of the long-standing scarcity of food, it had become a traditional greeting to inquire if somebody had eaten. It was not an offer to eat. It was the American equivalent of "How are you?" In America one replied, "Fine. How are you?" In China, one did not bore the asker with a long list of complaints.

The man with good shoes told Fu Hai that the Snake Ride would begin by boat down the Pearl River. He would travel inside a coffin to Hong Kong. The Chinese Army patrolled the border now, protecting Hong Kong from the flow of immigrants that tried to pour in from China to take advantage of the "other system." This was strictly prohibited by Beijing, but Fu Hai needed to cross into the New Territories to leave China.

"Hong Kong is forty miles downriver," the man with good shoes said. "You must jump in the water as the freighter rounds East Lamma Channel. You will swim ashore and find your way to the village of Wah Fu. There you must climb up a jungle gorge to Wong Chuk Hang, where you will find Neolithic carvings that look like spirals. They are at least five thousand years old. Wait there and Big-Eared Tou's cousin will find you," he said.

Later that night, Fu Hai was led by the man with good shoes down to the dock and a small rusting freighter with the name *Tai He Ping* (Great Peace) painted on the side.

He went aboard, past crewmen who didn't look at him or ask questions. He was led down into a dark, rusting hold where there were twelve empty coffins made from beautiful *bai mu*, white wood, the preferred material for coffins in China. It came exclusively from Liuzhou in the Guangxi-Zhuang Autonomous Region of southeast China. The coffins themselves looked like small boats with high, rounded ends. He knew they were very expensive, maybe ten thousand U.S. dollars each. The man with good shoes opened the lid of the farthest one and told Fu Hai to get into the coffin. Reluctantly, he climbed in, fearing it might be bad luck to spend time inside a casket.

"If soldiers board this boat and check the load, they will not open the casket. They are afraid of death," the man with good shoes told him. Fu Hai nodded. That was his feeling exactly. He closed his eyes as the man lowered the lid.

Hours passed in the hot, dank hold. Occasionally, he heard

people coming down the metal ladder or moving heavy boxes, but he couldn't understand what they were saying through the wall of the coffin. Then he felt the rumble of the freighter's powerful engine as it started.

Soon the boat was underway. The time passed slowly for Fu Hai, a living corpse inside the white wood casket. He wondered if the soldiers would board the freighter; if, as the man with good shoes said, they would be as afraid of the coffins as he was. He knew that all people weren't the same. Great ancient wisdom said that flowers look different to different eyes. He prayed that the man with good shoes was right.

When he heard the patrol boat, his heart almost stopped. It came roaring up alongside, its engine growling like an angry beast. He could hear voices shouting, and he pushed the lid of the coffin up slightly to hear better. Moist air came into the steamy, hot casket and cooled him. He heard footsteps ringing on the ladderway, as people came down into the hold. Through the crack in the lifted coffin lid, he caught a glimpse of two soldiers wearing the green uniforms of the People's Liberation Army. He softly lowered the lid. Fu Hai heard them slam their gun barrels on a few of the beautifully crafted coffins, undoubtedly leaving ugly, greasy gouges in the polished white wood. Then they turned and quickly left, in a hurry to get away from the baskets of death.

He heard the patrol boat start up and leave. He had been told by the man with good shoes that it would now be safe to get out of the coffin. Fu Hai pushed back the lid and clambered out. His body was drenched with sweat, his clothes damp and clammy.

There was a small porthole forward of where the coffins were stored, and Fu Hai went to it and looked out. The cold river air felt like rain on his face. He smiled as he saw the billowing, churning Pearl River flowing past the hull. In the distance, he could see the lights of Hong Kong. The huge skyscrapers lit low-hanging clouds with incandescent, man-made light. Fu Hai had never seen a sight like this before. The clouds were ablaze with the city's glow. It was as if they were on fire.

They were nearing the East Lamma Channel when the man with good shoes came down to the hold and got him. They went up to the deck and to the stern of the freighter.

"You must jump as far from the boat as you can to avoid the huge propeller," the man said. Then he motioned for Fu Hai to jump. Fu Hai was not a strong swimmer, but without thinking, he held his nose and leaped as far as he could, slipping slightly as he jumped, falling dangerously close, landing in the boiling wake at the back of the boat. He could feel the rush from the churning propeller as he kicked to get away. . . . Then his head came up and he swam as hard and fast as he could toward the shore.

The quick current took him and he was swept along in the oily sea, barely keeping his head above water. The harder he swam, the farther away the shore seemed to be. Jellyfish stung his legs.

Fu Hai began to panic. He would not make it. His life would end right here, a mile from Hong Kong. Brackish water filled his mouth. He accidentally inhaled it down into his lungs, coughing, choking, and sputtering. He swam harder, dog-paddling desperately to reach land but being carried farther down the coast like a small twig after a huge rain. He knew he was in trouble, close to drowning. Suddenly he saw an orange metal channel marker coming up at him fast. If he could only get to it, he might live. The current was moving faster now as it rounded the headland. The channel marker rushed up at him. He grabbed for it, and there was a loud clang as the metal buoy hit his head. His hands slipped down on the slimy sides, the barnacles there cutting his flesh to ribbons. Then he found an eye-hole down near the base and held on. Blood was in his mouth and all over his arms. He was gagging from the water in his lungs and stomach. The current ripped and tore at him, and then, because he was weak, he lost his hold and was swept away again, into the current toward the dark, mountainous side of Hong Kong Island.

Somehow, with superhuman effort, Fu Hai managed to keep his head above water as the current carried him rapidly along. He was about to lose consciousness when, without warning, he crashed into a rock jetty wall that protected the shoreline from the ocean flow. He was weak from the effort and tried several times to climb up on the hard, algae-covered granite rocks—each time slipping back into the water. Finally, when he had almost no energy left, he made one last try and managed to get half his body out of the current and up onto the rocks. He sucked in air until he had the strength to pull himself the rest of the way out of the churning water. His heart swelled. He had made it.

Zhang Fu Hai was finally in Hong Kong.

EIGHTEEN

Crossing Paths

Before Wheeler and Tanisha left Willard Vickers's house at eleven P.M., it had all seemed to make pretty good sense. He'd told them about a Hong Kong cop he knew. The Royal Police had been reorganized. The Chinese had brought in a contingent of police from Beijing, but some old-time Brits were kept on the force for continuity. Willard said maybe his friend could help. Using Wheeler's credit card, they called Hong Kong.

He had an English accent and the terribly British name of Julian Winslow. Julian said they'd been trying for six years to tie Willy Wo Lap Ling to the Chin Lo Triad, but Willy had been very careful, very thorough. . . . Two Hong Kong informants and two detectives had been murdered over rumors of his involvement. Nobody else wanted to talk much about Willy.

Wheeler and Tanisha had booked two rooms in the Cleveland Ritz-Carlton, downtown.

Tanisha had never stayed in a hotel like the Ritz-Carlton before. After they checked in, she walked around her room looking, in awe, at the antiques. She touched the crystal lamps, ran her hand over the beautiful terry-cloth robe in the bathroom, which had the Ritz-Carlton emblem embroidered on it in gold.

An hour later, she met Wheeler downstairs in the ornate bar. She sipped a cola while he took giant gulps of his double Scotch/rocks. She kicked off her shoes and was trying to figure out what to do when he blurted, "Let's go to Hong Kong."

"Huh?" she said.

"If that Hong Kong cop thinks Willy Wo Lap Ling is part of that Triad, and if Vickers thinks Willy's about to run for office, maybe we could find out what's going on. . . . I can't believe Wo Lap would run for government without a lot of money on the table. What if we could find out, get a police raid mounted or something?"

"This isn't half-time at the U.S.C.–U.C.L.A. game. You shoot beer on these guys, they won't just chase you around in short pants."

"You get that out of the police computer?" he asked, startled that she knew about it.

"No . . . it's not in the computer."

"Then how did you know?"

"I was there, Wheeler. I did my last two years of criminology at Bruintown. I was in the U.C.L.A. rooting section—you sprayed me with beer."

"It was a great stunt, wasn't it?" he grinned, warmed by the memory.

"You're a real project," she finally said, then they were both smiling. That incident, which had so defined their differences fifteen years ago, now seemed to bring them together.

"I loved my brother but I resented him too," Wheeler admitted. "Some part of me is saying, if I could find out what happened to him, if I could solve his murder, then . . . maybe . . . I don't know. Maybe it's the first step to things being different for me. I know it doesn't make sense, but . . . that's what I think."

It was the exact same thought that had been going through Tanisha's mind.

He looked up at her unexpectedly, and for the first time, they really saw into each other.

"Look, I'll pay for the trip to Hong Kong," he suddenly said. "You can get your passport overnighted to you here. I've got mine. Let's go ask the Hong Kong cop to help us. Who knows what will come of it? Maybe we'll learn something. Maybe not. Cost you nothing but two days of your life, and you'll get to see one of the most exotic cities in the world."

She sat there looking at him, wondering why she was drawn to the idea. Why she even gave a damn about Prescott Cassidy or Angela Wong . . . or Wheeler, with his Scotch breath and boyish charm. The world she came from was dark and terrifying. Hope was a scarce commodity on her block. Her friends, growing up, had had no future plans. Making it to tomorrow was the ultimate reward. They buzzed in aimless panic like bumblebees caught out after dark, until they crashed in some accidentally tragic way or were jailed for their rage and helplessness. At age thirty-five, she had almost no friends left down in the hood. The girls distrusted her; the boys were either dead or in jail. Worse still, she had failed despite her promise to her dead sister. She had made no contribution to the quality of their lives.

They said everybody in Black America was one relative away from the penitentiary or a drug collapse. It didn't matter whom you looked at—how high up you went. Dr. Joycelyn Elders had a crack-smoking son. Jesse Jackson's brother was in jail. They were all drawn back to their beginnings, circling the drain, drawn by circumstances or love. Everybody just precious moments from extinction. So why this—why consider this?

She looked at Wheeler, who sensed her distress and, for once, had the good sense not to speak. He was a black sheep like her. . . . He had become the same problem for the people in his country club bar that she was in Zandel's beauty shop. Could it be that simple? Or was it because when he looked at her, he seemed to see a woman—not a Black woman? She knew it would be dangerous to believe that. It was that kind of thinking that always ended up coming back and breaking you. But she pondered it anyway and then rejected it. She knew herself better than that.

Underneath everything else, her demon was survivor's guilt. Her kindergarten class had been social cannon fodder. How could that group of once shining futures be such a rat hole of failed expectations? What she really had was cultural guilt—guilt about moving out of the neighborhood—guilt about buying her clothes in West L.A.—guilt about trying to go someplace else . . . be something else. Because deep down in her heart, she hated "Rings" Williams. Hated that sloe-eyed little girl. Deep down, she wanted to be someone else. But she didn't know how.

Was she looking for redemption or escape?

"Make the reservations," Tanisha said to Wheeler, then she got up and left the bar to call Verba before she changed her mind.

"I'm sorry, Captain. I know it's late, but I had a family emergency here in Cleveland. I'll be in on Monday," she lied.

"Listen, Tanisha, these I.A. guys mean business. They're set to harpoon you. I asked for a look at the file. Everything's a big secret, so they said no, but one guy told me that some Blood G-ster named 'Blue Mandango' said you were transforming on the man."

So Blue had said she was turning in cases. Forget that Blue wasn't even in her old set, or even around when her neighborhood crew was still Cripping. He was an off-brand buster from the Rolling Sixties gang.

The Sixties and Tanisha's old friends got into it frequently over adjoining territory. She had dated two Crip ghetto stars while Blue was trying to slam her. Anything Blue said was bullshit. I.A. couldn't be so out of it they'd believe a rival gang member.

"You hear what I'm saying?" Verba interrupted her thoughts.

"I understand, Captain."

"Okay, I'm gonna tell the Shooflies ten o'clock Monday. You be there. Otherwise nobody can give you any cover."

"Nobody ever has," she said sadly. Then there was an empty sound on the line to L.A. Captain Verba had hung up. She wondered if she was making a horrible mistake.

Fu Hai sat on a rock in Wong Chuk Hang under the five-thousand-year-old Neolithic carvings that no longer had meaning, and waited. As night came, he fell asleep and didn't wake up until morning.

When he awoke, he was looking right into the eyes of a large, black *naja naja*. It had crawled up close to investigate. Its tongue slithered out as its prehistoric eyes gleamed, showing the viciousness of the ages. Fu Hai didn't move. He was terrified. He knew the hooded cobra was one of the most venomous in the world. His heart almost stopped beating as he stared at the deadly reptile. Then, unexpectedly, the snake just turned and slithered away.

Fu Hai sat up. He took a giant breath. He thought maybe this was an omen. He was "Riding the Snake" and this deadly snake had left him alive to go to America.

At a little after ten in the morning, Big-Eared Tou's cousin came for him. She was tall, slender, and very beautiful. She wore the old-style slit Chinese dress, which had made a fashion comeback with the repatriation of Hong Kong to China.

"I will take you to a place where you will stay. It is not very beautiful, but you will be safe from the police there until we can get you travel papers." She had a small suitcase, and she handed it to him. "Put on these clothes," she told him, "so you will blend in."

He went behind a rock and opened the suitcase. He pulled out a blue suit. The stitching was poor and the suit had little style, but still, it was the most beautiful suit of clothes he had ever had. He took out the new white shirt and tie and unfolded them. He put it all on, then took the socks and the cheap new shoes out of the suitcase. The shoes were two sizes too big, but he laced them tight, and cinched the belt holding up the new pants. Once he was dressed, he put the old clothes from the silkworm factory into the suitcase and came out from behind the rock.

"I will never be able to pay you back for these beautiful gifts," he told her.

"Yes you will," she said. There was something about the way she said it that unsettled him, as if her words held some dark secret. Then she handed him a cellphone to clip onto his belt. He looked at it in amazement.

"It doesn't work," she told him. "It has no mechanism, but with it on your belt, you will look like you belong in Hong Kong."

Then, without holding his hand, she led him down the hill to a taxi. They got in and she gave the driver an address in the New Territories of Kowloon.

They took backroads, but still Fu Hai was startled at the magnificence of the Colony. Rolls-Royce, Lexus, and Mercedes sedans transected the wide streets. People hurried to their destinations. The city, with its rickshaws and floating junks, skyscrapers and neon signs, mixed East with West.

They headed through the tunnel that went under the harbor, leaving Hong Kong Island. The pretty girl said nothing. She didn't look at him or even appear to notice that he was smiling proudly in his new Western clothes.

They finally pulled up across the street from what looked like a wall of crumbling buildings. She paid the taxi driver and got out of the cab, then motioned for Fu Hai to follow. Strangely, there was a beautiful Rolls-Royce parked in front of the shabby buildings.

"This is the Walled City of Kowloon," she told him. "It is a ghetto, but it is controlled by our Triad."

He nodded and looked at the Rolls-Royce. He had never seen such a beautiful car like this up close.

"That is the car of the new Shan Chu of the Triad," she told him as he stared at it. "His name is Henry Liu. He is very thin and very vicious. . . . He limps badly from an old wound. In the street, they call him Limpy Liu. When you are inside, he will tell you what you must do to earn your way. You must agree to whatever he tells you."

They walked across the street, and Fu Hai noticed that they were walking across hundreds upon hundreds of old human teeth.

She saw him looking at them in horror and smiled. "From the unlicensed dentist shops that line this street," she explained. "They like to show off their workmanship."

They crossed the road and were standing in front of the wall of buildings when suddenly a huge United Airlines jet, with its wheels down, came low over the Walled City, ready to land at Hong Kong International a mile and a half beyond. Fu Hai was startled at the noise, looking up as the jet thundered overhead, throwing a black shadow over him. Fu Hai wondered if the shadow was an evil omen.

"A flight from America," she said, smiling. Then she took him inside the dentist shop and out the back door and into one of the pitch-black, dank alleyways inside the Walled City. The stench in the garbage-strewn alley was unimaginable. She led him a short distance to a door. They went inside and she turned to him.

"You will wait here," she said.

He looked around the room in the dim light from a dull hanging bulb. An octagonal mirror hung on a wall above a small red-and-gold shrine to Amitabha, the Buddha of the Hereafter.

"The mirror keeps out evil spirits," she explained. "The spirits cannot stand to see their ugly faces." Then she turned and left him there, closing the door behind her.

Fu Hai leaned against the damp wall and sighed with relief. He had journeyed clear across China, from the Domes of Wrath to the edge of the South China Sea. He would do whatever they asked of him to earn his freedom.

Fu Hai didn't know he was standing in the same ghetto where Willy Wo Lap was born.

He didn't know that inside the huge airliner that had thrown its shadow over him were two Americans, who were on a course to change his life forever.

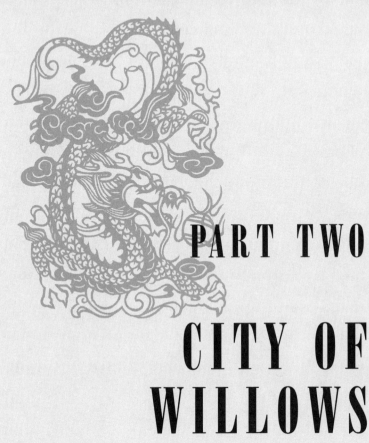

PART TWO

CITY OF
WILLOWS

Hong Kong

L ike a Dowager Empress, the Peninsula Hotel sat on Tsim Sha Tsui Point, its top-floor picture windows staring indolently out on Victoria Harbor. Its carved stone back was turned to the hustling cacophony of Salisbury Road, ignoring the ugly commercial squalor behind her.

The world-famous hotel was known by its guests as "The Pen," and that Tuesday it was almost completely full. Wheeler discussed this with a polite woman at the reservation desk and finally booked the two-bedroom Mandarin Suite in the new central tower on the twentieth floor, using his American Express card. It was more than he wanted to spend and he and Tanisha would have to share a sitting room, but it was the best he could do. Since they had no luggage, he told the room clerk that he would see himself up, then crossed the ornate marble-floored lobby to the rust-colored antique sofa where Tanisha was seated. When he told her that they were going to share a suite, she just looked at him, her beautiful black eyes pinning him mercilessly like a bug on a board.

"Paucity of rooms," he said nervously, using a canned British accent.

"Bear in mind I'm combat-trained," she replied.

They crossed the lobby adorned with massive Elizabethan antiques, found the elevator, called a lift, and rode silently in its polished mahogany splendor to the twentieth floor.

The Mandarin Suite was magnificent. It was on the next-to-top floor of the hotel and had a commanding view of Victoria Harbor. Louvered doors and ceiling paddle fans paid homage to its colorful past. The hotel was owned by Hong Kong Shanghai Hotels, Ltd., one of the largest companies on the Hong Kong Stock Exchange. The Pen had a rich historical background and had even once been the headquarters for the Japanese Imperial occupation forces in 1943. Recently it had been refurbished to bring out the original neoclassical design. From their windows, they could look south across the bay to Hong Kong Island. Tanisha moved to the plate glass and stood there for several minutes, her right hand up to her face, stunned by what she saw.

Multicolored Chinese junks seemed poised, motionless, on the bay. Heavy oatmeal-colored clouds were just sweeping in off the South China Sea, partially blocking the late-afternoon sun and throwing shafts of filtered light down on the blue-green water. Across the harbor, high and commanding, were Jardines Lookout and Victoria Peak. To the west, they could see all the way up the coast to the Macao Ferry Terminal in Sheung Wan. Water taxis zipped across the bay, throwing out frothy wakes in disappearing wedges. Wheeler thought it was as beautiful a view as there was in the world, remembering how it had stunned him the first time he'd been here with his mother and brother.

He and Prescott had been twelve and ten. His father had business in Sydney, Australia, and was supposed to join them, but something came up and he never made it. Even at the age of twelve, Wheeler had trouble deciding whether he was angry that his humorless father didn't make the trip or glad that he would be free of the relentless judgments. Wheeler never seemed to be good enough to please him. It was in this very hotel, when his mother announced that Wheeler Sr. wouldn't be coming, that he decided to stop competing for his father's love. That same night he'd flooded the hotel bathroom, causing a leak that swamped rooms two floors down. It was right here at The Pen where the Prankmeister made his first appearance.

His mother had taken them sightseeing, cramming their heads with Eastern culture and guidebook literature. Back then, they'd been staying in the Presidential Suite, which was just one floor above. He and Prescott had sat by the window, looking at the timeless and colorful junks tipping precariously with cargo. He had marveled at the mysteries of this place, the endlessly throbbing beat of Hong Kong. The Colony was now in the hands of the Chinese Communists, but from their window twenty stories up, very little seemed to have changed.

After a moment, Tanisha turned away from the view and looked at him. "My God," she said, her voice like a reverent whisper in an empty church.

"Pretty amazing, isn't it?"

All the way in from the airport, along South Chatham Road, through the teeming, overpopulated outskirts of Kowloon, to the Peninsula at Tsim Sha Tsui, Tanisha had remained silent, looking out the window of the Mercedes-Benz taxicab at streets overflowing with humanity and bright neon signs. Now she seemed to finally be digesting it.

"It's so beautiful," she said, "so different than I thought it would be." It was hard for her to imagine that this incredible place shared the globe with the ugly, graffiti-scarred four square blocks in South Central that had been her Crip turf. While she and her homies were shedding blood to protect those desolate street corners, all of this exotic beauty and splendor was half a world away, unknown to any of them. It made her sister's death seem all the more tragic. What had they all been dying for? What made them treasure a place so dangerous and ugly?

"We're prisoners of our environment," Wheeler said, reading her thoughts like a psychic.

She was surprised by the direct hit. "How did you know I was thinking that?" she asked.

"Because it's what I thought the first time I saw this."

"How the hell is somebody a prisoner in Beverly Hills?"

"You can be trapped anywhere, Tanisha. We make our own prisons. They're in the mind. You don't have to be from South Central to be a captive."

"Maybe," she said, but knew they weren't talking about the same thing.

Later that evening, they called Detective Julian Winslow's number and got him on the first ring.

"Why don't you pop over to the police headquarters in the A.M.," he said pleasantly. "I'd buy you a spot of supper, but I've got my Black Watch tonight. I play the pipes for the old Scottish regiment. We used to wear the kilts and tartan . . . march in parades and the like. The detail was disbanded by the Commies, but we still hold practice once a week to remind us of the old days, then we head off to some bag a' nails for hops and mischief. I think I should bring in Johnny Kwong to help us." He continued, changing subjects without taking a breath, "He's a right copper and he's got the juice we need with the new Police Department. What say we make a diary engagement for ten o'clock tomorrow?" His voice chirped through the line with high-tenor English cheer.

"We'll be there," Wheeler said.

"You know the which-way?" Julian Winslow asked. "It's at 2600 Harcourt Road in Wan Chai—any livery driver will know it, only we don't call it the Hong Kong Royal Police Headquarters any longer. It's now the bloody People's Police Building. These Commie blighters got damn little sense of color, I'll tell you that much," he complained. "I'll leave your name. Have the lad knock me up when you're in the lobby," he instructed before he hung up.

They had dinner in the Felix, the top-floor restaurant in The Pen, which was the vision of the world-famous interior designer

Philip Stark. Since it was during the week, they got a table by the window. Wedgwood china and sterling silver cutlery glittered on Danish linen. The room was framed with dark mahogany and crowned by chandeliers that hung above them like huge crystal mushrooms. Wheeler ordered French goose liver with truffles and the house trademark dish of roasted milk-fed veal on a ragout of baby potatoes, carrots, and pearl onions. Tanisha wrinkled her nose in thought and finally ordered a cheeseburger.

"Why did you become a cop?" Wheeler asked unexpectedly, jerking her thoughts off food and the princely decor, snapping her back like a ball on a rubber band to bang against dark childhood memories.

"You mean, instead of pursuing my short, ass-puckering career in gang warfare?" she said, dodging him deftly, not wanting to discuss Kenetta . . . Kenetta with her wide smile and nappy braided hair, Kenetta with the ugly, bubbling hole in her chest.

"You still don't like me much, do you?" he said. "I usually overcome that attitude with women well before this."

She sat there, looking at him for a long moment, not sure how she really felt about him. It was true, of course, she had hated him on sight, but it had been an unfair value judgment and she'd set it aside. She had come to a place where she actually respected him. For somebody who grew up rich and pampered, he had some unusual attributes. . . . He didn't kid himself. In fact, he was brutally honest . . . too honest. She had learned that a little self-deception, applied carefully on social or psychic wounds, stemmed emotional hemorrhaging. And he was brave. He had "come from the shoulder" when he'd faced down the three Chinese Tong gangsters in his brother's house. She wondered what exactly it was she was feeling about him. "We're not . . . compatible," she finally said.

"Funny way to put it." He was feeling strange with her now, unable to connect.

Time slowed as waiters scurried to clear dishes. Out the picture windows on the bay beyond, the listing Chinese junks moved in lazy disrepair.

"Why do I feel you judging me?" he said.

"I'm not judging you. The few things we have in common are nothing compared to the things that separate us," she continued. "Even though we're the same age and were born just a few miles apart, we aren't even from the same universe."

"What makes us so different?" he challenged. "People are people."

"Not to your Confederate great-grandfather. To him, people were property."

"What hopeless bullshit," he flared. "You want me to write his checks? I didn't even know him. He was dead seventy years before I was born. He's a name in a history book."

"It's okay, Wheeler," she said. "Calm down. We both still know you wouldn't trade skin with me. I'm not pissed off about it, but it's a fact. . . . You can't change it. It's still the main thing that defines us."

Again, they sat in silence. The sun was setting, dipping below the green sea, lighting the bellies of gray storm clouds with colors from some godly spectrum. Against her better judgment, she finally tried to explain her feelings to him. She hoped to hell it wouldn't sound like whining.

"While you were going to Sandy Hill Academy or John Dye Prep, or wherever your nanny chauffeured you every morning, I was at Walker Jones Hundred-and-third Street School. My friends started dying on me in the first grade. I was Crippin' when I was seven. Most of my friends were hooked to dope rides before sixth grade and off-line by high school."

He cocked his head in a silent question.

"Dead," she explained. "My first sexual boyfriend was Bobby Hughes. He was a Kitchen Crip from a Hundred-and-ninth Street. A tiny gangster whose street handle was 'Li'l G-Rock.' Bobby was already on State paper when I met him. We were only thirteen when he got me pregnant. He'd been busted a bunch for selling seams—that's crack or heroin in foil packets. He couldn't take another fall or he'd get sent to a C.Y.A. Farm. He got careless selling rock to help pay for the baby we had coming. The Crash Unit rode down on him and he took off running to avoid the bust and got faded by two cops in a cruising Z-car. It was on Halloween. 'Trick or treat, motherfucker.' Month after that, I miscarried. I had my first Department of Corrections appointment around then. My Doc-man was a boned-out redneck named Boyd Jeeter who always wanted to meet with me after work. He told me I could skip some of the appointment dates if I'd put out. He meant business, too. He seemed constantly on the edge of jumping me. I was so scared of him I kept a clean spout in my purse whenever I met with him."

Again, Wheeler looked confused.

"That's an untraceable handgun. I was so hard by then, if that ugly Gomer had tried anything, I woulda gauged him on the spot and never thought twice about it. Then, my baby sister died in a drive-by and mosta my friends got sent upstate. That was my childhood, Wheeler. Dead babies in pigtails. Friends boxed up in jail or coffins, and the strange thing was it seemed perfectly normal to me. So don't tell me about the prison you were in in Beverly Hills. I don't wanna hear it." When she finished, the anger in her voice hung there, distorting the atmosphere like cheap perfume. What about him made her so edgy? she wondered. "I'm sorry. I didn't mean to get angry. It's not you. It's me," she finally added.

Again, nothing to say. Waiters cleared the plates and time took the tension. After the busboys left, she went on, her voice softer now.

"When my mother died, I was at the mortuary," she said. "I was there to pick out a box for her, and I was in that room they have upstairs, where they have all the different coffins on display. I looked out the window and I saw this Beemer blow into the parking lot full of T.G.s. Not one of them was old enough to drive. I figured the car was probably a Valley hot-roller, but I was upset about my mother and I decided to let it slide. A few minutes later, these little boys are up in the same room with me. They're baggin', saggin', and braggin', struttin' around with their hats on backward. I thought they were trying to pick a coffin for a dead friend. Then I heard one say, 'Hey, J-Dog, this here be one top-rank box fer you t'possy out in.' It took me a minute before I realized those babies were in there to pick out their own coffins. They had so little belief in their futures that at age fifteen they came there with their drug money to pre-buy their own funerals, and they were right. Those little boys were all in the diamond lane to Forest Lawn, and there was nothing anybody could do about it.

"After my sister died, I made a promise to do something to help them. You wanted to know why I joined the police—I wanted to try and slow the carnage, but it was a stupid goal. The system doesn't want it, from liberal politicians with their welfare handouts that enslave us, to the conservatives who won't ban the guns that kill us. And we don't help either. The little T.G.s are being raised with such violent disregard for each other that their premature end is unstoppable." She looked down at her hands. "I haven't even come close to changing anything. And now I'm over here with you, on the other side of the world. I feel like a traitor to myself and to them. I think I'm just running away from my failures." She looked up at him. "I'm not judging you, Wheeler. I'm judging me. I don't like what I see. I think I need to go home."

They sat in the gathering darkness of the huge dining room as the sun finally set. Somebody turned on the chandeliers and adjusted them down until the Wedgwood china glittered gold. Wheeler signed the check, then looked up at her.

"I'm sorry," he said. "You're right. My problems growing up were nothing like that. But at least you had something to go after— to strive for. My silly, goddamn curse was I already had everything. Nothing seemed worth the effort. I had no reason to exist, so I played golf, fucked around, and got drunk. I'd have been much better off someplace else."

To be polite, she nodded, but didn't understand. He had money, and no matter what they always said, she knew that if money couldn't buy happiness, it could at least buy change. What on earth was he saying? If she'd had money, they wouldn't have been stuck south of Crenshaw. They'd have lived someplace else. Her sister would still be alive. She wouldn't have to carry the bur-

174

den of the two dead G-sters. Wouldn't have to wake up in the night, still seeing the disbelief in their eyes as she ended their zig-zag existence in the back of that market. She could still feel their flesh separating at the end of her blade. What on earth was he talking about? Money would have changed it all. The cultural gap between them was cavernous. They couldn't have been more different if they'd lived in separate centuries. About all they had in common was their age and a knowledge of the L.A. freeways. It wasn't his fault. He hadn't made the choice, but she hadn't either.

"Don't go home, Tanisha," he said unexpectedly, his voice a whisper. "This is my first try at something important. This is the first thing I've wanted bad enough to give up everything for. I've got to find out what happened to Prescott. I don't know the right questions to ask. Without you, I'll fuck this up. Without you, I'll fail."

TWENTY

Constables

A fter breakfast the next morning in the coffee shop of The Pen, Tanisha and Wheeler spent an hour shopping in the huge underground mall next to the hotel. Tanisha picked out a change of clothes, deciding on a tapered pair of slacks and a silk blouse made in China. Wheeler found The Gap and bought jeans, a black polo shirt, and tennis shoes. They both stocked up on cosmetics. They packed their old clothes in a canvas duffel bag they found in a luggage shop that carried everything from llama-skin purses to rhino briefcases, all made in Communist China. The mall went down four stories underground and covered four city blocks, and it was already teeming with customers at nine in the morning.

They cabbed over to the address Julian had given them in Wan Chai and stood outside the police station for a minute, inspecting it.

"Looks like a prison," Wheeler observed skeptically. It was an extremely ugly and foreboding gray-brick seven-story building with lots of tiny windows, many secured with iron bars. The building and courtyard out front were surrounded by a high brick wall, festooned along the top with long steel spikes that curved inward, toward the courtyard, like deadly skeletal fingers. The effect was impressive, but unfriendly.

They walked through the wrought-iron gates and up a steep set of stairs into an equally foreboding gray interior.

"Fun place," Wheeler grinned nervously as they moved into the lobby, which had a narrow waist-high shelf on one wall that held a slew of shooting trophies won by Hong Kong's finest. Above the shelf, on chipped gray walls, were recognition plaques for marksmanship and police service. Other than these two minor concessions to decorating, the lobby was just a big, gray rectangle with a high ceiling, turning paddle fans, and a yellowing linoleum floor. Like cop shops all over the world, it smelled of mildew and disinfectant. Even at ten A.M., the place was surprisingly empty. Wheeler and Tanisha moved over to a Constable's desk and smiled at the young Chinese Sergeant, dressed in a crisp olive-green uniform with a Sam Browne belt. His badge shone brand-new. The police badges had been redesigned after the hand-over of the Colony on July 1. The old badge had a delicate relief that pictured a trading junk with Hong Kong towers in the background. This new one showed a bauhinia flower, the Chinese symbol for the Special Autonomous Region (S.A.R.), which Hong Kong was now designated.

"How may I help?" the Chinese Constable said in cultured English, looking and sounding as if he didn't intend to.

"We're here to see Inspectors Julian Winslow and Johnny Kwong," Wheeler said. "I'm Wheeler Cassidy and this is Los Angeles Police Detective Tanisha Williams."

Tanisha opened her purse and took out her LAPD badge and laid it on the counter before him. The Constable picked it up and looked at it carefully, studying it with furrowed brow before handing it back and picking up a phone. He spoke quietly in Chinese for a minute and then hung up.

"I'll buzz you through. It's the third door on the right. Take the lift to six. He'll meet you there." His English was perfect but without a trace of warmth.

"Thank you. You've been most kind," Tanisha said coldly.

They walked to the indicated door. He buzzed the electric lock and they passed into another gray corridor with a linoleum floor and walked under harsh fluorescent lighting to the end of the hall. They punched the elevator button, and when one door opened, they entered and rode up to the sixth floor.

"Pleasant fellow," Wheeler said sarcastically, as the old elevator lurched upward.

"Asshole," she corrected.

The doors opened and they were looking at a man who was shaped like a medicine ball in pleated pants. He was short, jolly, plump, and bald, with a handlebar mustache that overpowered his round face. He wore a patterned tie over a striped Savile Row shirt with black suspenders. He smiled at them through tobacco-stained teeth as they stepped off the elevator. "I'm Julian Winslow. Welcome to the People's Police Building," he said and shook their hands. His handshake was firm, warm, and strenuous. "And you must be my colleague from the LAPD," he grinned at Tanisha.

"Yes sir," she said, smiling. It was hard not to like him on the spot. He was impishly friendly.

"Good-oh. Well, let's be off then. Johnny was out to court this morning. Had a rounder in the docket. Bloody heroin dealer. Lots more of that now that we're part of China . . . opium dens and the lot. Just get my jacket. Come along."

They followed him down another narrow hall and finally he turned into a tiny office not much larger than a prison cell, with two desks and four chairs crammed inside. Julian's tweed jacket was over one of the chairs, and he snapped it off. "Sort of a dungeon, but we just got a brand-new complement of coppers from Beijing, so we're at full stretch around here. Johnny Kwong will touch up with us at the Police Museum on Coombe Road. Dour sort of place, really. No windows, ghastly criminal relics all about in tiny little rooms. It's got some of the strangest photos you've ever seen. My favorite is a before-and-after of a mass execution in 1880 . . . all these pirates lined up on their knees in the courtyard in one shot, right next is a shot where the bloody pikers are still kneeling but their pig-tailed heads are on the ground in front of them. Photo was published in the Crown newspaper back then to set the blighters straight. 'Don't muck around with the Queen, what?' " he chuckled.

They left the small office and were moving toward a private elevator in the rear of the building. All of the offices they passed were just as tiny as Julian's and crowded with Police Inspectors— most were Chinese nationals, but there were a few "round eyes" mixed in. Julian pushed the elevator button.

While they waited, Wheeler said, "We need to find out as much as we can about Wo Lap Ling."

"Not here, laddie. This ruddy pile a' bricks has more spies than the Turkish Embassy. Let's wait till we're with Johnny; saves telling it twice."

The elevator arrived. An old, scarred, American-made Otis eight-man. They got in. It rattled and shook, but took them down to the street entrance. They moved into the police parking lot and got into Julian's unmarked police car, a two-door English Ford Popular. He pulled his gun and clip-on holster out of the glove box and pushed it onto his belt. "My new People's Police ordnance . . . piece a' Russian junk. I used t'have a keen nine-millimeter Beretta. The new Chinese Superintendent issued us all these Bic disposable gats. Bloody seven-point-six-five-millimeter auto-fires. Jam like Chinese sewing machines. Eject port, throws the brass back at you. Put your bloody eye out, you're not careful." He put the economy-sized English Ford in gear and pulled out.

They drove the short distance to the museum in Wan Chi and pulled up in front of a small block building surrounded by a children's park. There was another car in the lot. As Julian got out, he nodded at it. "Johnny's," he explained as he closed the Ford's doors and locked them. "One thing you should know about Johnny Kwong," Julian said, turning to look at them. "A few years back, he was working the I.C.A.C.—that was our Independent Commission Against Corruption. They were trying to purge the Police Department of Triad members on the force. Johnny had made a good connection and was lining up on the most powerful Shan Chu, their supreme leader, of the 14K Triad. The blighter got word Johnny was after him and set fire to his block of flats, burned the whole bloody apartment building. Poor Johnny got it pretty bad. When he arrived unconscious at Extreme Casualty, he was charred to a cinder and nobody recognized him, so his police insurance didn't cover him. Nobody was gonna pay for skin grafts on some unknown Chinese. They moved him to Cinderella Services, which is like your charity wards in the States. He was completely out of it, delirious for almost two weeks. I finally got onto it, got a dental match, and pulled him out of there, then paid to get him a private room, but by then it was too late for a graft, so the poor lad is a bit of a mess. Looks like he's been dragged through a hedge backwards."

"We won't stare, if that's what you're saying," Tanisha said.

They started walking up the path toward the museum.

"Underneath all that scar tissue is a great copper," Julian continued. "He's a department hero. Awarded the George Cross and the C.B.E. That's the Commander of the Order of the British Empire—it's for extreme gallantry. He got assigned to the Special Investigations Unit of the Serious Crimes Group. Only the best of the best get that. Yours truly is still out doin' street busts on weenie-waggers in Chan Chow. So there you have it." He led the way past the children's park, and they climbed the steep flight of stairs and entered the windowless building.

As promised, the Police Museum was completely deserted and the walls of the rooms were full of old photographs. Glass cabinets with artifacts from old cases stood on the hardwood floors. They found Johnny Kwong in the Narcotics Room. He was bent over a glass case, looking at a beautifully carved ancient opium pipe, a priceless work of art. When he turned, it was hard not to gasp. Johnny's features had been completely burned off. His nose was gone, his lips were shriveled yellow lines. His ears were nubby protrusions on each side of his scarred, bald head. He smiled at them and put out a disfigured hand that had only two fingers left. The rest had been sacrificed to the flames. He shook with Wheeler and Tanisha as they were introduced by Julian.

"I'm Johnny," he said in the same cultured English accent that characterized all educated speech in the Colony. "This place always amazes me." He continued, "That pipe there destroyed countless lives, but it's truly beautiful. Its inscription reads, 'The crisp air refreshes the mind, the evening wind delights the nose.' I rather fancy that. Many of the most dangerously seductive things in life are beautiful—from snakes and white tigers to opium pipes and, I daresay, even some women. The policeman's lament," he laughed.

"Thank you for helping us," Wheeler said, as Johnny edged to the threshold where he could command a clear view of the front entrance and see anybody attempting to enter the museum.

"Julian tells me you are interested in Wo Lap Ling," Johnny said, smiling, his manufactured lips stretching tight with the expression.

"That's right," Tanisha said. "We think he may be involved in the murder of Mr. Cassidy's brother, Prescott, and the death of Prescott's secretary, Angela Wong."

Johnny stood before them, his expression, through the scars, impossible to read. He finally nodded. "Willy Wo Lap Ling is a dodgy piece of work," he said. "Not an easy quarry . . . What say, Julie?"

Julian nodded. "Johnny and I had a go at pinning the tail on the blighter, but he had a severe kick. We lost two Constables on that play."

"You must have a big file on him," Wheeler said.

"He was born in Kowloon, in the Walled City," Johnny nodded. "He was a beggar boy operating in the biggest criminal grocery store on earth. There were no laws in the Walled City, due to a bungled agreement between Britain and China, where ownership was disputed."

"We know about that," Wheeler said, "but we think it's possible that Willy Wo Lap Ling has made a secret agreement with the Communists in Beijing. A deal to run, unopposed, for Chief Executive of the Colony in the mid-1998 election. We think that deal may be tied to criminal political bribes in the U.S., and my brother's and his secretary's murders."

"Hong Kong is full of misinformation," Johnny said. "Rumors are like homeless orphans hunting for shelter. They adapt themselves to fit any promising circumstance. It's best to rely only on provable evidence. Willy is a cagey one. As Julian said, we've tried to move on him more than once. We even picked up trusted aides and tried to roll them, but they were so scared, nobody flipped. With Willy, we were always a day or two after the fair. We'd show up at the jail and find our informant hanging from the over-beam in his cell. Tough bit of business that. The buggers would rather die than rat out Wo Lap Ling."

"What if there was a document describing his deal with Beijing?" Wheeler said. "Wouldn't that be provable evidence if we had it and could bring it to light? Wouldn't that end his chance of being Chief Executive of Hong Kong?"

"Probably so," Julian said, "and if Willy has made a deal with the Communists in Beijing, he probably would have it documented. Willy's not one to trust a handshake or any man's word on a deal."

"Where do you think he'd have it stored? We've been told he doesn't trust banks," Tanisha said.

"Most likely at Triad headquarters," Julian said, looking to Johnny Kwong for confirmation. Johnny nodded in agreement.

"Where's that?" Wheeler pressed.

"It's a temple," Julian said. "An old Buddhist temple, not used for religion anymore. But it would be impossible to get to it unobserved."

"The Chin Lo Triad Temple is in a huge park," Johnny added, "which I'm told is beautiful with cherry blossoms this time of year."

"And you haven't seen it?" Tanisha was surprised. "Can't you just get a warrant and go search it?"

"Hong Kong is not a Western city. A man with Guan-Xi can escape through influence," Johnny said softly.

"He lives in the Temple?" Wheeler asked.

"No," Julian answered, "he has an apartment in Hong Kong, but he would never keep anything of great value there. He would seek the security of the Triad safe."

"There must be a way to get in there," Tanisha said. "Nothing is impossible."

"Maybe not impossible but highly improbable," Julian theorized. "Believe me, we've given it a lot of thought but decided we'd be batting a poor wicket to try."

"Why?" Wheeler pressed.

"The Temple is in a park, surrounded on all sides by the Walled City of Kowloon," Johnny explained. "It is, in effect, a moat of corruption and evil that protects the Chin Lo headquarters. The Walled City has no maps. It is a dark, dangerous place. The alleyways that transect it are bloody and treacherous. Thieves and murderers will kill you for your shoes—or worse still, for being an Occidental or a cop. It's a maze of dead ends and banjo cul-de-sacs. Nobody but a resident could make it through that stinking, pitch-black maze to the Temple in the center of the Walled City."

"What about going in by air?" Tanisha asked.

"They'd hear a helicopter, and be gone, disappearing in a whit into the alleyways, with all the valuables. Willy has vanguards from the Triad's fierce fighting sections posted on the roof with powerful weapons. These men court death and fear no one. Believe me, the only way into the Temple is through the Walled City, and without a map, you'll get nowhere near. Even with one, you'd be risking everything."

They stood in silence for a long moment.

"What about Quincy Lee's map?" Julian finally asked the scarred Constable.

"We never could prove it out. Quincy was probably lying to save his skin."

"What's Quincy's map?" Wheeler asked, grasping at this faint hope.

"Lee Shu Lin, known as Quincy, was raised in that ghetto," Julian said. "He was a dope runner and bag boy for the Chin Lo. We busted him on narcotics when he was just fifteen. He panicked and rolled. We talked him into making Johnny a map of the Walled City in return for protection and a reduced sentence, but he committed suicide in jail before he completed it."

"Sounds like you get a lot of that around here," Tanisha said. "Don't you take their belts and shoelaces?"

"They find implements. The jail is a place of little courage. They would rather die than face Triad justice," Johnny said. "If Quincy's map is wrong, we could go in there with an army of police and be picked off in the dark, one at a time, while we wandered around helpless as blind children."

"What about Jackie Pullinger?" Julian suggested. "Show her the map maybe. She could confirm it and complete it."

Johnny smiled and shrugged. "Much has changed since we were partners. I went to see her in the hospital a year ago. She's ninety-five years old and crazy as a box a' birds. I can't trust that map, and nobody is talking. The rumor I have is that Henry Liu is the new Shan Chu of the Chin Lo. Willy has pulled way back, possibly to distance himself before the election. 'Limpy' Liu is even more violent than Willy. He will kill anybody who considers talking."

"I'd like to see Quincy's map," Tanisha said, "if you still have it. And I'd like to try to talk to Jackie Pullinger. If we can get a map, can't we originate a police raid and search the Temple?"

"If anybody could arrange that, Johnny can," Julian said, proudly. "Johnny has enough Guan-Xi to pull it off."

"I'd be grateful for the professional courtesy. One cop to another," she added.

"I can make you a photocopy of the map," Johnny finally said, "and you can go talk to Miss Pullinger. She was the only White person ever to live in the Walled City. They say she gave Wo Lap Ling his name, Willy, and taught him English. When he became a Triad leader, selling dope to other children, she vowed to get him. However, she's in the Colony hatch and not right in the head. You'd belong in there with her if you listen to anything that crazy old woman tells you now."

"We'd like to try," Wheeler concurred.

Johnny and Julian looked at each other. A silent message of some sort seemed to pass between them. "You'd be better served to just beetle off back to America and leave this be," Johnny said sadly. "But if you want to try, I guess we're good for another go. I'll get the map copied and meet you for dinner tonight, in Wan Chai, at the Black Swan." Johnny looked at the watch on his scarred, bony wrist. "I've got to get back to court. See you at eight then." He walked out of the museum, leaving them standing there.

"If you've got a jiff, let me show you something," Julian said, and he led them out of the Narcotics Room of the Police Museum and into the Triad Room. He searched the photographs on the wall and finally found the one he wanted. He pointed to a picture of a burned apartment house. Next to it was a shot of a man scorched beyond recognition on a hospital stretcher. "That's Johnny Kwong, right after the fire. It was published in the Hong Kong paper two days later, and I recognized the ring on his right hand. Took me a week to find him. They had him in the Adventist Hospital in Hong Kong under a John Doe."

Wheeler looked closely at the picture. He thought he saw something. He leaned in closer. "What's that?" Wheeler asked. "It looks like a 1414 written on his forehead." It was exactly the same as Angie Wong.

"Westerners often think that. It looks like two fourteens, but it's not."

185

"What is it?" Tanisha said, leaning in with Wheeler, studying the three-year-old photo of the terribly burned face of Johnny Kwong.

"It's Hakow writing, an old Chinese dialect mandated obsolete by the Communists. But the language is still written and used by some peasants in the Walled City."

"What does it mean?" Wheeler asked.

"It's a promise and a curse," Julian said softly. "It means 'Certain death, certain death.' "

TWENTY-ONE

Bridge of Clouds

It was just after one in the afternoon when Wheeler and Tanisha finally arrived at St. Mary's Hospital for the elderly and infirm in the northern New Territories. The hospital was a small one-story main building with several wings jutting off on each side. Painted white and perched in the center of a rich green meadow, it looked like something out of *The Sound of Music.*

They parked their rented Mercedes in the circular drive and walked inside.

Behind the reception desk was a Chinese woman in a nun's habit working diligently over a sheaf of papers. She looked up, smiling as they approached.

"We're looking for Jackie Pullinger," Wheeler said.

"Oh," the nun replied. "You're from her Solicitor's office. We've been expecting you. I have the final tally all prepared. Her nephew is in there now, clearing out her bureau and bedside locker."

"He's doing what?" Tanisha asked, an alarm going off in her head. "Clearing the room?"

"Yes," the nun said softly. "Because as you know, Miss Pullinger has left us. She passed on, God rest her soul."

"When?" Wheeler asked.

"Just two days past. So I daresay, if we don't know that, we're not from her Solicitor's office, are we?" the nun surmised.

"That's like an attorney?" Wheeler asked, and the nun nodded. "No, we're not. Sorry to bother you," Wheeler said, and started to go.

Tanisha was still looking at the nun. "Could we talk to her nephew?"

"I suppose so, if he's still there. Miss Pullinger didn't have many belongings. He may have already toddled off."

"Where's her room?" Tanisha asked.

"It's outside, to the right. Number six. There's a wing with cottages." She pointed in the direction of the room, and they thanked her and left.

"Her nephew?" Tanisha said as they moved quickly down the path to the right. "Didn't Julian tell us just an hour ago that she came here in 1929 from England, that she lived her whole life alone in Kowloon, never leaving that ghetto? What fucking nephew?"

"Damn! You're right," Wheeler said.

They quickened their pace until they got to number six. They paused at the door and could hear dresser drawers opening and closing. Tanisha reached into her purse and took out a .25-caliber Glock that she'd brought with her from Los Angeles. A policeman could check a gun with airport security and retrieve it at the other end. The Glock was a short-barreled, highly inaccurate weapon whose chief virtue was that it was extremely light.

She silently turned the knob and pushed the door open. They could see a man with his back to them. He was dark-haired, medium-built, and was looking through a jewelry box, working quickly and quietly.

"What are you doing?" Tanisha said.

The man spun, his eyes glazed with fright. He saw the gun in Tanisha's hand, and although she hadn't pointed it at him, she was

188

holding it at the ready by her side. The man was about twenty-five and Chinese. He was still holding the jewelry box. Suddenly he threw it at them and lunged across the room and out a side door that led onto a sunporch. As Wheeler bolted after him, he could feel the stitches in his right leg snap like buttons popping off a shirt. Pain from that week-old injury shot up his thigh. He kept going; in three strides, he was out the door, limping badly. He saw the young man vault the three-foot wall, heading toward the meadow and a stand of willow trees a hundred yards away. Wheeler hurdled the low wall, picking up precious yards with the more athletic maneuver, but his right leg almost buckled when he landed. He lurched on.

This is for Pres, his mind screamed. *Go . . . go . . . forget the pain!*

He was close enough to launch a flying tackle off his good left leg. With his outstretched right hand, Wheeler managed to catch the fleeing man's ankle as he fell. The Chinese youth hit the ground hard, rolled, and all in one motion came up on both feet, balanced and ready for combat. Because of his leg, Wheeler was slower getting up, and as he rose, he caught a mouthful of shoe leather as the young man's foot swept his face, busting his mouth with a perfectly executed spin kick. Wheeler went down. Blood started to flow from his mouth. He got up again and limped toward the man, who hit him three times with karate-hardened knuckles. Wheeler, who had had combat training in the Marines, caught two of the shots on his forearms but ate the third. It rocked him back. His bad leg folded, he went down, and the man moved in to finish him.

A gunshot ripped the silence and the young man froze.

About twenty yards away, Tanisha was in a Weaver stance, her legs spread wide for balance, the ugly square-barreled Glock aimed right at the young man's chest. Wheeler picked himself up slowly as Tanisha moved in, holding the gun on the Chinese man. Blood oozed from Wheeler's mouth and leg, staining his new Gap clothing.

"Who are you?" Tanisha asked, her voice quivering. "You speak English?"

"I'm Chan Chak," he said. "I'm Miss Pullinger's nephew."

"She's English, you're Chinese. Get a better story, sugar," Tanisha said as she moved close, still holding the gun on him, aiming for his midsection, where she had the largest target for the inaccurate short-barreled automatic.

"All of us, her students, her helpers, she called us her nieces and nephews. I loved her," he said.

"And that's why you were going through her things?"

"She promised me this," he said and held up a simple gold crucifix. "She said when she crossed the bridge of clouds, I should come over straightaway and fetch it. She wanted me to have it. She said not to wait for the State Solicitor General because the Chinese death taxes will take it." He was still breathing hard. Wheeler reached out and took the cross, looking at it carefully.

"There's something written on it. If she promised this to you, you should know what it is," he said.

"P-11-21," Chan Chak said, his chest still heaving as he struggled to catch his breath. "It's from the Bible; Proverbs 11, Verse 21: 'Though hand join in hand, the wicked shall not be unpunished: but the seed of the righteous shall be delivered.' That was her message. It was what her life was about. It was why she lived. To prove to all of us that we could be delivered. She gave it to me, it's my inheritance, my memory of her." He looked at Wheeler defiantly.

So Wheeler handed it back to him.

Wheeler had his pants off and Tanisha was looking at the week-old bullet wound in his thigh. "It doesn't look that bad," she said. "It's already healing on the inside. This slug musta had eyes— missed the bone and all the major veins and arteries. Just tore a hole in the fleshy part. Couple stitches and you'll be ready to rumble."

They were sitting in Jackie Pullinger's room. Chan Chak wouldn't tell them where he lived, so they had opened his wallet and copied his business address off one of his cards. The young man was now standing nearby, looking at them with a strange, fearful expression on his face. After a minute, a Chinese nun arrived with bandages and some disinfectant. She started to wash carefully around Wheeler's wound. It had puckered slightly at the edges as it began to pull together and heal. After painting on a disinfectant, she wrapped it tightly with a bandage and clipped it with fasteners. She spoke no English, so Chan Chak conversed with her in Chinese.

"She's a medical nurse and says you should have a doctor look at it, but she says it seems to be healing."

Wheeler pulled his pants on.

"You took off like an N.F.L. running back," Tanisha grinned. "Not bad for a guy with a bullet hole in his leg."

"You probably didn't see me soak up all that shoe leather Mr. Chan was delivering."

"Doesn't count," she smiled. " 'Cause technically, you're still on injured reserve."

Chan Chak closed the door after the nun left. "I have to go. I have things to do. Thank you for letting me keep the crucifix," he said and turned to leave.

"Did Jackie ever talk to you about Wo Lap Ling?" Wheeler asked.

Chan Chak froze, then slowly turned back again.

"Why?" he asked warily.

"I just wondered."

"She thought he was a devil, the nastiest sort. She thought he needed to be stopped." Chan Chak had no British accent. His English still rang with the singing lilt of Chinese.

"She wasn't crazy at all, was she?" Wheeler said. "When the police came, she only pretended to be nuts."

Chan Chak hesitated, started to answer, then stopped. It was as good as an admission.

"Why didn't she want to help the police if she felt Wo Lap Ling was such a devil?" Wheeler continued.

"I don't know. She was old and frightened. She had given

her life to others. She deserved a little peace before she crossed her bridge."

"And you were one of her nephews?" Tanisha asked. "You were a disciple of Miss Pullinger's?"

"Yes. I was chasing the dragon by the time I was ten. She got me off drugs, taught me English. She named me 'Chauncy.' "

" 'Chasing the dragon' is heroin," Tanisha said to Wheeler.

"Wo Lap Ling had also been one of her nephews," Chauncy Chan continued. "She prayed for him because she had once loved him, but he went bad. He became one of the Triad devils. He sold poison in the Walled City and joined the Chin Lo. He ended up being the Shan Chu, the worst of the worst. 'A dreadful piece of mischief,' she called him. And she devoted her life to stopping him and others like him, but she also had to co-exist with him. There is no way an English woman alone can destroy the mighty Chin Lo or its most powerful Shan Chu. She had to swim in their ocean and avoid being devoured."

They looked at him, both thinking Chauncy Chan could be a valuable resource. Tanisha finally stood and moved closer.

"You were raised in the Walled City. You lived there, didn't you?"

He looked frightened for a minute, then the look passed and he nodded.

"We need your help, Chauncy. If we brought you a partial map of the Walled City, could you tell us if it is accurate and correct, and complete it for us?" she asked him.

"Anybody who draws a map of the Walled City of Kowloon will die the Living Death." His voice was stretched tight with fear. "The Living Death takes three days. They keep you alive with medicines, they use acupuncture needles to awaken the dying nerves so you can feel the pain more clearly. They cut your muscles and tendons a strand at a time so they snap back against the bone. They feed you to rodents who crawl up your anus and devour your insides while you are still alive. It would be better to set yourself on fire."

"We're at the Peninsula Hotel," Wheeler said after a pause. "If you can help us . . ." And he stopped because Chan Chak looked away from them, casting his eyes down.

"She was very brave," he finally said, his voice reverent in memory, soft as a rustling wind. "She could somehow swim in their water and avoid the stinging fish. I am just a shoemaker. I work with leather. I have two children and a wife who is very sick from malaria. I am not as strong as Miss Pullinger, I am only human. She was the Lord Buddha's child. I do not have her courage. I never will have. I cannot help you." And then he turned and left them there, alone.

TWENTY-TWO

The Mucky Duck

T he Black Swan restaurant was on the second floor of the Corral nightclub in the Wan Chai district of Hong Kong. The music vibrations came up through the floorboards from the strip club below. Wheeler and Tanisha sat in a booth in the small back room, which the restaurant reserved for VIPs like Johnny Kwong, and watched in fascination as the famous scarred inspector spooned cooked brains out of the skull of a dead tree monkey. The furry head of the primate had been severed, the top of the skull cut and removed at mid-forehead; the brains were cooked at the table. Julian Winslow was eating another traditional dish called pork-ball soup, which emitted a strong, pungent odor in the hot, enclosed back room. Tanisha and Wheeler had both lost their appetites when the monkey head had been sawed. On the table in front of them was uneaten fish-ball soup and a copy of Quincy's map. It was a baffling drawing that showed a hundred or more crisscrossing lines, some dead-ending, others wandering aimlessly and turning back on themselves like a spilled plate of spaghetti. There was Chinese writing all over the map, which

194

Johnny said indicated approximate distances. The map was incomplete, confusing, and almost impossible to read. Worse still, Johnny explained, it only depicted the front two blocks of the Walled City, which stretched for ten, in all directions around the central park where the temple sat.

"Bloody shame," Johnny said between spoonfuls of monkey brains. "If I coulda got the whole thing, we might have run a raid on Willy Wo Lap and caught him on the glimmer."

Wheeler was still looking at the map, distressed at the myriad of transecting, wandering lines. "Who designed this place?" he finally said.

"Nobody did," Julian said. "It grew like a jungle fungus, one floor over another, took whatever shape it wanted. If a block of flats tumbled down, the people would scavenge for what was usable, bury the dead, and just build right over it. Reeks in there from garbage and rot. Got no proper sewage."

"I understand Miss Pullinger is no longer with us," Johnny said as he finished the last bite and wiped his napkin across cracked yellow lips.

"Yes, but we met a man named Chan Chak," Wheeler said. "He was one of Jackie Pullinger's disciples, if that's the right word for it. A man about twenty-five. He was raised inside the Walled City. He's a shoemaker. We got his business address."

Johnny put out his hand, and Wheeler dug the address out of his pocket and handed it to the detective. "I know this place. It's in Kowloon," Johnny said, handing it back. "He won't talk. The peasants are even more scared of Limpy Liu than they were of Willy. Evil, skinny, limping bastard's got a complexion like lunar lava, and a heart yellow as piss. If anybody goes up against him, he'll have their guts for garters."

Tanisha had remained silent through most of this. She was looking at Julian Winslow and Johnny Kwong, using her cop's instinct to see into the dark corners of their complex relationship. Something wasn't right. There was too much intrigue in Hong Kong. She could already tell that there was almost no fraternal trust among the police. Everybody was a potential spy. Julian ate with his eyes down, not looking at them. Something unhealthy was going on, but she couldn't pin it. It was a feeling she had learned to trust. Her instincts had saved her more than once in the street. Now they were screaming at her, but she couldn't figure out which way to look, or even what was going on. She didn't know the rules here. She was lost.

After dinner, they went downstairs to the Corral nightclub. It was a grind joint with nude Philippine and Thai dancers, slithering onstage and humping brass poles. A loud band played American rock-and-roll badly, slots rang, and mah-jongg tiles and dice clicked on twenty green felt tables. They moved to a game room and watched through an atmosphere thick with cigarette smoke, while Johnny Kwong stacked the little tiles in front of him and made a large bet. His scarred features revealed nothing. The fire had done him one favor—it gave him the ultimate gambler's face.

Johnny Kwong seemed to be well known at the Corral. People waved to him and shouted greetings while he played. Julian led them to the bar and ordered for them in Chinese. Tanisha had a wine cooler, Wheeler ordered a cola. She looked over, surprised at the choice. She had been mildly aware of the fact that he hadn't been drinking since they left Cleveland. At dinner, he'd passed on the wine list; he hadn't opened the mini-bar in the suite or even had a free drink on the plane. She looked down at his hands to see if they were shaking but he had them tucked safely in his pockets.

"This is one of the big clubs in the Wanch," Julian said. "The Wanch is the whole tenderloin district in Wan Chai."

"It's also a Ho-tel," Tanisha said matter-of-factly.

"Beg pardon?" Julian asked.

"Those are the Ho's over there," she said, pointing to a string of B-girls lounging on stools at the far side of the room. They were wearing fuck-me shoes and lacy see-through tops, with slit skirts that showed they wore no underwear. "The grind rooms are back there, behind the curtains," she said, just as two girls got off their stools and approached some Chinese men. Then they accompanied the men across the room and through the curtains. "Cha-Ching," Tanisha grinned.

"You're right," Julian nodded. "This is a bit of a knocking shop. Prostitution is illegal in Hong Kong, but everybody looks the other way. The girls take the customers back to the plastic-lined rooms and manipulate them to orgasm. A while back, one of our British legislators, Dame Lydia Dunn, inspected this place for the Health Ministry. She insisted on looking back there. They didn't have time to freshen up the stalls, and when she looked down and saw all the tissues on the floor, the Lady said, 'It must be very unhealthy here, because the poor girls all have colds.' Bloody true story," he grinned. "But the Black Swan, upstairs, is one of the best Chinese restaurants in the city. Johnny calls it the Mucky Duck, 'cause the illegal proceeds from downstairs help fund the restaurant overhead. Johnny also likes it because he can pop down here after and get his oil changed. Lookin' like he does, it's his only play with the ladies."

Julian looked over at Johnny, who was winning now, a small fortress of chips in front of him. "You should have seen him before the fire," Julian said reflectively. "What a figure of a man he was, like a cinema star. Women everywhere. He certainly paid his dues to the Crown, that one has." There was a tinge of anger mixed with the remorse. "The only way to get inside Willy's temple is a full-on police raid. Be a big operation," Julian continued. "Johnny has good connections with the Independent Commission Against Corruption. There still are straight coppers on that detail. If we can get a map drawn, you can bet Johnny will find a way to put a raid together."

"We're gonna take off," Tanisha finally said, "unless you want to stay, Wheeler."

"I'm outta here, too," Wheeler said, picking up his cue.

"There's a taxi rank directly outside," Julian told them.

"Something is very kinky," Tanisha said, "and I'm not talking about what goes on in those plastic-covered booths."

They were back in the Mandarin Suite at The Pen and she had changed into the hotel robe. It was belted around her slender waist. She had her feet up under her, curled in the club chair that faced the window. She was holding the incomplete Xeroxed map of the Walled City.

Wheeler was standing next to her, looking out at the harbor. "Are we getting jerked off?" he wondered aloud.

The neon across the harbor threw shafts of light on the water that reached across the bay toward them, like the ivory fingers on a Chinese fan. The speedboats raced in the dark, their fast-moving running lights streaking like fireflies under the heavy cloud-black sky.

"I can't shake the feeling that something isn't right," she said and dropped the map on the table, "but I'm too tired to figure out what. I'm bushed. Going to bed." And that's what she did.

The phone woke him up at four in the morning.

"I can't find Johnny," Julian's slightly drunk voice announced. "His phone isn't picking up."

"You can't find who?" Wheeler was clawing up from a deep, dreamless sleep. Finally, he broke surface and reassembled his thoughts.

"Johnny Kwong," Julian said. "He sounded different when he called me two hours back, like some bloke who just lost a shilling and found a sixpence. Then, all of a sudden, he was sort of saying good-bye. Hard to explain, but I partnered with him for five years. I couldn't get to sleep, worrying, so I paged him. He's not returning. Something's gone whacker."

"Where are you?"

"I'm . . . I'm, well, laddie, I'm not in church."

Then Wheeler heard a woman laughing and he knew where. "Okay, what's his address? I'll meet you there," Wheeler said. "We'll all take a look."

"He lives in a flat not fifteen minutes from you, on Queens

Road East, two thousand six. It's going to take me a little longer."

"We'll wait outside till you get there."

The row of flats was old and architecturally unimpressive. It sat in nondescript blockiness on the corner of Queens Road and Swallow Street. Tanisha and Wheeler had been waiting for fifteen minutes when Julian pulled his English Ford Popular over to the curb in front of their Mercedes rental and joined them by the car.

"Nice of you to come over. Didn't want to call headquarters and make a muck of it for Johnny. The new Commie Supers are lookin' for any reason to cashier all us old Royal Constabulary coppers," he said. He looked to Wheeler and Tanisha, who both thought he was still drunk. They all moved across the street and into the apartment building. It was almost five A.M. and the sun was beginning to lighten the distant horizon.

They took the lift up to the third floor, then Julian stopped in front of an unmarked door and knocked. There was no answer.

"How do we get in? Pick it?" Tanisha said.

"I know where he keeps the drop key," Julian said. He moved down the hall to the fire extinguisher, opened it, reached in, and found it on top of the coiled hose. "No sprinklers in this building. You'd think, after what happened, Johnny would get a flat with overhead water." He fit the key into the lock, turned it, and they entered.

Johnny's apartment was a mess. Somebody had thoroughly searched it. The contents were strewn everywhere. The upholstered chair seats were overturned and ripped open from underneath. The shelves were emptied, books and small artifacts strewn everywhere. It reminded Wheeler of his brother's house after the Chinese gangsters had been there.

"This is a spot of too bad," Julian muttered, pulling out his 7.65mm Russian automatic.

They moved through the place carefully, but it was empty. Then they began their own thorough search.

Tanisha used her thumbnail to swing the bathroom cabinet open. It was still full of cosmetics and pills, indicating that Johnny hadn't left on his own. She could see a tube of Tiger Balm ointment, and some lotions and creams on the shelves which, she assumed, Johnny used to keep his horribly burned scar tissue lubricated.

When they finished searching the apartment, Tanisha came out of the bedroom and found Wheeler looking down at a silver-framed photograph in his hand.

"You shouldn't be touching that," she reminded him.

He turned and showed it to her. It was a picture of Angela Wong, a little younger, maybe five years before. Her hair was bobbed and she was in a Disney World T-shirt. In the picture with her was a handsome Chinese man, about twenty-five. As Tanisha looked closer, she saw it was the same man whose picture had been on Angela Wong's stomach in her basement workout room in Torrance, California.

"Who is this?" Tanisha asked Julian, pointing to the handsome young man.

Julian crossed the flat and looked at the picture. "That's Johnny, before the fire," he said. "With his mum, who lives in America."

TWENTY-THREE

Sleeping with a Tiger

T he assault on his senses had been overpowering. Fu Hai had walked blindfolded in the dark for twenty minutes or more, flies buzzing in his ears, his hand on the belt of the tall man in front of him. He fought desperately to control his gag reflex. Then, as if by magic, he felt afternoon sunshine on his face and arms. The stench of human waste and rotting sewage was replaced by cherry blossoms so sweet he could barely contain his sensory joy. His feet moved across grass now. He could hear birds singing. A man's voice spoke softly to him in Mandarin.

"You will wait here."

Strong hands disengaged his grip from the belt he had been clutching and placed his hands at his side. Fu Hai wanted desperately to please these voices who now controlled his life and future.

He had lost track of time waiting in the dark Key Room just inside the Walled City. He had been able to endure the smell because of an air shaft that connected to the street. A young boy brought him tasteless food once a day but didn't talk to him. Fu

Hai sat on the floor, his head on his knees, and prayed that he would soon be released from this dungeon without a lock. He had wanted to get up and run out into the street, but he had no place to go. The thing that held him there had been his dreams of America. He didn't know how much time had passed, several days, maybe longer. Then an extremely tall man, about thirty years old, came and handed him a blindfold. He was told to put it on, that it was time to leave.

He had been led blindfolded through the stench-filled Walled City and was now someplace else, someplace very different. He was standing in the sunshine with the sweet smell of flowers and fresh-cut grass in his nose. Then, after a great deal of time had passed, the tall man came back and, without removing the blindfold, led him a short distance farther into a building. His feet were now on hard tiles and he heard a heavy door close behind him.

"Take off the cloth," the tall man said.

Fu Hai reached behind his head and removed the knotted rag. He was in a beautiful place: A magnificent carved ceiling was above his head; gold-leaf statuary of dragons and snakes sat on stone-carved pillars in the entry where he was standing. The windows looked out on a huge meadow, and in the distance maybe a hundred meters away, he could see the backs of rotting buildings that he assumed were the ghetto in the Walled City through which he had just come. He could hear wind chimes somewhere nearby.

"Prepare to meet the great and most powerful Incense Master," the tall man said.

"How will I prepare?" Fu Hai asked.

"You will make yourself humble. You will realize that before such wisdom you are nothing. Prepare to accept any wish he commands of you, or you will go no farther."

"Will he send me to America?"

"You must not ask for favors. To attempt to bargain will only bring disgrace. One must serve the powerful to achieve one's destiny."

The tall man left, and Fu Hai remembered a Confucian wisdom taught to him at school: *"Serving the powerful is like sleeping with a tiger,"* the Master had warned.

Soon the door opened and four old men in flowing red robes came into the magnificent enclosure. They were all very impressive, with gray hair and eyes that reflected ageless knowledge. Fu Hai was instantly both afraid of them and drawn to them. Then the most impressive of the four men approached him.

"I am Jiang Hu," he said. In Chinese, *jiang hu* meant "the rivers and the lakes," and the name referred to any man who had a floating lifestyle, a sense of detachment from society. The old man was telling Fu Hai that he was a member of the Chinese subculture, a gangster.

"You are privileged to be brought to this holy place," the old man said. "This Temple is called the City of Willows. You are just inside the east gate, which, if you choose, is the beginning of your journey. Few get this far, but after accepting this road, none may leave. Many things happen in this place. . . . It is the opening flower, a place of extreme awakening. The first step on a path to a new life and the place where all recruits must register. Do you understand?" Fu Hai nodded.

"From here there is no return. If you go forward, there is either success or failure, life or death. There is no other option. Do you wish to continue on this journey?"

Fu Hai wanted to go to America. He wanted to save his beautiful sister, who had been made ugly by her life. He knew no way but the path he was on. He nodded his head to show he understood the consequences.

"Good," the old man said. "I am the Incense Master of this great and secret society. To enter here, you must do whatever I instruct. Is this your wish?"

Again, Fu Hai nodded his head.

"That door," he said, "leads to a life of power." The Incense Master pointed to a door with a sign above it that read *Yap ki mun fei chung mat wong,* which meant "Go no farther if you are not loyal." The man in the red robe wrote Fu Hai's name in a book of recruits and then opened the door. Fu Hai walked into a small inner room with another door and one window. The Incense Master and the three men with him encircled Fu Hai.

"There are four entrances to the City of Willows," the Incense Master said. "The City of Willows is open to all men who can prove worthy of being Brethren. The Red Flower Pavilion beyond this door embraces all, regardless of class or rank. A peasant from the Western Provinces is as valuable to us here as a wealthy, powerful businessman from Beijing or a policeman in Hong Kong. If you obey our laws, you will never again fear other men, but there is much to learn," the Incense Master instructed. "To become a member of this secret society you must experience three days of spiritual evaluation and teachings. During this time, you must prove that you are willing to sacrifice yourself for your Brethren. But once a recruit has passed into the City of Willows, he is defined only by his association here. He is no longer a sparrow who flits from tree to tree, looking for lint to build a nest. He becomes instead an eagle who swoops from on high and slaughters life, grabbing it in his talons, but always obeying the three great rules: the rules of this society, the rules of nature, and the rules of the Lord Buddha."

Fu Hai couldn't believe his ears. Was it possible that in three days he could become knighted with such power? Become the equal of the wealthy?

"Is this your desire?" the Incense Master asked.

"Yes," Fu Hai said, bowing his head to show respect.

"But we are a Society of strict laws. As there are great rewards, so are there great penalties. A traitor to the Brethren must suffer a Living Death. It is important that you understand. Are you strong enough to experience our rewards as well as our penalties?" the Incense Master asked him.

"Yes," Fu Hai said.

"Then you will wait here," the Incense Master said. "It will not be long. You are a caterpillar who has asked to become a butterfly. Prepare to attempt to change yourself forever."

They left him in the small room just inside the east gate of the Temple the Incense Master had called the City of Willows. Fu Hai sat on a hard bench and smelled the flowers through the open window and tried to imagine what it would feel like to not be afraid of other men. He could not do it.

An hour passed, maybe more, before they came and got him. He was led out of the room, and a novitiate's plain white robe was slipped over his head. It went all the way to the floor.

"You are safe here. It is important that you know that," the Incense Master said. "The four gates of the City of Willows are guarded by the four great and ancient faithful ones. The spirit of Lee Cheung Kwok guards the north gate, Hon Fuk the west, Chang Tin the south gate, and Hon Png the east. No enemy of the Triad, mortal or spiritual, can reach you here." Then he opened a door and led Fu Hai into the magnificent Red Flower Pavilion.

There were approximately a hundred other people in the huge open room. All were dressed in identical red robes, the only exception being Fu Hai and four other initiates in white, who were just inside the first gate, which was a freestanding threshold in the back of the Pavilion. The initiates were led past the second threshold. They skirted the edge of the hall, moving around two other symbolic gates. They were told they had not yet earned the right to pass beneath them. The Incense Master led them to a spot where they had an unobstructed view of a magnificent altar at the front of the room.

The Incense Master spoke softly to the initiates, describing important symbols in the City of Willows. "Before us, farthest from the altar, is the Heaven and Earth circle," he said, pointing to a large symbolic circle on the floor, farthest away from the huge, beautifully decorated altar. "It blends the mortal qualities of the earthbound with our great spiritual ancestors. Beyond that is the fire pit, which you will soon cross and which will symbolize your lack of fear and pain. Then, closer to the altar, you see the large stepping-stones that symbolize the righteous path of the Brethren of the Chin Lo. Finally, the two-planked bridge that leads to the altar. Only the most surefooted traveler can cross this bridge to experience the true power of life," the Incense Master said. "You undoubtedly will wonder at the trials before you. You may even question their value, but as a muddy river will one day become clear, so will the wisdom of these trials. To be persistent in this task, from start to finish, is a virtuous thing," he told them.

Fu Hai couldn't believe the splendor of the place. Great sayings hung from ornate banners on the walls all around the hall. But more important than the splendor or the spectacle was the way the Incense Master spoke to them. It was as if they were important guests, valued additions to this place. No powerful person had ever before addressed Fu Hai in this fashion.

The Incense Master pointed to one thing after another, giving them brief descriptions of everything and explaining what each object stood for. He pointed to the engraved tablets on the walls which honored other Triad chapters.

On the huge, festooned altar he pointed out each of the symbolic articles. The Tau, which was a large wooden tub filled with rice, each grain said to represent a society member, all equal in size, shape, and importance. He pointed out the flags of the ancients, including the Five Tiger Generals, and the flags of the Four Great Faithful Ones. The current Shan Chu's own flag was there—the beautiful gold warrant banner of the most high and holy leader. In a large holder near the front of the altar was an ugly red club, which the Incense Master told them was the symbol of Triad punishment. Also adorning the altar was the Sword of Loyalty and Righteousness, which he said represented the sword of Kwan Kung, God of War. It was used only for initiation of the holy and execution of Triad traitors. He went on pointing out everything: the yellow umbrella, signifying the Ming Emperors who had allowed the first Triads to flourish in the 1500s; a large white paper fan, constructed of bamboo with thirteen ribs, representing the administrative divisions of China under the Ming Dynasty; the abacus, which once calculated the sins and debts of the Chinese people, and now represented the economic power of the Triad; and the beautiful, ornate scales of justice to weigh and guarantee the equality of all Triad members. The banners that hung over the altar preached great wisdom in glorious gold-threaded Chinese symbols. Fu Hai read as many as he could see:

FAITHFUL ONES MAY JOIN THE SOCIETY.
DISLOYAL ONES MUST OFFER INCENSE HERE.
THE HEROES ARE SUPREME.
THE BRAVE HAVE NO EQUAL.

Then the doors opened on the north gate and a man with a hood over his head was led into the hall. He walked slowly and seemed to be in great pain. He was led by a very thin, ugly man who limped badly when he walked. The limping man wore a magnificent white robe adorned with beautiful gold thread. It was the only robe in the Pavilion that had any decorative symbols. The Incense Master whispered that the man in the hood was a traitor to the Triad, and that the skinny man in the beautiful embroidered robe was the most powerful Shan Chu, President and Supreme Leader of the Chin Lo. He pointed to another man who was standing on the platform of elders and whispered that he was the Vice President of the Society, the most powerful White Fan.

The Shan Chu led the hooded man to the altar and pushed him down before it. Then the Shan Chu reached down and snapped off the hood. The kneeling man had been severely beaten; his face was bloody and there were only a few teeth left in his mouth. Stranger still was the fact that the man was covered with scars. He had once been horribly burned. His face and bald head were grotesquely altered by flames. Several of his fingers had been burned off. His yellow lips were stretched thin in pain and resignation.

"You have betrayed the oath and you must pay the price of sin against your brothers," the Shan Chu said loudly in the hushed Temple. Then he pulled the Sword of Loyalty and Righteousness out of its ornate scabbard. Five muscular vanguards from the Triad's honored Red-Pole fighting section moved forward and tied thongs around the scarred man's hands and feet, then he was pushed down to the floor. His clothing was removed by the van-guards, cut from his body with short knives. Fu Hai could see that the rest of the man's body was also horribly scarred.

What happened next was a riot to Fu Hai's senses. He watched in fascination and horror as the most powerful Shan Chu performed the Death by a Myriad of Swords on the horribly scarred man, slowly drawing the Sword of Loyalty and Righteous-ness across the man's body, first here, then there. With each cut, the man screamed in pain. The five vanguards held him down as his bloody body bucked, arched, and jerked in agony, but the scarred man was held firmly in place before the altar.

It went on for almost a half-hour until the traitor was covered in his own blood and his horrible screams had died to whimpers. When he was finally silent, Fu Hai knew he was most surely dead.

It was ghastly and inhumane, yet it was also somehow spec-tacular and awe-inspiring, because it demonstrated the immense power of the Shan Chu. That he could commit this horrible crimi-nal act in front of hundreds of witnesses, without fear of discovery, certainly displayed his supreme power.

Fu Hai wondered who the scarred man was and what he had done to deserve such a terrible death.

They came for him in darkness. He was lying on a grass mat in the garden pavilion of the great Temple building. They shook him awake as, nearby, the other initiates slept, unaware. They led him silently, under a quarter moon, out of the garden pavilion into the main building, just inside the Temple entrance. The red-robed In-cense Master was waiting for him in candlelight, holding a large, magnificent yellow gauze quilt embroidered with Chinese calligra-phy. Fu Hai was still rubbing the sleep out of his eyes, but his heart began to beat faster.

"This is the Sha Tz'u Pei," the Incense Master said, holding up the quilt for him to see. "It contains all of the sacred oaths of the Chin Lo society. Even though you are just an initiate, tonight you have been chosen for a great mission, but you must swear that you are worthy of our trust. . . . Can you do this?"

"Yes," Fu Hai said.

"You have been chosen because you have already received a tremendous gift from the Society. We have given you a new life and asked for nothing. No member of your family has been pledged to us if you default. You have been embraced as few have and given a long journey for which you owe us a great accounting. Tonight you must begin to repay. As our proposed brother and one who has asked to join our number, we have trusted you for many million *yuan*. But you must do certain extra things to repay our great trust and generosity. For this reason, you have been chosen. Tonight is the beginning," the Incense Master said. "Do you understand your duty?"

Again Fu Hai nodded.

"Before you go on this mission, you must read one oath of fealty and four oaths of allegiance and you must swear to each oath. These oaths must not be taken lightly. To fail in this will bring dishonor and terrible death. Do you understand?"

Fu Hai nodded. He did not want to end like the scarred man in the Red Flower Pavilion. The Incense Master took the gauze quilt and placed it on a low table before Fu Hai. He gently pushed Fu Hai to his knees and pointed to the thirty-sixth and last oath. "Read and swear," he said softly.

"After entering the Chin Lo gates, I shall be loyal and faithful," Fu Hai read aloud. "I shall endeavor to overthrow the Ching and restore the Ming by coordinating my efforts with those of my sworn Brethren. Our common aim is to avenge our five great ancestors."

"This is a historic oath of fealty. It deals with our great and bloody past, with the historic plight of the Five Tiger Generals. To appreciate the past is to see into the future," the Incense Master told him. "This morning you will perform a work of honor for your Brethren . . . but there is some risk. Should things go badly, the Brethren must know you can be trusted. For this reason, you must swear the four oaths of allegiance." He pointed to the fifth oath embroidered on the Sha Tz'u Pei. "Read and swear," he instructed.

"I swear I shall not disclose the secrets of the Chin Lo family, even to my parents, my brothers, or my wife. I shall never disclose the secrets for money. If I do, I will be killed by a Myriad of Swords." Fu Hai read these words in a soft voice, again shuddering at the memory of the horrible ceremony he had witnessed just a few hours before.

The Incense Master then pointed to oath number six:

"I swear I shall never betray my sworn brother," Fu Hai read. "If through a misunderstanding or mistake I have caused the arrest of one of my brothers, I must give my life to attempt to release him. If I break this oath, I will be killed by Five Thunderbolts."

Then the Incense Master pointed to oath number eighteen:

"If I am arrested after committing an offense, I swear I will accept my punishment and not try to place blame upon my sworn Brethren. If I fail this oath, I will die by Five Thunderbolts."

Then the Incense Master pointed to the last oath he wanted Fu Hai to read. It was oath number twelve:

"If I have supplied false information about myself for the purpose of joining the Chin Lo secret society, I will die by a Myriad of Swords," Fu Hai said softly.

Suddenly, he was pulled to his feet and embraced by the Incense Master. Fu Hai could smell the soft, sweet fragrance of flowered soap on the old man. Then the Incense Master held him at arms' length and looked at him as a father would a beloved son.

"There will be many trials for you, Fu Hai," he said. "This is but your first. It is the first step along the path of true believers."

Fu Hai was taken out of the Temple to the grass park. On all four sides, he could see the backs of buildings that made up the inside of the Walled City. Four young men dressed in black waited for him. Two were holding Russian AK-47s. Fu Hai looked at the ugly machines of death and wondered what he was supposed to do. Then, one at a time, all four men embraced Fu Hai and called him brother. They again placed a blindfold over his eyes. He was spun three times in a circle until he lost his bearings, then they put his hand on the belt of the man in front of him. He was led out of the grass park and into a building a short distance away. He could not smell the stench of the Walled City, but he knew he was inside one of the buildings that backed up to the central park. Then he was being led down a set of stairs. The sounds of their footsteps echoed in a narrow stairwell. He could no longer smell the sweet cherry blossoms. Damp air now filled his nose. Then Fu Hai was helped into some kind of vehicle. Once it was in motion, he knew it was an electric cart. It hummed as they sped along. Cold, musty air filled his nostrils and blew past his ears. Fu Hai thought they were underground.

After only a few minutes, they stopped and he was helped out of the cart. They climbed another set of stairs. Fu Hai heard several men speaking in low tones. He was frightened and yet very exhilarated. It was like being part of some huge adventure. For the first time in his life, Fu Hai was part of the group; he was no longer a peasant sweating in a silkworm factory while supervisors yelled at him, cursing his stupidity. These men talked to him softly and with respect. He was treated as if he possessed great Guan-Xi.

He was placed in the back seat of a car. He heard men talking about street directions, and then he heard an electric garage door open. Fu Hai felt the car start, and it began to move out of a garage. They were driving now. He heard traffic and buses. One of the men in the car told him, politely, to remove his blindfold. He took it off and saw that he was still with the men who had embraced him in the park. The same two were still holding the Russian machine guns. Fu Hai's heart leaped with conflicting emotions, excitement and fear. He wondered what he would be asked to do. More than anything, he wanted to go to America, but a new feeling had been sweeping over him, coloring his thoughts, making him proud. For the first time in his life, Fu Hai belonged. For the first time, he was part of something much larger than himself.

TWENTY-FOUR

Johnny, We Hardly Knew You

It was just eight o'clock in the morning and they were in Victoria Park, near the swimming pools. Julian said it was best to do your planning outside the People's Police Building, where one didn't have to worry about listening devices. Off to the west, they could see the cars streaming along the elevated causeway. A new workday had begun in the oxymoronic Communist Democracy of the Special Autonomous Region known as Hong Kong. Julian Winslow was looking at his hands as he sat on the wooden bench under an elm tree, deep concern creasing his round, cherubic face.

"Why would they search his apartment? What's going on here, Julian?" Tanisha asked. She was trying to read the cagey nuance in his watery blue eyes. She had sensed something was wrong between Johnny Kwong and Julian Winslow, despite Julian's overwhelming praise of the scarred inspector. Now, before going on, she wanted to find out exactly what it was.

"He was on to the blighters," Julian said, his eyes focused on the distant traffic. "Had been for years. Caused a ruckus for bad cops and criminals alike. Johnny liked putting the cat among the pigeons. The Triads and some of our own bent coppers wanted Johnny dead, you can bet on it."

Tanisha was on the bench beside him, and she leaned over and found his eyes with hers, forcing him to look at her. "Julian, I've been playing cops and robbers since I was ten years old. I've been on both sides of the game. It doesn't work that way in L.A., and my guess is it doesn't work that way in Hong Kong."

Doubt and confusion fought for control of his round face.

"Gangsters don't go after cops, because it's always a stupid play," she continued. "It gets front-page news coverage. It makes politicians crazy. The heat gets turned up on the gangsters. Angry cops start playing catch-up, people die, everybody loses. So something else is going on, and I think you know what it is," she said. "Johnny didn't just disappear because he was investigating the Triads. If that was all it was, it would have happened years ago. There's something very wrong between the two of you. I could feel it last night at the Black Swan and again after dinner. You and Johnny aren't the same as you once were. And, as long as we're at it, I should tell you I also don't like coincidences. I don't like the fact that we called you from Willard Vickers's house in Cleveland, then you bring in Johnny Kwong, who just, by the way, happens to be Angela Wong's son. Angela, whose murder I started out investigating a week ago in California. So just what the fuck is going on?" she demanded.

Julian's arm jerked once in an involuntary reflex, then he took a deep breath, letting it out slowly. "I didn't know about Johnny's mum being murdered, and then, after the fire, Johnny changed," he said, his voice thin and sharp as rusty wire. "Everything was different after that. It's why we stopped working together. I mean, it probably would have happened anyway, because he got famous and won all the Queen's tinware. But still and all, he was different . . . bitter and mad. I was glad to call it cappers. Then, about six months ago, the Independent Commission Against Corruption started a Queen's Inquiry into Johnny himself. It was all a bit close to the knuckle, because

Johnny was a hero and it would have been a mess, should it get out. But everybody knew that Johnny was in the broth."

"What were they investigating him for?" Wheeler asked.

"They thought that after the fire he went over and started working for the Triads."

"Let me get this straight," Tanisha said, amazed. "You mean Willy Wo Lap sets Johnny Kwong on fire and then Johnny goes to work for him? How does that track?"

"You have to understand the way it was here. Johnny was a respected copper, an untouchable, as you Yanks call it . . . part of an elite group who were investigating policemen who had joined the Triads. He was going after the most supreme Shan Chu and his vanguards. Then somebody sets Johnny's flat on fire. They burned him to a cinder, and the bloody Royal Hong Kong Police wouldn't even give him his disability or get him skin grafts. They didn't look for him in the rubble even though they knew Johnny was somewhere in that blaze. The reason for that was he'd become a problem for both sides. They let him rot in a hospital bed as a John Doe. He felt like after all he'd done for the Royal Police, they buggered him off. So he got bitter and mad. Some thought he went to work for the Triad, making Charlies of us all in the bargain."

"And do you believe that?" Wheeler asked.

"Johnny was a hero. He would have helped us if he could. I always thought the corrupt cops were trying to get him before he got them, but who knows, it could be true."

"So what happened to the Queen's Inquiry?" Tanisha asked.

"The bloody Queen took a hike. She left with Bonny Prince Charlie on the royal yacht, *Britannia,* last July. So you go figure the rest."

"And what about our coincidence?" Tanisha asked. "How did this all get so claustrophobic?"

"I can't help you there, Miss Williams. Johnny came to me two days back, said he'd heard two Yanks were asking questions about Willy Wo Lap. Said he knew more about Willy than anyone, and that he'd help give it a go when you arrived. I said okay. He was the only one around here with the guts and connections to go after Willy. He might have worked for Willy once in a while, cut a deal here and there, but I still trusted him. This city is a place of intrigue. You've got to be on both sides of the table occasionally. But if they killed his mother, you can bet he would have gone after Willy." Julian sat looking off at the noisy overpass.

As Wheeler listened to all of this, he had a growing sense of dread. "So, is Johnny dead?" he asked.

"I don't know. He wouldn't just disappear like this. His flat wouldn't be rummaged unless something bad had happened."

"Why would they kill him?" Wheeler asked.

"The Chinese have a saying," Julian said. " 'Water can both sustain and sink a ship.' Who knows what happened. Things change, laddie."

"If Willy is running for Chief Executive in three months, then maybe he's shutting down all the people in Hong Kong he doesn't completely trust," Wheeler said. "Maybe he's afraid his affiliation with the Chin Lo will be made public and ruin everything. Prescott and Angela were being questioned by the FBI about campaign funding. Maybe that's why the Triad had to eliminate them."

"There's still something wrong with it," Tanisha said. "Why leave the picture of Johnny on her as a warning? They must have known it wouldn't scare him off but just make him furious."

Julian had been quiet. Finally, he looked up at them. "Not necessarily. He would have realized he was a dead man when his mother died. . . . He would want revenge, but Johnny was a survivor. He would want to pick the timing. Johnny was Chinese—he could play the waiting game. He might have offered Willy something of value in return for his life . . . a swap to buy him time."

"What would he trade?" Tanisha asked.

"Us," Julian said. "Johnny tells Willy we were planning to get a troop of coppers inside the Temple. But Willy doesn't keep the bargain and kills Johnny anyway. Wo Lap Ling is not a man you trust when his vital interests are at stake."

215

"If that's true," Tanisha said, "then we made a terrible mistake with Johnny."

"What's that?" Julian asked.

"We never should have told him about Chauncy."

They left the Mercedes and took Julian's English Ford Popular, because it had a police light and siren. They roared across the business district of Hong Kong Island, turned on Gloucester Road, and raced down into the Cross Harbor Tunnel, heading toward Kowloon. The morning traffic was heavy, and Julian had to slam on the brakes. They found themselves in an eight-thirty A.M. tunnel traffic jam. They crept through the noxious fumes beneath Victoria Harbor, the green lights on the tunnel walls inching past their windows with maddening slowness. Finally, they escaped the underground congestion and shot up the ramp and across Hong Kong Road, toward the New Territories.

If they had been just a few seconds later, they would have missed the whole thing. As they reared the front of Chan's shoe shop, they could see three young men, dressed in black, struggling to pull Chauncy Chan out the side door of his store. Chauncy was screaming for help, but nobody was responding. Pedestrians watched in disbelief as one of the Triad hoodlums pulled a knife and held it to the struggling Chauncy's neck. Tanisha yelled at Julian to stop the car. He hit the brakes, and while the car was still skidding to a stop, she yanked the plastic Glock out of her bag and started banging off rounds, pouring lead just past Julian's chest and out the far window. She could see her rounds sparking off the side of the building. She was firing for effect, not trying to hit the three hoodlums, because she didn't trust the inaccurate handgun and didn't want to hit Chauncy. The barrage scared the Triad killers, who were still trying to wrestle Chauncy Chan over to their car, where another man dressed in black pulled a Russian AK-47 out of the back seat.

Julian put the Ford in gear and tromped down on the acceler-

ator. It shot into the parking lot, but then, as if from out of nowhere, a cart vendor rolled his trolley right into their path, and,
for a second, Tanisha and Wheeler were looking into the frightened eyes of Zhang Fu Hai. Fu Hai was there with the stolen cart
to block the drive if anybody came. He desperately held the cart
handles while Julian's English Ford skidded into the contraption.
The three young gangsters now dove for their car, and one came
up with another AK-47. Without a second's hesitation, both armed
men started spraying lead at the entangled English Ford. The little
vehicle rocked with the impact of the rounds, the bullets shredding
the interior, coming dangerously close. The windows on the car
shattered, raining crystallized safety glass all over them. The sound
of tearing metal and ricochets filled the street.

"Bloody bastards," Julian screamed. He had his Russian
7.65mm auto-fire out and was blowing off rounds. The hot brass
was ejecting, bouncing down, burning Tanisha's legs. She didn't
react. She fired the Glock until it locked empty; then, ducking
below the window, she dropped one clip and slammed in her
backup, chambered the gun, and came up firing.

While this was happening, Wheeler, who was unarmed, dove
out of the car on the far side. The AK-47s continued to burp death
at them from the parking lot until both Russian weapons pin-
locked. They heard the gangsters start up their car and roar out
past the now-disabled English Ford, pausing just long enough to
pick up the terrified Fu Hai, who had been hiding behind his bullet-
mangled trolley. He dove into the back seat of the Triad car, which
then roared away, up the crowded street.

Tanisha, Wheeler, and Julian had lost sight of Chauncy Chan.
They took off, running toward the shoe shop, exploding into the
store. "Police!" Julian yelled, and they saw Chauncy bent over a
wounded Chinese woman, who was bleeding from a bullet wound
in her chest. Chauncy was talking to her softly in Chinese.

Chauncy Chan looked up. He had blood streaming down his
neck where the point of the blade had stuck him. "My wife. They
shot my wife," he said in terror.

Julian moved to the phone and called for an ambulance. Wheeler was standing in the center of the shop when all of a sudden his legs and arms began to shake. It was all he could do to stand up. This time, the reaction was not from alcohol, but from adrenaline. He looked at Tanisha. The residue of combat fear still lingered on her face; the plastic Glock hung hot and empty in her hand.

"I don't know about you," Wheeler said softly, "but I'm starting to get pissed."

TWENTY-FIVE

Powwows

W illy Wo Lap Ling sat in his living room and listened while Henry Liu explained what had happened. The Hong Kong apartment was modest but had exceptional Feng Shui. Feng Shui was the Chinese practice of having a house or business "read" by a Master to see if the layout of space and the directions the windows faced, along with the position of the bathrooms and kitchen, would bring good fortune or bad. Wo Lap had had the house read by the best Feng Shui Master in Hong Kong. As a youth, he had not had time for such indulgences, but now he took no chances. The Feng Shui Master said the apartment was cloaked in good fortune: It was facing north, toward the harbor, which guaranteed wealth; the main windows faced away from the mountains; the front door to the apartment was east; and the kitchen was farthest from the bedroom. The Feng Shui Master said this layout guaranteed favorable health, sexual prowess, and good fortune. Willy hoped the Master had been right as he listened, in distress, while Henry Liu told of the difficulties now facing the Triad.

Johnny Kwong had been careless. His mother, in California,

had allowed the United States government to find out about their payoffs, forcing Willy to order the death of an American attorney, as well as Johnny's own mother. Since he could no longer trust Johnny, Willy had also ordered his Death by a Myriad of Swords.

Willy feared the loss of his Guan-Xi with Beijing. He was on the eve of his political career and was not willing to accept blunders from Limpy Liu. He listened with rising anger as his old White Fan, and now most powerful Shan Chu of the Triad, explained the many problems.

"The Americans who came here believe that you have made an agreement with Beijing and that it is on paper. That is what Johnny Kwong told us before we executed him. They have a partial map of the Walled City and had contacted one of Jackie Pullinger's disciples to try and complete it. We failed when we went after this man earlier. He is just a shoemaker, but somehow he escaped. I think we may have fallen into some jeopardy," Limpy Liu said, his ugly, pock-marked features and protruding teeth giving him a scary but comical appearance. He limped slowly over to the picture window that looked north and protected Willy from the dual dragons of greed and avarice.

"This cannot be a serious threat," Willy said. "If it was serious, would they send a woman, a racial, who has limited Guan-Xi, even with Americans?"

"If they try to breach the Walled City with a force of police, we could have a bloody confrontation," Limpy Liu warned. "We might lose the City of Willows because of interfering Western politicians who will demand to know why it exists here, why our Temple hides in the park. Our secrets will be exposed."

Willy sat still for a long time, his liver-spotted hands thrust forward on his knees. "The cunning hare always has three burrows," he finally said.

Limpy Liu nodded. "So you believe we are protected? The police here don't know of your arrangement with Chen Boda."

"I believe that it will be almost impossible for the police to move against me. Beijing will instruct their police not to kill the hen to get one batch of eggs. They have much to lose. But you must take great care not to make matters worse," Willy told the Shan Chu. "And you must be ever vigilant. You must place our best Red-Pole fighting section on the roof and around the perimeters of the park. You must protect the City of Willows with your lives."

Henry Liu moved painfully to the door. His bad leg had been his life's biggest curse. He had been shot in the leg by an English policeman when he was fifteen. The butcher surgeons in the Kowloon clinic had repaired it badly, and it had never healed correctly. He had had it amputated just below the knee three years ago, but it was now worse than before. It ached when he walked on his prosthesis. His stumped leg was always rubbed raw from the appliance, and late in the afternoon he found it difficult even to stand. Now he stoically endured both the pain and Wo Lap Ling's stern warning. He left with his new instructions: He would guarantee the safety of the City of Willows or give his own life in failure.

After he had gone, Willy sat in silence on the sofa in his darkened apartment. He was too old to run from weak enemies. He would not scurry in fear from a Black woman. He had no better place for his money and political papers than where they were now sequestered. He had fashioned a set of Chinese boxes he felt were impenetrable. The documents were currently locked inside a safe, inside the altar, inside the Red Flower Pavilion, inside the City of Willows, inside the Walled City of Kowloon. He had been at this game for three-quarters of a century. He had come a long distance in his life and crossed many treacherous rivers. He also knew: *Distance only tests the endurance of a horse. It is time that reveals the character of a man.*

Wheeler's own thoughts pestered him like begging children. He was tired of evaluating himself, but he couldn't stop. Every thought he had led him back to his own performance. And then, making it worse, he had not been able to shake the memory of Chauncy

Chan being dragged out of his shop, or the sight of the woman bleeding on the floor, or the look of panic and loss in Chauncy's eyes when he turned to them and said, *"They shot my wife."*

He felt guilt for all of it. He was the conduit that had brought destruction into Chauncy's shoe shop. And then, changing channels on this screen of bad memories, he began reviewing his sorry performance that morning. . . . With the smell of cordite in his nose from Julian's and Tanisha's gunfire, and panic in his chest, he dove out of the car, fearing for his life, unable to move fast enough, ducking for cover while Julian and Tanisha returned fire with grim expressions.

"What the fuck did you expect, you stupid asshole?" the Prankmeister whispered, but his voice had grown dim. Wheeler had become disgusted with himself. But still, what *was* he doing? What did he expect? There seemed to be almost no upside in it for him. He could destroy his brother's legend and devastate his mother, sister-in-law, and nephew, Hollis. He could easily end up dead, half a world away, perhaps the victim of a horrible, torturous death. So what the fuck *was* he trying to prove? And then he felt a surge of protective love and a sense of loss for Pres. He began to choke up in the darkened hotel room, but he still couldn't cry. Something was stopping him. Some sense that he had not purged himself of selfish thoughts. He had failed his little brother. He had not protected him. If after Prescott's murder there had once been some part of him rooting for his brother's exposure, at least that part had finally died. He no longer felt anything but shame for not being there to guide Pres. All he wanted now was to solve his murder and make the ones who had done it pay. In that effort, he could recapture some portion of his self-respect.

Wheeler couldn't live with who he had been; he couldn't stand the memory of the Prankmeister. His old life now looked sad and comical to him. As he lay in bed on the twentieth floor of the Peninsula Hotel at one in the morning, he could finally see how he must have appeared to others. He could finally understand his father's disdain. His cheeks stung with embarrassment for himself and for the hollow waste his life had been.

Then the door opened and she was standing in the threshold of the bedroom, back-lit by the sitting room. She had on the terry-cloth robe that she never seemed to believe was complimentary.

"Wheeler?" she said softly. "Are you awake?"

"Yes," his voice a whisper.

"Can I talk to you?"

"Yes."

She moved across the room slowly and sat on the edge of his bed. She didn't say anything for a long moment, but he could feel her body trembling slightly.

"I'm scared," she said. "I'm scared and lonely."

He reached out and took her hand. "Me too," he said. Then he put his arm around her and tried to comfort her. She pulled away, unsure what she wanted.

"I need to hold somebody," he said softly. "I need to hold you."

She looked down at him. "I'm afraid we may die before we get home. I'll never see my grandmother or my niece again," she said.

He pulled on her wrist, and this time she allowed him to pull her down on the bed, next to him. He could smell her hair, sweet and fresh from a recent shower. Her body was firm and yet tender. She lay next to him, but somehow apart from him. He could hear her breathing, feel her breath on his neck. He reached out with his right hand and brushed the hair off her forehead. In the dim light, he looked into her black eyes. He could see the strength of ages there. Not just generations, but centuries of Black courage looked back at him. She had been forged by her past relationships, her racial history, and the violent streets of South Central. She was a fierce warrior, but somehow she had not lost her humanity. She had fought to retain it while he'd given his away at a country club bar for free. As he lay there, looking into her eyes, he wondered how he'd gotten so far off the road, how he'd managed to place value in such a string of asinine accomplishments. Then she took his hand and put it against her face, reached forward, and kissed him. He was surprised by it. Surprised she found anything worth cherishing in him. But some of his fear and self-loathing melted with that kiss.

He looked in her eyes and wondered how he could ever be good enough for her.

TWENTY-SIX

The Other Woman

"**F**or a crook, this bloody fool was an ear-bashing bore,"
Julian said as he led them down the steps of the Royal
Hong Kong Yacht Club, across the grassy park in front
of the Colonial Club House, and down onto the concrete docks.
The Yacht Club was just around the point from Causeway Bay and
looked north, toward Kowloon, across Victoria Harbor. The docks
were tucked in behind a massive concrete jetty wall. A magnificent
collection of sailboats and motor yachts were nestled there, floating
evidence of the Colony's past European splendor. Some of the
boats were now falling into disrepair. Their owners had fled Hong
Kong, and the dock workers hired to maintain them had taken a
holiday. Other vessels had found new owners, with government
titles, and they still sparkled in the midmorning sunshine.

Julian headed down the main concrete pier. "The lout was
basically a drug-runner," he continued. "We seized his apartment
and his office building, which was in his mum's name, then we find
out he's got this piece of all-right floating down here. This was in
July, just before the hand-over. I didn't bother to tell the lads in

the police building I found the thing. With all of the confusion, this bauble slipped beneath the radar."

They were now approaching a fifty-five-foot, pearl-white, custom motor-sailer with teak decks and a large center cabin. Its name was painted across the stern in English script:

The Other Woman
Hong Kong

Julian jumped aboard and unlocked the main salon with a key that he pulled from a hook under the aft starboard seat locker. They moved into the beautifully appointed salon, and Julian started opening the teak shutters to let the light in.

"This is a bit more cozy," he said. "I've been taking her out, from time to time, keeping the brightwork fresh, but the marine licensing board is about to have a go at it and I'll be forced to step away. Been lucky to have use of her these last six months," he said, then went down the few steps to the galley, opened the refrigerator, got three beers, and moved back and handed one each to Wheeler and Tanisha.

Wheeler smiled and looked longingly at the frosty bottle of English Red Crown in his hand. His mouth watered for a swallow. He could almost feel the alcohol going down his throat, unlocking and warming his stomach, washing away the burning nausea that he experienced every morning.

"What is it you wanted to see us about?" Tanisha said.

Julian had called them at nine and asked them to meet him at the Yacht Club. Now he sat on the big sofa in the main salon in tan slacks, a T-shirt, and boat shoes and looked at them.

"I just came from the hospital over in Ling Tim where we took Mrs. Chan. She'd been on the critical list since yesterday, but she packed it in this morning at eight thirty-five."

Wheeler's heart sank. He looked at the beer in his hand. His throat burned. He wondered if there was any Scotch whisky aboard.

Julian continued, "Chauncy went into a flat spin after she

died. Started screaming at the docs and the like, then he took off. I tried to stop him, but he was in a bloody lather. I found out an hour ago that he got his kids and disappeared.

Tanisha realized that with Johnny probably dead and Chauncy gone, they had just sevened out.

"You want my take?" Julian continued. "This was always a doggy business. Even if we got to that park, we wouldn't be able to breach the Triad headquarters. They have fighting sections, suicide assassins, called vanguards. They're martial artists armed to the teeth with Russian weapons. You saw the firepower they had yesterday. We'd need a division of Royal Marines to get in there," he said, with a sigh. "I've decided to bugger off. Been thinkin' about it for months. I can smell my own death coming, so I'm gonna leave."

"You mean you're gonna run!" Wheeler said, setting the untouched beer down.

"It's over. I'm out of rope and up to my knickers in trouble with my Chinese chums in the Colony police. You'd best be off, too. The police and the Triads are obviously in league, and Willy's at the center of it. We didn't endear ourselves to that buncha tearabouts yesterday when we fired on them. Johnny's in the orchard and I don't need my name on a bloody invitation to the Ice House to know I've used up my stay."

"Where are you going to go?" Wheeler asked.

"That's not something I plan on sharing with you, laddie. . . . Not that I don't trust you, but it's bloody hard not to talk when somebody shoves a live fucking rodent up your arse."

When Wheeler and Tanisha got back to the hotel, she had managed to convince him that without Julian and Chauncy, they had no way of proceeding. Tanisha wanted to go home. She had called and left a message with Captain Verba earlier, saying that she had more family problems in Cleveland and needed a two-week leave. She asked his voice mail if he could postpone her I.A.D. hearing. Now it was time to face that situation.

While Tanisha went upstairs to change, Wheeler sat in the lobby and tried to think of some way to continue. After reviewing everything, he realized they had no options left. He had failed Prescott in death, just as completely as he had in life. Wheeler watched the flow of people in the Peninsula lobby, feeling such a depression he almost couldn't deal with it. Self-loathing swept over him. Finally he stood and walked to the concierge desk and ordered two tickets on the next flight out to Los Angeles. The first available seats were on a Singapore Air red-eye that left Hong Kong's Kai Tak Airport at one A.M. that next morning. While Wheeler was at the concierge desk booking the seats, Tanisha called from the suite and said she would meet him in the Pen Room grill off the lobby. He arrived there and found her in the leather booth in the back. They hadn't eaten since breakfast, but neither was hungry, so they just ordered Cokes.

"I'm sorry," Tanisha said. "I know this meant a lot to you, but I don't think we could have pulled it off, even if we had Julian and Chauncy and half the honest cops left on the Hong Kong police force. It was a nice try but it wouldn't have worked. We needed to find an edge—a smart way to do it—and there doesn't seem to be one."

He knew she was right. It had been insane, and it might not even have solved Prescott's murder. If only they had been able to prove Willy had cut a deal with Beijing. Wheeler was sure he could have exposed their plot and at least made the bastards pay for Prescott's death. But they couldn't go up against the most powerful criminal organization in the world in their own backyard without help. All he had managed to create in Hong Kong was more misery and death.

Then a shadow fell across their table and Chauncy Chan was standing there. He seemed to have shrunk in size, his shoulders slumped, head down, his eyes sunk deep in his head. He was rubbing his hands together in front of him. He looked like he hadn't slept since they last saw him, a day ago. "I was waiting in the lobby," he said. "I saw you come in."

"I'm so sorry about your wife," Wheeler said.

Chauncy nodded, the pain and sorrow visible on him like a second skin. "I've taken my children to my cousin's house," he said, his voice now almost frightening in its coldness. "My wife was very ill. She had a sickness, but she was my life," he said. "She was my strength. Her death cannot go unpunished."

Wheeler got up and motioned for Chauncy to sit, but he remained standing.

"I know how to get into the park inside the Walled City," he said.

"Can you draw the map? Complete Quincy's map?" Wheeler asked.

"There is no need for a map. Jackie Pullinger told me there is a much easier way." He stood in silence, still rubbing his palms together.

"I will take you there," he finally said. "I will show you the way."

TWENTY-SEVEN

City of Willows

It was a little after one in the morning.

There was a strong chop on the bay as they cleared the jetty that sheltered the Hong Kong Yacht Club, leaving the dock lights behind. They were under power, heading east, the sturdy forty-horsepower, four-cylinder marine engine moving the sailboat at a stately seven knots. Easterly swells were breaking against the bow of *The Other Woman,* throwing a light sea-spray into the air, blowing it back into their faces or to splatter on the main salon windows. They were running without lights as they turned into Victoria Harbor to begin the four-mile journey that would take them past the huge man-made peninsula landing strip of the international airport. Their eventual destination was Lei Yue Mun Point, which was across the harbor in the Yau Tong district.

It had been an exhausting twenty-four hours since Chauncy had made his surprise appearance. They had spent hours with Julian trying to decide if Chauncy's information gave them enough of an edge to try to get into the Triad headquarters. Julian told them that with Johnny gone they could not count on police help. They would have to go it alone. . . . They never really took a vote or decided in so many words, because they all knew they were going to try it. Each had a personal reason.

Their plan focused on one rule: Don't do anything expected. With this in mind, Wheeler and Tanisha had rebooked their air reservations, securing two first-class seats for the eight A.M. Singapore Air flight to L.A. the next morning. Chauncy had taken their rental car and parked it across from the east end of the Walled City. They had fully provisioned the sailboat with food and water, and were now headed across the bay, where they would meet up with Julian.

Chauncy was sitting on top of the main salon, looking out at the moonlit water, lost in feelings too complicated for him to talk about. All of them shared a need for revenge. Wheeler was at the helm, Tanisha beside him in the cockpit. Wheeler had operated boats since he was a kid in Newport Beach, often stealing his father's sportfisher for fraternity parties. The only fish they'd ever caught were sorority tuna. Now he adjusted his course, heading the fifty-five-foot sailboat a few points higher into the wind to allow for drift, rechecking the compass on the navigation panel next to the wheel.

"Are you okay?" Tanisha asked, looking at the tightly drawn expression on his face.

"Scared pissless," he admitted ruefully. "I only made it halfway through Special Forces training, and in most of our war games we were using rubber bullets or paintballs."

"One thing to remember," she said. "Nobody hits anything they're aiming at in a street action. The direct hits are all pure accident."

"Even these vanguards? These suicide assassins? They sound pretty kick-ass."

"Everybody is blinded by adrenaline. If it gets hot, just move fast and keep zigging," she said.

He nodded, hoping she wasn't just trying to build his courage.

They dropped anchor an hour later in Yau Tong Bay. They could see the lights on the warehouses, and beyond the tall loading docks they could see occasional late-night traffic on Kow Ling Road.

Chauncy was quiet as he helped them get the rubber Avon off the stern davits and into the water. Wheeler stood in the tippy little launch while Chauncy handed him down the two-and-a-half-horsepower American-made Evinrude engine. It had a Chinese cowling which read "Yellow River Outboard" in Mandarin.

They were all dressed in dark clothing, which they had purchased in the underground mall earlier that day. Tanisha locked up the yawl's salon and boarded the rubber boat. Wheeler pulled the cord and started the motor. The three of them headed across the little bay in the launch toward the docks.

Wheeler's heart was fluttering in his chest and his head felt light. He wondered if he was entering the last few hours of his life.

They arrived at the huge wharf, which towered fifteen feet above them to accommodate the freighters that loaded there. They putted slowly around the dock until they found a service ladder, then Wheeler brought the Avon in and Chauncy tied the bow line to the ladder. They scrambled up out of the boat, carrying almost nothing with them: no wallets or identification, no weapons, no flashlights. Each had a few hundred Hong Kong dollars in red hundred-dollar bills. They climbed the ladder to the dock, and Wheeler checked the rubber boat, which had now drifted under the pier out of sight. He nodded at Tanisha.

The three of them took off at a jog across the parking lot. The huge shipping warehouse loomed in the background. The moon lit them with unwelcome silver light.

They moved silently. The only danger here was being spotted by a security guard. Finally, they found themselves out on Kow Ling Road. Up ahead, an old, rusty plumbing repair van was parked. It blinked its lights once, and the three of them took off, running toward it. The side door was unlocked and they clambered in.

The interior of the truck was lit by a red overhead light. They had stepped from a desolate commercial roadside into a state-of-the-art mobile command center. The rusted-out wreck of a van turned out to be a high-tech miracle inside.

Julian was seated behind the wheel. He looked back at them, his face tight with pre-game anxiety. "Everything kipper?" he asked.

Wheeler nodded. "No problems," he said, looking at the racks fitted with extensive surveillance and combat equipment. "This is amazing," he said.

"Bit of a gasher, what?" He grinned. "The Royal Police have three of these lorries. You have to check them out, but I waited till the motor-pool watchman went to the loo and I took 'er on unauthorized loan. At least we won't want for firepower," he said.

Wheeler took down an Uzi submachine gun from a wall case of various automatic weapons. He checked it quickly before returning it to the rack. Everything Julian had said they would need was in the truck: night-vision goggles, safe-cracking equipment, even laser sights that could be fitted to the weapons.

Julian put the truck in gear. "It's getting on. We'd better cut the stick," he said as he pulled out, swung a U, and headed north to Kwun Tong Road.

As they rode in silence, Wheeler looked up to the front seat at Julian, studying the cherubic English Inspector's constantly changing profile in the overhead street lamps. When Wheeler called Julian that afternoon and asked him to reconsider, he had never expected him to say yes. The cagey, paranoid cop had set up another meeting outside the People's Police Building in the same park, and listened while Chauncy, Wheeler, and Tanisha described the bones of their idea.

"Pretty long odds," Julian said, after he'd heard it all. "We cock it up, we're all gonna kiss the gunner's daughter."

Wheeler couldn't figure out why the Inspector had agreed to help. A few hours later, while they were working out the exit plan, he'd finally asked Julian why.

"I'm not doin' this for you, laddie," he said. "I'm doin' it for me and Johnny, and for all the good coppers who've been scuttled. We had it good here. This was a special place, then the Commies came and left us to carry the can. There was a time when Johnny was the best. But it got too bloody hard, too much moving around under the covers. Johnny couldn't hold on with the Triads and the Commies in business together. So I guess they turned him and burned him. Time to set that right." And that was all he would say.

Julian turned on Prince Edward Road, and it didn't take them long to get to the Walled City. He drove slowly past the ugly line of slum buildings that stretched for miles in every direction. The place was huge, much bigger than Wheeler had ever imagined. A few of the apartments were lit with dim lights, from kerosene lanterns or from electricity stolen from power lines. The overwhelming color of the Walled City was concrete gray.

Finally, Chauncy moved up to the shotgun seat beside Julian and looked at the passing buildings. "There," he said, pointing to an apartment house across Tung Tsing Road, on the other side of the street from the Walled City.

Julian parked the van and turned off the lights. They sat there for a long moment and looked at the darkened apartment building. It was much better maintained than the ghetto buildings just across the road.

"They bring the money back here from their criminal take in Hong Kong every night at about two-thirty," Chauncy said. "Usually a car with two guards. There are one or two armed men inside the garage to meet them."

Wheeler again felt light-headed. He looked at Tanisha, who squeezed his hand.

"Let's get ready," she said.

Tanisha and Wheeler moved to the back of the van and were joined there by Julian and Chauncy.

"I loaded up the knappies," Julian said, pointing at four backpacks. "Everything's in there we talked about. Flak jackets are in the lorry boxes."

They opened one of the built-in boxes in the van and took out the bulletproof vests. Tanisha was surprised to see that they were the same "second chance" American-made Kevlar vests that were issued to the LAPD. They were light and could stop just about anything but a full-load Rhino or a Winchester nine-millimeter Black Talon. She put one on and handed one to Wheeler. They were all working under the single red light, bathed in its seductive glow.

"Pick your poison, mates," Julian said as he took one of the automatic weapons from the gun wall in the van.

Wheeler selected a Browning fully automatic rifle, because he had used them in the Marines. He grabbed two banana clips and a laser sight and began to assemble it. Then he slammed in the clip and tromboned the slide.

"You look like you know what you're doing," Tanisha said, impressed.

"And you thought I only knew how to field-strip coeds?" He smiled weakly as they saddled up.

They were jacked and flacked, and now they waited.

At a little past two-thirty A.M., a car with three men pulled up the street, turned, and nosed into the driveway, its headlights making hot circles on the garage door. A second later, the electric door opened. Two other Chinese men were standing in the under-lit garage with guns out as the car pulled in.

"Now," Julian said.

They pulled back the side door of the van and jumped out. They ran the short distance across the sidewalk and exploded into the garage, shoving their weapons into the faces of five startled Chinese gangsters. One of the lookouts in the garage turned to fire, but he got clubbed to his knees by Chauncy's rifle butt before he could discharge his AK-47. Chauncy swung the automatic weapon a second time, hitting the man in the jaw, knocking him backward. Julian and Tanisha pulled down on the three men in the car, their guns trained in the windows. Wheeler was left in a standoff with the last garage guard. They were facing each other, gun barrel to gun barrel. They stared in fear at one another, seconds from death, both frozen in desperate indecision.

"Drop it!" Wheeler shouted.

"Fuck *him*," Julian said, then turned and fired a short burst. The bullets flew into the Chinese man's chest, blowing him off his feet and across the garage, dead before he landed.

"You didn't have to kill him," Wheeler said.

Julian grabbed the garage opener out of the other Chinese guard's hand and closed the door, shutting them off from the street. "This ain't a bloody Boy Scout trip," Julian said angrily. "We take 'em without shooting if we can, but if one a' these buggers pulls down on you, you put the effin' bastard in the mummy bag!" He was boiling mad.

"He's right," Chauncy said. "These men are killers. They'll have no mercy. You can't hesitate."

Wheeler looked at Tanisha. She caught his look and nodded her agreement.

"Watch that door," Julian instructed. "If there's more upstairs, that's the way in here."

They were still holding their guns on the three other men. They got them out of the car, and using plastic cuffs that Julian had brought with him from the truck, they cuffed the gangsters to the wooden column supports in the garage, then gagged them with their own socks. Tanisha removed their weapons and took their cellphones. There were two canvas bags of money in the trunk of the car, which they left.

"Okay," Julian said, "let's sweep this flat, make sure we got 'em all."

They moved upstairs from the garage and went room-to-room through the apartment. It was deserted. They found one unexpected piece of good fortune in the bedroom closet: Six red Triad robes were hung there with cellophane cleaning bags over them.

"This is a spot of sunshine," Julian said as he pulled them out of the closet and started passing them around. The robes had hoods, and once on, went all the way to the floor.

They quickly found a staircase that led down to the basement. Julian turned on the lights. The basement was very small and looked as if it had been dug under the house by hand. Cold, musty air began cooling their skin and icing their nerves. At the far end of the basement was a door. They opened it and were looking at a four-seat electric golf cart and a tunnel that extended beyond, into the darkness.

"There's the tunnel," Chauncy said. "Just like Miss Pullinger said."

"Bloody fucking marvelous," Julian grinned.

They all moved to the cart and got in, with Julian behind the wheel. "Okay," he said, patting his machine gun, "from now on if we have to use these things, we've blown it. . . . We fire as a last resort." He started looking for the key to turn on the cart. He found it under the seat.

"If these guys were delivering money from the nightclubs in Hong Kong, maybe there's going to be somebody at the other end to receive the bags," Tanisha reasoned.

"Good thinking," Julian said. "Somebody go get the money bags out of the trunk of that car so we'll have something to distract them with."

Chauncy and Wheeler turned and moved quickly back up the stairs, into the garage, to get the money from the trunk of the gangsters' car.

While they were gone, Julian looked at Tanisha. "Is Mr. Cassidy up to this?" he asked, concerned. "He really froze back there."

"He went up against L.A. Tong members in his brother's house in Bel Air, and got two out of three. He'll be fine," she said, hoping she was right.

They whipped along the narrow hand-dug tunnel in the dark, the single finger of light from the golf cart poking the blackness, their red robes billowing in the cold underground air. It was a surprisingly short journey. They pulled up at another staircase a few minutes later.

There was a lone man lying on a cot in the darkness. He rubbed his eyes and started to rise. Chauncy spoke to him in Chinese and started to hand him one of the sacks of money. As he reached for it, Wheeler got out of the other side of the cart and clubbed him into unconsciousness with the Browning.

"That's a good lad," Julian said, beginning to feel a little better about Wheeler.

They tied the man up and moved up the staircase, still lugging the heavy bags of money. At the top of the stairs was a small room and a door. They opened the door slowly and found themselves peering out into a beautiful central park lit by moonlight. They could smell the sweet cherry blossoms on the night wind. Somebody outside near the door spoke to them in Chinese. "It's us," Chauncy replied in Cantonese. "Here, give us a hand." Then he handed a bag of money through the opening. An unseen man reached for the canvas bag, and before he could control it, Chauncy dropped the bag and pushed hard on the door, smashing it against the man, knocking him down. Wheeler, Tanisha, and Julian all exploded through the door, into the park.

There were three men there, waiting for the money. All of them were now busy clawing under their red Temple robes for handguns. This time, Wheeler didn't hesitate. He kicked his man in the nuts and brought the Browning down in a chopping motion as he'd been taught to do long ago, in Special Forces. All three gangsters were disposed of quickly, without a shot fired.

They dragged them back into the tunnel, cuffed and gagged them, then looked at each other as they caught their breath. They still had the two heavy bags of money before them.

"Okay," Julian said, "we don't know how much time we're going to get, so from now on, we move fast, take advantage of everything." He looked at the strained faces of Wheeler, Tanisha, and Chauncy. "Ready?" he asked.

They all nodded.

They went back up and stepped out into the beautiful central park, pausing for a minute to get their bearings. Across the open field was the Triad Temple, known as the City of Willows. They started to move cautiously across the wet grass, their heads down, their monk's hoods up to disguise them. Because his Cantonese was flawless, Chauncy was in the lead in case they needed him to talk. Wheeler brought up the rear, his shoulder blades tingling as if any moment they would be separated by a bullet.

They reached the Red Flower Pavilion without incident. An old man was standing there; he reached out for the bags of money. Chauncy handed him both bags, then Julian stepped forward, pulled his rifle from under his robe, and hit the old man, up from under, with the butt of his gun. The man went down like chopped wheat and immediately started snoring at their feet.

"Can't be this effin' easy," Julian muttered as they moved into the Pavilion, past pedestals that held golden art. Snakes and carved dragons watched with cold ruby eyes as they passed.

They opened the inner door of the Red Flower Pavilion and looked in at the magnificent altar.

"All of the Triad secrets are supposed to be stored in the altar safe," Chauncy explained. "It's a sacred place. Only the sacred elders can open it. If Willy has a secret document here, that's where it will be."

They backed away from the east gate and headed across the huge hall. Then they moved up to the altar to the very spot where, two days before, Johnny Kwong had died.

The prostitutes were nude dancers from a Triad club in Mong Kok, and they arrived in a van at two A.M. They sat in the back, rubbed their sore calves, and wondered how quickly they could bring the gangsters off and get home to bed.

The driver of the van banged his hand on the garage door. When he couldn't get an answer, he took out a key and walked around to the narrow wood staircase and climbed the half-flight up to the main door of the flat. Once inside, it was just minutes before he reached the garage and found the four gangsters tied to the support posts and one dead on the garage floor. He untied the man nearest him, removed the gag, and listened in dismay as the man began to babble out the story of the assault. Within minutes, he had untied the others, and they discovered that the electric cart was gone. They started looking around for one of their flip-phones so they could call the Temple in the park and warn them. They found their four shorted-out cellphones under water in the kitchen sink, where Tanisha had left them.

They turned and rushed back down into the basement to the tunnel. Stumbling in the blackness, they ran toward the City of Willows.

Julian found the safe directly behind the altar, mounted in the stone floor. He took an electronic safe-cracking tool out of his backpack and hooked the electrodes to the safe dial. He turned it on and watched the small LED screen in his hand as the unit electronically scanned the safe dial, looking for the hollow tumblers. The LED screen locked first on the number 25, then the number 42, and finally a third number, 19. When all three were locked in, a small bell tone confirmed the combination. Then Julian reached out and spun the dial to 25-42-19 and opened the safe. It was then that they heard the first shouts in Chinese, coming from the park outside.

Wheeler was guarding the east gate of the Red Flower Pavilion. He saw several men in red robes running across the moonlit park, looking up at the Temple roof, and screaming their warning to the Red-Pole vanguards up there.

"We've got a situation here," Wheeler called back to Julian, who was just reaching into the safe, removing its contents.

"Goddamn to bloody hell and hereafter," Julian mumbled as he threw the stacks of banded money and jewels aside, looking for the Agreement. "Chauncy, get your arse over here and help me read this shit," he yelled.

They could now hear people coming down a staircase from the roof above. Wheeler turned and fired his B.A.R. in that general direction. A stream of bullets chipped and whined against the staircase and Temple walls. They heard somebody scream and a lone body rolled down the staircase, sprawling dead on the Temple floor. Tanisha was now kneeling and firing out of the north gate, into the park. She watched as Triad gangsters dropped on their faces and rolled in panic to escape her fire.

Fu Hai had been awakened in the middle of the night by gunfire. Unsure of what was happening, he was pulled up off his mat with the other initiates and told by the Red-Pole vanguard that bandits were in the Red Flower Pavilion trying to steal from the Triad. It was very dark. He could hear automatic gunfire marked by flashes of muzzle fire in the park. A Russian AK-47 was thrust into his hand. He didn't know how to use it, but the vanguard pulled the slide, cocking the weapon for him. The vanguard told Fu Hai to just aim and pull the trigger. He was ordered to run across the grass toward the Red Flower Pavilion, get inside, and kill the bandits. Without even thinking, he started running with the other initiates toward the Temple. A Black woman was shooting at him from the door of the Pavilion with an automatic weapon. He felt a rush of air from one of her bullets as it zipped past his ear. The initiates from his class continued on, screaming for courage, charging through the park toward the Pavilion.

He lost track of the others, but somehow made it to the side of the building. He opened a side door and ran into the Red Flower Pavilion. . . . He dove to avoid being hit, then slid on his stomach on the polished wooden floor.

Chauncy was pawing through the large safe, glancing at the documents. Some were real estate leases or Triad business agreements which extorted payments from restaurants or shops in Hong Kong.

Gunfire erupted all around him as he kneeled below the stone altar, sweat pouring into his eyes, stinging them. He couldn't read with his eyes smarting, so he gathered up everything that looked possible and stuffed it all into his robe pockets. Then he stood and wiped his eyes, just in time to see several armed gangsters moving into the back of the Red Flower Pavilion from the west gate. They were all carrying automatic weapons. He flipped on his laser sight and fired at them. Several went down, wounded. The others fired back; bullets ricocheted off the stone altar, screaming and whining away into the night, before shattering unseen wood and glass.

Fu Hai fired his weapon without aiming. He did not want to kill anybody. A round-faced White man with a handlebar mustache, who he thought he remembered from the gunfight in front of the shoemaker's shop, returned his fire. Automatic bullets thunked into the wood bench he was hiding behind. He felt a blow to his side as a round knocked him backwards. He started bleeding but felt no pain. When his clip was empty, he grabbed another weapon from a fallen comrade.

"We're outta here!" Julian yelled. "Gotta find a back door."

They all started to fall back toward the south wall, firing as they did, dropping spent clips and slamming in new ones, using the heavy wooden benches for cover.

The Temple was now filling with Triad members. They made low, suicidal charges through the east and north doors, sliding on their stomachs, their weapons held before them, firing streams of hollow-point death at the escaping foursome.

Tanisha arrived at the south gate first. The door was locked, so she fired a burst of bullets from her Russian assault rifle. The wood frame and the door disintegrated, coming off its hinges. They ran through the shattered opening into a small adjoining Temple library. They could see the park out the window, just beyond.

"Stay with the exit plan!" Julian shouted, and they started for the door on the far side of the library. Then, almost by accident, as Wheeler's eyes swept the crowded bookshelves, he spotted something familiar. He jerked his gaze back, even as gunfire splintered the threshold behind him. On the library shelf were twelve leather-bound, gold-stamped volumes: *The History of California,* by Father John Stoddard. The same collection he had given Prescott, one volume at a time, every Christmas.

"Son of a bitch!" Wheeler said, as more gunfire erupted, tearing the walls of the library.

"Let's get bloody scarce!" Julian shouted.

They opened the library door to the park and began their own suicidal run across the grass, toward the back wall of the low buildings on the south side of the Walled City. The vanguards on the roof were armed with tracer rounds. They opened fire. Mud divots and flying sod exploded around them as white-hot tracers shattered into the ground at their feet. The sound was deafening, like fifty jackhammers all starting at once.

"Over here!" Chauncy yelled, taking the lead.

They zigzagged across the park, switching directions as more tracers streaked above and around them.

With anger and adrenaline fueling his pursuit, Fu Hai chased the enemies out of the Temple library and into the park, running on ever weakening legs. Finally, he fell from loss of blood, his cheek hitting the cool wet grass. Before he lost consciousness, he remembered the sweet smell of cherry blossoms in his nose.

They got to a small wooden door that led down some stairs into a small flat. As Chauncy worked to pull the locked door open, Wheeler, Tanisha, and Julian turned and laid down some cover fire, aimed at the Temple roof. The Triad gangsters up there were forced to duck down behind the parapets, while the three of them emptied their weapons. Then the Triad roof guards reappeared, their assault rifles armed with fresh clips.

Floodlights on the Temple roof clicked on and quickly found the four of them against the south building wall, pinning them in blinding light.

"Shoot the floods!" Julian screamed, slamming in a fresh clip. Just as he turned to fire at the roof lights, he was doubled over by a burning tracer. The hot round knocked him off his feet. He stumbled backwards into the wall, grabbed his abdomen just below the vest line, and went down hard. His legs splayed out in front of him, and blood started oozing through his fingers. "Bloody fucking damn!" he groaned.

Tanisha fired at the roof, getting two of the three floodlights, just as Chauncy got the locked door open and jumped down into the small opening. "I'm in, let's go!" he yelled. Tanisha jumped down.

Now only Wheeler was in the park with Julian. He turned to grab the Englishman while bullets sparked the wall all around him. Miraculously, Wheeler wasn't hit. The huge distance he was from the Temple roof helped throw off the gangsters' aim. He felt one round tug at his sleeve, a reluctant warning.

"I'm a goner," Julian croaked. "Get out of here."

"You're through giving orders," Wheeler said and struggled to pull the overweight detective up over his shoulder. Then he jumped down into the room, pulling the wooden door shut over him. Julian was heavy, and Wheeler's wounded leg almost buckled. His senses were immediately greeted by the worst stench he had ever encountered. It was pitch black. He felt Tanisha's hand on his sleeve. He couldn't see her; his eyes had not adjusted to the dark.

"This way," she said, and with Julian in a fireman's carry over his shoulder, Wheeler stumbled blindly after Tanisha, down the stairs of the darkened house.

They found Chauncy waiting for them in a doorway that led out into a blackened alleyway.

"Follow me," he said.

"What about the night goggles?" Tanisha asked. "I can't see anything, and this stink is about to make me puke."

"Breathe through your mouth," Chauncy said. He looked over at Wheeler. "We've got to leave him. He'll slow us down."

"Not leaving him," Wheeler said stubbornly. "I'm not losing another one." But he wondered how long he could carry the overweight detective. Wheeler could feel Julian's blood running down the back of his own neck, down his rib cage, into his underwear. He tried to blot the feeling from his mind, and the unsettling stench from his nostrils.

Tanisha and Chauncy put on their night-vision goggles. Then Tanisha reached into Wheeler's backpack and pulled his goggles out, adjusted the focus, and put the heavy contraption on his head. Reaching around to the top, she flipped on the power. Immediately, in green hue, Wheeler could see a small alley out the apartment doorway. It was only about two feet wide and twisted away in the darkness. Then he saw the glint of half-a-dozen rodent eyes looking at them from the garbage-strewn alleyway.

They heard a door open behind them in the park, then footsteps coming down the stairs, and the sound of Chinese voices.

"Let's get out of here," Wheeler said. He turned, and with his right hand still on the trigger, let a stream of lead fly in the direction of the voices. No one cried out in pain as his bullets crashed into the walls.

Chauncy led the way. He had been born in the ghetto and, as a child, had memorized every inch. But that gave them no advantage, because he shared that same history with the men pursuing them. The foursome moved along, picking their way over piles of garbage and human excrement. It seeped into their shoes and clung to their pant legs. Then they heard a burst of machine-gun fire. Bullets chipped the walls, sparking light all around them.

Tanisha grunted in pain but said nothing.

"You okay?" Wheeler asked, still struggling with the almost-dead weight of Julian Winslow.

"Fine," she hissed.

They moved along the narrow alley path, turning right, then left. The Walled City's corridors were an ungodly maze of dead ends and blind switch-backs. Only once did Chauncy turn the wrong way. "Gotta go back," he said, and they headed back up the alley toward the pursuing Triad assassins. Chauncy and Tanisha took the point, and with the advantage of the night-vision goggles, they laid down a withering fire, hitting three of the Red-Pole vanguards and forcing the Triad gangsters to back up fast to find cover. Chauncy finally found the right path and they followed him into an intersecting alley.

Wheeler was now completely lost. He thought they were going back the way they came. Occasionally the pursuing gangsters would blind-fire in the dark, the whining tracers screaming over their heads or ricocheting off apartment walls. Then they were heading up a small flight of stairs. Wheeler's wounded leg buckled. He could go no farther and was forced to sit down in shit and garbage with Julian still over his shoulder. He turned, and through his night goggles he could see a few gangsters moving along at a trot twenty yards back, their weapons at port arms in front of them, appearing in his night visor like eerie green ghosts. Wheeler set Julian down, almost shrugging him off his shoulder. Then he found his Browning under his arm, hanging from his shoulder strap. He rotated it up, holding it underhanded. Without sighting, he let a blast go and watched in awe as several of the pursuing men were picked up by the powerful stream of lead and flung backward into the reeking, garbage-filled darkness. He heard them screaming in pain as their lives ended.

"Bloody fucking marvelous," Julian whispered, surprising Wheeler with his consciousness. Then Wheeler heard Chauncy at his right elbow.

"Come on. It's not much farther."

"Gotta help me. Can't carry him," Wheeler said.

With Chauncy now bearing half the weight, and with one of Julian's arms around each of their shoulders, they dragged him along, through the stench and darkness. It was a terrifying journey, almost as if they had been dropped onto an alien planet. Ungodly rats, the size of small cats, sat on piles of human waste hissing in the dark. Occasionally they would pass a flat that had a light burning, and the night-vision goggles, unable to handle the light, would white out, blinding them until they could tip them up. Once they were past the light source, they would pull them down again and continue on.

It seemed like they were in the narrow, twisting alleyways forever. Then finally Chauncy turned and broke down a door with his shoulder and led them into a house. They dragged Julian up a short flight of stairs and into a small living room where a Chinese family slept.

"I lived here once," Chauncy whispered as he moved through the flat, tripping over a sleeping man. They heard a child cry, and one of the sleeping men awoke and screamed at him. Then Chauncy was out a back door, and he led them into another narrow alley.

Wheeler momentarily lost track of Tanisha. He was too busy dragging the fat detective, worrying about his footing, and trying not to throw up from the horrible smell.

Finally, Chauncy opened a door and they moved through a low doorway. Like magic, they had stepped out of hell and were back on Tung Tsing Road. The street, the moonlight, and the cold air revived their tortured senses.

They laid Julian down against the side of a building and looked into his face. He had almost bled out. His eyes were open, but he was a ghastly pale color. Blood was all over his shirt and Wheeler's back. Then Tanisha came through the door from the Walled City.

"They're right behind us. I can hear them coming up the alley," she said as she shut the door.

About two hundred yards away, they could see the rented Mercedes that Chauncy had parked there yesterday for their escape. Chauncy took off, running toward it, and in a few seconds he had it going and was speeding back toward them. He pulled the car up just as the door behind them opened and a Chinese Triad member cautiously looked out. Wheeler was closest to the man and stepped up and hit him with his best husband-bashing left hook, knocking the man back into the ghetto. Then he threw the car door wide. Chauncy and Tanisha got Julian into the Mercedes. Wheeler dove in as Chauncy jumped behind the wheel and floored it. The car screeched away just as three more Triad gangsters ran out into the street, firing automatic weapons. Their gunfire starred the back fenders and shattered the taillights.

The Mercedes sped away into the night.

An hour later, they had returned to the dock and lowered an unconscious Julian aboard the Avon. It took two trips to get them all back to *The Other Woman.* Wheeler turned on the anchor winch and pulled the hook. Then he started the marine engine and powered the sailboat back out into Victoria Harbor.

It was then that he noticed blood on Tanisha's shirt. "You're hit," he said. She didn't reply, but she looked pale.

He pulled her shirt up and checked the wound. The bullet had caught her under the armpit right above the protective vest, cutting out a furrow of flesh between her rib bones. The bleeding had stopped, but some of her shirt was buried deep in the wound.

"We gotta get you both to a hospital," he said.

"Can't do it," Chauncy said, glancing at his watch and recalling the exit plan. "We're supposed to clear this harbor in half an hour." He was now watching Julian, who they had laid out on the sofa in the main salon. The English cop hadn't said anything in over fifteen minutes. But now his eyes opened and he looked at them through dull slits.

"Julian's lost too much blood. He'll die," Wheeler argued.

Their original exit plan had been to cast off from here and head directly out of Victoria Harbor. They figured their enemies would check the airport and discover their eight-o'clock airline reservations, then waste valuable time staking out that flight, while they cleared Chinese water and headed off across the South China Sea to Sydney, Australia. Wheeler doubted Julian would ever make Sydney alive. Tanisha had a chance, but she had become listless and he was sure she was going into shock.

"The Chinese will be looking for us. The police will have warrants out. They're all working for Willy," Chauncy said. "We can't go back to Hong Kong."

"We can't just let them die," Wheeler insisted.

Chauncy looked at him, trying to come up with a new plan. "Maybe we could get to Macao," he said. "It's only forty-six miles from here. It's still a Portuguese province and doesn't get handed back to China until 1999. All you need to get in is a valid passport. But it's dangerous—the population is ninety-five percent Chinese, and they have agents everywhere in Macao."

"Let's try," Wheeler said. He grabbed some charts off the navigation table and found Macao on one of them. It was a little island colony off the eastern coast of China, north of Hong Kong. As Chauncy had said, it was only forty-six miles away, about five hours at ten knots. Wheeler grabbed a new navigation chart and found the heading for Macao Harbor. He plotted the course, then went up on deck and reset the autopilot. The moon and cold night wind seemed to clear his thoughts. It was finally up to him to take charge.

As they headed out into open water, Wheeler organized what he had to do. He rechecked the autopilot and listened as the little servomechanism clicked and hummed, then he moved back into the cabin. Julian had again closed his eyes. He looked bad. Chauncy said Tanisha had gone forward and was stretched out on the bed in the master stateroom. He found her there and put a pillow under her feet to try to stave off shock and get blood to her head. Then he found a blanket in the overhead and spread it over her. He reached out and took her hand.

"I'm fine," she said, reading his concerned expression. "You can't drop a homegirl with a wing shot. You gotta hit the ten-ring."

"I've got to get Julian to a hospital," he said. "We're headed to Macao."

"You saved Julian's life. You know that, don't you?" she said, still holding his hand. "I'm proud of you, baby."

Ten minutes later, when Wheeler came down from the wheel to recheck on Julian and Tanisha, he found Chauncy holding a document they had removed from the altar safe. It had been sealed in a bright red envelope of very heavy bond. The flap had been dipped in cinnabar paste and stamped with beautiful, intricate ideograms. The document inside was on very thin rice paper, the writing was brushed calligraphy. Chauncy handed it to Wheeler.

"I think this is the one you were looking for," he said.

Wheeler looked at the Chinese calligraphy. He could make no sense of it. "Does it say he's going to run for Governor of Hong Kong?" Wheeler asked.

"It does," Chauncy answered.

"Does it say Beijing has made a deal with Willy?" Wheeler asked again.

"It does." Then Chauncy turned the page and pointed with awe to the gorgeous red stamped imprint. "This is the seal and signature of Chen Boda, the head of the Chinese Military Commission," he said. "One of the three most powerful men in the world."

Macao

I t was nine-thirty in the morning when they dropped anchor in the Bay of Praia Grande. They could hear music
drifting across the water. Wheeler got the binoculars out
of the cabin and inspected the coastline. In the distance, along the
Avenida de Republica, a parade was winding through the outskirts
of Macao. A line of costumed, dancing people serpentined along,
carrying a huge Catholic crucifix.

"What the hell is this?" Wheeler wondered aloud.

"The February Festival," Chauncy said, looking off across
the bay.

At this distance Macao looked misplaced. It didn't seem to
belong on the east China coast. The Spanish architecture and old
steeple church of São Paulo gave it the look of a sleepy Mediterra-
nean village, but the picturesque image was destroyed by a line of
modern hotel casinos on the water. The monstrously ugly Hotel
Lisboa, with its tall white circular architecture, sat like a misplaced
visitor from Las Vegas amidst the Spanish ambiance.

Wheeler had been reading a guidebook he'd found aboard

and already knew that Macao was technically part of the Chinese mainland, connected by two bridges to the islands of Colôane and Taipa. In the hill section of central Macao, overlooking the sea, was the São Paulo Cathedral, built in the fifteen hundreds, and right next to it, a huge stone garrison, Fortaleza de Monte.

Wheeler was amazed that Julian was still alive. His color was ghastly. They had done their best to stop the external bleeding with towels, but God only knew what was leaking inside him. He had slipped into a coma and it was now impossible to awake him. Tanisha was sluggish, as well. He had to get them both medical help immediately. Wheeler and Chauncy decided on a plausible story to explain the gunshot injuries. They knew Tanisha would be questioned, and they had to make sure she was straight on the basic points. They ran it past her while she lay on the bunk in the forward stateroom. She seemed strangely uninvolved. Wheeler knew that shock could be fatal and that you had to keep the patient warm with the feet elevated, but he wasn't sure how else to treat it.

They got the Avon rubber boat in the water and Wheeler made the trip alone across the bay to the inner harbor. Off to his right were tugboats pushing barges laden with dredging sludge. Near the shore he saw floating homes on rafts tied up against the concrete pillars of the dock. The intense sun beat down, burning him, sticking his shirt to his back.

He got ashore, found a phone, and called the police.

Willy made the trip back to the City of Willows riding on a golf cart through the tunnel he had ordered dug ten years before. The tunnel had allowed his enemies to short-circuit his defenses. For the sake of his own personal convenience, he had weakened his perimeter. It had been a stupid mistake. He had said very little since being informed that the Temple safe had been breached, instructing only that the contents of the safe not be reviewed until he got there. If, miraculously, the Agreement he had negotiated with Chen Boda had been left behind, he didn't want it to be read by anyone.

He moved with quickening strides across the park. Triad assassins from the Red-Pole fighting section flanked him on both sides. He had been told of the raid by phone at five A.M. by Henry Liu. Willy had listened in silence as the acne-scarred, limping Shan Chu explained the disaster. Anger seethed. Willy intended to personally administer the Living Death to Henry as payment for his horrendous failure.

When Willy got inside the Red Flower Pavilion, he moved to the building where the Triad safe was located. It was then that he got his first big surprise. The body of Henry Liu was sprawled before the altar. He had shot himself in the mouth, the back of his head disintegrated by a 9mm slug, saving him from a more torturous end.

Willy had known Henry for most of his adult life, but in the end, Henry had failed him. Without so much as a moment's sadness, he moved around the body to the back of the altar and looked down at the plundered safe. When he saw the stacks of money and jewelry that had been thrown aside and left behind, he feared the worst. Quickly, he sorted through the contents of the safe. In less than a minute, he knew that the document outlining his arrangement with Chen Boda and Mother China was missing.

The meeting was in the Shan Chu's quarters on the top floor of the Temple. From the windows they could look out over the park. Willy had run the Chin Lo from this space for almost thirty years, before relinquishing it a few months before, to Henry Liu. Now he sat, his hands folded impassively in front of him, and looked at the Triad's section leaders, who sat on mats before him.

The White Fan and the most powerful Incense Master sat in the front row. Behind them was the Red-Pole vanguard who was head of Triad Military Operations and leader of the most feared of the two fighting sections. He had his eyes cast down in shame; he had also humiliated himself in failure.

Arranged behind him were the three old men who had accompanied the Incense Master at Fu Hai's oath-taking two days before: One was the head of the Recruiting Section, one was head of Liaisons, the last was head of the Education Section. Behind them, seated on the floor, was the organizational leader of the Triad. The two remaining fighting section leaders were seated behind him. All of the men wore the red robes except for Willy, who was in a double-breasted blue English worsted.

"In 1580, the Five Tiger Generals were outrageously accused of crimes they did not commit, and were forced by the Siu Lam Monastery to become outlaws," Willy began, his voice soft but clear in the still room. "One day, in their travels, they met with Chan Kan Nam, who was also wanted by the evil monks of the Siu Lam Monastery for killing a man who had molested Chan Kan's wife and child. Owing to his high moral character and magical powers, Chan Kan Nam was made leader and the First Shan Chu of the Secret Society of Six, which they had just formed. The new Brotherhood traveled the countryside until they came to a Red Flower Pavilion." Willy was speaking softly, in perfect Mandarin. His captive audience leaned forward to catch every word. "While they rested in the Pavilion from their travels, a red flame suddenly burst from the floor in the center of the room. The flame had great heat but made no smoke. It burned clean, leaving no ash or residue. The Five Tiger Generals and their new Shan Chu knew that this was a sign from Heaven. They believed that the Deity wanted them to devote their lives to avenging the kind of treachery and cowardice they had experienced at the hands of the evil monks of the Siu Lam Monastery, but they could not be certain. They had no divining block, no Oracle of Wisdom, to guide them.

"They drank tea during this evening and continued to ask Heaven if they should go forth and avenge the wrongs of the Siu Lam Monastery, which was, after all, a house of Heaven, but had lied wrongfully, persecuted them, outlawed them, and caused them to be fugitives. There was no sign. No answer from God. In anger, they all threw their empty teacups against the wall, but when the fragile clay cups hit the stone wall, they did not break. This they immediately accepted as a sign of Divine approval."

The men in the room nodded. They all knew the story, but it grew in importance for them as Willy retold the historic fable.

"Then the Five Tiger Generals and their Shan Chu all pricked their fingers, and mixing one drop of blood from each with a chalice of wine, they drank it and swore an oath of brotherhood, pledging themselves to undertake revenge against treachery. They also swore to give everything they had to their secret society, including their lives.

"We must take that oath again, all of us," Willy said. "For now, just as then, our Society is at stake." Willy clapped his hands and the doors opened, and men carrying silver trays with silver wine goblets entered the room. Another man carried an ornate chalice. As they passed the chalice to the section leaders, a third man stepped in front of it with a ceremonial dragon-head dagger wrapped in a red silk cloth. Each man pricked his finger and let a single drop of blood fall into the chalice. After each man had finished, they poured in a bottle of sacred wine. Willy stood and retrieved the chalice. He pricked his own finger and let a sole drop of his blood fall into the blood-tinged wine. Then he led them in a prayer of fidelity as he poured wine into each man's goblet. They all drank the mixture until the silver goblets were empty.

"Three men and one woman broke into this sacred palace and stole something of great value to our Society," he said. "They must not be allowed to survive. They must not be allowed to leave mainland China. We must return this document to the sacred safe beneath the altar and punish them with death. We must use all of our Guan-Xi. Check every airplane leaving Hong Kong, every hotel and hospital. The brother who brings me the stolen document will achieve a great lasting gift from this Society." The men were frozen before Wo Lap Ling, waiting for him to explain, wondering what the gift would be.

"The one who is successful will become the new Shan Chu," Willy said. "He will join the line of honored leaders that stretches down to us from Chan Kan Nam and the Five Tiger Generals. But if any of you work against your brothers to secure this victory, to him will go the Death by a Myriad of Swords. We have just taken an oath of solidarity. Like the first Shan Chu and the Five Generals, we must all work together to prevail."

The ambulance took Tanisha and Julian to the São Paulo Catholic Hospital. Wheeler and Chauncy were held behind to tell their story to the English-speaking Constable who had been called in specially to interview them.

"I don't really know too much," Wheeler said. "They were in the water, almost dead, when we rescued them. They told us they were out on a fishing excursion and their boat was boarded and stolen. Both had been shot. We pulled them out of the ocean and brought them here. That's all we know."

The Constable furiously wrote it all down in his book. "Pirates," he said, giving the word no emphasis one way or the other. Since they had no more information to give, he concluded that his interrogation with them was over and closed his book.

The Constable drove them slowly across the cobblestone streets of Macao, being forced several times to stop because of the parade. He said it was the Festival of Our Lord of Passos. He explained that a likeness of Christ on the crucifix was carried all around the city. It was a two-day festival participated in by everyone—Catholics and Buddhists alike. The festival had little religious significance to the mostly Chinese population, but it had been going on since the Portuguese founded Macao in 1549, and now was just a good party.

They arrived at the São Paulo Hospital at eleven, and Julian had been in surgery for almost an hour when they got there. The Constable took Tanisha's rehearsed statement in a separate room. Her wound had been cleaned and dressed, and she had been given antibiotics for infection and adrenaline for shock. She told them she had been a passenger on Julian's boat and was wounded by the pirates when she jumped into the water.

Wheeler and Chauncy sat in the sterile waiting room, turning pages in Portuguese magazines they couldn't read.

Finally, Chauncy said, "You have to leave soon. It is important that you get this document out of Macao and back to the United States. Here it will get buried and never be seen."

Wheeler nodded. He took the paper out of his pocket and looked at it again. The intricate Chinese calligraphy, on delicate, transparent rice paper, whispered evil. It was artistic and filled up two pages. He closely reexamined the signature of Chen Boda.

Tanisha joined them around noon. She walked with exaggerated stiffness. They went to the hospital cafeteria and used some of their S.A.R. money to buy a Portuguese lunch, which consisted of a steak roll called a *prego* and *batatas fritas*, which turned out to be soggy French fries.

While they ate, they decided that once they knew Julian's condition, Tanisha and Wheeler would go directly to the airport in Macao and book the first flight out to L.A. They had not yet had interviews with Customs or Immigration, because of the unusual circumstances surrounding their arrival. Wheeler hoped that wouldn't cause them a problem at the airport when they left.

At two in the afternoon, a Chinese doctor found them in the waiting room. Wheeler knew when he looked into the surgeon's face that the news wasn't going to be good.

"The Englishman has died," he told Chauncy in Cantonese. "I'm sorry, he lost too much blood. We could not save him."

After the doctor left, Chauncy told them the news.

They sat there in the cold waiting room, each with their own thoughts of the cherubic Inspector. Wheeler wondered when and how it would end. First Prescott had died, then Angela, then Tanisha's partner, Ray Fong, and the three men in Prescott's house, two of which he'd killed himself . . . then Chauncy's wife and Johnny Kwong, and now Julian. Who knew how many others had been killed in the shootout at the Triad headquarters? All had died in one way or another because of the paper he now held in his hand.

———

Wheeler and Tanisha had no trouble booking the flight out, but they had to show their passports and therefore reserve seats under their own names. They got on American flight 821 in seats 10-A and 10-B in first class. Wheeler knew it was stupid to relax, but just being on the American L-1011 was like being on U.S. soil. They waited in tense silence, expecting that at any moment, a regiment of Macao police would come aboard, arrest them, and turn them over to the Chinese Embassy.

At five in the evening, the plane's door was finally closed and they pushed back from the ramp.

Wheeler and Tanisha held hands for luck as the plane thundered down the runway and took off into the evening sky.

After the gunfight in the City of Willows, Fu Hai's loyalty to the Triad was never questioned. The bullet wound was dressed and heavily taped. He was initiated into the Chin Lo a day later. He had stood at the east gate of the Pavilion in his new red robe, and tried very hard not to show pain as they hung his Blue Lantern— the symbol of his acceptance into the Triad.

He then had to undergo a symbolic death before being reborn as a Chin Lo hero.

The Incense Master waved the Sword of Loyalty and Righteousness over his head, and Fu Hai fell to his knees. The Incense Master then stepped in front of the altar, and while the elders in the Triad listened, he told the Brethren of Fu Hai's many virtues. The White Fan described Fu Hai's heroic fighting and described the injury he had sustained in his valiant attempt to protect the Red Flower Pavilion. When Fu Hai rose, he was offered a bowl of water and the Face Washing Ceremony began, symbolizing his purity.

Then Fu Hai was told to remove his shoes and walk across the path of red-hot stones. He was so filled with the glory of the moment that miraculously, his feet were not burned. He had chosen the path of righteousness and his unblistered feet had proven him worthy. He then read aloud the tablets that were placed before the two-planked bridge. One tablet said: *Having a beginning and an end makes a true gentleman.* Another said: *The confluence of three rivers flows for a myriad of years.* Then the Incense Master retrieved and read aloud the allegorical poem found in the precious censer dish, next to the symbolic blood-stained robes that commemorated the loyal monks who were murdered at Siu Lam Monastery in 1580. The poem was beautiful in its simplicity:

> *"Three years, three years, two years, three*
> *Blood stains a river, bones cover the hill*
> *White flower open, red flower blooming*
> *Three, three makes nine, eighteen years*
> *Master and servant stop shedding tears*
> *Brightness regained, eyes wiped dry*
> *Blood stains a river, red flower and sky."*

Then Fu Hai crossed the two-plank bridge, walking slowly, with more pride in his heart than he had felt in his entire life. At the other side of the bridge, he was kissed on the cheek by both the White Fan and the Incense Master. Then Wo Lap Ling embraced him and welcomed him to the Family. The Shan Chu thanked him for his incredible bravery.

Fu Hai had never felt more alive.

Tradition said that after the initiation, there was to be a three-day feast, but Fu Hai had been singled out for a great honor. As a new member of the Triad who had requested passage to America, he would now be in charge of 180 Snake Riders. He would be an honored Snakehead who would travel with them, supervising their journey and finally delivering them to the Bamboo Dragons in Los Angeles.

Fu Hai's dreams were all finally coming true.

———

An hour after they left Macao, one of Willy's vanguards finally got around to checking the Macao airport. Using his Guan-Xi, he got into the American Airlines computer manifest. On the passenger list of flight 821 to Los Angeles, he saw the two names he was looking for: Wheeler Cassidy and Tanisha Williams. He called Willy Wo Lap from the airport and told him of the discovery.

Before American flight 821 had even cleared the Pacific Rim, Willy was already making arrangements for his enemies' arrival in Los Angeles.

PART THREE

THE SMART
MONKEY

Dry Dragon

L o Sing's favorite Zodiac animal was the Dragon. Dragons were said to be strong and commanding. Lo Sing felt he was also very strong and commanding. Dragons were supposed to be leaders, and Lo Sing headed up a fighting section of the L.A. Bamboo gang, which was one of the largest and most vicious street gangs or Tongs in Southern California.

Because he admired the qualities of the Dragon, Lo Sing chose Dragon as his gang name. He had been Dragon until somebody in his L.A. Tong found out that he couldn't swim and was desperately afraid of the water. Magically, after that, he had become Dry Dragon, which was a name that pleased him not at all. However, it had stuck, and now Dry Dragon and two of his enforcers waited outside the Customs area of American Airlines in Los Angeles. All were armed with 9mm Berettas and physical descriptions of the two Americans they were to "capture, search, and then kill without mercy," although Dry Dragon intended to change that sequence.

Lo Sing looked over at his best enforcer, White Wolf. White

Wolf was Tsang Lo Jin and, like Dry Dragon, was originally from Fukien Province in China. He was tall, with long, stringy muscles which made him lightning-quick. White Wolf would kill on command for Dry Dragon. He had proved this already, several times.

Over at the terminal gate, scanning the first passengers coming off American flight 821, was Lo Sing's cousin, Luck Wu, whose gang name was Blue Dog. Dogs were supposed to be watchful and alert, responsible and patient, all qualities that Luck Wu lacked in startling proportions. He was distracted, dull-witted, irresponsible, and barely alert. He did share one characteristic with the Zodiac symbol he had chosen for his gang name. He was defensive. Never would Luck Wu stand still for any criticism, always blaming others for his failures.

Dry Dragon would have preferred to leave his shirking cousin home, but had promised himself to try and teach Luck Wu the art of street warfare.

There were three other Bamboo Dragons in cars at the airport parking lot. Dry Dragon would contact them by walkie-talkie the minute he spotted the handsome, dark-haired man and the Black woman. He had decided not to try anything at the airport. There were several reasons for this decision. First: There were new Snake Riders coming in on phony passports from Hong Kong one terminal over on Singapore Air, and he didn't want to chance a shootout that would close down the airport and make it harder for those immigrants to post entry. Second: There was always a large police presence at the airport, and he didn't want to run that risk. Third: There were too many witnesses and too many cameras. And last: The airport traffic was accessed by one road, and they could too easily get trapped on the premises. So they had chosen another way. Dry Dragon and his two enforcers stood near the Customs area and waited with relatives of passengers from Macao.

It was unseasonably hot in Los Angeles. He could feel the desert heat in the wind as it blew across the loading zones from the parking lot, scattering leaves and scantily dressed L.A. women.

He inched closer as he watched the passengers coming up

the ramp from Customs and Immigration: Chinese businessmen carrying their computers and overnight bags; old Chinese ladies pulling airport luggage carts stacked with suitcases and taped-up boxes. And then he saw them.

The man was larger than he had expected, over six feet. He moved with athletic grace, and Dry Dragon promised himself to take no chances with him. The woman was a beautiful, light-skinned Negro. She walked with a purposeful stride, her eyes scanning the waiting crowd as if she expected trouble. Dry Dragon looked over at the vigilant White Wolf, who had also made the identification.

Over at the far gate, his cousin, Blue Dog, was leaning on the rail, paying no attention, looking at a girl standing by the magazine stand. Dry Dragon quickly moved to his cousin and punched him on the back. Luck Wu snapped his head around, glaring with mean, violent eyes. Blue Dog may have been shifty and irresponsible, but he was also homicidal and prone to violence.

"They have arrived," he said in his native Fukienese. As they moved toward the curb outside, Dry Dragon pulled out his walkie-talkie and told his soldiers in the parking lot to pull up. He watched with interest as the two targets moved out of the terminal and across the airport center island, heading back toward the parking lot for the domestic terminal. Dry Dragon, White Wolf, and Blue Dog followed, twenty yards back, not sure where they were headed. Then the handsome man and Black woman entered the United Airlines parking lot and approached a red Jag XK8. It was covered with dust and looked like it had been there for at least a week.

"United parking lot, red Jag, move up now," Dry Dragon said in Fukienese into his walkie-talkie. He had never been able to learn Mandarin, finding the new mandated language of his homeland impossible to grasp.

They followed at a distance as the two Americans got into the dust-covered Jag, backed up, and pulled out of the lot.

The Tong members separated now. Blue Dog and White

Wolf got in a green Ford with another Tong gangster. Blue Dog took over behind the wheel. Dry Dragon joined two more teen-aged shooters in a white Pinto. They followed the red Jag out of the airport and up onto the 405 Freeway toward San Diego. They had two Russian assault rifles in each car, and each Bamboo Dragon wore a bulletproof vest.

They had practiced all afternoon and knew exactly what they planned to do. Once they were out of the airport, Dry Dragon would pick a spot and give the signal on the walkie-talkie. The white Pinto in the lead would then scream up and head the Jag into the curb. The green Ford would lock it there from behind. They would surround the targets, killing them with a blast of withering automatic gunfire. Then Dry Dragon himself would get behind the Jag's wheel, and in seconds they would be headed back to a waiting garage next door to the Chin Lo headquarters in Chinatown. Dry Dragon had been told what he was looking for— a document written on rice paper in Mandarin Chinese. Since he could not read Mandarin, the document had been carefully described to him. It was two pages long, with a seal that looked like a brilliant red square with a maze of characters inside its border. Once within the safety of the garage, they would search the bodies and the car and take back what the Americans had stolen from the Triad's Red Flower Pavilion in Hong Kong. Dry Dragon would be honored for his bravery. He would be rewarded and gain much Guan-Xi. . . .

It didn't happen exactly the way he'd planned.

Tanisha checked the Glock, chambered a round, and turned to look again out the back window. She could see the white Pinto following behind them on the freeway, then saw a green Ford changing lanes, hurrying to catch up. She reached into her purse for her cellphone, turned it on, and got nothing. In the six days since she'd charged it, the battery had died. "Where's the car phone?" she asked.

"In the trunk. I always lock it in there when I leave my car at the airport."

She watched as both cars changed lanes to stay behind them.

"How did I miss these guys at the airport?" she said. "We're being followed. Two carloads. At the interchange, take the One-ten south. Get off on Manchester. It's about two miles."

"You're gonna take these guys into Watts?"

"Three good things happen when we get into South Central."

"I gotta hear this."

"One: There are more cops to the mile down there than in all the other police divisions in the city, so we've got a much better chance of backup and capture. I want to jack these guys. Two: I know the terrain and I can even the odds down there. And three: These G-sters are gonna be in unfriendly territory. If they get caught out of their cars in my hood, they're gonna be fighting to save their own wallets, watches, and balls. The homies don't give a damn, 'cause everybody's strapped down here. Once we're off on Manchester, turn left on Broadway, one block east of the free-way—we'll make a run for the South Division Station. It's on Seventy-seventh Street. It's a fortress. We get there, we're safe."

They took the 110 Harbor Freeway and headed south, toward the most dangerous ten square miles in L.A.

Dry Dragon was surprised when the red Jag transitioned onto the Harbor Freeway, heading south. He was surprised again when the car took the Manchester Avenue off-ramp. He pressed the key on his walkie-talkie. "Move up," he instructed.

Now both pursuing cars pulled into the slow lane and took the Manchester turn-off. Manchester was in the D.M.Z. between L.A. and Watts. Like most border areas, it had taken on the protective coloring of its rougher neighbor: Steel grates were pulled down in front of bulletproof windows; graffiti-scarred liquor stores seemed to dot every street corner; motels and tire stores sat side by side.

"We're going to do it now," Dry Dragon said nervously over his walkie-talkie.

The Pinto, with Dry Dragon inside, squealed up to overtake the red Jag. Two of the four Bamboo Dragon gangsters in the Pinto leaned out of the windows, waving assault rifles, as the Pinto attempted to run the Jag to the curb. But Wheeler saw it coming and immediately turned right on Broadway. The Pinto missed the turn and went shooting off, down Manchester.

"Turn left!" Tanisha shouted, her voice shrill in the closed plush interior. "There's a narrow alley ahead, goes for six blocks. Go right at the alley," she yelled.

Wheeler found it and started to speed along, hitting the rain run-offs that transected the alley at every block corner. Only the green Ford was behind them now, trying desperately to stay up with the faster Jag.

Inside the Ford, Blue Dog cursed in anger as he fought the wheel. He had never been down here before. He didn't know his way around; worse still, as he glanced out the window, he thought this might be L.A.'s Black ghetto. White Wolf, sitting beside him, triggered the walkie-talkie and started screaming out street names to Dry Dragon, hoping the leader in the lost white Pinto would intersect and get back in the game, but that wasn't going to happen, because the white Pinto had already crashed into a chain-link fence that surrounded an outdoor basketball court on the corner of Manchester and Elm, knocking down the backboard.

Dry Dragon and his two accomplices got out to check the damage and found themselves staring at ten angry Black basketball players.

"Hey, chump! You fuckin' with our B-ball. We gonna break on yer Chink bullshit asses."

"Huh?" Dry Dragon said. What happened next was painful and not easy to watch. The three Bamboo Dragons were surrounded and punched into unconsciousness.

In the alley a few blocks away the Jag miraculously slowed, allowing the green Ford to get closer.

"Pull up, get alongside," White Wolf said, not seeing the trap. Blue Dog pulled the green Ford up, and White Wolf leaned out the passenger window, firing a long stream of bullets at the foreign car. His aim was badly skewed as the Ford hit one of the rain run-offs, bouncing hard on its shocks. Most of the rounds either chipped off the pavement or went wild into the air. White Wolf yelled at Blue Dog to pull back up alongside. Then, unexpectedly, the Jag swerved left and Blue Dog saw a chance to pull even by passing on the right. He shoved the accelerator down and sped up next to the XK8.

"No . . . no, not this side!" White Wolf screamed, but it was already too late. White Wolf, holding his smoking Russian machine gun, was trapped on the wrong side of the car. Blue Dog found himself looking down the barrel of Tanisha's plastic Glock, which was pointed out the passenger window, only inches from his nose. His Chinese features contorted in distress. He finally achieved two of the mythic characteristics of his Zodiac animal: In the brief seconds before Tanisha pulled the trigger, Blue Dog finally became watchful and alert. As the gun fired, he swung the wheel and skidded the green Ford sideways. The bullet missed. The Ford swerved out of control, and as the Jag sped away out of danger, the Ford hit a telephone pole. The explosive impact stood the car up on its nose. All three Kevlar-vested Bamboo Dragons flew head first out the front windshield and bounced on the rough asphalt. None of them survived.

The South Division Station was heavily guarded. There were parking lot details that worked a constant beat; there were also police marksmen on the roof. The division was in the worst crime area in the city and the station had been bombed more than once, so it was protected like a fortress. The parking lot guards, armed with M-16s, looked up in surprise as the red Jag screamed down Broadway toward them, the horn honking, the high beams flashing. The guards brought their weapons up to firing position and sighted on the Jag.

"Is this one of our undercovers?" one of the guards screamed.

"An XK8? You fuckin' nuts?" the second guard answered.

They were getting set to fire when the Jag turned left on 77th Street and crashed through the fence and barricade, shuddering to a stop inside the parking lot.

The two parking lot guards ran toward the red Jag, weapons cocked and ready.

"Out of the car, hands in the air!" they shouted.

"Detective Williams," Tanisha shouted back. "Asian Crimes. I'm a cop." She had her badge in her hand, out the window.

"You fuckin' nuts? You don't come roarin' in here unannounced like that," the parking lot guard said, his heart pumping adrenaline, his finger tightly wrapped around the trigger. Then both guards stepped back, and still pointing their assault rifles, ordered them out of the car.

THIRTY

If It Has Four Legs
and Is Not a Table, Then Eat It

Ellen Ming sat in the small room that housed the switchboard at Asian Crimes and listened in on the phone call she had just patched through to Captain Verba at his home. The call had come in from Tanisha Williams. It was two in the morning. Ellen had made the connection, waking the grumpy Captain, telling him that Tanisha had an urgent situation, and then she stayed on the line, undetected, and listened as the Black detective gave a brief description of what had happened on her way in from the airport. Tanisha told Captain Verba that she was still at the new South Division Station in South Central and needed to see him right away.

"Jesus, Tanisha, it's the fucking middle of the night," Captain Verba said, his voice filled with sleep and anger at being awakened. "That could have just been an attempted car-jack. You say you were in a new XK8?"

Ellen listened as Tanisha spoke slowly for emphasis. "Captain, it wasn't a car-jack. This is big. Bigger than anything we've ever worked on down there. Wait till you read this document we got out of Triad headquarters in Hong Kong."

The Captain agreed to get up, but he didn't want to drive all the way to South Division in the middle of the night. "I'll meet you in the coffee shop at the Westin in half an hour," he said, the Westin being a fifteen-story hotel on Hill Street that catered mostly to Asian businessmen. It was familiar ground, an Asian Crimes after-work watering hole.

"Captain, I don't think—"

"Listen, Detective, you got a pile of trouble right now." Verba's voice was gaining strength as he woke up. "I.A. went into your Police Academy ap. You told me you had family problems in Cleveland. According to them, you don't *have* any relatives in Cleveland. They think you're ducking them 'cause you're guilty, and frankly, so do I. I'll see you at the Westin in half an hour," and he hung up.

Ellen Ming disconnected the phone patch and sat very still in the Dispatch Center. She was thirty-six and delicate, with exotic Asian features. She had been in America for only four years, having grown up in Shanghai. She had gotten married at fifteen and had two children there. Her husband had died of dysentery, and her children had left China in their mid-teens, Riding the Snake to America. In order to secure their passage, she had personally guaranteed the huge cost demanded by the Chin Lo Triad. She had been a schoolteacher in Shanghai, but had lost her job. In order to pay for her children's voyage, she had finally been forced to dance at Triad nightclubs in Hong Kong. After three years of nude dancing and prostitution, she had finally gained favor with a powerful Triad enforcer who eventually arranged for her to join her son and daughter in L.A.

She managed to avoid dancing in Triad clubs in L.A.'s Chinatown by getting another job teaching school. She was extremely quick with language and soon mastered English. But her family still owed large sums of money to the Chin Lo, and they lived in squalor as she and her son and daughter all struggled to pay back what they owed. The Bamboo street gangs took everything her children made working in a Chinatown restaurant, plus what she made teaching school. They ate only what they could steal. Since she was a child in the streets of Shanghai, hunger had pursued her like a ravenous dog, growling in the pit of her stomach. There was a Cantonese joke about hunger: "If it flies in the air and is not an airplane, if it swims in the sea and is not a submarine, if it has four legs and is not a table, then eat it."

Her life in America seemed hopeless until one afternoon her Snakehead in Los Angeles called and demanded a meeting. She had been frightened that she or her daughter would be forced back into a strip club or, worse yet, prostitution.

But that was not what the Snakehead wanted. "There is a job for somebody who speaks many Chinese dialects," he said. "How many dialects do you have?"

"I speak Mandarin and Cantonese, Hakka and Fukienese," she said, naming only a few of the dialects that she had mastered.

"The Los Angeles Police need translators. It's always nice to be kind to your enemy." He grinned.

She had easily won the job.

Working at the LAPD, she had paid back much of what her son and daughter owed to the Snakehead. Soon her family would be free of the Triads. But until that day, she had to continue to perform acts of "loyalty" to survive. She picked up the phone and dialed.

The coffee shop of the Westin Hotel was completely empty at two-thirty in the morning. Tanisha and Wheeler sat in a booth with their backs against the wall. Both faced the room as a half-asleep Asian waitress moved to them with two cups of coffee, which she gently set down in front of them. At a quarter to three, Rick Verba moved into the restaurant and joined them. His hair was badly combed and he still had sleep in the corner of his eyes, not having bothered to shower.

"Okay, this better fucking blow the roof off my day, Tisha," he said without even saying hello.

"Captain Verba, this is Wheeler Cassidy," she said, introducing Wheeler.

Verba looked over but didn't bother to shake hands. Instead, his eyebrows climbed his forehead in surprise. "*The* Wheeler Cassidy?" he said disdainfully.

"What's that supposed to mean?" Wheeler countered.

"Well, not counting half-a-dozen D.U.I.s and assault charges where you kicked the shit out of angry husbands in country club parking lots, aren't you the trigger-happy citizen who peeled a clip of nines at three Bamboo Dragons and sent two of them off to live with their cloud ancestors?"

"You're packing more than your share of attitude, Captain. Why don't you slow down and look at what we've got," Wheeler said, unintentionally slipping into his snotty country club voice.

"Because Detective Williams, who happens to be under my direct supervision, keeps putting her booty in the bucket. She lied to me and to Internal Affairs. She's working this case off the board, and she's about to get drop-kicked into a no-pension retirement."

"Detective Williams is the best goddamn cop you've ever been around, and if you weren't such a constipated asshole you'd know that, and defend her instead of attacking her," Wheeler said hotly and with way too much emotion.

Verba looked at Tanisha, nonplussed. "Jesus, dear God in Heaven, don't tell me you're fucking this guy," Verba said. "He's on your case sheet, for Christ's sake."

"Can we get past the bullshit and deal with what we're here for?" Tanisha finally said, blushing, which is hard to see on black skin, but nobody missed it on her in the brightly lit Westin coffee shop. Tanisha pulled out of her purse the document that they'd stolen from the Red Flower Pavilion and put it on the Formica tabletop in front of him. "You can read Chinese, can't you, Captain?"

"I'm taking classes. I struggle along," he said, opening the document and looking at it.

"That agreement says that a Triad Shan Chu in Hong Kong

named Wo Lap Ling has cut a deal to run, unopposed, for the Chief Executive of the S.A.R. in mid-'98. That's Governor-General of Hong Kong."

Verba looked at the document, scratching his head and yawning. "So what?" he said. "What's that got to do with Asian crime in Los Angeles?"

"It's why my brother and Angela Wong got murdered," Wheeler said, pulling a typed sheet out of his pocket. "This is a transcript of a tape we found in my brother's car. When we were in the Walled City at the library of the Red Flower Pavilion two days ago, I saw a collection of antique books on the history of California by Father John Stoddard. My brother has the same collection. What would a Chinese Triad leader want with a Dominican monk's description of the California gold rush?"

"How the fuck would I know?" Verba said, beginning to get annoyed.

"Because volume ten of that collection was the volume they were using for their key book code. All these numbers on this letter correspond to pages and letters in that book. I can explain how the key book code works, if you want."

"I know how a key book code works," Verba answered, looking at the document.

"What it comes down to, Captain," Tanisha said, "is Prescott Cassidy was a cut-out man for the Hong Kong Chin Lo Triad. The Triads have been flooding our markets here with illegal aliens, guns, and heroin. It's why 'China White' has made such a huge comeback in the last five years. Prescott was a local fund-raiser for politicians here in the U.S., funneling Triad cash into political campaigns. He also bribed I.N.S. officials to get green cards or political asylum for Snake Riders. His secretary, Angela, was a Chinese national. Her real last name was Kwong, not Wong. Her son, Johnny Kwong, was a Hong Kong cop. They were part of the Triad criminal pipeline—mostly working on illegal immigration, I think, but probably some dope and gun deals, too. Prescott Cassidy had been contacted by the FBI. They were asking him questions. He and Angela were killed because the Triad was afraid Prescott would spill to the FBI.

"Willy can't let this document come to light. If the two signatures at the bottom of that agreement can be verified as his and Chen Boda's, and I think they easily can, then this paper is political dynamite.

"The Communist leaders in Beijing want to convince us they're living up to the Sino-British Joint Declaration, but they're not. All of these paid-off Senators and Congressmen, the d's and r's in this letter, are supposed to carry the ball in Congress to get Wo Lap political acceptability in the U.S., so our government will support his election in Hong Kong. Our current political fund-raising scandals reach right back to this criminal empire," Tanisha said, tapping the document as he struggled to read it. "This represents proof that the third-largest banking center in the world has been sold to an international criminal organization."

There was a long silence while they waited for Verba's response.

"Gimme all that again," he finally said, looking up and then waving at the waitress for a cup of coffee.

Twenty minutes later, they had gone through it again, this time adding a detailed description of their Hong Kong adventures in the Walled City. They described the deaths of Johnny Kwong and Julian Winslow, their penetration of the City of Willows, the escape from Macao, and the attempt on their lives coming in from the airport. When it was over, Rick Verba sat in the booth looking at them speechless, his eyes peeled open in wonder.

"That is the most preposterous fucking story I ever heard," he finally said. He folded the document and put it in his pocket just as four Chinese businessmen in suits arrived in the coffee shop carrying briefcases. The group sat at a table directly across the restaurant from them. Tanisha kept her eye on the men over Captain Verba's shoulder, as he motioned for the bill. Tanisha thought two of the Chinese businessmen were improbably young, maybe nine-teen or twenty. The suits all looked brand-new and very cheap. Now two of them opened their briefcases and started to rummage inside, pretending to look for papers.

"Captain, are you packing?" she said softly.

Verba looked up, "Huh?"

"You strapped?"

"Yeah," he said, "a nine under my wing and a twenty-five on my ankle. Why?"

"Give him the twenty-five and get the nine unhooked," she said, still watching the Chinese businessmen over his shoulder.

"Why?" the Captain asked.

" 'Cause right behind you is a four-man posse. We're five seconds from getting splashed on. I'll call it for you. . . ."

Without turning, Verba reached under his arm with one hand and down to his ankle with the other. He slid the .25 across the table and yanked the 9mm out of the upside-down rig he wore under his arm. Tanisha had the Glock out of her purse. Suddenly, the four Chinese men got up. They all had 9mm automatics in their hands.

"Now!" Tanisha shouted as the Chinese stood, and Verba spun, gun hand outstretched. Wheeler and Tanisha dove right and left, firing. Simultaneously, seven guns barked in the over-lit coffee shop. The waitress screamed, running for cover.

The Chinese assassins didn't expect a simultaneous counter-attack from their "unsuspecting" targets, and hurried their initial volley. It was a costly mistake, as their first rounds went wild, breaking a bad Chinese brush painting on the wall behind their intended victims. Tanisha, Wheeler, and Verba got three of the four with their first shots. The three gangsters went down, raking the far side of the room with automatic gunfire as they fell. The fourth man turned and ran. Verba pulled down on him and hit him between the shoulders, blowing him out into the lobby, where he landed and slid on the polished floor.

The suddenly quiet coffee shop was filled with the lingering memory of gunfire and the coppery smell of blood and cordite. Only one of the Chinese gangsters was still alive, croaking like a hooked flounder, his mouth opening and closing, barely audible sounds coming out.

"Call an ambulance," Verba said to the waitress, who was still screaming hysterically.

"Call a fucking ambulance, dammit!" he bellowed at her, and she ran to the phone.

Tanisha looked at Verba, who had been nicked in the ear by gunfire. Blood was running down his face. "How preposterous does it seem to you now?" she asked.

THIRTY-ONE

The Smart Monkey

I t was ten o'clock in the morning before Tanisha, Wheeler, and Captain Verba were through with the Major Crimes Investigators from Parker Center. They had all filled out field shooting reports and given statements. The four dead Bamboo Dragons were now parked on gurneys in the morgue, next to the three who had died in the car accident in South Central. A Chinese gurney traffic jam. The lone survivor of all of the carnage was in the L.A. County Trauma Unit with one of Rick Verba's 9mm half-loads still buried in his back. His condition was critical and doubtful.

All the dead Chinese Dragons had been fingerprinted, but the print run had failed to turn up anything. They didn't exist in the LAPD computer files and were being listed as John Does. They had been further categorized as probable illegal immigrants.

Tanisha, Verba, and Wheeler were now back in the Captain's office at Asian Crimes, with strict instructions from the Investigators at Major Crimes to let Parker Center handle the follow-up investigation.

"They couldn't find shit in an elephant's asshole," Verba said bitterly, pulling the blinds in his office to cut out the stares of the other Asian detectives. Everybody out there knew that Rick and Tanisha had just washed out four Bamboo Dragons, and that Tanisha had DOA'd three others in a South Central car chase.

As he sat in Verba's office, Wheeler's mind felt sluggish. He was still on Hong Kong time and he had cooked too much adrenaline. His muscles felt burned-out and unresponsive, his mind running at quarter-speed.

Rick Verba reached into the inside pocket of his jacket and pulled out the document taken from the Red Flower Pavilion. He set it down on the desk. "Now, how the hell do we get these signatures verified?" he said.

"You kept it? I thought you were supposed to give everything over to Lieutenant Miller, downtown," Tanisha said.

"This is my beat, our case. Those Parker Center cowboys aren't going to run the maze down in Chinatown," he said. "So how do we prove this paper?"

"Xerox it and I'll fax it to Willard Vickers," Wheeler said. "He'll get it verified."

Tanisha nodded and gave Wheeler a smile that turned into a yawn. "Sorry," she said.

"Go home, get some sleep," Verba ordered.

"I don't think she should go home. And I don't think I should, either. This makes two attempts on our lives since we landed," Wheeler said, "and, as long as we're on that subject, how did those Bamboo Dragons know we were going to be at that hotel restaurant in the first place? How the hell did they find us there?"

"Good question," Tanisha nodded.

"Maybe they followed you from South Division," Verba speculated.

"Not unless they were in a chopper," she said. "We took every precaution. Nobody was tailing us."

"Then I don't know," Verba said.

"Did you tell anybody?" she asked him.

"No. I came right from my house."

They sat in silence.

"Could your car have a tracking bug planted on it? Or your suitcases? Or clothes?" Verba finally asked them.

"It's possible," Tanisha said.

"Okay, we'll go through everything, luggage, clothes, the works," Verba said. "I'll get the Jag swept in the garage downstairs. If that comes up clean, I don't know what to tell you."

After they left Verba's office, Tanisha ran into Al Katsukura in the detective squad room.

"You okay?" the Japanese detective asked her.

"Yeah, thanks for asking. How you doing with Ray's murder?"

"I'm nowhere. It's sitting in my casefile. Meanwhile, I'm back on Snake Patrol. Operation Dry Dock now."

"What the hell is that?" she asked.

"Some Chinese guy tried to rent the *Hornblower* down at Marina Del Rey. It's one of those big party boats you can charter for a wedding or office party. Only he wanted it stocked with enough fuel to go over thirty miles. The guy at the boat company thought that was a weird request, like maybe they wanted the boat for some drug deal, so he called us. We put an undercover in there. We're playing along with it. Looks like they're going to use the *Hornblower* to off-load some Snake Riders from a mother ship outside the three-mile limit. Only this time, I finally convinced Verba to play it smart. We're gonna be set up to follow them. Trace 'em all the way to the end user. Throw a net over the whole operation."

"Good way to play it," she said, yawning again.

The bug detectors went through their luggage, their clothes, and the car, but found nothing. Tanisha and Wheeler watched as they put the carpet back in the trunk, and when they were finished, Wheeler hooked his cellphone back inside the car.

"We gotta find a place to go where we won't get dead," he said.

"My grandmother's house," she said. "My grandmother still lives there with my niece. It's south of Crenshaw. Not the most scenic neighborhood in L.A., but you can't beat the hood for keeping out off-brand G-sters."

"Sounds good to me as long as it's got a soft pillow and a dark room."

"Let's go then."

They got into the Jag and left the safety of the Asian Crimes parking lot. Wheeler drove onto the freeway, but instead of going south, he took the turnoff heading west toward Bel Air. She looked over at him in wonder. "I've got one stop I want to make first," he said.

Liz Cassidy stood in the entry hall of Prescott's Bel Air house and glared at Tanisha until Wheeler finally returned from the den with volume ten of John Stoddard's *History of California.*

"Where are you going with that?" Liz asked.

"I'll bring it back, Liz. I promise."

"We missed you at Prescott's funeral." Her voice was brittle in the air-conditioned foyer.

"I'm sorry."

"Are you and your policewoman friend here having a nice time?" she asked coldly. "Have you managed to destroy Prescott's reputation yet?"

"Liz, I'm sorry. I know you can't understand what I'm trying to do. I don't expect you to."

Tanisha felt like a spectator at a family hanging.

"I understand, Wheeler. *Oh boy, do I understand,*" Liz said, her shrill voice filling the entry. "Prescott tried to help you. He tried to explain your hopeless lifestyle to your mother. He stood up for you when nobody else did, and in return you're hell bent on destroying his legacy. You are the most pathetic excuse for a human being I've ever seen."

"I'm tired of this. . . . I've had it, Liz. Consider what would have happened if this 'pathetic excuse for a human being' hadn't been here a week ago and stepped up. You and Hollis might be dead too. I didn't start this. It wasn't me who invited this tragedy into our family, but I'm gonna for damn sure get it out. I'm going to find out who killed my little brother. . . . I'm doing this for Pres. He wanted it. He asked me to." Then they turned and left Liz standing there, speechless.

As they got back on the freeway heading south, Wheeler was thinking of the last time he had seen Pres alive, sitting across from him in the Westridge Country Club dining room. It was one sentence that had made no sense back then, but now gave him the strength to go on: *"Whatever happens,"* his brother had said, *"promise me you'll do the right thing."*

Sometimes Willy thought about dragons. He had read books on the mythic Chinese power symbols. Dragons were the chief lizards of the 360 scaly reptiles that lived on the planet. Dragons had four legs but often walked on two. The Imperial Dragon had five claws on each foot, other dragons only four. The dragon was said to have nine resemblances: Its horns resembled those of a deer, its head that of a camel; it had the eyes of a devil, the neck of a snake; its abdomen was like that of a large crocodile; it had the scales of a carp, the claws of an eagle, the feet of a tiger, and the ears of an ox. The small dragon was like the silk caterpillar with many legs and little to protect it. But the large dragon filled both Heaven and Earth.

Willy sat in his magnificent jet, thinking of dragons while the U.S. Customs officials made their final entry marks on his visa. He was traveling on his British passport, so entry into the United States was still quite easy.

His jet was parked in front of the LAX Executive Jet Terminal. Finally, Customs and Immigration signed him off, stamped his passport, and left his plane without checking the luggage hold where Willy had a secret compartment containing a deadly suitcase.

Willy walked down the ramp and got into a gray Lincoln Town Car. He waited while his pilots retrieved his luggage from the plane. The last suitcase came from the secret compartment and had Russian writing on its side. It was placed in the trunk with his other belongings.

The man behind the wheel of the Town Car had introduced himself as Lee Chow, saying his American name was Danny. Danny Lee put the car in gear and drove Willy off the tarmac. Willy said nothing to him, choosing his own thoughts over meaningless conversation.

As they drove toward Chinatown, Willy remembered "The Legend of the Foolish Dragon." The way the story went, the Foolish Dragon had a very sick wife. They lived at the bottom of the ocean. The Dragon's sick wife said to him, "I must eat the heart of a Smart Monkey to survive."

The Foolish Dragon then said to his wife, "But how will I get such a heart?"

His wife said, "I don't know, but you must try or I will surely die."

The Foolish Dragon left the bottom of the sea and went up onto shore, looking for a Smart Monkey. He finally found one, sitting on the highest limb of a huge willow tree.

"I will take you wherever you want to go," the Foolish Dragon said. "Just climb on my back. It is much easier to ride than to walk."

"But I don't need a ride," the Smart Monkey said. "I can swing from vines."

"You can go much farther and faster on my back," the Foolish Dragon coaxed.

So the Smart Monkey climbed down onto the Dragon's back and the Dragon rushed back into the sea. As the Monkey's eyes and mouth filled with water, he cried out, "Why are you taking me into the sea?"

"Because my wife is very sick and if she can eat the heart of a Smart Monkey, she will not die."

"Oh, this is terrible," the Smart Monkey said. "Your wife will die, for I have left my heart back in the tree. If she needs to eat my heart, we must go back and get it."

The Foolish Dragon turned and lumbered back onto land, then the Smart Monkey grabbed the limb of the tree and scurried back to safety.

"What are you doing, my little friend? You must come back. Bring your heart, my wife is dying."

"You must be a very Foolish Dragon," the Smart Monkey said, laughing at him from the highest limb of the tree.

Willy had been a Foolish Dragon. It was now time for him to be the Smart Monkey.

THIRTY-TWO

South of Manchester

T he house was an old, run-down two-story that was trying hard to look Victorian. A wooden porch and circular corner turrets should have helped the effect, but somehow only managed to look like add-ons. The house was located south of Manchester Boulevard, in the Leimert Park section of South Central on Bronson Street. They pulled up the drive and parked behind a '63 Impala bomber, known as a "glass house" because both front and back windows were wrap-arounds. The Chevy was dripping oil like an Italian gigolo.

The red Jag had been drawing street-corner attention ever since they passed La Cienega. "Pull around on the grass in back," Tanisha said. "Your car will be a duck in half an hour if you park it out here."

They drove down the drive under an exposed telephone wire that went from the phone pole at the street to the eave of the house. Hanging by their laces over the wire and visible from the street were a pair of old tennis shoes. Tanisha glared up at them as they drove underneath. "Shit," she said to herself softly.

The back of the house had a small dirt yard with an old, rusted swing set next to a woodpile, where several sections of metal fencing were stacked. Wheeler parked and turned off the engine.

"That's my nephew LaFrance's glass-house Impala out front. He's a kitchen-table drug dealer and a big family problem. Those tennis shoes hanging on the phone line are a ghetto advertisement to anybody driving by that you can buy drugs inside. My grandmother, Nadine, is old. She can't handle him. I thought I ran LaFrance out a month ago."

They moved up onto the back porch, where Tanisha found a key under an empty, cracked flowerpot.

"Clever spot," Wheeler said.

"Honey, if you can still find anything in this house worth stealing, then the immediate family musta gone blind."

They entered a very dark hall with overstuffed chairs and old wooden furniture. The hammering beat of a Puff Daddy rap song was blasting the windows in the front of the house. They moved toward the laughter and music, into a room where ten teenage boys and girls were skinnin' and grinnin'. There was a strong smell of laced cigarette smoke.

"What the fuck is this, LaFrance?" Tanisha demanded.

The roomful of Black teenagers turned and looked at her as if she had just been beamed down into their midst from outer space.

"It's the PO-lice," a tall, muscular seventeen-year-old drawled in amusement as he stood and moved away from his friends. He had eyes lidded by marijuana and a graceful indolence. Tanisha could see bags of narcotics and money on the coffee table behind him. Several of his crew got busy gathering up the baggies and the cash and stuffing them in Raider jackets or sagging pants.

"Where's Nadine?" Tanisha said, glaring at her nephew.

"She upstairs, boned-out, like she do," LaFrance said, performing a gangsta lean, bobbing his head for his friends. "It don't matter no way. What come 'round go 'round. I call the play now."

"You still rotating, LaFrance? I thought we got that straightened out last time you hit the numbers." "Rotating" was gang talk for selling drugs; "the numbers" was jail.

"That's my stack money," he said, indicating the money on the table. "Saved up from my job." She knew he didn't have a job. LaFrance was rocking on his heels now, almost as if he wanted to take a step away from her, but was afraid to show weakness to his homies. "Who dis gray cat you got with you?" he finally said, to change the subject.

"Friend of mine."

"You givin' this ice-slice, Gumby motherfucker some play? No wonder you be cracked on down here."

Wheeler unsnapped the gold band on his Rolex watch and let it slip down his wrist into his left pocket.

"Is that you, Breezy?" Tanisha said, looking around La-France at a young girl barely in her teens. She was LaFrance's half sister and sat on the sofa with both a cigarette and her adolescent beauty smoldering.

Tanisha glared at her nephew. "You gonna hook your own little sister to a dope ride?" Now Tanisha was angry, and she took a step toward LaFrance. He backed up slightly. "I oughta bust you myself for this pile a' candy cane and these laced blunts," she said, grabbing a bag of white powder off the table and holding it up. She shook the baggie and glared at her nephew. "This isn't coke. You sellin' heroin? I oughta nine-one-one your sorry ass."

"What you call yourself doin' here?" LaFrance said, his voice rising. "You bess be jaw-jackin', 'cause I ain't gonna stand here, whatever, let you call no blue light motherfuckers in. I be comin' outta the bag, you try that."

Wheeler took a step forward. "Anytime you feel froggy, dick-wad," he said softly.

LaFrance looked at his homies. He had to do something. He couldn't be fronted off by a middle-aged honky. His homies returned the stare, watching, calmly waiting to see how LaFrance would handle it.

Without warning, LaFrance let go with a wild right uppercut aimed at Wheeler's chin. Wheeler had been waiting for it and La-France had telegraphed the punch. Wheeler wasn't very good with

Uzis or nine-shot Italian target pistols, but he still had one of the best left hooks in Beverly Hills. As LaFrance swung his uppercut, Wheeler moved to the side and bent his knees, which dropped his center of gravity a half-foot. The uppercut went wild over his right shoulder. Simultaneously, Wheeler swung his left, connecting with LaFrance's midsection, directly under his exposed armpit. He could feel a rib snap as the hook landed. LaFrance stumbled back, screaming and holding his side. He crashed down on the coffee table. They glared at each other. "The fuck you be doin'?" LaFrance whined.

"Kickin' your ass," Wheeler answered.

"We rollin'," one of the gangsters suddenly said. They got up and moved quickly out of the living room, onto the front porch, all in different directions up the street, disappearing in the dingy neighborhood like cockroaches under a baseboard.

LaFrance stood slowly, groaning in pain. He turned and looked at Tanisha. "You a fuckin' transformin' ho'," he said. "Turn on your own."

"I can't believe you're still dealing drugs in your own family's living room. What the hell's wrong with you?" she scolded.

LaFrance didn't answer. He turned and walked out of the house, still holding his side. A second later, they heard the Impala start, and, with mufflers rumbling loud through torn glass packs, he backed it out of the driveway and roared away. Now only Breezy was left.

"I'm sorry, Auntie," she said, standing and beginning to straighten up the living room, emptying the ashtrays.

"Girl, you gonna end up somebody's bag bride. You gonna be off doing a telephone number, and when that happens, none a' these busters gonna cut you any time." A "bag bride" was a coke addict prostitute; a "telephone number" was a long prison stretch. Tanisha was home now. She was back in the hood, her U.C.L.A. education undetectable as she talked street to her thirteen-year-old niece.

Breezy finished picking up the paper-clipped marijuana blunts in the ashtray and threw them into the downstairs toilet.

"How's Nadine?" Tanisha asked.

"She sleeping most of the time. The medicine they give her for arthritis be what's doing it to her."

"If LaFrance comes back, I want to know."

"I will, Auntie," Breezy said without conviction, and she nodded her head. "I gotta go. You gonna be 'round later?"

"I'm gonna ask Nadine if we can stay here a few days."

Breezy smiled, showing beautiful teeth. She was going to be a stunner someday if the laced joints and double-ups didn't get her first. Tanisha made herself a promise to watch her niece much closer. She was only one or two bad decisions from disaster. "Don't worry about LaFrance," Breezy suddenly said. "He gonna be right one day."

They both knew it wasn't true. LaFrance was headed toward self-destruction at warp speed.

Upstairs, Tanisha found her grandmother. She was in a four-poster bed, propped up with pillows, "sleeping with her eyes open," as she called it. Wheeler was standing in the upstairs hall.

"Granny . . ." Tanisha said, and waited until recognition flitted across Nadine's face. Her grandmother was a short, overweight woman who had completely lost her ability to smile.

"Hi, chile," she said, her jowls sagging as she struggled to sit up straighter. "You been a long time away."

Tanisha kissed her grandmother and then sat down on a chair next to the bed. "Granny, I just caught LaFrance downstairs doing a heroin deal. I don't want him bringing gangsters into your house to sell dope. I'm worried about Breezy."

"What I gonna do, chile? I can't move all de way downstairs ever' time I hear dey music. My ankle's been swellin', hurt somethin' awful."

"You call me. You tell me if he comes over and I'll get him out."

Nadine looked at Tanisha and nodded. If eyes were the windows to the soul, hers showed a tired, reluctant spirit that had given up all hope to pain and poverty. Tanisha went to the door and pulled Wheeler into the room from the spot where he'd been waiting.

"This is my friend Wheeler Cassidy," she said. "We'd like to stay here for a couple of days."

"Now, what you go be doin', girl? You bring a White man to visit, we gonna get ourselves in mo' trouble than Jack's stray cat."

"Granny, we had nowhere else to go. Somebody's after us, but they can't get to us down here."

Nadine closed her eyes. When she opened them, they showed tired acceptance. "Lord God a'mighty," she whispered softly. "What we gettin' our foolish selves into now?"

It was the same question Wheeler had been asking himself.

They were gathered before him, sitting on wooden chairs that they had dragged in from the meeting hall. The room was small and over-heated and everybody was shiny with sweat, except for Wo Lap Ling, who sat patiently, cooled by his iron willpower. He listened as Dry Dragon recited the events of the botched assault at the airport. Dry Dragon still showed the effects of the terrible beating he had taken in South Central. His face and lips were swollen. He had been left barely conscious and had finally managed to get a taxi out of there, by using fifty dollars he always kept hidden in his shoe. He finished the miserable tale and looked in terror at the powerful Shan Chu.

"You have brought disgrace on yourselves and this Brother-hood," Willy said. Shame and culpability instantly shot up, heating Dry Dragon's cheeks, painting his ears red. "Do we have any idea where they might be?" Willy asked in Fukienese, because most of the Bamboo Dragons in the room were from Fukien Province and didn't speak much Mandarin or Cantonese.

"No, Shan Chu," the White Fan of the Los Angeles Triad said. He was a fifty-year-old, extremely fit Chinese gangster who had come from Taiwan in the late sixties. His name was Chu Lu. He wore his Bamboo Dragon fighting colors: black pants, black shirt, and a red bandanna. He was afraid that the most powerful Shan Chu of the Hong Kong chapter would simply raise a hand and have him disposed of for his failures. "We have an ear inside the Police Department," the White Fan added, looking for any way to appease Wo Lap Ling's judgment of him. "A switchboard operator. She can listen in on their calls. The Black woman detective has already called her Captain and left a phone number. She didn't give an address, but the prefix is two-one-three, and the first three digits of her phone number are four-eight-five. That means the call was made from somewhere in South Central."

"Where is South Central?" Willy asked. "Is it far?"

"It's a part of L.A.," the White Fan said respectfully.

"L.A. has over three million people. Are you suggesting we drive around looking for her? Surely this can't be your solution," Willy said. He was tired from his flight and angry at their failures. The local Chin Lo brethren were violent men, but seemed to have no sense of ingenuity or guile.

"Most Honorable Shan Chu," the White Fan said, bowing his head to show subservience, "South Central is a Black ghetto, where people are shot for no reason. However, we have great Guan-Xi in this place because the gangs sell our China White. We supply many dealers. The gangs control everything in that neighborhood, but they need our heroin. We have already told them there is a great reward for finding the Black policewoman, Tanisha Williams, and her White boyfriend." The White Fan looked into Wo Lap Ling's stoic face. He suddenly wondered if he had made a mistake telling the Shan Chu that he was relying on coloreds to solve this problem. "It does not matter if the cat is black or white as long as he catches rats," the White Fan added, using one of Deng Xiaoping's famous sayings.

Willy Wo Lap felt events had turned against him. Now that the two Americans were back inside their own country, how hard could it be for them to get the stolen document into dangerous hands? Time was now his most virulent enemy.

In less than two hours, the word was on the street. Tanisha Williams was worth fifty keys of China White.

At three that afternoon, LaFrance was sitting in front of the Payless, drinking Forty-Nine out of a paper bag. His side was killing him and he was still angry. A Santa Ana wind had started that afternoon and was blowing hot air out of the desert and the temperature was climbing, which didn't help his attitude. He could hear Bad Sam and Li'l T-Bear shooting hoops in the parking lot around the corner, doing lay-ups against an invisible basket, their voices drifting to him on the hot afternoon wind.

"Man, I be bust outta this shitbag, y'know, have me some fine pussy, be rollin' deep," Bad Sam said as Li'l T-Bear bounced the basketball, in no hurry to play because of the heat.

"Fifty keys, da man say?" Li'l T-Bear asked, and he stopped bouncing the ball. "This be pure or we talkin' ganker shit been stepped on a hundred times?"

"Dis ain't decoy. Da shit s'pose ta be pure. Dat what de China-man say," Bad Sam grinned.

Li'l T-Bear then made his move, dribbling around Bad Sam and doing a lay-up where a chalk line high on the wall marked the pretend basket.

LaFrance got up painfully off the low wall next to the liquor store and moved around into the parking lot. "What's this hoo-rah you be talkin'?" he asked them.

When they told him, LaFrance grinned for the first time since his ganja high left him. He knew he was about to become a very rich man.

THIRTY-THREE

Godfather

anisha and Wheeler snuck out of South Central at 8:30 the next morning while the local G-sters were still sleeping. They had breakfast at a coffee shop near the airport, then headed north, arriving in Beverly Hills at nine.

"My God," Tanisha said, looking at a huge Colonial house on Outreach Drive. "This is your uncle's place? Looks like a hotel."

"He's not really my uncle. I just call him that. He was one of my dad's oldest friends. When I got baptized, he was my godfather. Although we've never had any deep religious discussions, he's always been there for me."

Wheeler parked the Jag in the circular drive next to a swimming-pool-sized fountain that was two feet deep and guarded by a flock of iron sculptured herons. Their long necks pointed skyward, water spurting high out of their pointed beaks into a catch basin, where it overflowed and rained back into the pool below.

The house was Cape Cod Colonial with architecturally designed turrets that fit the motif perfectly and seemed to mock the memory of the turrets on Tanisha's grandmother's house, south of Crenshaw. An Asian gardener was blowing leaves off to one side of the huge property as Wheeler and Tanisha moved to the front door.

"Uncle Alan is a Superior Court judge. He's very big in the Republican Party. If anybody can help us get the right pressure on this thing, he can."

"But will he?" Tanisha asked.

Wheeler shrugged and rang the front doorbell. The door was opened by his aunt Virginia, a refined sixty-eight-year-old woman with a lean, no-nonsense body. Her feathered hairstyle glinted gray and she was wearing a short-sleeved silk blouse and a nubby-textured Chanel skirt. Her jewelry was expensive but understated. She offered Wheeler her cheek to kiss.

"Aunt Ginny, this is my friend Tanisha Williams," Wheeler said.

Virginia turned to Tanisha and offered her hand, palm down. "Well, come on in, you two. Alan was so glad to hear from you this morning. He's in the Hunt Room trying to rewire our speakers." She smiled. "God only knows whether we'll ever hear anything out of that system again."

She led them through the magnificent entry hall and down a three-step flight of stairs into a large room adorned with the heads of wild animals. Lions and antelope looked down on them with glass-eyed indifference. A zebra rug, head attached, sprawled under a glass-topped table made of elephant tusks and period rifles. A gun rack on the far wall displayed a deadly variety of scoped, oiled artillery.

Over by the fireplace, working with the speaker system, was Judge Alan Hollingsworth. He was wearing blue jeans and an old cardigan sweater over a green-and-white striped shirt. When he turned to them, Tanisha was treated to the most beautiful pair of bright blue eyes she had ever seen. They were set in a ruddy-complexioned face topped by a head of bushy, thick silver-white hair. Judge Hollingsworth was the poster boy for aging gracefully. He grinned at Wheeler. "Damn woofers or tweeters, or whatever they are, went on strike. No amount of judicial anger seems to convince 'em to work right.'' He moved to Wheeler and shook his hand, then turned to Tanisha as Wheeler made the introduction.

"Tanisha Williams,'' Judge Hollingsworth repeated after hearing her name. "Seems to me I remember reading that somewhere. Aren't you the police detective working on Prescott's murder?''

"Yes sir, I am, or at least I was.''

"We were really distressed. Prescott was such a comer. It's impossible to believe he was murdered.'' There didn't seem to be recrimination in his remark, just a fact, stated bluntly.

"That's why we wanted to talk to you, Uncle Al,'' Wheeler said. "We've been looking into his death and got more than we bargained for. We ended up with a tiger by the tail.''

"Well, you're in the right room for that.'' He smiled, waving an arm toward all his shooting trophies. "Can I get you anything?'' he said.

"No sir, we're fine,'' Wheeler answered.

"Okay then, gimme the gist of it.''

"To begin with,'' Wheeler said, "I think I need to tell you that the people who killed Prescott are dangerous, violent men. They're members of a Hong Kong Triad known as the Chin Lo. They have vicious street gangs over here called Bamboo Dragons. They've already tried to assassinate us, twice. If you help us, you may be at risk.''

The remark hung there like ugly art until their thoughts were interrupted by the front doorbell.

"That must be Kay,'' Virginia said and moved out of the room toward the front door.

"You called my mother?'' Wheeler asked in shock.

"She's been very worried about you. When you didn't come to Prescott's funeral, she called me. I know she wants to see you.''

"Jesus, Uncle Al,'' Wheeler said, distressed. "I can't do this with my mother here.''

"I highly doubt that your mother's presence here will alter anything," he said, judicial bearing on full display.

They waited until Katherine Cassidy entered the room behind Virginia Hollingsworth. Kay, as usual, looked astonishing. Still in mourning, she was dressed in basic black and pearls. She turned to Wheeler, her expression cool, making no attempt to embrace him. After one glance, she completely ignored Tanisha.

"I understand from Liz that while we were burying your brother, you spent the week in Hong Kong," she said without preamble.

"Mother, I'll try and explain this to you, but I can't do it if you attack every sentence before it's out of my mouth."

"Maybe I'll go ask Esmeralda to fix us something to eat," Virginia said, moving out of the den, anxious to be away from what promised to be an awkward family confrontation.

"Okay," Judge Hollingsworth said, "let's get at this, whatever it is."

"Mother's right. Tanisha and I went to Hong Kong. We brought this back with us. . . ." He handed the stolen document to his godfather.

Judge Hollingsworth examined the graceful hieroglyphic Chinese characters, and his expression darkened. Before he could comment, Wheeler handed him the translation that Willard Vickers faxed back to them at Captain Verba's office at Asian Crimes. The Judge read the first page, then passed it to Kay. It took only a few minutes for them to read the document.

"Okay," Judge Hollingsworth said. "Pretty amazing, if true. But what does this have to do with Prescott's murder? I don't see the problem. Take it to the *L.A. Times.*"

Wheeler took a deep breath. "If I do that, most of these people will disappear or destroy the evidence and Prescott's involvement in this is going to become public."

"Prescott's what?" Kay said, fire coming into her eyes. "Prescott doesn't have a damn thing to do with this, Wheeler. How did Pres have anything to do with this silly election in Hong Kong?"

"Because, Mom, he was working for the Chin Lo Triad. He and his secretary were killed because the FBI was on to him, and the Triad leaders in Hong Kong were afraid he was going to—"

"I will not hear one more word of this. That is the most insane, trumped-up—"

"Why don't you stop shouting and listen to your son?" Tanisha said.

Kay's head snapped around. "I beg your pardon?"

"No, you don't. You resent the hell out of me. But the fact remains that Prescott was guilty of crimes against his country. The proof is right here." She handed Kay the translation they had made of the tape from Prescott's car, using volume ten of John Stoddard's *History of California*. "You can see Prescott says he was contacted by the FBI. He was involved in illegal bribes and campaign funding violations. The 'r' numbers and 'd' numbers in that letter are Republicans and Democrats. We matched them to initials and districts of U.S. Congressmen and Senators. Their names are listed on the bottom of the page there."

Alan Hollingsworth took the page out of Kay's hand and quickly read the letter.

"This is utterly ridiculous and without corroboration," Kay said.

"You can say that, Mrs. Cassidy," Tanisha shot back. "You can even try and believe it. But this is going to come out. Too many people have already died, including your own son. I would think, instead of trying to keep it quiet, you'd want some justice."

"You couldn't possibly have a clue what I want. Accusations and disgrace won't help Prescott's family—won't help his widow and son hold up their heads in public. . . . Not that I believe, for a minute, any of this is true." She was almost screaming at Tanisha as the dusty glass eyes of dead animals stared impassively down at them.

"Let's all calm down," Judge Hollingsworth said.

"I think if we can get the right political help," Wheeler said, "we can close all of this down and maybe nobody even has to know Prescott's part in it."

"What about her?" Katherine said, pointing a slender, diamond-jeweled finger at Tanisha. "She's dying to get her pound of flesh."

"Mrs. Cassidy, I'm not trying to destroy the memory of your son, but what we've discovered has almost cost your other son his life. He's been shot at and nearly assassinated. He just wants to get his brother's killer. Why don't you worry about what could happen to him? He's still alive."

Katherine Cassidy stood, holding her purse with a claw grip in front of her. Her fingers dug into the leather like the talons of a meat-eating bird. "You are certainly a sad, misinformed little Nigra," she finally hissed. "You couldn't possibly understand what I want or need. You come from dirt, so naturally this all makes perfect sense to you. To me, it's an abomination, an unfounded figment of your imagination, and I will hear no more of it." She turned and glowered at her eldest son. "Wheeler, if you insist on pursuing this course of action, I will have you removed from your father's estate. I am the sole executor and I have that power. I will see that none of your inheritance ever reaches you. You'll be out there on your own, buddy, and I don't think you've got the guts for it."

"Then you don't know him," Tanisha said softly.

"Finally, something we can agree on," Katherine said, then turned and walked out of the house.

A few seconds later, Virginia returned and looked at them. "Did Kay leave?"

"More or less," Alan said, turning to Tanisha. "I apologize for Kay's racist remarks. She's a product of her upbringing. She doesn't understand we're in a new world from the one she was raised in."

"Are we really?" Tanisha said levelly.

Alan let the sarcasm pass, as Wheeler started to pace the room. He moved to the window and looked out at the beautiful yard and pool beyond. He kept his back to the Judge, Virginia, and Tanisha for a minute. Then he turned and looked at his godfather. "I don't mean to hurt her, I really don't. But can they just kill my brother and walk away?"

"They can't," Alan said. "So let's start at the beginning. Tell me every single detail."

Wheeler and Tanisha were still there when the sun went down. Judge Hollingsworth was astonished by the tale and by his godson's obvious bravery. He called Willard Vickers in Philadelphia and talked to him at length. By eight o'clock, the Judge was convinced that Wheeler and Tanisha were not only telling the truth, but were on to something so big that it would rock the world.

"No wonder they're trying to kill you," he said. "It was foolish to risk your life."

"It was worth the risk, because—" Wheeler stopped. He had been about to say, . . . *because I've finally found out who I really am,* but that was not true. At least not yet. It was also a melodramatic overstatement, so he finished the sentence differently. " . . . a lot is at stake," he said.

"God only knows how deep or high up in our government this corruption goes," the Judge said, looking at the names of well-known Senators and Congressmen. "If we pull on the wrong string, it could explode on us. We need to be very careful. We also need to get this into the right hands so it will be dealt with correctly and efficiently. You were right to bring it to me and keep it out of the media. This would've destroyed Pres's reputation, hurt his family terribly, and, as you say, it would have given the unknown guilty a chance to scurry and hide. We need to get everyone—not just the names on this list. I think I might know the right man to help us . . . and let's just pray to God he isn't on somebody's payoff sheet."

The name he mentioned was Cameron Jobe. Jobe was the crusading Attorney General for the State of California, and had run on a reform ticket. Tanisha hoped they weren't making a huge mistake, but there was one thing about the state A.G. that gave her some reassurance. After having spent six months on Asian Crimes, she knew, first-hand, how the Chinese felt about Blacks. She didn't think the Chinese in Beijing would invest in a Black politician.

Cameron Jobe was a brother.

THIRTY-FOUR

Fu Hai's Journey

he trip had started well for Fu Hai. They had all been given false travel documents, made in Triad print shops in the Walled City of Kowloon. They had flown out of Hong Kong on a chartered airplane, right under the noses of the Immigration inspectors. Fu Hai knew that the powerful Triad he was now a member of had made arrangements so that no questions would be asked. They had then flown to Madrid, Spain, and then had been put aboard a cargo plane and flown to Tijuana, Mexico. Fu Hai had been given a phone number to call when he got there. They were held at Mexican Immigration. He could not speak to the inspectors, but he had been given an envelope to hand to the man from Immigration. Shortly after he gave over the sealed envelope, he was allowed to make one call. He was soon speaking to a Chinese doctor from Taiwan who had immigrated five years before to Tijuana. The doctor told him everything had been arranged, but they were held in a deserted hangar for half a day. There were babies in the group, who cried in the oppressive heat. There was no water. An old man passed out and they could not revive him.

Two hours later, he died. Then, in the middle of the night, the hangar was opened and they were all loaded onto two stake trucks and taken over dirt roads for several hours to a dock. There they were loaded aboard the *Golden Hind*.

It was here that the worst part of the journey began. The Chinese peasants he was in charge of spoke many different languages. They huddled like children on the deck of the rusting trawler. The captain was Mexican and very drunk. There were three crew members; two were Koreans and constantly ate kimchi, a hateful Korean habit. The odor came out through their sweat glands, making them reek horribly. The third crewman was a surly Japanese with tattoos all over his body. Fu Hai could not speak or communicate with any of them. The Snake Riders had no place to sleep and had to share the few bunks below. Because Fu Hai was a Chin Lo vanguard and was the leader, he was given his own bunk, but he hated being belowdecks in the hot, smelly quarters, and gave it up to others who were unable to sleep outside in the wind and ocean spray.

The *Golden Hind* had left port and chugged north. The one propeller pushed them along slowly. The boat rolled in the heavy sea. Everyone, including Fu Hai, got seasick. As he leaned over the rail and vomited into the ocean, his taped wound ached miserably.

Suddenly the engine stopped and they were rolling in the swells off the coast of Southern California. Fu Hai was on deck, looking at a shiny white speedboat moving toward them fast, bouncing off the waves. He waited as the boat got nearer and the two men aboard threw lines over to the surly crew. A slender man climbed out of the speedboat's passenger seat and came aboard the *Golden Hind*. Fu Hai moved through the crowd of Snake Riders, across the deck to where the man was standing.

"I am in charge here," Fu Hai said in Mandarin, but the man spoke no Mandarin, so Fu Hai switched to broken Fukienese, which he had learned in Khotan. The man introduced himself and said he was called Dry Dragon. His face was swollen, as if he had recently been beaten.

"We will be out with a large boat to get you tonight," Dry Dragon said.

Fu Hai didn't think he could stay on the rolling, rusting *Golden Hind* another minute. "Is it not possible to get off sooner? There are some infants whose mothers have gone dry. They have not eaten in several days," he said. "There is almost no water."

"I wish I could honor your request, but for safety we must wait until long after dark to come ashore. I will try to accomplish it as early as possible." He was speaking to Fu Hai with great respect, so Fu Hai nodded, proud to be a member of the powerful Chin Lo Triad from the City of Willows.

The speedboat left and Fu Hai stood at the rail, watching. He knew he was close to the end of his journey. Somewhere, not far to the east, was the coast of California. He would live like a Party official in America. He would send for his once beautiful sister. He would nurse her back to health. He would accomplish everything he had set out to do.

If Fu Hai hadn't felt so seasick, he would have been very happy.

THIRTY-FIVE

T. for Tyrone

T here weren't nearly enough chairs in Rick Verba's over-crowded office. Wheeler and Tanisha ended up standing, because he was a civilian and had no business being there to begin with, and she was the lowest-ranking municipal employee in the room. Verba had given his desk over to Deputy Chief Gene Pitlick from Parker Center. Pitlick was tall, angular, and bald. He had brought with him two uniformed captains from Major Crimes: Captain Dan Lamansky, head of Administrative Affairs, and Captain Justin Meyers, head of Press Relations. Seated next to that parade of protocol was Captain Verba, and to his right was Al Katsukura, primary detective on the Ray Fong/Prescott Cassidy/Angela Wong murder cases. Judge Alan Hollingsworth was in a wooden chair, all but forgotten in this sea of blue.

The most space in the room was taken up by T. Cameron Jobe, coal-black and handsome. He seemed to be constantly aware of the impression he made. Cameron was a strutter. He wore a very expensive, well-tailored suit which Wheeler would have gladly put in his own closet full of European labels. His tie was pearl-gray with almost no pattern. It lay neatly against his crisp white English linen shirt. He projected arrogance, and Wheeler hated him on sight. Tanisha knew in five minutes what he was: a consummate politician who used both his black complexion and his Harvard education for maximum effect. She had found out the T. stood for Tyrone. He'd been born in the Compton ghetto, but now acted more like the crown prince of an African nation. He had swept into the office ten minutes earlier, with his two White female paralegals, and had immediately taken the unstated position that nothing was going to happen unless he fully endorsed it. Wheeler and Tanisha had already taken him through the whole story, starting with Prescott's and Angela's murders and ending with the shootout at the Westin coffee shop. Cameron Jobe was now holding the two documents: one taken from the Triad headquarters in the City of Willows, and the other transcribed from Prescott's dash cassette. He was looking from one document to the other, his magnificent face arranged in a theatrical, puzzled frown. "The attempted assassination in the Westin restaurant was because of these?" he finally asked.

"That's what we believe," Wheeler said, trying hard to keep the edge out of his voice.

"Mr. Cassidy, this is a police matter. As much as you would like to contribute, I'm more interested in the opinion of the police professionals." He turned and looked at Tanisha. "Go ahead, Detective."

"What he said," she replied.

For a moment, the mask on T. Cameron Jobe's face slipped slightly and the two ghetto children traded eye-fucks straight from the corner of 103rd Street.

Cameron finally looked over at Judge Hollingsworth. "And you support this epic story, Judge?"

"Yes, I do."

"Okay," Cameron said, "if you're correct, then what we're looking at is a situation with heavyweight political overtones. You're talking about Congressional bribes involving powerful U.S. politicians. It's also got serious multinational implications."

"Does all this bullshit mean you're about to pussy out?" Wheeler challenged.

"Wheeler, that will be quite enough," his uncle Al said sternly.

"I've had people dying all around me for two weeks. Hell yes, this is big and full of international danger! Does that mean we're gonna just cover our asses?"

"You obviously haven't spent much time trying to make headway in the treacherous corridors of government," Cameron shot back. "There are a few important bases that need to be hit before we run off on something this complex and potentially explosive. You've got U.S. Senators on this list." He waved the document at the room full of cops. "Including Senator Arnold White, who is Chairman of the Foreign Relations Committee. You have any idea how many phone calls he has to make before this whole mess gets classified as a foreign security matter and all of us are bombed into career oblivion?"

"Who the fuck cares!" Wheeler said, stepping forward. He was so angry he could barely keep his voice from shaking. "This isn't about your fucking career, it's about justice. It's about solving Prescott's and Angela's murders. All we have to do is break the windows and let the world press sort out the assholes. You wanna stand around and debate protocol? We've gotta bust this local Triad headquarters and search the place for murder weapons. You've got the two bullets out of my car. You've got the ones from Ray Fong's body. You can run ballistics, or whatever it is you do. The place is probably full of undocumented aliens or immigrants with doctored passports. Make some trouble for these guys, get 'em playing defense, maybe one of them talks. You wait much longer, everything and everybody's gonna disappear."

The room was quiet.

"Mr. Cassidy, I understand your anger," Captain Verba said, "but Cameron's right. We don't want to end up just making hash here. This thing is jurisdictionally complicated. We need the right probable cause or they'll lock up our search in court. We need a valid warrant to go through Triad headquarters, and the jurist who signs it is gonna have his ass way over the line."

"I'll sign it," Judge Hollingsworth said. "I'm set to retire in a year—they can't do much to me."

Then, almost like spectators at a tennis match, all heads simultaneously turned to Cameron.

"You think I'm playing politics," Cameron said, "and you're right. It's only because I've been wrapped up in this kind of thing before. If everything you're saying is true, we're gonna be in a shitstorm from Washington. We're going to have a squad of raincoats from the National Security Council in here on the next Con Air flight. These assholes will be grabbing everything. After N.S.C. gets through closing embarrassing loopholes, you people are all gonna be standing in your underwear, pleading for help. I'm gonna be washed out because I didn't come in with unbeatable jurisdictional control. Judge Hollingsworth is a state judge. This is most certainly a federal, as well as an international, crime. That brings in the spooks from CIA. You haven't lived until you've had a jurisdictional beef with those guys."

"My brother's murder is a Los Angeles homicide," Wheeler shot back. "He was killed with an acupuncture needle through the heart, in his office in Century City, California. His secretary was sliced up like a honey-baked ham in Torrance, *California*. I'm no lawyer, but if those aren't state crimes, I'd like to know why."

"Why can't we seek an injunction against Wo Lap Ling and file Prescott's and Angela's murders in Judge Hollingsworth's court?" Tanisha asked. "If Judge Hollingsworth won't transfer the case over to the federal court, how can they beat his jurisdiction?"

"Because you don't have enough evidence to get a murder conviction on this Wo Lap guy for conspiracy, and even if you did, the Feds will pull every string in Sacramento," Cameron said. "They'll have an ex parte meeting with the Chief Justice of the California Supreme Court. They'll get him to dismiss the case, with a decision to transfer jurisdiction over to the federal government, *terminus ad quem*." Off their looks, he translated, "The end . . .

But there won't be an end, 'cause forty corrupt Congressmen are going to fall on the fumble and we won't sort it out for fifty years."

"If you agree to file the charge against Wo Lap Ling, I think I can hold the Feds off," Judge Hollingsworth said. "At least I can slow them down. I can set up a crack media team and we'll help the national press vet it. *Tempus omnia revelat.*" He smiled at Cameron before translating, "Time reveals everything. We'll leak anything to the press that helps us. That'll keep the Feds honest, because once this is uncovered, it's going to have its own life."

Cameron stood in the office now, his big, handsome profile turned to the window, where the lights of Chinatown twinkled in a night sky cleansed by Santa Ana winds. Finally, when Cameron turned, he had a narrow smile on his face.

"Okay then, I'm either the next Governor of this state or I'm back in the Compton Carwash cleaning windshields."

Tanisha had spotted the first three letters on the license plate of the white Pinto when it shot past them on Manchester Avenue several days ago. She had scribbled down "PTC" in her notes and added it to her crime report. The computer had tried to match up a white Pinto with the partial plate, but had come up with nothing. The plate was either stolen or had been altered. Al Katsukura had decided to wander around in the five square blocks of Chinatown with the partial plate letters and look for the car. He didn't expect to find anything.

Sometimes, in police work, you just get flat lucky. Al found it parked in the lot adjoining the Chin Lo headquarters. He got close enough to see that the P was an I that had been doctored. The C was an O that had been whited out on one side. When he got back with that fortunate piece of news it gave Verba probable cause for a hard entry. Judge Hollingsworth had immediately written the search warrant, sitting at Tanisha's old desk in Asian Crimes. He signed it and handed it to T. Cameron Jobe, who looked at it before sticking it in his pocket. "Okay," he said, without emphasis or excitement. *"Veritas praevalebit."*

"Truth usually prevails," Judge Hollingsworth said, "but not always."

They all waited in Asian Crimes for an hour while detectives from Metro SWAT gathered in the parking lot outside the Hill Street building. Tanisha and Wheeler went to the lunchroom and got coffee. It was machine-made but hot, and they sipped it, sitting at a linoleum table. She looked at him for a long moment, her expression impossible for him to read.

"What?" he finally asked.

"You amaze me sometimes," she said.

"What does that mean?"

"Back there, in Verba's office, chewing out that pompous Latin-quoting Oreo cookie. . . . You were . . ." She stopped and looked at him. " . . . different than I ever saw you."

"Different like crazy, out of control, certifiable?"

"Kinda sexy." She smiled at him.

"Sexy?"

"Unrestrained, primitive anger. I always find that sexy. Must be my African blood."

"Jesus, I hope so." He smiled, giving her his W.C.C. bedroom eyes.

At ten-thirty P.M. the SWAT team was organized, flaked in body armor, and gathered in the ACTF parking lot. Wheeler was allowed to sit in a car a few blocks away with Alan Hollingsworth, who was judicial home plate and available to render on-the-spot legal opinions or write additional paper if needed. Tanisha sat in the SWAT van next to the Communications Officer. From there she could monitor the action on the team radios. Team One was the I.I., "Initial Incursion," Unit. It was scheduled to storm the front. Team Two would remain in the back just outside, to seal off the rear exit. It would not make an entry, because they expected gunfire and didn't want to catch each other in a crossfire. Team Three in the second SWAT van was held in reserve.

The SWAT raid started at quarter to eleven. Al Katsukura, carrying a pizza box, knocked on the door of the Chin Lo headquarters. The door was opened by a Chinese youth dressed in black, who looked at the pizza in confusion. Without warning, Team One rushed into the headquarters, knocking the youth down, then cuffing him to an old iron heater. "Police! Everybody on the floor!" the squad leader shrieked at half-a-dozen startled Bamboo Dragons. Several Chinese youths pulled handguns and started firing.

Willy heard gunshots and yelling. He came out of the room where he'd been going over an operation plan with the White Fan. Gunfire now erupted everywhere around him in the small wooden building. Bamboo Dragons, screaming in anger and for courage, had grabbed up Russian automatic weapons and were now shooting at the SWAT team. Willie was quickly surrounded by four Bamboo Dragons, all of them armed and firing wildly at anything that moved. They pumped out copper-jacketed lead as they tried to hustle him out the back door of Triad headquarters.

The front hallway was suddenly full of SWAT. The young gangsters who were escorting Willy sprayed more copper-jackets at the swarming police, hitting two officers in the face, blowing them back in a blood mist, killing them instantly.

The back door of the Chin Lo headquarters was thrown open and Willy and his escorts ran down the steps. Unit Two was shoulder-ready. They opened up with automatic weapons. The deadly muzzles of the second SWAT team sprayed 9mm death. Bamboo dragons with no fear for their own lives shielded the most powerful Hong Kong Shan Chu with their bodies. They scrambled back into the house under a rain of gunfire, stumbling as bullets tore into them. All but one was killed before Willy, miraculously still unhurt, was back inside the building with no place to escape.

Two SWAT officers, their guns in firing position, sprang around the corner into the hall where Willy was standing.

"Freeze, motherfucker!" one shouted.

"On your face, asshole!" The other screamed.

Willy had risked his life countless times in his rise to power, but he was always one to quickly and carefully calculate his chances of survival. Not anxious to join his Cloud ancestors, the Smart Monkey put his hands in the air and waited as the SWAT members quickly surrounded and cuffed him.

It had happened so quickly and brutally that Wheeler and Tanisha had not been ready for it. The entire adventure, along with their trip to Hong Kong, had been a quest for validation, and now after all the death and destruction, Willy Wo Lap was in custody. It was almost impossible to grasp. They looked at each other outside the mobile command center, unable to put their feelings into words.

An hour later, Willy Wo Lap Ling was in Parker Center, which he knew was the main police building in Los Angeles. He was in a windowless holding cell. Nobody had spoken to him since he had been delivered there in handcuffs almost forty minutes before. Willy had a good understanding of American law. He knew that he was allowed one phone call and had the right to an attorney. He knew that he had not yet been charged, as his Miranda rights had not been read to him. He would demand his phone call as soon as possible. But Willy didn't need a lawyer. He knew that two SWAT members had been killed in the foolish shootout at the Chin Lo headquarters. He assumed that he was going to be eventually charged as an accessory to second degree murder. Worse still, he had failed in his mission in the United States. He had not retrieved the precious document, and he was now a terrible threat to Beijing. He could only expect the worst from Chen Boda.

There was only one person who could save him.

THIRTY-SIX

Reflections

he reflections streaked across the windshield from the overhead freeway lights. Wheeler pushed the Jag up past sixty-five. His jaw was locked, but his thoughts were whirling. Next to him, sharing similar but separate feelings, was Tanisha. She had her eyes pinned on the road ahead.

Somehow they had drifted into a new zone. They were now physically aware of one another in a way much different from before. Wheeler remembered the moment in the Pen Hotel when he had lain next to her on the bed and looked into her eyes, wondering if he could ever match her courage or deserve her respect. They had both known it was better not to pursue a physical relationship, and they had abruptly swerved back to structure. Now, their thoughts were exploring a new list of "maybes."

"You've gotta watch for Manchester, it comes up fast. You've gotta get over to the right," she said.

He changed lanes, and quiet again filled the car. Wheeler was reviewing, with shame, old White boy fantasies. He remembered tales told by fraternity brothers, their minds dulled by all-night keggers. Doug Pooley had said Black pussy was ten degrees hotter than White pussy. "No shit," Doug had insisted, to the room full of half-drunk Sigma Chis. "You put your hand down there and I swear you can feel it. Black pussy radiates heat." They laughed, hooted him down, but wondered if it was true. For them, interracial sex was raw sex. It was sex without commitment, tenderness, or love. Pooley called it the ultimate jungle-fuck. Wheeler knew this was racist horseshit, but it wasn't something any of them challenged outwardly, only inwardly. He knew it was damaging because it reinforced racial barriers by creating mythic differences. Tanisha had once told him, "The first thing Whites always see is color. African-Americans are Black before they're people." That difference fed the imagination and spawned the frat-house sexual fantasies. Tanisha had also said, "Color is the most basic thing defining them, and Whites either feel superior or guilty. Very few buy into the concept of racial equality."

Wheeler remembered once fifteen years ago going to a performance of *The Wiz,* a Black musical, which was good, but not spectacular. He had gone with some buddies from U.S.C. and was sitting next to a Black friend, a drama student, named Clarence Simmons. When the curtain came down the entire audience at the Dorothy Chandler Pavilion sprang to its feet in a standing ovation. He looked down at Clarence, who had not risen. "What are you doing down there?" Wheeler asked.

"The show is good, but come on, man, it's not great. This standing ovation is horseshit. White guilt," Clarence had correctly pointed out.

Wheeler thought he was immune to racial hypocrisy, but now wondered if he could trust his emotions. Were his feelings for Tanisha real, or was this just White guilt, another standing ovation?

If he made love with Tanisha, he wanted it to be much more than sex. He wanted it to be the consummate coming together of souls, not bodies. He questioned whether the pool of his emotions was deep enough to accommodate her.

Amidst these uplifting worthwhile thoughts, the jungle-fuck still haunted him.

Tanisha sat watching the traffic, but not seeing it. She vaguely saw them turn off onto Manchester and head across Baldwin Park toward her grandmother's house, where they were hiding. How could it be that she was falling in love with the great-grandson of a Confederate general?

Her life growing up had failed all the traditional social tests for normalcy, but in her neighborhood it had been the norm. Her early gang life had been centered around the concept of loyalty. Loyalty to a drug culture, and friends who shattered rules with violence. She had lived a nickel-slick existence that ended with the death of the two off-brand gangsters in the back of a 7-Eleven, and finally with Kenetta's murder. From that freewheeling, gang-banging life, she had rebounded in the exact opposite direction. No time for anything but the books.

Since birth, White people had been the enemy. They were the big white wall holding her back.

Wheeler was everything she had been taught to despise. The stereotype for honky hatred: a country club cocksman; a privileged drunk who lived off family money, with absolutely no direction in life unless he was following his own tee shots.

But it was Wheeler who had struggled to get mortally wounded Julian Winslow up on his shoulder. With tracers zipping the air all around them, only Wheeler went back for the wounded detective.

It was Wheeler who, back in the Walled City, treated her with more honesty and respect than any other man she had ever known.

To him, she wasn't homeboy property; and she wasn't a racial trophy, a hip way of flipping off his country club friends. She was a valuable, cherished entity. She could see it in his eyes. She had never been respected like that before, not by her homies or her teachers, not by the LAPD or even her family. She could see and feel his respect, tangible and sweet as a lover's touch.

But she worried about her responsibility to herself as a Black woman. She had pledged her life to a goal after Kenetta's death. To do any good for her people, she needed their respect. The hoochie mamas at Zadell's would write her off. They'd say, "She was jus' climbin' White rope."

But she knew that she was in love with Wheeler. She didn't know if it was a lasting love, but for now at least, it was an important one. She wanted to feel him and touch him. She wanted to feel his tenderness around her and his hardness inside her. She was shamelessly ready for him. All he had to do was make the first move, and she could sense it was coming.

A half-hour later they were sitting in the living room in the empty house on Bronson Street. Nadine wasn't upstairs. She had somehow left, which Tanisha thought strange, because her grandmother had such difficulty moving. Somebody must have helped her downstairs. Breezy was also gone, and the lights were off in the front room. They stood in the quiet house. Suddenly, they were in a new emotional arena.

Wheeler took her hand and pulled her down onto the sofa. He gently brushed his lips against hers. They kissed for a moment, first tentatively, then with deep, unrestrained passion. His hand was on the side of her face, touching her softly.

"I . . . I . . . I don't . . ." he stuttered.

"Shhhh," she said and slowly unbuttoned her blouse and put his hand on her breast, his fingers touching her hardening nipple. He caressed her while he unzipped her skirt. She undid his belt, and together they found all of each other's snaps and zippers. Then they were on the sofa, naked. He let his hand wander and found the delicacy of her stomach, her thighs, and then her center. Slowly, they kissed, exchanging moans and whispers of pleasure and intimacy. They came closer. It seemed more meaningful to both of them than any act of love had ever been. Wheeler was a good lover, with too much practice; but his need to possess her in an emotional way, now for the first time in his life, matched his physical need. As he entered her they both felt excruciating joy in the gentleness of human coupling, unplanned and without masks or artifice. Slowly and with great tenderness they made love. Finally, the moment for them had come. It was both hypnotizing and delirious, ending in a climax that shook them to the center of their souls. They were kissing deeply at the moment of release.

Wheeler had never felt such glorious completion, because he had never made love before with such unselfishness.

After it was over they lay still. Both breathing hard. Both afraid to speak . . . not wanting to change the magic of the moment.

Outside the house, LaFrance pointed at the red Jag's bumper, which was sticking out around the corner from the backyard. "Dat be d' gray cat's ride," he said to the four 103rd Street Crip gangsters from Tanisha's old set. "Dey inside. All you gotta do is walk in an' serve d' motherfucker."

The four Crip gangsters got out of the car and silently closed the door. They left LaFrance at the wheel, telling him to be ready to bone out after he heard the gunfire. Two of them shouldered Russian automatic assault rifles that they got out of the trunk. The guns had been bought for top dollar from the Chin Lo several months ago. The other two grabbed cut-down shotguns known as "street sweepers."

All four killers moved silently toward Nadine's darkened house.

THIRTY-SEVEN

Irish Charlie

I t was a complicated string of events that had put "Irish Charlie" McGuire aboard the *Hornblower* charter boat on Thursday night. The deal had started two days before, when a barely understandable skinny Chinese teenager named Lo Sing had booked a charter for Friday night. He wanted to rent a seventy-foot, triple-deck party boat. The youth had put down nine hundred dollars in cash to secure the deal, and had said in horrible broken English that he wanted enough fuel to go at least thirty miles out. The suspicious charter boat company called the LAPD. The call had been kicked over to Asian Crimes and had landed on Al Katsukura's desk. Al called Parker Center to get help on the surveillance, and that's how Irish Charlie McGuire, the Major Crimes detective with the most boat-handling experience, got tapped to stand in for the *Hornblower* charter boat captain.

At a few minutes past eleven on Thursday night, the same skinny Chinese asshole had reappeared with a handwritten note, demanding that the time of the charter be changed. The note said he wanted to move it up twenty-four hours, to just before midnight, which was a bitch, because Charlie was at home sound asleep when the boat company called and told him the *Hornblower* was out on the bay with a load of Orange County insurance salesmen, celebrating their annual bonuses.

"Then get the fucking boat back to the slip. I don't give a shit about the insurance guys," Charlie had told the booking agent.

The rest of it had been your standard slide-for-life last-minute police bullshit. Charlie McGuire had called the three other undercovers he'd already recruited from Major Crimes, waking them up, listening to them bitch and moan before telling them to shut up and haul ass. Then he dug around in his wallet for the phone number of the owl-eyed Jap who had tapped him for this shit detail in the first place.

"Yeah," Al Katsukura said. He was at Parker Center, talking on his cellphone.

"Operation Dry Dock is happening," Charlie told him.

"Now?" Al whined, not wanting to leave Parker Center because he was beginning to suspect that the Cassidy case was going to be an all-time, Hall of Fame, once-in-a-lifetime hot grounder. They had allowed Wo Lap Ling his one call an hour ago. Al had been a short distance away from the pay phone trying to overhear, but Willy was speaking Fukienese in a soft voice. Al was fluent in Japanese, but knew only a little Cantonese and even less Fukienese, so he missed all of it. Since then, they had been sitting around waiting for the next shoe to drop. Tanisha Williams and Wheeler Cassidy had left; so had Cameron Jobe. Al had decided to spend the rest of the night there so he wouldn't miss out on the pinch. Now, of all times, his fucking immigration case had come alive. He had to beat ass out of Parker Center and get all the way down to the marina in less than an hour. His part in Operation Dry Dock was to maintain "on the water" surveillance from a harbor patrol boat, then be on hand to call in and coordinate the ground units in the resulting full-scale surveillance.

He moved quickly to the parking lot across from Parker Center, found his P.O.V., and pulled out. He grabbed the list of numbers for his hand-picked surveillance team and began waking up angry Asian cops while he drove too fast with one hand.

Everything was in place when Dry Dragon, using his real name, Lo Sing, walked down the pier with Long Snake and Fighting Rooster, his two Bamboo Dragon accomplices. All three were dressed in black. Charlie McGuire was waiting next to the yacht with two U.C.s from Major Crimes: Detectives Leo Huff, overweight, red hair; and Clark Johnson, overweight, no hair. Both were dressed up in cornball *Hornblower* crew uniforms that looked ridiculous on them: white bells, with striped blue-and-white T-shirts under white linen jackets. They looked like a couple of badly cast gondola drivers from a fifties musical.

"You go now," Dry Dragon said, pointing at the boat.

The three Chinese teenagers all had backpacks on, and Charlie hoped to God they weren't packing guns.

"You got the rest of the cash?" Charlie said. "You only put down half. This boat is nine hundred an hour. Minimum is eighteen hundred."

"Go *now*," Dry Dragon repeated, putting a little oomph in it this time for emphasis.

"You got cash money?" Charlie rubbed his fingers together in the international signal for greenbacks, and Dry Dragon finally got the message. He dug into his pocket for a wad of hundreds, then handed Charlie a piece of paper with a compass heading on it. "Go now!" he demanded one more time, pissing Irish Charlie off.

Fifteen minutes later the three Bamboo Dragons and three undercover Major Crimes detectives were on a moonlight cruise together, clearing the harbor bell buoy in an empty, barely seaworthy boat heading straight out to nowhere.

"You shit fingers sure ain't being too subtle about this," Charlie muttered.

The *Hornblower* chugged along under its single-screw diesel engine at its top speed of seven knots. It had been designed for bay cruises, and in open water it rolled like a pregnant hog. After ten minutes Charlie was amused to see all three of the tough teenagers hanging over the rail, emptying eggrolls and wonton soup into the drink.

Charlie McGuire checked his Department-issue .38-caliber Smith & Wesson Airweight revolver to make sure it wouldn't stick on his waistband and, if necessary, would be easy to pull from under his shirt. He wasn't too worried, because he didn't think three skinny seasick boys in black PJs would be hard to handle. The one called Lo Sing moved back into the cabin. He looked white from throwing up. He also had sweat on his face, even though the warm Santa Ana winds had stopped blowing and it was turning cold outside. There was panic in his teenage eyes. He looked to Charlie like a man who was scared of the water.

Finally Charlie spotted the running lights of a distant boat. As he got closer he could see the moonlit silhouette of a rusting trawler.

The *Hornblower* approached the *Golden Hind* from the east to take advantage of the new, cold, onshore breeze. Irish Charlie backed down the single engine and tried to get the boat alongside the rolling trawler without bashing his starboard-side paint. He yelled at his cops to throw over the fenders as he backed the throttle down. He could see groups of Chinese huddled on the deck of the old boat, leaning over the rail, anxious to get off the rusting hulk.

Once they made the lines fast, Charlie moved from behind the wheel and climbed up onto the trawler. He was greeted by a Mexican captain with oily hair, greasy skin, and a sweat-stained T-shirt.

Charlie could not believe the stench aboard the trawler. It was unlike anything he had ever encountered: a mixture of old engine oil, mildew, human excrement, and vomit. He looked into the frightened, seasick faces of almost two hundred Asian immigrants, who were whispering in half-a-dozen different languages. Three women were holding scrawny babies; the rest were clutching soiled bundles containing their meager possessions. A young Chinese man seemed to be in charge of the Snake Riders. The skinny asshole in the black pajamas approached that man. They spoke for a minute and then the asshole came back over to him.

"We go now," the boy ordered, pointing at the *Hornblower*.

"Can you say 'Eat my dick'?" Charlie replied.

"Go now!" Lo Sing said again, and pointed with greater emphasis to the *Hornblower*.

Charlie nodded, and they began to load the Chinese Snake Riders aboard. They grinned and pointed at the clean toilets. They kneeled and touched the shiny, polished linoleum deck. The *Hornblower*'s interior had been finished in plywood by an apartment building contractor and Charlie thought it looked about as nautical as a tax auditor's office, but to these Chinese immigrants it was the *Queen Mary*. They sat down on benches, their knees together like good children waiting for the school bus. The *Hornblower* rocked heavily in the trough, banging against the rubber fenders and occasionally trading paint with the trawler as it crashed against its rusting hull.

Finally, they were finished loading the immigrants aboard and his two U.C.s got busy untying the two boats. Charlie went out to supervise the operation.

Dry Dragon nodded at Long Snake and Fighting Rooster. All three quickly pulled 9mm automatic pistols from their backpacks. Long Snake and Fighting Rooster went to where the two U.C.s were leaning over the rail to catch the lines from the trawler's crew. The boats were banging together, rocking precariously.

Dry Dragon moved up behind Charlie. "Go on inside, sit down. We got it," Charlie yelled in anger at the skinny teenager.

"Fuck you, Joe!" Dry Dragon said, using his only other English expression. Then he unloaded the pistol into Charlie McGuire, knocking him over the rail and into the water. Simultaneously, Long Snake and Fighting Rooster did the same, firing in unison at the unsuspecting U.C.s, amidst the screaming of terrified Snake Riders. In seconds, the three L.A. cops were dead and overboard.

Fighting Rooster moved to the helm. He loved boats. This one looked slow, but easy to operate. He studied the dash and turned the key. The *Hornblower* started. He throttled up and pulled away, leaving the rusting trawler behind.

Fu Hai stood on the back deck, bile still in his throat. He watched in fascination as one of the dead policeman rolled in the moonlit wake, his blue-and-white shirt billowing with trapped air like the belly of a bloated fish.

Al Katsukura was hoping he wouldn't vomit into the sea. The Marina Del Rey Harbor Patrol boat was rolling badly, because it had to run at slow speeds to stay out of sight of the lumbering *Hornblower*. At about one A.M. the weather had suddenly turned cold. The Santa Anas had been blowing hot all day, and now, without warning, the winds had stopped and a thick marine layer began descending over the water, coming out of nowhere. In twenty minutes they were wallowing around in a pea soup fog.

"The fuck," Al said, looking at the wall of white air.

"We got radar, no sweat," the patrol boat skipper said, turning the Furuno radar on.

Using the radar they followed the *Hornblower* down the coast, which in the Santa Monica Bay area runs roughly east and west. Unexpectedly, the *Hornblower* bypassed the Marina Del Rey Channel and continued southeast.

"Where the fuck is Charlie going?" Al said, not realizing that Charlie had stopped going anywhere, and was now sinking in the water five miles away. Then suddenly the *Hornblower* stopped moving and just parked out in the ocean about a mile south of Del Rey. The skipper of the patrol boat throttled back, and again they began rocking in the thick fog. Fifteen minutes passed and the party boat still hadn't moved.

"Whatta you wanna do?" the patrol boat captain asked.

It was now almost two-thirty in the morning and Al was out in Buttfuck Nowhere, rolling in the tide, swallowing air like a guppie, trying to keep his dinner down.

"I don't know," he finally said.

"I can just park here and let whatever happens happen, but this doesn't look good. We could buzz 'em. Ask 'em if everything's all right, and then if it is, just move off like we're patrolling out here."

"Okay," Al said. "Let's try that."

The boat captain put the vessel in gear and moved forward. The heavy gas engine vibrated under Al's feet as they finally gained speed. The forward motion steadied the boat and Al's stomach. Although the radar said they were close, almost without warning the stern of the *Hornblower* loomed up at them, out of the fog. The patrol captain hit reverse and backed his boat down. They drifted about five yards off, watching the huge, unwieldy triple-deck party boat wallow and roll in the three-foot swells. All of its lights were out. The Harbor Patrol captain grabbed the mike.

"Hello, *Hornblower,* everybody okay?" he asked over the loud hailer.

No answer from the darkened vessel.

He put the patrol boat in gear and moved slowly around the starboard side of the *Hornblower.* There didn't appear to be anybody aboard.

"I wanna get on," Al said, his heart pounding in panic. He moved to the rail as the Harbor Patrol captain jockeyed the boat into position so Al could grab a trailing rope and pull himself up. His feet slipped and skidded on *Hornblower*'s rub rail and he almost went into the water, but managed to finally clamber aboard.

There was nobody on the first deck. He checked the toilet: nothing. He ran up the stairs to the second deck, clawing for his service revolver as he ran. The second deck was also deserted. He checked the toilets there, then moved to the top deck. Again, nothing. There was not a soul aboard the huge boat. He moved back down and started walking the decks.

"Everything okay?" the patrol captain shouted from a few yards off. Al didn't trust himself to answer. When he got to the port side, his heart froze. There, in the scuppers, washed with seawater, was Charlie McGuire's police-issue S&W Airweight. He turned and looked around the decks. His gaze fell on a line which was lying in a tangle on the front deck. He bent down and stared at it. The rope was soaked with blood. Al knew that Irish Charlie and his two U.C.s were dead.

Everybody else had vanished into thin air.

THIRTY-EIGHT

The White Man's Nightmare

Something wasn't right. Tanisha could feel it, tangible as a silent touch. She rose up on the sofa and looked out the front window. LaFrance's "glass house" was again parked in the driveway. She could see the occasional hot glow from the tip of a cigarette inside the car. She looked at Wheeler, who was beside her on the sofa, sexual satisfaction still alive in his blue eyes.

"LaFrance is sitting in his car in the drive," she said.

"He's a hard little shit to get rid of," Wheeler grinned.

"Damn," she said, and scrambled up, grabbing her skirt and blouse. Wheeler sat up and watched her. He was still naked.

"This ain't right," she said, looking out the side window into the driveway. She thought she saw a shadow moving out there; dark clothing against a green hedge. It was just a glimpse, she wasn't sure. "Get dressed. Let's go," she said, zipping her skirt and snapping her bra.

"What's wrong?" he said as he started looking around in the dark for his Jockey shorts. He found them and tried to get them on, almost falling as he jumped around on one foot trying to find the leg hole in the dark.

They heard the back door open and close. "Shit," she said, grabbing her shirt, purse, and Wheeler's hand, dragging him toward the stairs.

Wheeler had managed to get his undershorts on, but was still clutching his pants as they ran, Tanisha pulling him along behind her, taking the stairs two at a time. As they got to the landing they heard the door downstairs in the den open and close. Tanisha dragged Wheeler down the upstairs hall and into Breezy's bedroom at the end of the corridor. She closed the door silently behind them and ran to the window, which looked out onto the roof at the far side of the house. She unlatched it and pulled it open.

"What's going on?" he said, as she got the window open. They could hear footsteps in the hall, and Tanisha pulled the Glock out of her purse, jacked a round into the chamber, and held the piece with both hands out in front of her just as the door flew open and a nineteen-year-old shaved-bald gang-banger stood there, unexpectedly looking right into her gun barrel.

"Sheee*it,* Mama, what you doin'?" he squealed, as he tried to inch the barrel of a sawed-off shotgun over at her.

"Don't!" she yelled at him, and he froze. "Wheeler, get out the window, now!" she commanded.

Still holding his pants in his right hand, he clambered out the opening onto the roof, while she held the gangster in a deadly standoff.

"What the fuck is this?" the banger said.

"Drop the breakdown or I get busy and start peeling caps!" she said.

He quickly dropped the shotgun, and she heard more footsteps on the stairs.

"Why?" she said.

"Not my doin'. You worth fifty keys a' China White, Mama," he said. "Everybody be gettin' ovah on yo' ass for dat much racehorse." He was holding his palms out to indicate he was no threat anymore. "I be on E here, baby. Don't pull no jack move!"

Then two more gangsters appeared at the far end of the hall behind him. They had assault weapons. She stepped forward and pushed the banger in the chest, forcing him back into the hall. Then she kicked the door shut and locked it. Two shots rang out, splintering the door by her head, and she quickly moved across Breezy's bedroom, then dove headfirst out of the window onto the roof. Wheeler helped her up and they ran across the flat roof to the edge of the house. They could hear the door of Breezy's room being kicked in. "Follow me," Tanisha said, then grabbed the limb of an elm and started climbing down. The trunk of the tree was in the neighbor's yard.

One of the gangsters appeared in the window of the room and yelled out at them, "We don' wan' you, baby, we want da snow brother."

"Who?" Wheeler asked, as they landed in the next yard.

"That's you, Casper. Let's go." She grabbed his hand and started to thread her way through a backyard full of junk cars and old refrigerators. She knew where she was going and moved fast, not hesitating for a moment as she ran. Then she ducked through a hole in the fence and they were suddenly in a narrow alley. They took off running. Pebbles and broken glass cut their bare feet as they ran, still carrying their clothes.

Tanisha led him through a broken fence into the backyard of another house, then through a back gate, and finally stopped next to an old shed. They were both breathing hard.

"Jesus," he said, trying to catch his breath. "Naked in Watts—the White man's nightmare."

"This is Monster C.'s house. He used to be my boyfriend. He's in Lompoc, but I think I can trust his mother." She held her blouse up in front of her, looking for an armhole.

"Tanisha, we can't trust anybody here. Nobody."

"This is my hood."

"This is their hood. You heard that punk. Fifty keys of China White, Chinese dope. Willy supplies these assholes. They all work for the Triad. We're fucked down here," he said, desperately trying to put on his pants.

"Shit," she said, finally finding an armhole.

"You still got your cell in there?" he said, grabbing her purse. "Get us some help!"

"I must be losing it," she said, pulling out the cell and dialing a number.

"Who out there?" a woman's voice yelled, as the lights over the back porch went on.

"It's just me, Mrs. Crawford, Tanisha Williams."

"My land . . ." They could hear somebody unbolting the back door. Wheeler was finally into his pants and was fastening his belt as the door opened and a fifty-five-year-old Black woman looked through the safety-chained door. "What you doin' out there with no clothes on, chile? It's two in the mornin'," she said. Then she saw Wheeler, bare-chested, standing next to Tanisha. They could hear footsteps running in the alley.

"It's okay, Mrs. Crawford. Go back to bed," Tanisha whispered, cellphone in her right hand, getting her shirt on as the call finally rang at Parker Center. Mrs. Crawford didn't move; she kept her eye to the slit in the door. The police switchboard answered.

"Officer needs help, shots fired," Tanisha said, using the ultimate police call for help. "Detective Williams, badge number four-seven-six-nine-eight. I'm in a jackpot, being chased by three black males armed with assault rifles. I'm pinned down in a backyard, corner of McClung and Stocker in Leimert Park, South Central. I'm a Black female with a White male civilian and we're not going to last long."

"Stay on the line, Detective, I'm putting out the call."

"What you doin' with a White boy, two A.M.?" Mrs. Crawford called out. "What you think you be doin', girl?"

"It's okay, Mrs. Crawford. Stay inside," she hissed.

And then somebody rattled the back gate. Tanisha swung in that direction, the Glock in front of her, as one of the G-sters yelled, "She down here!" Then as the Crips started to break down the gate, Tanisha and Wheeler heard the distant sound of a helicopter. In seconds it was overhead, then a xenon belly light snapped on, sweeping the area, quickly finding them. Tanisha held her badge up to the light. The helicopter pilot immediately swung the light off her and found the four AK-armed gang-bangers in the alley next to the back gate.

Seconds later, two squad cars screeched down the alley. The gangsters disappeared into backyards and over fences, chased by four uniformed cops and a belly light. When Tanisha heard sirens in front of the house, she took Wheeler's hand and led him around to the street. Two minutes later they were in the back of a squad car, streaking toward Parker Center, Code Three.

THIRTY-NINE

The Superior Man

Confucius said, *A superior man is sincere, and has the ability to recognize truth, just as surely as he can recognize a bad smell.*

Willy had always recognized the truth.

Confucius said, *A superior man is watchful over himself when he is alone, because what is true in a man's heart will be shown in his outward appearance. Just as wealth beautifies a house, so does character beautify a body.*

So Willy sat quietly alone in his cell at Parker Center, with his jacket buttoned and his hands clasped restfully in his lap. Willy was a superior man even though he suspected that like all mortals, he had some inferior qualities.

Confucius said, *The superior man develops up, but the inferior man develops down.*

Willy had no clue what this meant. He had made deals with criminals, as well as great national and religious leaders. He had come from great poverty and had assumed great power. He had climbed a slippery, treacherous ladder to gain prominence, living in a world so complex that the concept of up and down, good and evil, had become completely obscured by other men's nature and the complexities of modern life. He had developed in any direction that looked plausible just to survive.

Willy knew that in order to survive, he had to find a way to get out of the United States. He had great Guan-Xi in America and could contact people at the very top of the U.S. government. They would pick up his call quickly, because he had invested heavily in their campaigns. However, he did not trust American politicians; they fit most of the Master's definitions for inferiority. They would sense the danger in helping him and begin issuing denials of their associations with him. For this reason, he had made the one call allowed him not to a politician or a barrister, but to a skinny teenage Tong gangster named Dry Dragon. He knew the boy had gone to pick up 180 Snake Riders. Willy had been given his cellphone number in case there were problems. He had called and instructed Dry Dragon on what to do. Willy could only pray his exact orders had been carried out.

He had decided not to deal with the American justice system. Western lawyers were all inferior men who prized wealth and ego over principle. He had decided to take the situation into his own hands. He had an exit plan in mind. The only problem would be to get the men who arrested him to recognize his sincerity as surely as a bad smell.

Willy hoped to give these inferior men a stench that would gag them.

At ten the following morning Willy was taken from his cell on the third floor in the correctional wing of Parker Center to a large, windowless interrogation room on the fifth floor. He entered and found himself looking at a handsome, well-tailored Black man in a three-piece charcoal suit. Willy felt Blacks were sly, unmotivated people. He viewed them as a hopelessly inferior race. The Black man introduced himself as Cameron Jobe and said he was the Attorney General of the State of California . . . something Willy found hard to understand. The American system seemed determined to reward guile over accomplishment. Also present were two people Willy had never seen before. A police Captain named Verba and a white-haired, distinguished-looking man with blue eyes, who was not introduced.

Willy was shown to a seat. On the table in front of him was a folder. Cameron Jobe turned on a tape recorder and stated for the record the location of the meeting, the date, and the time. Then he read Willy his Miranda rights.

"We know you speak English very well," the Black inferior man said, "but would you like an interpreter?"

"That is very kind, but not necessary," Willy replied in a calm voice, hiding both his pride and contempt.

"You are about to be charged as an accessory to the second-degree murder of two police officers, with attempt to avoid arrest, as well as conspiracy in the murders of Prescott Cassidy and Angela Wong. With the exception of avoiding arrest, these counts are all Class A felonies. Due to the serious nature of these crimes and the international implications, I would like to strongly suggest that you retain counsel," Cameron Jobe said, as he seated himself across the table from Willy.

"I will not require a solicitor," Willy said softly.

"I disagree," Cameron said, "but in that case, I want you to sign this sheet. It states that you have been offered an attorney and read your Miranda rights; that I have recommended you take advantage of legal counsel and that you have declined of your own free will."

He handed the sheet of paper to Willy, who read it quickly and then put his hand out for a pen. One was handed to him and he signed it.

"Before you, Mr. Wo Lap, is a folder. Open it please, and inside you will find two documents. One is a copy of an Agreement that was taken from a temple inside the Walled City of Kowloon, which is your Triad headquarters in Hong Kong. The other was transcribed from Prescott Cassidy's automobile tape."

"I have no such headquarters in Hong Kong," Willy said. "I know nothing of anybody named Prescott Cassidy."

"The document is a contract between you and Chen Boda, who I'm sure you know is the head of the Chinese Military Commission in Beijing." Cameron continued, unfazed. "The Agreement states that you will run, unopposed, for Chief Executive of Hong Kong in the mid-'98 elections, in return for huge financial considerations from Beijing outlined in paragraph three. Paragraph six of this Agreement also says that, in the event you fail to be elected, the Chinese government will help you reattain your position as Shan Chu. I understand a Shan Chu is like a president or head man of a Triad. The document is, of course, written in Chinese, but I have an accurate translation before me. Would you please read the paragraph I'm talking about?"

Willy looked at paragraph six of the document written in Mandarin. He had supervised its writing the afternoon of his historic meeting with the President of China, in the beautiful Zhong Nan Hai Garden in Beijing.

Willy reread paragraph six, even though he knew the document by heart. Then he looked up and nodded, indicating he had finished.

"Is that your signature?" Cameron Jobe asked. The Attorney General was ready for a denial. He had already had the signature authenticated by two separate handwriting analysts. Cameron and the room full of observers were surprised when Willy leaned forward, looked at the signature at the bottom of the document, then said, "This is my signature."

"Good," Cameron noted. "Mr. Wo Lap, I am now going to charge you with the aforementioned crimes. Again, I feel it is imperative for you to hire an attorney before we proceed."

"I wish to make a statement first," Willy said.

Cameron looked over at Rick Verba, who was in the corner of the room, then at Judge Hollingsworth, who shrugged.

"I do not wish to make this statement twice, and it is very important to me that I am believed. Therefore, I would like to suggest that I make this statement while attached to a polygraph machine." Willy could see that the remark took them by surprise. "I assume," he continued, "you have the equipment in this building and we can proceed quickly. When you hear what I have to say, you will agree that it is in your interest not to waste precious time."

Cameron Jobe looked at his colleagues in the room, again ending with Judge Hollingsworth, who nodded. "Okay, we can arrange that," Cameron said, then nodded to Rick Verba, who left the room to set it up.

"You're aware of the nature of polygraph examinations?" Cameron asked. "You can't just make a statement. You have to be asked questions that are answered yes or no."

"I'm aware of that," Willy said calmly, in his perfect, unaccented English. "To that end, if you could supply me with a paper and pen, I will prepare a short list of five questions."

Wheeler and Tanisha had been watching Willy's interview through a one-way mirror in the adjoining observation room. After Rick Verba had gone to get the polygraph machine, Cameron Jobe and Judge Hollingsworth left to get coffee, leaving Willy Wo Lap alone. Tanisha left the observation room and followed them into the coffee room, also leaving Wheeler alone.

Wheeler looked through the mirror at the Triad leader, sitting quietly in the room just beyond the glass. The man he was staring at had ordered his little brother's murder. Wheeler felt guilt for not protecting Prescott, guilt and intense, uncontrollable anger. Suddenly, he lost all control. Wheeler wanted to see fear on the Triad leader's face. He wanted Wo Lap Ling to realize it was Prescott's death that was causing his demise, but the Shan Chu didn't seem at all worried. He had a look of passive indifference on his aged face.

"Whatever happens, promise me you'll do the right thing."

Now Wheeler was out of the observation room and into the corridor. Before anybody could stop him, he opened the door to the interrogation room and barged in, not even sure what his mission was, or what he was about to do.

As Wo Lap Ling looked up, Wheeler saw recognition flicker in Willie's eyes. Since they had never seen one another, it was all the confirmation of guilt Wheeler needed.

"I just wanted to tell you that it doesn't really matter what the result of this fucking lie detector test is or what you tell the police," Wheeler said, "because if they don't get you, I will." Wheeler's rage was burning. "You're finished! You'll never get out of jail!"

"Do not mistake inactivity for defeat," Willy said pleasantly. "The superior man lives his life without one preconceived course of action. He must decide, from moment to moment, what is the right thing to do."

Wheeler moved across the room and yanked Willy out of the metal chair and up onto his feet. Willy was only five foot five and Wheeler held him erect, by his lapels, towering above him.

"Hey, asshole, I want you to know exactly why this is happening." There was a moment of powerful silence in the room. "You had my brother killed. You had your street thugs push an acupuncture needle through his heart. That's why you're going down, because you killed Prescott Cassidy."

"Take your hands off me," Willy said, his voice now hissing with anger, fear, and hatred. "Your brother was willing to take our money, but not willing to accept his responsibilities. You may have more courage, but you have his same mistaken sense of direction."

"Wanna bet?" Wheeler yelled into the Triad leader's face.

The door opened and Rick Verba entered with two uniformed police officers pushing a polygraph machine on a rolling cart. Tanisha came in behind him. "What the fuck is going on here?" Verba asked, as he saw Wheeler with his hands on Willy's lapels almost lifting him off the floor. "Let go of him."

Wheeler turned Willy loose.

"Jesus Christ, you're threatening him? You're gonna fuck up this investigation."

"There isn't going to be an investigation, is there, Willy? Willy can't stand an investigation. Look at him—he's already found a hole to wiggle through."

"Get the fuck out of here," Verba said, and the two uniforms pulled Wheeler and Tanisha out of the room.

Willy watched them go, hatred contorting and twitching on his face. He tried to regain his sense of calm, but the raging anger he had fought to control his entire life would not leave him.

The superior man develops up, but the inferior man develops down. Suddenly, Willy saw the truth in Confucius's ancient warning. From impure acts come bad results.

For the first time in almost fifty years, Willy had a sudden paralyzing moment of fear.

Five minutes later the polygraph operator arrived. She was a forty-year-old woman named Helen Staggs and was the best the LAPD had on staff. Willy removed his coat jacket and was hooked to the machine. The electrodes were extended around his chest, the clips attached to the fingertips of his left hand.

Mrs. Staggs turned on the machine and set a level to determine skin electrolysis and respiratory function. She asked Willy a few test questions to be sure it was functioning correctly, then she looked up at Cameron and nodded.

Tanisha, Wheeler, and Rick Verba were now in the adjoining room watching through a mirrored glass window.

Wheeler was still enraged. Willy had again assumed a look of indifference.

"Is your correct name Wo Lap Ling?" Cameron began.

"I will not answer any of your questions," Willy stated. "I would like only to answer the five questions I prepared. I think you will find it well worth your while."

Cameron looked over at Judge Hollingsworth, who shrugged. Willy withdrew the handwritten note from his pocket and handed it to Cameron Jobe, who opened it and read the questions to himself. First a puzzled look crossed his face. Disbelief quickly followed. "You can't be serious?" Cameron said. "This is outrageous!"

Willy fought to exhibit a serene exterior. "Ask the questions," he said. "You will see by this machine that I am telling the truth."

Cameron glared down at the list of questions as though it were dog shit in his hand. "Do you have a nuclear device in your possession?" he began.

"Yes, I do."

"Is it a portable Russian knapsack bomb?"

"Yes, it is."

"Is it currently in Los Angeles?"

"Yes."

"Is it set to explode today at four P.M.?"

"Yes," Willy said, keeping his voice gentle and superior in the quiet room.

"Is it somewhere at Los Angeles International Airport?"

"Yes, it is."

They looked at the polygraph operator. "These are nine-plus-range responses," she said. "Very truthful."

"Obviously you will try to find this device," Willy said. "That is your job. My plane is at LAX. You undoubtedly will search it first, but you will be wasting your time. In the meantime, I want my jet provisioned and fueled. My pilots must supervise this operation. I will take off at exactly three P.M. Once I have cleared American airspace, I will radio you the position and the instructions for disarming the nuclear device. That should give you adequate time to disarm it before it explodes at four o'clock. You should now ask me if I intend to live up to this agreement. Your machine will verify my response."

There was an awkward silence in the room.

"Ask him," Alan said.

"If we let you go, do you intend to keep your end of the bargain?" Cameron asked.

Everyone except for Willy turned to look at the polygraph operator.

"Yes," Willy said. "I would never break my word." The Triad leader was rewarded with a nod from Helen Staggs. "You must not waste your time. I want my plane ready to depart no later than three."

"What if we put you at the airport and let the bomb, if there even is one, take you up with it?" Cameron said.

"You can pursue whatever course you choose."

Willy sat quietly and waited to see what his enemies would do. They were inferior men, and as the Master had once said, inferior men were liable to do anything.

FORTY

Carter DeHaviland

anisha and Wheeler could not remember the name of the man who told Willard Vickers that Willy was dealing in nuclear weapons. They called Vickers in Cleveland and he gave them the name. Twenty minutes later, Carter DeHaviland showed up at the fifth-floor office in Parker Center. He had rushed over from the CIA's office on Wilshire Boulevard as soon as they'd called. Carter DeHaviland was stoop-shouldered, with wire glasses, and wore an out-of-date narrow-lapeled seersucker suit. He was an E-5 company Indian, and told them he was assigned to the Agency "Scare Book," which investigated black market nuclear ordnance from the old USSR armory, alleged to have been sold to terrorists. The hundred missing suitcase bombs were already under investigation. He listened while they filled him in, finishing by showing the results of Willy's lie detector test.

"I think this is pure bullshit," Cameron said, after the briefing was complete. "I think he's bluffing."

"I don't," DeHaviland said. "This has been a CIA front-burner scenario since slightly before Russian General Alexander Lebed made the charge public on *60 Minutes* in September of '97."

"You mean this is true?" Cameron asked. "We can't let this guy threaten us with a nuke in a suitcase and just let him walk out of here."

"The lie detector says he's telling the truth," Wheeler reminded him. "You have any idea how much damage that bomb would do?"

"Whatta you know about lie detectors or bombs?" Cameron responded. "Besides, the polygraph isn't foolproof. It's possible to beat the box. This guy is Chinese—maybe he was in some sort of yoga trance or something. Who the hell knows?"

"That's sorta bullshit," Verba said hesitantly. "I've been giving lie tests for twenty years. They're ninety to ninety-five percent accurate. So on that scale, we've got at least a ninety percent chance Mr. Wo Lap is telling the truth."

Then Alan Hollingsworth asked a question that needed an answer. "What makes you think this suitcase bomb even exists?"

Carter DeHaviland pushed his wire-rim glasses up on his nose, trying to decide how much classified information to give them. "First," Carter said, "I think we should notify NEST immediately. That's the Nuclear Emergency Search Team. I checked before coming over. They're on a field op right now. NEST is usually on a five-hour string. They are a self-contained unit, traveling in four C-141 cargo jets. Since they're presently gathered in New Mexico for training exercises, we can probably get 'em here by two. First you have to notify the FBI, because they have lead agency authority over NEST and have to call them in. You should also immediately notify the White House that you suspect a foreign agent placed a nuclear device at the L.A. airport, and simultaneously, you must clear the area, notifying the police and National Guard."

"We've already informed the Governor," Verba said. "He was going to take care of the White House."

"Okay, good. The first thing you must understand is, in the

intelligence community, we deal with both factual and counterfactual probabilities. Every story has a counterclaim. People don't always give you the whole truth. We assign probability quotients to casual factors to determine counterintuitive scenarios."

"Jesus, talk English, will ya?" Wheeler said.

"General Lebed made these charges initially in '97," Carter went on, "He had just been fired by Boris Yeltsin. We know the General is planning to run for President of Russia in 2000. It therefore could be considered in his best interest to embarrass President Yeltsin, and this story about a hundred missing nuclear suitcase bombs could be counterfactual disinformation."

"Go on," Cameron said.

"On the other hand, we have some independent corroboration that one hundred nuclear suitcase bombs are, in fact, missing. This came last year from a Russian Deputy Defense Minister, named Andrei Kokoshin, who confirmed everything General Lebed said. A few weeks after Kokoshin made his confirmation, he was also fired by the Russian High Command . . . a bad sign, we thought, in the hallowed halls of Langley. Kokoshin's firing was as good as a confirmation. After that, the CIA started taking Lebed's claim very seriously. We know these suitcase bombs exist in theory. It's not at all difficult to reduce nuclear technology down to the size of a suitcase or a backpack."

"How destructive are these things?" Cameron asked.

"They're not Start I or Start II nuclear devices, which means they're not covered by any international arms agreements. These are much smaller NUTS units."

"They're what?" Cameron asked.

"NUTS units. It's an acronym, stands for Nuclear Utilization Targeting Strategy. It's a theory based on the idea that it will be military targets, not cities, that will be hit in a nuclear exchange. These knapsack or suitcase bombs were designed to destroy tactical targets like power plants, airports, hotels, and munitions centers. Russian paratroopers could parachute in with them and wreak havoc on hard targets behind enemy lines. To the best of our knowledge, the missing suitcase weapons were deployed to Ukraine and Georgia, just before the break-up of the Soviet Union. This is much more disturbing to us because those governments are even less stable than the Russian government, and it's quite possible that their military establishments, or individuals therein, chose to steal the bombs and sell them on the world munitions black market.

"China would be a big buyer of this kind of ordnance. Their Poly Industries in Beijing is one of the biggest brokers of Russian armaments in the world. In theory, that would make it very easy for Wo Lap Ling to purchase one or two of these devices."

The room was now totally silent. Cameron Jobe got up. His chair squeaked as it slid back. He walked to the window and looked out, his broad back to the rest of them. "You're telling me this criminal has actually put a nuclear bomb at LAX?"

"Let me put it this way. . . . Nothing you have said surprises me. I don't believe this information is counterfactual. We have assigned a very high probability percentage to Lebed's claims."

"Shit," Verba said

"How big are these damn things?" Alan Hollingsworth asked. "How much damage will they do?"

"According to Lebed, these are what we call NO FUN weapons. Another acronym, meaning No First Use Nuclear devices. They are only one kiloton, weigh sixty to a hundred pounds, and could kill a hundred thousand people if detonated in a populous area. They would take an average person less than a half-hour to activate, and once activated, can be detonated by radio wave. If Wo Lap Ling has one placed at LAX, he'll turn the airport into a pile of rubble and the resulting ejecta will most probably knock out a good portion of Marina Del Rey, as well as points north and south. Nuclear fallout will be dangerous, but not immediately critical, depending on how 'clean' the device is. I can't speak to increased incidents of cancer and the like."

They sat in silence.

"In fairness," Carter added, "I owe it to you to say that there

is some countervailing opinion. The chairman of the Foreign Relations Committee has gone on record as saying Lebed's charges are
nonsense. He says they are political in nature and not substantive."

"Really?" Alan said. "Senator Peck said that?"

"Jesus Christ," Wheeler said, grabbing for the sheet of paper
with the translated code names transcribed from Prescott's car
tape. On the bottom of the page he found it:

SEN. JOHN L. PECK (D) WYOMING.

FORTY-ONE

Cash Flow

After Carter DeHaviland's briefing, Wheeler and Tanisha were told to go home.

Alan said there was nothing they could do.

Verba said this was completely out of their hands.

T. Cameron Jobe said if they interfered he would personally bring charges against them for obstructing justice.

Then they were left standing alone in the fifth-floor corridor of Parker Center as activity swirled around them.

They were out of it. They left the building and found Rick Verba standing in the parking lot across from Parker Center. The hot noon sun was beating down on them. The outside of the architecturally uninteresting granite building showed no sign of the intense activity inside. Somewhere on the third floor, Willy Wo Lap Ling was sitting in a holding cell, his hands clasped on his lap, waiting to see what would happen.

"You guys did great work," Verba said to them. "If this turns out to be true, you've saved thousands of lives."

"Captain, can this bozack Attorney General just blow us off

345

the case? We've been working this for almost two weeks," Tanisha said.

"What're you gonna do while NEST does its job, take pictures? You're counterintuitive or whatever. . . . Go home, get some sleep. You look bushed," Verba said.

"I can't go home. That piece of Triad gangsta shit upstairs put a bounty of fifty keys of pure heroin on our heads. The gangs in South Central aren't going to know that Willy is busted. Wheeler and I are marked anywhere south of Crenshaw."

"You can sleep in my office at ACTF," Verba said.

That was finally what they decided to do. They followed Captain Verba back to Hill Street and left the Jag in the parking lot at the side of the leased Asian Crimes building.

Things took a strange turn once they got upstairs. Al Katsukura was complaining to anyone who'd listen. He grabbed Tanisha and told her what had happened last night. While they were dragging Wo Lap Ling out of the L.A. Triad headquarters, he was out in the ocean, in pea soup fog, losing a boatload of illegal aliens and three Major Crimes detectives. He had spent the night answering angry questions from Deputy Chief Pitlick. Al had just finished his paperwork, and the owl-eyed Japanese detective was frustrated beyond anything Tanisha had ever observed in him before.

"These three U.C. dicks from Major Crimes aren't missing, they're dead, Tisha," he said, glancing only occasionally at Wheeler. His Asian poker face twisted in anguish. "I was bobbing around out there like a fucking asshole while they got washed out. I let those guys get taken. Operation Dry Dock was my deal. I feel like shit."

"Let's get something to eat," Tanisha said. "We all need lunch. I'll buy."

"Anyplace but the fucking Westin coffee shop," Wheeler reminded her.

They found a little greasy spoon on North Hill and Alpine, just outside of Chinatown. They picked the diner because the place was absolutely empty.

They sat in the back and ordered sandwiches and steaming hot coffee. Wheeler told the Hispanic waitress to keep the coffee coming.

When the food arrived, Al was still on a talking jag, retelling his story, trying to find a version that didn't make him feel quite so shitty.

"Where was this?" Wheeler asked when Al finally paused to eat.

"Where was what?"

"Where you found the empty boat?"

"We were in the ocean, somewhere south of Marina Del Rey."

"How far offshore?" Wheeler asked.

"I don't know. Mile, mile and a half, maybe five. It's water out there. They don't have mile markers."

"That's roughly out by the airport then," Wheeler observed, picking at his fries with a fork. "How often do undercover officers get shot on a deal like that?"

"It shouldn'ta happened. These Bamboo Dragons couldn't have known my guys were U.C.s. They were dressed like a *Horn-blower* crew in corny sailor outfits. They weren't carrying any badges or I.D.s. They weren't there trying to make a bust. The deal was strictly Watch and Report. There would be no reason for them to get killed. That's what makes this screwy. If I'd thought there was any danger, I would've had half-a-dozen guys with me on that patrol boat and I woulda had troops stashed on the *Hornblower*. We'da been screwed tight into their assholes."

The waitress brought more coffee and left the carafe, while they all sat, thinking.

"What if all this shit is connected?" Wheeler finally asked Tanisha.

"It is, but not like you think," Tanisha answered. "The boys on the boat were Tong gangsters connected to the Chin Lo and to Willy, but the Bamboo Dragons are doing a whole menu of crimes. Nothing would stop just because Willy came into town. This immigrant smuggle probably started in Hong Kong a week ago. Besides, what does a bunch of Snake Riders have to do with a bomb scare at the airport?"

"I don't know. But once the immigrants were off-loaded, why kill three guys for no reason?" Wheeler pondered.

"Because they're jacked up on speed or adrenaline," Al said. "Who knows why they pull this dumb violent shit? It happens all the time now. It's just what they do."

Wheeler poured himself more coffee out of the carafe. "Is anybody out there looking for these missing Snake Riders?"

"We had a full-scale helicopter search in place as soon as the fog burned off. Nothing out in the ocean. Empty as a junkie's wallet."

"Let's go look for ourselves," Wheeler suggested. "My uncle Alan has a boat at the marina. I'll call him. It used to be my dad's boat. He left it to Alan when he died. I've run it a bunch. I know where the key is."

"Why? Whatta we gonna find?" the Japanese detective asked.

"I don't know. Probably nothing, but to tell you the truth, I'd a helluva lot rather sleep on that boat than on the couch in Verba's office."

It was hard to get to the slip in Marina Del Rey. The National Guard was already evacuating the marina. They had barricades up and stern-faced young men in *Hogan's Heroes* helmets that said HAZMAT, for Hazardous Materials, on the back were stopping traffic and turning it around. Al asked why the city was being evacuated. The HAZMAT lieutenant said, "Gas leak," and that was all he would say. Al and Tanisha had to badge him and threaten to arrest him to get them through the barricade. Cops were at every intersection in Marina Del Rey directing evacuation traffic. It took them almost half an hour to get to the dock on Palawan Way.

The boat was named *Cashflow*. Alan had contemplated renaming it *Legal Ease,* but in the end had not changed it out of respect for his dead friend.

The boat was a fifty-two-foot Bertram Sportfisher with a tuna tower. Wheeler was on the flybridge with the twin engines burbling as Al and Tanisha threw the lines off. He backed it out of the slip, using the twin screws to rotate it in the channel before heading it out of the harbor at the mandated five miles an hour. They moved toward the jetty, past the junction of Ballona Creek, past the channel markers, and then turned left, heading toward the general spot where Al said the empty *Hornblower* had been drifting on the tide.

After the marine layer had burned off, it left behind a calm sea and a beautiful day. Wheeler and Tanisha stood on the flybridge while Al sat morosely in a fighting chair just outside the main salon. He was lost in a deep depression over his failure to protect the three detectives.

Finally, they were offshore about a quarter-mile out, looking in at LAX. Wheeler throttled back and watched as a United 747 took off, roaring out over the ocean six hundred feet above their heads. The jet thundered in the cloudless sky, raining sound pollution down on them. As soon as the jet was away, another took off from the parallel runway.

"I thought they closed this airport down," Tanisha said.

"I've been watching since we turned out of the marina channel," Wheeler said. "Everything is leaving, nothing is landing. I think the airlines are trying to get their equipment out of here."

Another jet roared overhead, banking right and heading east.

Al Katsukura got out of the fighting chair on the deck below and climbed the ladder to the flybridge.

"Is this about where the *Hornblower* was?" Wheeler asked.

"How would I know? You couldn't see shit. It was socked in. I didn't hear any planes, but the fog was so thick the airport was probably closed."

Wheeler put the binoculars to his eyes and again looked at the airport a quarter-mile beyond. Through the lenses he could see several olive-green canvas-covered military trucks driving around on the field. Off to one side, parked near the Federal Express hangars, were four military C-141s with no markings. He wondered if they were the four NEST aircraft from New Mexico. He looked at his watch. It was one thirty-five. Carter DeHaviland had said two hours would get NEST to LAX. He could see men in olive uniforms running between hangars.

"This either happens or it doesn't in two and a half hours," he said. Then he turned his binoculars on Dockweiler State Beach. It was a broad strip of sand that started at the Del Rey Channel marker and stretched all the way past the airport to the housing development at Vista Del Mar. Wheeler scanned the beach carefully.

"What is it?" Tanisha asked.

"If the *Hornblower* was around here and they off-loaded it with small rubber boats from the shore, then Dockweiler Beach would be perfect. Nobody is ever there because of the noise from the airport. Could be this is where they landed."

"If that's true, they'd be long gone by now," Al added.

Wheeler didn't know what he was trying to prove or why this seemed so important, but something was driving him, pushing him to go ashore. Maybe it was the look of indifference in Willy's eyes when Wheeler accused him of killing Prescott, or the fury that had flashed when Wheeler had challenged the Triad mobster. "I'm gonna put the Avon in the water and go take a look," he said.

"And leave us floating around out here? I did enough of that last night," Al whined.

"According to my depth finder, it's only fifty feet deep. I can anchor, and you both can come with me."

After backing down on his Danforth anchor to set it, Wheeler shut the engines down. He used the davit to put the rubber Avon boat with the fifteen-horsepower Yamaha outboard in the water. The two Asian Crimes detectives got in the Avon while Wheeler unlocked his uncle's gun cabinet aboard the sportfisher. He took out the shark rifle and two long-barreled Smith & Wesson .44 Magnum "Dirty Harry" revolvers, with drop-forged aluminum frames and full checkered walnut stocks. He grabbed a box of Remington ammunition. In a few seconds they were in the Avon headed toward Dockweiler State Beach.

He had to surf the boat in on the medium-sized breakers to get it ashore, gunning the motor as the wave broke, shooting ahead of the cresting surf, cutting the motor at the last minute, and running the light Avon high up onto the beach. They all jumped out and pulled the boat to safety ahead of the next breaker.

The sand on Dockweiler Beach was windblown and smooth.

"Let's split up, look for footprints," Tanisha said. "A whole boatload of Snake Riders should leave a pretty good trail."

Tanisha and Al went up the beach to the east, Wheeler went west. He had walked about 250 yards before he saw it: a windblown trail of footprints heading from the shore, up the beach to where he was standing. "Over here!" he shouted, but his voice was overwhelmed by a departing jet. He soon realized they were too far away to hear him over the thundering surf. He let out a shrill whistle, which they finally heard. He waved his arm and they began moving back toward him.

The footprints led to a huge round concrete drain, almost ten feet in diameter. It was a gigantic underground water run-off that headed diagonally back toward the airport; inside the dark tunnel was a small river of dirty water. In a storm, Wheeler guessed, it would be a raging river of spill-off from LAX that emptied flooding runway water into the ocean. The metal grate across the opening, which was designed to keep people out, had been cut out and removed. The white-hot burn of an acetylene torch had scarred the remaining ends. While Wheeler waited for Tanisha and Al, he saw something buried in the sludge and water, at the bottom of the concrete drain. He reached down and picked it up. It was a sodden black backpack. As soon as Al and Tanisha got to him, Wheeler showed it to them.

Al examined it, saying, "That looks a little like one of the packs those Bamboo Dragons were wearing. Hard to be certain— I was two piers over, using binoculars." Wheeler turned it inside out, looking for a manufacturer's tag. He found it sewn to the inseam. It said: MADE IN CHINA.

FORTY-TWO

Food Fight

They were gathered in the Situation Room in the basement of City Hall. It was a big, windowless, half-basketball-court-sized underground chamber, connected to fifty phone lines and satellite TV communications. There were screens on two walls that could project maps or satellite images, and now reflected graphic line drawings of the huge Los Angeles airport's runways and support buildings. There were two dozen desks in the room, and several private offices around the perimeter with curtained-off glass windows looking back in toward the room. There were ten TV screens, which were set to monitor the four national networks, plus the four local TV stations in Los Angeles, along with CNN. A separate screen was for remote TV cameras.

The room was almost never used, the exceptions being two earthquakes and one race riot, which had all been dealt with from this underground chamber.

The Mayor was on the phone in one of the perimeter offices. The Governor was in the air flying to L.A. from Sacramento. They had a direct line to the White House Situation Room, where half-a-dozen specialists on nuclear threat scenarios were gathered to heckle and raise the level of confusion.

Nobody was in charge. It had become that horrible phenomenon of modern government: a jurisdictional food fight.

Present in the L.A. bunker was one-star Air Force General Robert "Kicker" Clark, head of the California National Guard. He was a jet pilot and ace from the Vietnam War, a no-nonsense kick-'em-in-the-ass kind of leader. Next to him was the southwest section's FBI Special Agent in Charge, Douglas Pardee. Then there was CIA Area Director Rogers St. John. Behind him sat Carter DeHaviland, looking dismayed. There was a gray, colorless man from State, named Lew Fisher. He had been in Los Angeles on other business, and the State Department had rushed him over. Next to him was the geek from FEMA (Federal Emergency Management Agency). L.A. Police Chief Carl Leddiker was dressed for a parade, looking like a high school band leader in full uniform. Everybody had his own "secure" phone jockey. The room was full of tension, snapping and buzzing like a broken toaster.

"You can't tell the fucking citizens there may be a nuke at the airport. We're gonna have a stampede," Chief Carl Leddiker was saying to FBI SAC Douglas Pardee.

"You've got how many people living out there by the airport?" Pardee responded, "A million, give or take a few hundred thousand. They're all in the fall-out radius. You can't clear a million people driving down streets with bullhorns announcing a fucking gas leak. They won't leave. You gotta put it out straight on the network news what the situation is here."

"You'll panic the whole damn town. We've done studies on mass evacuation. The freeways will jam. We've got traffic flow chart analyses that say we'll have a world-class cluster-fuck."

"I don't give a shit. You gotta tell 'em what's going on. It's our asses if the airport mushrooms up and we knew the bomb was there and kept it quiet," Pardee argued.

Then his phone rang and he snatched it up. It was his NEST Commander at the airport. Everybody got quiet as Pardee listened to the report, then hung up.

"Okay, NEST is deployed on site. They already have one detection platform on a helicopter and they're about to take off and scan the field. Two more are in jeeps and are starting at opposite ends of the field, working toward the center. Most of the heavy commercial airliners are gone, but in half an hour I'm locking the field. Nothing else leaves. We're getting the rest of the civilians off the premises. My NEST Commander says he can do a thorough sweep of the field and buildings in six hours. We only have two. In that time frame he can give the place a once-over lightly, scanning for nuclear trace elements, move in and narrow down if he gets any Geiger ticks."

The room was silent.

"How does the detection platform work?" Chief Leddiker asked.

"Classified," the FBI SAC shot back.

"I still wanna know what we're gonna do with the perp," Lew Fisher from State said. "You gonna put him on his plane, fuel it up, and send him outta here if we can't find the bomb? Then what? We pray he keeps his word? You want my opinion, that plan sounds motivationally deficient."

"And from a tactical point of view, it sucks," General Robert Clark said. "This guy isn't going to keep his word. He's a low-life criminal. He'll leave and never look back. We're gonna be hunting around in radioactive rubble trying to find each other's dicks."

"He passed the lie detector test when LAPD asked him that," CIA Director Rogers St. John said.

"You show weakness to a guy like this, you encourage him," General Clark said. "Let's make him wonder what the fuck is happening. It's gut check time. The best show of strength wins in a deal like this."

"It's my city. I'm in charge," the Mayor said. He had come

out of the side office to join the argument. "I'll make the decision."

"Not hardly," Pardee replied.

And so it went, until the National Defense Team at the Situation Room in Washington cut in on the speaker phone. "You had better pull it together, fellas. Stop arguing and get proactive," somebody back there boomed over the large telephone speakers.

"I think we let him go. Trust the lie detector. We'll never find a bomb in two hours," the Mayor said, thinking he didn't care about Willy one way or another. If LAX got nuked, his career in politics was over.

"I have three Tomcats at Edwards ready to go," General Clark shot back. "If you put that bastard in his plane and let him take off, I'll scramble those three birds and torch him on my own authority. I don't give a shit about airspace or corridors of neutrality. This guy gets a heat seeker up the ass. That's my promise."

"Who's gonna take responsibility for that bonehead move?" Pardee asked.

"I will!" the General replied. "They can have my star if they don't like it. We gotta stop coddling these bastards."

"Let's just all calm down," the Mayor said. "We're not shooting him down. Let's go back and take this one step at a time."

They had retrieved the flashlight and walkie-talkie from the survival kit on the Avon, and Wheeler handed Tanisha one of the matched Smith & Wesson .44s. He kept the shark rifle, which was a thirty-ought-six, with a sportsman's nine-shot clip. They had asked Al to go back to the *Cashflow* and radio their position to Major Crimes. They helped him get the Avon out through the surf, then they walked back into the tunnel, wading through the sludge and ankle-high water until the light behind them had completely disappeared and they were moving along blindly in inky blackness. The battery on the flashlight was weak, so Wheeler only turned it on from time to time, shining it up the cavernous concrete pipe looking for offshoots, trying to conserve the power. The drain they were in seemed to be heading back toward the north side of the airfield. Then without warning the tunnel began to vibrate and shake. They both froze in fear, unable to see anything as the terrible noise enveloped them. Then the sound slowly disappeared and the vibrating stopped.

"Airplane," Wheeler said "We must be right under the runway." They stood in stunned silence trying to get their hearts slowed.

Tanisha had thought it was an earthquake and they were about to get buried alive.

"This is all related," Wheeler said, talking as much to calm them as anything. "What did you call it in Hong Kong? Claustrophobic? Never trust a coincidence. We've got way too much activity in one place. It's gotta be tied together," he said. "Ready?"

She nodded in the dark. "You're sure beginning to sound like a cop."

"Is that a compliment or a slam?" he asked.

"Depends if we get out of here alive."

Another jet thundered down the runway above them, rumbling and shaking the cement tube. They both froze until it was gone. "Shit . . . I wish they'd stop with that," she whispered.

They moved farther down the tunnel in the darkness, not sure what they would find. Their hearts were beating wildly, their faces shiny with sweat, even though the deeper underground they went, the cooler the air was becoming. They continued along silently for almost twenty minutes, turning on the flashlight every so often to make sure there were no tunnel offshoots they should examine. Occasionally, rodent eyes shone back at them in the flashlight's dim beam. Tanisha didn't look too close. She didn't want to see how big they were. As they continued sloshing on, both lost track of time. Finally, Wheeler thought he heard something. He stopped abruptly and put his hand out to warn her. They stood silently in the ankle-deep water, holding their breath, their ears straining to hear any sound. Then Wheeler heard it again. . . .

The distant sound of a baby crying.

FORTY-THREE

No Feast Lasts Forever

Fu Hai was huddled in the wretched flickering darkness, soaked from the waist down. He had fallen several times in the concrete tunnel. The moss and algae growing there were so slippery it was sometimes impossible to walk. All 180 Snake Riders were now deep underneath L.A. International Airport. Dry Dragon had brought candles, and once they had stopped moving he had lit some. Every half-minute or so the tunnel would rumble and vibrate as jumbo jets took off over-head. Each time it happened it seemed to Fu Hai as if the world was about to end. He felt helpless and insignificant. The Snake Riders whimpered in the candle-lit gloominess, terrified of this rumbling, dank place.

They had stopped at a wide spot where two tunnels inter-sected the main one. Dry Dragon made them stand and wait. There was a ledge where the side tunnels intersected, and Fu Hai placed his burning candle there. Several of the other Snake Riders put theirs up beside his. The babies in their mothers' arms were crying loudly from starvation. Their screams echoed in the enclosed concrete darkness, fraying everyone's nerves. Then Dry Dragon took off his large backpack and handed it to Fu Hai.

"Put this on," he said in Fukienese. "I must leave to go tell the Red-Pole vanguards that you are safe and waiting, so we can get the trucks to take you to a nice place where you will spend the night."

"What is in the pack?"

"It is provisions for later," Dry Dragon said, because he had been told to say that. "You must not open it." This he had also been instructed to say.

Fu Hai took the backpack and shouldered himself into it. It was very large and extremely heavy; the straps cut into his shoulders. "How long will you be gone?" he asked.

"Not long. You must keep these peasants quiet. They will panic unless you talk to them."

Another jet took off, vibrating the concrete. Everybody froze, including Dry Dragon, until it was gone.

"I must have the flashlight and the gun, or I cannot protect them," Fu Hai said. "The candles will be gone soon, and in the dark they will be uncontrollable."

Dry Dragon gave Fu Hai the Russian machine pistol he had been carrying, because he still had a Russian 7.65mm automatic tucked in his belt. Then he gave Fu Hai the flashlight, because he thought that even in the dark he could find his way out. There were no intersections between here and the beach to confuse him. "I will not be long," he said, then he turned and left Fu Hai in the flickering candlelight.

Fu Hai was deep underground with almost two hundred people, but he had never felt so alone. He tried to concentrate on America. He tried to picture the wide streets and beautiful cars he had seen on the one television the laborers in the silkworm factory in Khotan were allowed to watch. The Communists had banned American programs after Tiananmen Square. He thought of the bright, beautiful kitchens in the homes on those programs. He remembered the blond women with perfect hairdos and beautiful white teeth. They never seemed to have to clean their houses. He thought of his pitiful sister, Xiao Jie, who struggled to keep house in a windowless hovel with dirt floors. Almost toothless, with unwashed hair, she toiled while her husband scraped shit out of latrines. Fu Hai was determined to change her world and save her from an early grave. He would finally bring happiness into her sorry life.

Fu Hai was so close, so near. Only hours separated him from his new life.

"I cannot keep him quiet," a woman said into Fu Hai's ear, startling him and interrupting his thoughts. She was holding a screaming baby. "His crying is making the others mad."

The child was skinny and filthy. They had had no water to wash with on the Mexican boat. Fu Hai looked at the child in the flickering candlelight, looked straight down into his squalling face, down his open mouth, to his tonsils that quivered as he screamed.

"He is just hungry," she said. "If there was food . . ."

Fu Hai decided he would give some of the provisions from the backpack to the child. He took it off his shoulders, unsnapped it, and pulled out a heavy metal box about a foot and a half by two feet in dimension and two and a half inches deep. It had Russian writing on it. Perhaps, he decided, the box contained Russian field rations. The box was locked, with a padlock attached to two leather straps. Fu Hai tried to pull the lock off, but it was secured through strong metal hooks.

"Li Feng has a knife," the woman said, and moved away to fetch it. She returned a few minutes later and handed Fu Hai a crude, short-bladed knife with a handmade wood-block handle. He stuck it under the leather strap and twisted hard. In a few minutes the strap was broken and the lock was pulled free. He opened the box wide.

Inside was a very strange contraption. Two cylinders and several tubes extended from a smaller enclosed box. The top and sides of this inner container had been welded shut. Some sort of timing mechanism was attached by colored wires. He put his ear down to the mechanism, listening. He could barely hear the buzzing sound of a clock over the screaming baby.

"What is this?" the woman asked.

Fu Hai didn't answer. He was confused, but he thought it looked very much like a bomb.

Al Katsukura called the Coast Guard on channel 16, using the radio on the bridge of the *Cashflow*. He told them his LAPD badge number and said that he needed to be patched through to Rick Verba. He gave his office number. In a few minutes he was talking to the Captain.

He quickly told Verba what had happened and that Tanisha and Wheeler were underneath LAX, in the sewers, looking for the lost Snake Riders.

"You've gotta be kidding me," Verba responded.

"Captain, there's something going on out here. We found a backpack just like the ones those Bamboo Dragons were wearing when they went aboard the *Hornblower*. It was made in China."

"Half the shit sold in L.A. is made in China," Verba growled, but the Captain's tired mind was already working on it. Like all cops, he also distrusted coincidence. Coincidences in law enforcement weren't happenstance occurrences . . . they were usually criminal mistakes that could be capitalized on. "They think the bomb is *under* LAX?" Verba asked.

"They didn't say it in so many words, but yeah, I think that's where it's going."

"These bastards are gonna blow up maybe hundreds of their own innocent people along with the airport? Why?" Verba wondered.

"There's an old Chinese saying that Ray Fong used to hit me with all the time. 'When the rabbits are dead, the hounds that track them will be finished.' The Snake Riders are rabbits, Cap. We're the hounds. These people die, we've got nothing, no case. Nobody can testify against Willy, and—"

"Okay, okay, I get it," Verba interrupted impatiently. "Where are you?"

"I'm on a fishing boat anchored a quarter-mile off the end of the north runway. We're way outnumbered. Look for the fishing boat, Cap. A white fifty-two-footer with a tuna tower. The drainage tunnel's in front of where it's anchored, about two hundred yards south. Send back-up. I'll monitor channel seventy-two on this hand unit, but I think once I get in the tunnel, I'll be out of range."

"Don't go in there," Verba commanded. "I don't need three people lost under the airport. Stay on the beach and wait for the back-up."

Rick Verba was stopped once he got down into the basement at City Hall. There were two National Guardsmen with Browning rifles blocking his way. He showed them his badge, and they glared at it like leftover food.

"Lemme at least talk to Carter DeHaviland," Captain Verba said.

The two guards shook their heads. Then the door at the end of the hall opened and General Clark moved toward the bathroom.

"Hey, General!" Verba yelled. "I know where the bomb is!"

It was something of a stretch, but it stopped Clark dead in his tracks, one hand already on his fly, the other on the men's-room door.

Two minutes later Rick Verba was inside the Situation Room telling his story.

When he finished, General Clark looked at him with disdain. "You don't *know* there's a bomb down there. You just *think* there are some illegal immigrants hiding from I.N.S. in those drainpipes."

"It could come out that way," Verba admitted, "but these Snake Riders just happen to be brought in by the Chin Lo Triad out of Hong Kong. That Triad just happens to be the one that Willy is head of. This bomb scare just happens to be on the very same day this delegation of illegals comes in from Hong Kong and just happens to end up right smack underneath the airport where your NEST team just happens to be looking for a nuke twenty feet over their heads. I like a nice coincidence once in a while, but this is my all-time Hall of Fame favorite."

"I think he may have something here," DeHaviland said. "Maybe we should look for the bomb down there."

"Wait a minute," Pardee said. "Are you suggesting I pull my NEST team off that search so they can run around in a maze of sewers under the airport?" He looked at his watch. "We only have an hour before we either put Willy on his plane or let him know his bluff didn't work. Whichever way it goes, we gotta deal with the fallout, no pun intended."

"What does it hurt to look like we're going to play along?" Verba said. "Put him in a SWAT truck, under close guard, take him out to the airport. At least it keeps our options open, buys time."

Rick Verba was the lowest-ranking official in the room, but it was hard to argue against common sense, so that's what they did.

Wheeler and Tanisha moved slowly in the inky blackness. They were holding hands because the tunnel was curved pipe, full of slippery algae and moss. Occasionally, one of them would stumble and have to rely on the other for balance.

Then Wheeler heard splashing in the pipe in front of them. He squeezed Tanisha's hand to get her to stop moving.

Sure enough, somebody was close to them in the tunnel. The sloshing sound of footsteps cut through the darkness. Wheeler couldn't risk turning on the flashlight; he had to assume it was a man and that the man was armed. He stood with Tanisha in the darkness, tucking the light into his back pocket to free his right hand. He reached into his waistband to check the .44. He had the thirty-ought-six shark rifle slung over his back on the sling. He silently pulled it off and held the barrel in front of him, aiming toward the sound. It was inky black, but he could hear breathing now, mixed with the footsteps. The man was just a few feet away. Wheeler could taste stomach acid in his mouth.

Then he heard Tanisha grunt as somebody crashed into her. Wheeler could feel motion as air stirred by his left arm. Tanisha went down with a cry. Wheeler heard a brief struggle as Tanisha and the intruder splashed around in the dark. He couldn't see, but moved blindly toward the sounds of the struggle, his outstretched arms waving in the air trying to feel them. Tanisha screamed, but the scream was cut off by a gurgling sound as water filled her mouth.

Wheeler was grabbing helplessly in front of him in the dark, trying to find the intruder. He could hear Tanisha gagging and choking, but he still couldn't find her in the pitch black. Finally, he remembered the flashlight, grabbed it, and turned it on.

They were about ten feet away from him. A young Chinese man was on top of her, pushing her head down into two feet of brackish water. Wheeler tried to chamber the rifle, but in his haste, it slipped in his wet hands and dropped into the water. Dry Dragon turned to look at him, his eyes demonic in the dim beam of the flashlight. Then he let go of Tanisha, pulled his 7.65mm automatic, and fired it once at Wheeler.

The sound in the tunnel was deafening. The bullet whizzed by Wheeler's ear. He jerked back and lost hold of the flashlight. It splashed as it hit the water and sank. It was still lit and put a watery glow on the tunnel walls, dimly illuminating all of them.

Wheeler got the S&W .44 out and was pointing it at the dim outline of the Chinese teenager. Panicked and disoriented by the watery blackness, Dry Dragon fired wildly again, and Wheeler's ears echoed with the concussion. The bullet chipped the tunnel near his head, flinging concrete particles into his face and neck. Wheeler drew aim, praying Tanisha would not rise up into his line of fire. He pulled the trigger. The gun barked just as the flashlight flickered out, and they were again in pitch blackness. Then he heard footsteps running toward him. . . . Suddenly, a body hit him on the shoulder, brushing past on his way *up* the tunnel. Wheeler was knocked down on one knee. He spun in the direction of the disoriented fleeing man and fired twice at the splashing sound in the darkness. He heard his bullets hit the concrete and whine away. He listened for a grunt or the sound of a body falling in the water. He heard neither. Then he edged slowly back to Tanisha.

"Tisha," he whispered in the dark. "Tisha, you okay?"

He heard her cough deeply next to him, and then retch and spit. "Tastes like shit," she said, as she heaved up more brackish water, clearing it out of her lungs.

"You okay?" Wheeler said, finally touching her shoulder with his hand in the darkness.

"If you don't count drinking a quart of sewage. You get him?"

"I don't think so."

He helped her to her feet, and they stood there for a long moment and listened to silence so profound it roared in their ears.

The planes had stopped taking off, and all they could hear now was their own breathing.

"You got the rifle?" she whispered.

"Dropped it."

"Turn on the flash. Look for it. Maybe the cartridges are still dry."

"Dropped the flashlight."

"Good going."

"I never claimed I'd be good at this," he said, "just available."

"Let's go," she said, and again they held hands in the darkness. With their matched .44s out in front of them, they walked slowly and as quietly as possible up the tunnel.

Fu Hai heard the gunfire. It sounded like distant fireworks in the tunnel. He crouched low in the darkness, clutching the unlit flashlight in one hand and the gun Dry Dragon had given him in the other. The Snake Riders were in a panic, all talking at once. Fu Hai crouched even lower, cradling the deadly Russian machine pistol in his arms. Then, more to calm himself than the others, he started to sing a very popular Chinese song about persimmons that every child in China knew, regardless of dialect. One by one they joined in, until all of them were crouched around him, squatting, with their buttocks in the water. The children miraculously stopped crying. As they huddled in the flickering candlelight singing softly, Fu Hai wondered what he should do next.

Willy was in the back of the SWAT van as it sped Code Three down the Santa Monica Freeway. He sat quietly on a wooden bench opposite four stern-faced young men in SWAT uniforms and tried hard to remain impassive. He looked neither right nor left, up nor down. He sat restfully and waited.

Willy knew that the first stop on his way to victory was this ride to the airport. They wanted to keep their options open. If in failure they didn't intend to let him go, they would have left him downtown.

The SWAT truck stopped after thirty minutes. He heard low conversation, and then he felt the van moving again. Soon they came to another stop and the door to the back was opened. He could see the tail of his jet behind the young uniformed police lieutenant who looked into the back of the van.

"Sorry it's so hot back here. I'll keep the engine running and the air on," he said to the guards with Willy, then closed the door and bolted it.

The Stupid Dragon had carried the Smart Monkey back from a certain death at the bottom of the sea, and had brought him up on dry land. The LAPD was about to put Willy safely back up on the highest limb of his willow tree.

Time was running out. The flimsy constraints of order in the Situation Room were beginning to break down. What had started as a jurisdictional squabble had degenerated into open warfare. They had divided up into two groups. The "Turn Willy Loose" faction consisted of the Mayor of Los Angeles, the Governor of California, and L.A. Police Chief Carl Leddiker—the hometowners. They saw Willy's life as meaningless when measured against their civic responsibility and the destruction of the airport by nuclear explosion. The "Keep Willy Here" contingent consisted of all the Feds, who the hometowners said intended to sky out of L.A. as soon as it was over and leave the shit-digging and body-bagging to the locals.

The geek from FEMA never said anything. He kept his head down, working on fallout patterns, weather charts, and wind graphs.

"I'm taking authority for letting him go," the Governor said. "I don't give a shit what the federal government thinks." The Governor had just arrived ten minutes ago and was turning the tide. "We put him on his plane and cut him loose. He's just one life. One person. I have a potential disaster here. Hundreds or even thousands of deaths. Who knows how many more will die from radiation? We'll go after him later. He can't hide."

"Who says he can't hide?" St. John said. "He'll disappear just like those two fucks Megrahi and Fhimah, who blew up the Lockerbie flight. Can't hide, my ass. Those two rag-heads are in Libya right now, flipping us off."

"Put Wo Lap Ling on his plane. Get him out of here," the Governor instructed the L.A. Chief of Police.

Chief Leddiker moved into a perimeter office, snapped up a phone, and started dialing.

"I won't allow this," Lew Fisher of the State Department said.

"How're you gonna stop it?" the Governor shot back. "The police and National Guard are under my command. It's gonna take you forty-eight hours to nationalize the Guard. You don't have forty-eight hours. You're fucked, Mr. Fisher."

"Is that true, General?" Fisher asked. "Does it take forty-eight hours?"

They all turned to look for General Robert Clark, but Kicker Clark had slipped out of the room three minutes before.

The back of the SWAT van was opened and Willy stepped out into the sunshine. He moved with newly recovered dignity across the tarmac to the boarding ramp of his Falcon, strolling as if it was Sunday afternoon in the park. His pilots were both former German fighter pilots. Willy had always used Germans to fly him, because of twin German traits he viewed as essential for airplane pilots: anal meticulousness and rigid control. Once Willy was aboard, the pilots closed the door. In a few minutes they had the three jet engines wound up and were taxiing off the ramp, away from the Executive Jet Terminal. They crossed Service Road E and turned right on Taxiway C. Then the pilots hurried the big three-engine jet along, past the Department of Airports maintenance yard, where the NEST team had gathered, past the four C-141s with no tail markings, past the LAX Sky Lounge perched like a giant concrete spider in the airport's center parking lot.

Willy was standing in the doorway to the cockpit. "I would appreciate it if we can depart as quickly as possible," he said, not wanting to appear frightened or anxious, but not wanting to remain in Los Angeles a second longer than necessary.

The chief pilot was named Gunter Hagen. He nodded to his copilot, and they added ten percent more power. The jet moved faster, passing the empty United and Continental terminals. It rushed across the Sepulveda Boulevard overpass into the international section of LAX, past Air France and Singapore Air, past JAL and Indonesian Airlines. The airport was almost completely deserted. No planes were parked at the ramps. Except for Willy's Falcon jet, only one other vehicle was moving on the field.

Willy looked down and saw that a military jeep with four soldiers was racing along with them, just under the wing. "As soon as possible," he said to his pilots.

Now Gunter was at the end of the runway, and he pressed the yoke mike. "Dis is eight six eight Charlie Papa, requesting runway two four nine left."

"I don't think, under the circumstances, it's necessary to obtain permission," Willy urged. "We should leave now."

"Ja," Gunter said, and he taxied the big jet onto runway 249-L and looked at his copilot, who nodded and pushed the three throttles forward slowly.

The sleek Falcon jet thundered away from the trailing jeep, blowing dust and gravel into the faces of the soldiers. It was airborne halfway down the runway, then climbed steeply into the sky, all three powerful engines trailing exhaust and reverberated sound.

Wheeler and Tanisha heard the jet take off. It was the first jet they'd heard in almost half an hour. They stopped in the blackness and listened as it thundered down the runway, shaking the tunnel with distant sound and vibration. The noise abruptly abated as soon as the jet was off the ground. Suddenly it was quiet again. Slowly, Wheeler and Tanisha continued up the tunnel.

They began to hear hushed singing. It was in Chinese and coming from up ahead. A few yards farther on, Wheeler could see dim light flickering on the wall, and then his foot brushed against something submerged in the water at his feet. "Hold on," he whispered. He reached down into the water with his hand and felt for what his foot had hit. Something mossy and stringy floated in the dirty sewage. He pulled at it but it wouldn't move. He reached down with both hands and felt around in the inky black water. It was then he realized what he had found.

He had both his hands on the submerged head of Dry Dragon.

"Shit," he whispered, "I guess I hit that guy after all."

Tanisha reached down and helped him sit the dead Chinese gangster up as water drained out of his open mouth. They could barely see him in the distant flickering light. Wheeler managed to pull the body over to the side of the tunnel, and they left him there. Then he took Tanisha's hand and they continued on.

The tunnel was bending right, and as they moved along, they

could see flickering candlelight coming from a spot just ahead. Wheeler and Tanisha stopped, stood very still, and listened. They could hear the singing very clearly now. The song was simple in melody and very sweet. In the small amount of light that leaked back at them from the candles, they could see each other clearly. Wheeler took the first two fingers of his hand and pointed them at his eyes, then up the tunnel, indicating he would go up and look. She nodded, then he moved very slowly toward the light, trying hard not to make a sound, or slip and splash water. He hugged the far wall as he crept up on them. His hand was gripped tight around the checked walnut handle of the S&W .44. If the Snake Riders were near the candles, then, he reasoned, this position on the far side of the wall would give him the best early view. He would be on the edge of the light and hard to see. It should give him an advantage.

Slowly, Wheeler snuck up on them. He raised the cocked Magnum and pointed it out in front of him. Then he saw them: hundreds of people in a widened intersection where four drainage pipes came together. They were huddled knee-deep in the water. The babies were not crying now. He could see that these people were scrawny and undernourished. Their filthy hair hung down in their faces.

Then a man not far from him got up and started walking toward Wheeler. Wheeler was afraid to move for fear of splashing water and making noise. He didn't think the man had seen him, but still, the Chinese man kept coming straight at him, his head down. Then, when he was only a few yards from Wheeler, he reached down into his pants, pulled out his penis, and started to urinate into the water. When he finished, he suddenly looked up. . . . They were staring directly into each other's eyes.

The man shouted and all hell broke loose.

Willy was watching his pilots carefully. He had not moved from the doorway of the cockpit.

They were almost out of U.S. airspace when the copilot pointed out his side window at something off the right wingtip. Willy looked out the window of his Falcon jet, and there, tailing them a few hundred feet to the right, was an American F-16. Gunter twisted his head and looked to his left.

"Von ovah heah, too," he said, and Willy looked out the other side of the plane at a second American fighter jet on the left side.

"I was going to call and tell them where it was," Willy said. "I told them. They had the polygraph. It was not a lie."

And Willy had intended to do just that. It made no sense for him to blow up LAX with a nuclear weapon once he was free. Such an act of terrorism would make him the most sought-after criminal in the world. The first terrorist to explode a nuclear device in a Western city would be marked and dead in a year. This is why Willy fully intended to tell them where the bomb was, but the inferior men he was dealing with had not trusted him, had not given his plan a chance to work.

"Call them, tell them." His voice had ceased to be calm. "Tell them if they don't turn back I will not tell them where the bomb is. They are running out of time. It is less than forty minutes until it detonates," Willy said, glancing at his watch, sounding more and more like an inferior man.

Willy felt his vicious tiger stir. He was losing control of the terrifying beast.

Gunter picked up the mike and relayed the message.

A few minutes later he got his answer. It was short and to the point. "Fuck you, Charlie," General Clark said, from the pilot's seat of the lead F-16. Then he switched his radio over and went plane-to-plane. "This is Kicker to Killshot," he said to his wingman. "The bogie is about to leave U.S. airspace. He's a terrorist making a run for it. I gotta splash this dink on our side of the line, so he just became an upgrade. We now have a hot target. Follow me in."

General Clark kicked his F-16 over into a right roll, looped quickly around, and came back up on the tail of the Falcon, closing in from behind. Killshot did the same.

Gunter craned his neck to try and see the two jets behind him.

"I told them I would radio the location. I told them," Willy whined.

"I think dey vant to shoot us down," Gunter said.

General Clark let a Sidewinder go. The missile streaked across four hundred yards of cold Pacific sky and directly up the right-engine tailpipe on the Falcon. Willy felt the impact. The plane lurched, throwing him down onto his knees on the beige carpet of the jet. A second later the missile exploded, and the plane disintegrated, blowing Willy and his two pilots into a fine mist.

When the debris hit the ocean, there were only a few pieces larger than a phone booth.

Fu Hai heard the Snake Rider scream, turned toward the sound, and saw the shadowy figure of Wheeler Cassidy standing on the periphery of his group, gun in hand. Fu Hai had fired without aiming in the Red Flower Pavilion, and he had paid the price when he had been wounded. This time he pulled the machine pistol up and aimed carefully. The gun spit out a stream of Russian lead.

The bullets ricocheted in the tunnel. One hit Wheeler in the right side of his chest and took him down hard. He had the Magnum .44 cocked in his right hand, and he squeezed off four blind shots as he fell. Wheeler heard Fu Hai scream going down, then heard splashing water as he landed. Wheeler was now sitting on the floor of the concrete drainpipe, cold, brackish water swirling over his lap. He looked at his chest and saw heavy arterial blood oozing down his shirt.

"This ain't good," he said to himself. Then Tanisha was kneeling over him. "Make sure he's dead," Wheeler groaned. "He's got a machine gun. Be careful—may be other guards."

She looked down at Wheeler's wound, and her heart froze with dread. Could this be happening? Could she have found her soul mate only to lose him in this dark underground sewer? "Hurry," Wheeler whispered through gritted teeth.

Tanisha stumbled up, her mind and senses reeling. She moved toward the huddled Chinese immigrants, hesitating at the edge of the group. They glared at her. She saw no other guards. Just frightened, wretched immigrants. When she moved forward they parted to let her pass. She waded through them to the spot where Fu Hai was lying and kneeled. He had two bullets in him, one in his chest, one in his neck. His eyes were open, but they were beginning to look distant and afraid. Tanisha bent over him, grabbed his wrist, and took his pulse.

Fu Hai had felt the bullets hit him. Just as before, when he was shot in the City of Willows, he had felt absolutely no pain, just the dull, jerking sensation as the bullets hit his body and flung him backwards, out of control. Then he was lying in the water, his head against the side of the tunnel wall. He could not breathe, he could not move his legs. His arms were leaden, but were pawing the air in front of him, as if they belonged to somebody else.

Then the beautiful Black woman leaned over him. She was backlit by the flickering candles. She looked down at him with no expression. He tried to focus his vision on her, but she was slowly fading away from him. He had to do something. What was it he had to do? He could not remember. Then his right arm fell on the backpack with the strange mechanism in it. He clutched it like a lifeline, holding it tight, straining against its bulk. Then he was no longer looking at the Black woman, but at his little sister. . . .

It was a bright sunny day, in their backyard in Beijing. Xiao Jie was ten. She was walking with him in their courtyard garden. His mother was inside, cooking dinner. Soon his father, Zhang Wei Dong, would be home from his calligraphy shop. Fu Hai had made a paper bird for Xiao Jie. It was very intricate and had many folds. Fu Hai had worked on it all afternoon. When you pulled the tail, the wings would flap. Fu Hai showed his adorable little sister how it worked. Her bright child eyes twinkled with excitement; her round face with its perfect complexion shone. Her white teeth and black eyes glittered. As always, she sparkled for Fu Hai, clean and clear as a diamond. He loved her so much his heart could almost not contain the feeling.

"Fu Hai," she said, "is it really for me?"

"Nothing is too good for you, little sister." He smiled. "I would give my life to make you happy."

And he reached out to give her the paper bird, reached high so she would be sure to get it. He was so proud to have once more put the light of happiness into her beautiful eyes. He would never fail her. Would never let any darkness stain her happy face. She took the paper bird, smiling. Overhead, through the graceful curved branches of the ginkgo trees, shone the pale blue, cloud-wisped sky of northern China, ageless and serene. And then, as if the act of giving brought final peace, the darkness closed around him and Zhang Fu Hai was gone.

Tanisha saw his hand come up as if to give her something. And then she saw that he was struggling to lift the backpack, his arm twitching, his eyes pleading, as if giving it to her was the most important thing on earth.

She grabbed it from him and opened it up. She pulled out a metal box, which she could see had been opened before. The leather straps had been cut or broken. There was Russian writing on the side. She opened the box and she was looking at what she was sure was one of the missing Russian suitcase nuclear weapons. She stood, holding the box carefully in front of her. Then she inched back through the mass of huddled Snake Riders to Wheeler.

He was now on his back in the water, his head lolling against the side of the tunnel.

"Oh Jesus, Wheeler, don't go, please don't go, baby."

He opened his eyes. "Where would I go?" he mumbled. "I'm

a fucking care package." He saw what she was holding. "What's that?"

"I think . . . I think this is . . ."

"Get out of here with it. Gotta disarm it."

"What about you?"

"I'm fine. Feel great." And then he coughed and blood came out of his mouth.

"Shit, you're dying."

Then, unexpectedly, the Prankmeister's grin was on his sallow face. "Go," he said. "Go or we're all dead."

She got up and started moving down the tunnel, running with the bomb cradled in front of her. But her thoughts were back with Wheeler in the flickering candlelight. She pushed on, slipping once and going down on one knee, almost dropping the box. She clutched it tighter, afraid if she lost it, she would never find it again in the inky blackness. Her breath was coming in gasps, tears were filling her eyes. She could see nothing.

She didn't know how long she'd been running in the dark, but finally she thought she saw light way down the tunnel. She moved faster, and then a few minutes later, she was blinded by a five-hundred-watt xenon light.

"Freeze!" the NEST Commander yelled, as the light targeted her in the tunnel.

"Don't shoot her, she's a cop," Al Katsukura said, pushing his way toward Tanisha.

"Detective Williams, LAPD. I got it," she said breathlessly, as she held the bomb out in front of her. One of the NEST commandos moved forward and carefully opened the metal box. He recognized what she had handed him. "She's right," he said, and quickly put it in a baffled NEST carrying case they had with them.

"You've gotta help him. He's in the tunnel," she said. "There are hundreds of immigrants back there. Please help him. He's dying."

"Who's dying?"

"My partner," she said, refusing a more elaborate or accurate description. Al didn't correct her.

"Get this out of here!" the Commander yelled at one of his men, then looked at his watch. "You've got less than ten minutes to disarm it. I'll find these people. Take her out with you."

"No, I'm going back in there."

The Commander turned toward her. "You're going with them," he ordered. "Where is your partner? Is this a maze of tunnels here?"

"There's only one pipe into where they are," she said. "I'm going—I'll show you."

"Listen, lady, this is a fucking nuclear emergency! You do what I tell you!" he said, his anger and anxiety spewing.

"I don't know who you think you are, Chuck, but I don't work for you!" she shot back.

Then he hit her, stunning her and knocking her backwards. "Get her the fuck out of here!" he yelled. "Barker, Watts, Ferguson, you're with me."

"You asshole, why'd you hit her?" Al screamed, knocking the Commander backwards with a forearm shiver.

"She's in the fucking way. She's arguing against orders. We got a nuke alert going here, pal." Then the Commander turned and yelled at his men, "Let's go!" They headed up the tunnel, shining the xenon light ahead of them. Al grabbed Tanisha by the arm and helped her out of the tunnel.

They found Wheeler where she'd left him. He was unconscious. His pulse was faint. Two of the NEST commandos lifted him and carried him back toward the beach, while the rest of the NEST team gathered up the frightened Snake Riders and herded them out of the tunnel.

When they got Wheeler to the beach, the NEST helicopter had arrived from the airport, and they loaded him aboard.

Tanisha was standing next to the door of the Bell JetRanger as they strapped him in. Al Katsukura was with her. "I'm going with him," she said, as the NEST Commander moved up to her. He put a restraining hand on her shoulder, and she spun, shoving the Magnum .44 into his face. "Ain't gonna work twice, sugar," she said. "Now, back off."

They let her climb into the helicopter. She sat next to Wheeler, holding his hand as the chopper revved up and lifted off the beach. It flew over his uncle's anchored fishing boat and headed east toward Long Beach General Hospital. She looked down at Wheeler's pale face and squeezed his weak hand. "Jesus," she finally whispered, "are you ever something special."

FORTY-FOUR

Gold from the Rainbow

I n bomb disposal work the rule is "No news is good news," especially if you're unplugging a one-kiloton nuclear bomb. They had averted disaster by mere minutes.

Wheeler was in critical but stable condition in Long Beach General Hospital, a lucky choice, because that hospital had the best gunshot trauma ward in the state.

Two days after they had opened Wheeler up and dug the bullet out of his chest he had been downgraded to serious, and shortly later moved out of ICU into a private room on the sixth floor. He awoke with vivid memories of the gunfight in the drainage tunnel, but nobody in the hospital had heard anything about it, or the bomb. None of it had even made the evening news. There was a guard outside his door, and he was allowed no visitors until he was debriefed by somebody from the State Department. When he was strong enough to sit up and talk, he was visited by Lew Fisher. The narrow-shouldered bureaucrat pulled a chair up next to his bed and looked down at Wheeler, smiling without warmth.

"Glad you pulled through," he said disingenuously. He had

378

really been hoping that Wheeler would die on the table. Nothing personal. But nobody needed to know how close L.A. had come to a nuclear disaster. "That was quite a heroic thing you did."

Wheeler thought so too, but didn't quite know how to answer.

"At any rate, I think you and I need to come to an understanding, and I need to get some assurances. While you've been unconscious, the story we put out for the news was that we had a chlorine gas leak at the airport. Canister broke coming off a cargo jet. Deadly gas seeped into the atmosphere, blah-blah-blah. We made it as boring and humdrum as possible. The story made one news cycle and died quickly. We said the evacuation of the airport and surrounding area was simply precautionary."

"Is that counterintuitive or counterfactual?" Wheeler asked sarcastically.

"It's disinformation."

"A lie."

"Look, let's not get sideways with each other over this. Fact is, if the real story got out, we'd have more confusion, not less. We'd have government commissions and political speeches, and, in the end, nothing good would happen. We need to keep the panic level down to efficiently track the rest of these missing devices."

"That's reassuring, but from what I've seen so far, you guys couldn't track mud onto a carpet. What happened to Willy?"

"Willy attempted to leave the United States and had an engine malfunction. A gas tank exploded on his jet and he didn't make it. I've read the documents you brought from his Hong Kong headquarters. Looks like the Reds in Beijing lost their hand-picked candidate. With that Agreement, I think we can persuade them not to meddle any further in Hong Kong's elections. If they do, we'll make that document public. On the homefront, the FBI is investigating those Congressmen and Senators. We'll eventually get to the bottom of that." Lew Fisher hitched his chair closer, "We need to know, Mr. Cassidy, that you intend to keep this incident to yourself . . . no press statements, no book, no TV interviews."

Wheeler smiled. "What if I don't want to cooperate?"

"That would be unfortunate and momentarily tricky. But we're not entirely scenario-dependent. Let's suppose you say exactly what happened, but the California Governor, the L.A. Mayor and Police Chief, as well as everybody in the federal government who is in a position to corroborate your story, say Mr. Cassidy is just a little confused after his accident. With no corroboration, you're gonna look like a guy who took a ride on a spaceship."

"Got it," Wheeler said.

Lew stood up and looked down at Wheeler. "That is not to say that your nation isn't immensely grateful to you for your part in this. You helped avoid a rigged election in Hong Kong and a nuclear explosion here, and you brought down a powerful Triad leader who had targeted the United States. You are to be commended and congratulated. However, that having been said, you are also just a two-dollar chip in a billion-dollar board game."

"No Civilian Medal of Honor, huh?"

Lew Fisher stood. " 'Fraid not. By the way, the official story on your wound is, you were out on your uncle's boat, cleaning your shark rifle, and it accidentally discharged and you got shot in the chest."

"That should play. I usually can't seem to do anything right. Did my big toe accidentally get stuck in the trigger?"

Lew Fisher shook Wheeler's hand. "If I can ever be of service, Mr. Cassidy, don't hesitate to call."

"You wouldn't be interested in clearing all this up with my mother?"

"We stay out of family situations," he said, and walked out of Wheeler's life, never to be seen again.

Wheeler wondered what had happened to the Snake Riders, and what had happened to Prescott's and Angela's murder investigations, and if they had caught Ray Fong's killer. He guessed that his brother's part in the smuggling of illegal aliens and influence-peddling in the corridors of government would probably go unreported. Too much was at stake, and for that he was glad.

Tanisha had slept in the hospital, and as soon as the guard

was taken off Wheeler's door, she spent her days seated on an uncomfortable chair in his room, playing cards with him or just holding his hand till he could get to sleep.

"Your mother still hasn't come to see you?" she asked one evening after dinner.

"Nope. But she sent me some mail." Wheeler handed her an envelope. It was a legal letter informing him that he had been removed as a beneficiary of his father's estate.

"Shit, you're kidding."

"Beverly Hills is a tough town," Wheeler said.

Ramon Delgado took time off from behind the W.C.C. bar and visited the hospital one afternoon, bringing his family. He stood respectfully by Wheeler's bed. The children and his Spanish-speaking wife were dressed in their Sunday church clothes, smiling awkwardly at him. "You're getting better, Mr. C.," Ramon said, his handsome features lit by his grin. "You'll be back at the club any day now."

Mrs. Delgado had cooked him chicken and beef enchiladas in casserole dishes, covered with Saran Wrap. Ramon had smuggled in a bottle of Wheeler's trademark hops, Vat 69. After Ramon left, Wheeler gave the bottle to his night nurse.

Days stretched into weeks. The drains and catheters were unplugged and Wheeler was finally released. He left the hospital in a wheelchair. When he stood up in the parking lot next to Tanisha's old yellow Mazda, he felt ten feet tall and one foot wide. He teetered the two steps to the passenger seat, then lowered himself in with a sigh.

Rick Verba had managed to get the Internal Affairs case against Tanisha dropped. This unprecedented career feat had been accomplished with the help of the LAPD Superchief, Carl Leddiker. He, like Wheeler, had been briefed by Lew Fisher. The Chief couldn't tell the I.A.D. Shooflies what Tanisha had done. Instead, he just wiped her slate clean with no explanation.

Then, one Sunday afternoon, two weeks later, they were sitting in Wheeler's apartment, curled up on the silk sofa in front of the window that overlooked Bel Air Country Club. A light rain was falling through scattered clouds, and a four-color rainbow arched magnificently over the greens and fairways. It was the best rainbow Wheeler had ever seen. It seemed to contain a message that there could still be value in life, and gold at the end of his rainbow. Wheeler had gained back half of the weight he'd lost and was beginning to think he would eventually get back to normal. But he was worried about how he was going to pay the rent on his penthouse. With his inheritance gone, he decided he needed to go out and get a job. They had the Sunday paper open and were looking at the want ads.

"Here's one," Tanisha said. " 'Painting Contractor seeks Sales Executive.' "

"Yuk," he said. "I'm crazy enough without inhaling paint fumes all day. How 'bout this? 'Position for in-house Advertising Exec, Southern California Volkswagen Dealership.' "

"You have a colorful history with Volkswagens," she said, remembering his prank fifteen years ago.

"I'm surprised I ever got away with that shit," he said ruefully. "Somebody shoulda knocked my lights out."

She put down the paper and nestled into the crook of his arm. He felt her breath on his neck and her hair against his cheek.

"My place is too small, but we could live at my grandmother's house," she said. "It's cheap."

"I don't think I went over too good down there." And then they sat quietly on the sofa. He was looking at her. He reached out and touched her hair. "When I look at you, you know what I see?" he asked.

She shook her head.

"I see royalty. I see strength and nobility. I'm completely diminished by it. I want to be so much for you. I want to make you proud. All my life I've been a fuck-up. I'm almost forty, and I'm sitting around looking in the want ads, trying to get my first job. But I want you to know something, Tanisha. I'm gonna make it work. I'm gonna beat the odds . . . and you know why?"

"Why?"

"Because I have somebody to do it for. I finally found my reason."

She kissed him and held him, then put her head on his chest and listened to his heart beat. They sat in the apartment and watched the late-afternoon sun. The gold, red, green, and purple rainbow slowly faded. As he watched it go he realized he had never been happier. One day soon, when he had a steady job and both feet under him, he would propose marriage to her, and he knew she would say yes. He would marry her and never give her a reason to be sorry.

She snuggled closer, and he could feel her heart beat with his, feel her warmth against him, and then, after almost six weeks, he knew it was finally time. His eyes fell on a shelf full of pictures. Some were of his mother and father, some were framed shots of Wheeler with old girlfriends. His eyes sought out the picture that was his favorite. He could barely see it across the darkening room. It was a shot of him with Prescott, the day his brother graduated from junior high. Wheeler had an arm around Pres, who was looking up at him in awe. In Prescott's eyes there shone a look of hero-worship and love, in Wheeler's was a look of protective determination. It was a picture of a promise that had not been kept.

"Will you teach me how to throw a football, Wheel?"

"Will you show me how to skateboard?"

"Will you get her to go out with me?"

And then he was crying for a brother he had loved, but not protected. Tanisha held him while the sobs racked his body.

As the sun set, Wheeler finally said good-bye.